MARJORIE KING

Maverick Gambit

Book One of the Maverick Series

First published by Starscape Media, LLC 2019

Copyright © 2019 by Marjorie King

This novel is entirely a work of fiction. The names, characters and incidents portrayed in it are the work of the author's imagination. Any resemblance to actual persons, living or dead, events or localities is entirely coincidental.

First edition

ISBN: 978-0-578-47665-0

This book was professionally typeset on Reedsy. Find out more at reedsy.com

To Keith

Contents

1

The Attack

Knox muscled his way through the space station's delivery floor. His crates, hovering on a cushion of air, huddled together and followed behind. Soon the boxes would be safely in his cargo hold heading across the galaxy. At least that was the plan.

This rush shipment of custom products would fetch a nice price on the open market... which could attract unwanted attention. The perishable products had been boxed on the planet below, New Terra, and launched to this space station for a quick delivery to another colonized planet. So, with a steady hand and vigilant eye, Knox guided his floating payload forward.

Several bodies back, two space truckers wandered. They had no cargo and looked away at Knox's gaze. *Pirates.* Knox flared his nostrils and inhaled their scent.

His adapted sense of smell picked out the pirate's unique essence like picking out distinct voices. The woman liked too much garlic, and the man, cologne. Both predators reeked of mantle mud, the bacteria used to break up and fertilize the sterile crust of the colonized planets.

Knox tasted the roof of his mouth, memorized the stalkers' odor, and set his hand atop his boxes. No one crept up on Knox. No one.

Electromagnetic barriers flickered ahead, the gates between the delivery floor and landing dock beyond. Knox shoved his way forward and staked his spot in line for a smaller gate, '10-100 Crates'. He circled behind his boxes and checked the crowd. The pirates had slipped away.

He inched forward in line until it was his turn. The security detail scanned Knox's brainwave ID and his shipments with their data pad. Three seconds later, their handheld beeped.

"Clear," the watch said, staring over Knox's head and refusing to make eye contact with a lowly space trucker. Not that Knox cared.

The shimmering barrier turned off, and Knox and his goods entered the safety chamber. The wall reactivated behind him, swirling like oil on water, while the one before him stayed operational. The shimmering curtains were made of electricity and magnetism. If a person accidentally touched them, the voltage would give them an unpleasant, but not deadly, shock that would stop them in their tracks.

For five seconds Knox lived in rare silence, then the hazy veil before him dropped, and the raucous shipyard came into sharp focus. Knox stepped forward into a land with only one law, Darwin's.

Ivy, used to filter the air, draped from the ceiling like the bowels of a giant rainforest. Misters sprayed the vines, fogging the area with a haze. Even with all of humanity's advancements, plants still converted a human's carbon dioxide to oxygen more efficiently than any technology. The open area brimmed with a reek of plant-life and body odor that thickened inside his nose.

Knox inhaled and tasted the roof of his mouth. Mingled with the odors of ferns, bodies, and lubricant was the reek of garlic and cologne. The two pirates must have entered through the 'No Shipments' gate, and were waiting in ambush for him.

If Knox started shooting, a riot would break out. That's how stray shots put holes in the people he loved. He'd lost enough that way. But how to shake his stalkers? A familiar whiff of shea butter lotion and spiced beans wafted his way.

Knox spun and box-jumped his hovering crates, facing Garlic and Cologne. The boxes sagged under Knox's weight, until the hover-brackets adjusted and rose. The thieves set their feet and reached for their pistols.

"So, Sid, how's your sister?" Knox asked someone standing behind them.

"Two months and she finishes her training at SUSA's E & M Academy," answered a man with a booming deep voice.

Both pirates' eyes went wide. They turned and saw Sid towering over them with shoulders twice as wide as theirs. He was a heavy-set man with plenty of muscle to match his padding and twin plasma pistols on his hips. Garlic and Cologne crept away, to find easier targets.

There is another law in the docks after all: the Law of the Pack.

"Bet you're proud of her," Knox said to Sid and hopped down from his shipments.

"Oh yeah." Sid's overalls strained at their seams.

Knox shook his friend's hand. Sid's skin gleamed like his famous black beans against Knox's dark copper tones. His hands were soft as butter in Knox's rough palms.

3

"Thanks for watching my back," Knox said.

"Right place at the right time." Sid waved like he was shooing away a fly.

"We both know better." Knox turned to lead his crates to his ship.

"I'll always owe you for setting me up with—"

"Can some of your beans for me," Knox cut him off. "And we'll call it even."

Sid had almost let slip Knox's connection to the Nichev Shipping Co. Didn't need anyone in this landing dock knowing that. Knox circled his crates and pointed his nose home toward *Maverick*.

"I'll find a way to even the score!" Sid called over the noise of whistling power tools.

Knox gave a thumbs up but kept walking. Sid didn't owe him anything. The man had worked hard for Knox and more than earned his new job. So what if Knox had made some calls?

Darting his eyes across the spaceport's hangar, Knox dodged other space truckers, mechanics, hired hands, mechbots, ships taking off, and ships landing. His ears rang with metal creaking, engines revving, shouting, and cussing. Engine grease and sweat fogged his sensitive nose along with the ivy to concoct an overpowering bouquet.

He swerved onto a row of small-crew cargo ships and finally stopped before his: *Maverick*. It was dented enough to look old, but not blasted enough to be interesting. Knox slapped its hull.

Don't worry, Dad, we're still going strong.

He arched his eyebrow at a pair of steel-toed shoes sticking out from under the ship's belly. Knox nudged one with his boot.

4

"I didn't know the ship needed maintenance."

"That hum was driving me nuts," Ximena said back.

Clanks and hisses grumbled from under *Maverick*, and Ximena fumed as she worked.

"Go back in, you stupid, no, not there, here... right... *here*... thank you!"

Knox knelt down, and the rest of his wife came into view, her arms shoved up to her elbows in the bowels of their ship.

"How much longer?"

"¡Espera un momento!" *Just a minute.*

That could mean anything from a literal minute to a few days, but Knox sure as bloody hell wasn't pressing further. Something had upset her, and Knox prayed it wasn't him.

Ximena extracted her arms and tapped the digi-scroll on the ground next to her. The trapezoid panel on the ground floated up, slid along the ship's surface, and bandaged the exposed section. With a metallic whirr and click, the panel sealed into place. Ximena closed her scroll and stuffed it into a baggy pocket on her cargo pants.

"Finished."

She pushed off the hull, and shot out from under the ship. She stood and smiled up at him.

He was not a tall man. Knox stood a hair's breadth higher than most women, but generally had a clear view up guys' noses. At least his shoulders were broad and muscular. But Ximena managed to be even shorter, the top of her head even with Knox's eyes. On the plus side, she could wiggle into every nook and cranny of the ship's innards for repairs. Knox had never needed to rent a robomech.

Ximena wiped her greasy hands on her pants while the hoverpad folded itself into a tight package. Her fingers extracted a delicate necklace from under her collar, and her cross settled over the buttons on her coveralls. Lastly, she gently lifted her long, black braid from the back of her shirt. The noise of the dock fell away as Knox watched that silky rope slip free of her collar and swing down to her hips, such lovely hips.

"We've got a problem," Ximena said and stuffed the hover-pad under her arm. "Shields on. Open ramp."

The air shimmered as shields enveloped the ship and Knox's shipments. The electromagnetic bubble muffled the curses and metallic creaks of the space station's hangar. *Maverick* was an island. Cameras all around the ship monitored for any human or robot that wandered too close. Stun guns aimed for defense. No one approached a ship on lockdown without powerful shields of their own.

The ramp creaked open, and Knox and Ximena entered and walked through the intimate tunnel of crates packed tightly into their cargo bay. Ximena pulled her digi-scroll out of her pocket. She pulled open the thin rods that served as handles, unrolling the scroll's beige parchment. The "paper" stiffened and words glowed dark blue a centimeter above its matte surface. With a caress of her finger, it gathered the information on Knox's shipments. One tap and her loading program started. The boxes in the cargo bay lifted and floated aside as the shipments outside drifted in.

A crate of fresh strawberries joined the shipments to planet Aurora, mostly settled by the European countries of Old Earth. Coral Reef cuttings went to Yichen, the planet of China, Japan, and some of the southeast Asian countries though Indonesia, Vietnam, Cambodia, and Laos had settled with India on Naya Surya. They were getting an enormous carton of live worms.

Easier to ship than the box of bees from two months ago. Pollinators might be necessary for terraforming, but Knox still kept the cargo bay locked when he shipped them.

Another pile was slated for New Islam, Knox's next stop on his shipping run, and of course there was the frozen mutton for Siku Mpya, the planet settled by Africa. Last but not least, a tiny pile of hover brackets and the latest digi-scrolls were tucked in the far corner and slated for delivery to Old Earth. Knox mentally checked off his list of pick-ups and ran through his schedule.

Every crate, carton, and box in that cargo bay was a rush job. Within four days' time, each would be delivered and replaced with a shipment to one of the other Six Planets or Earth. Non-perishables like clothes, toys, or canned goods could take their sweet time in barges, the blue whales of space shipping. But plants, fresh food, or animals were rush jobs and required small cargo ships like Knox's *Maverick*.

Ximena's program found a place for everything and put everything in its place. Knox continued down the hallway to the galley.

"So, what's wrong?" he asked.

"Atienna called," Ximena said. "Klundah's village was attacked."

Klundah's village? We just volunteered there three months ago.

"No," Knox said, as if that would undo the damage. "Where's Atienna?"

"Kikuyu, Siku Mpya."

Knox marched through the galley to the cockpit. He took his usual spot, the pilot's chair, and Ximena sat to his right in the co-pilot's. Her gaze swept over him, and he could feel her diagnosing his mood just like she picked apart every creak, whistle, and vibration of the ship.

Ximena pressed one of the few physical buttons on the console. A panel slid back and seven marbles rose, one marble for each solar system of the Six Planets and Earth.

"Call Atienna, Head of Serving Hands," Knox said to the ship's computer.

For calls across a planet, wireless technology worked with a split-second delay at most. For planet to planet communications, however, only quantum entanglement crystals would do.

"Which planet?" *Maverick*'s computer asked with a voice that sounded exactly like Knox's late-father, Liam.

"Siku Mpya," Knox said. "Country: Kikuyu."

"Ruth Atienna Kamathi, I assume?"

"That's the one."

"Leaving a message," Liam's voice said. "Those fancy algorithms say she'll answer in about five minutes, but I bet she'll get back to you sooner."

In under a minute, Atienna's upper body appeared, floating above the cockpit's console. Her curly hair, kissed with touches of gray, circled her head like a black dandelion, and she wore a sleeveless dress splashed with the colors of the sunset. She spoke in Swahili and the computer translated.

"Thank you for calling back so quickly." The translated English preserved her rich alto. "I know you are in the middle of a shipment run."

"Don't worry about it," Knox said with a wave. "What happened?"

"Pirates snuck between the Earth spaceports and raided three villages in Taluk."

There weren't many space stations orbiting Earth, of course.

8

Why live in orbit when the planet was finally habitable again? In contrast, the Six Planets spread across the Milky Way still had at least eight vibrant, bustling stations each. Yes, the Six Planets had terraformed enough for their masses, but the cultures had developed a dependency on the orbiting cities.

"Which three?"

"Which three indeed. The three you helped Serving Hands get back on their feet. The three that had their first good crop in years. The three you aligned with a business to pay fair price for their produce. Ngalo-ngalo, Openyenge, and Klundah's village. That's why I called you."

"What did they take?" Ximena asked.

"Not what," Atienna answered. "Who."

Knox's stomach hardened around the rock dropped into it. *Who.* They'd stolen people and sold them to warehouses for cheap labor.

"How many?" Knox asked, his voice hoarse.

"I'll send the file," Atienna said.

On her end, she touched a scroll, and on their end, faces and names appeared. Smiles. One teen boy had big ears, one girl's hair shot out in every direction, and one little boy had lost his two front teeth. Lost children and furious, grieving parents. Knox forced his voice to work.

"Was the pirate ship ID'd?" he asked.

"I'll send you what we recorded, but they probably changed their signature as soon as they jumped."

Information on the pirate ship, a mid-sized transport, popped up on Ximena's scroll. It had passed close enough that an Earth spaceport captured its digital signature, but those could be switched by a talented hacker. She ground her molars hard enough for Knox to hear it. If she had access to their FTL nozzles right now, that would be the last trip they would survive through space.

"How long ago?" Knox asked.

Atienna bowed her head. "Almost a day ago."

"No!" Ximena yelled. She covered her mouth.

"Klundah had to travel for hours to reach a quantum comm-link that could call me on my planet. As soon as I heard, I sent workers to Earth to check the other two villages." Atienna slammed her fist into her thigh. "No matter how hard I work, someone is always waiting to destroy it."

Knox flicked through the faces on his scroll. All children that he couldn't help, couldn't save.

"Atienna, it's too late to save them," Knox said, numb. "They've already been sold by this time."

"Then we save those that remain." Atienna's tone was steel.

"What do you need?" Knox asked.

"Shields. Pirates can't raid the colonized planets because of their domes. They're protected. But Earth is exposed and vulnerable. I need one large shield to protect the whole country, all of Taluk."

Humans on the Six Planets lived inside domes, energy shields that protected them from the uninhabitable atmosphere of the unterraformed planet. Only a few hundred years more, and the planets would be converted enough that the shield-domes would be unnecessary. But Earth didn't need domes, so it didn't have them. This made it a lot easier for pirates to get access from space.

Ximena had been holding the scroll to her face, but at the mention of the shield, it started a slow drift toward her lap. Her eyes glossed over, focusing on a point in the middle of nowhere. Knox knew that look. She was in a math-trance.

"I need you," Knox said. "I need you to talk to Atienna and find a solution."

With a shaky breath, Ximena dug deep and pulled up her voice.

"Shields big enough to cover an entire country have to be powered by massive quantum relays from a spaceport solar grid. Earth's solar panels aren't sized for shields that big."

Her mouth stopped speaking and hung open. Then her lips started flinching. She tapped her thumb to her index finger, whispered to herself, touched her middle finger, scrunched her black eyebrows, then moved to her ring finger.

"That could work." Ximena woke from her hypnotic state. "Oh, umm, sorry."

"What did you work out?" Knox asked.

"Facility-sized shields. They're smaller than the country-sized domes. Volatile industries use shields this size to protect the surrounding communities."

"And?" Knox asked.

"I'll have to verify my calculations, but I think a facility-sized shield with six photocells for each would cover an entire village, plus surrounding fields. Those could be powered and operated on Earth for," another calculation, "well over a century."

"Then I need three of those," Atienna said.

Ximena gagged. "Atienna, those are expensive."

"We'll figure it out and get back to you," Knox said.

"Thank you."

Atienna touched a light on her side, and her body dissipated like smoke. Ximena's jaw dropped.

"Knox. We can't."

"Not alone," he said.

11

"Even the Nichev Company can't afford to give away shields. If those shields were protecting a facility that was producing a massive profit, maybe. But a village producing meat and barrels of fruit twice a year? It's not enough to pay for itself."

Knox's right hand balled into a fist. "Then others will pay for them."

"They won't voluntarily." She sat up. "Oh, I see."

"Other companies have been given more than enough time to *voluntarily* do the right thing."

Ximena didn't jump up and agree with him. Instead, she pushed back into her chair and winced. Knox had trained as a fighter, but not his wife. She was a mechanic. Could he really ask her to join him in this? Stealing shields for a country that so desperately needed them?

Her eyes returned to the faces shining above her scroll. One face stuck out, Kiara, Klundah's niece. That girl had asked so many questions about spaceships when Ximena and Knox had volunteered at her village. Who knew where Kiara was now? Knox's mind wandered to all the awful fates that could have befallen Kiara, and then shut it off with disgust. This couldn't be allowed.

"We'll need help," Ximena said. "We can't gather the 'donations' alone."

Knox's fist relaxed. "You're with me on this?"

"Always."

"We have a week and a half to finish this run of shipments," Knox said. "That gives you time to verify your math and research the shields."

"And then?"

"And then we hire professional soldiers to help us do the job right. I know just the ones."

Ximena took a deep breath and nodded. They were going to do this.

2

IAS

TrysKa sat cross-legged on her fold-down cot and nibbled her lower lip. She peeled a bit of dead skin off with her teeth and cut her eyes at Willow and Amalie sitting on Willow's cot. It was a tight squeeze to fit TrysKa and Willow into their dorm room, but they'd made room for Amalie too. TrysKa needed them both; she couldn't make this call alone.

"You can do this," Willow said. She held up her index finger. "Make the call." She held up her next finger "Ask for your mom." Ring finger. "If she's not there..." Willow motioned to TrysKa.

"I'll call back later," TrysKa recited.

"Faster. You have to say it faster, and then disconnect."

TrysKa nodded, inhaled, and exhaled. Why did her family force her to do this? Why couldn't she just be nice, and people listen and understand? Especially the people she loved most.

"LaDonna Carter, Alamo, Texas, SUSA, New Terra."

The holoball sitting on her cot lit up. Colors swirled inside the grapefruit-sized ball like a tornado twister. It connected, and the miniature form of one of her sisters, Shawna, popped into focus.

"Oh, thank goodness you called back."

"Is Momma there?"

"She's busy with Andre, but she'll be here in a minute."

Willow made a slashing motion across her throat. TrysKa screwed up her courage.

"OK, well, I'll just–"

"She hasn't told you, but we need help."

Amalie winced, and she pointed to the disconnect button. TrysKa tried again.

"I can talk to her–"

"Did you hear me? *She* won't tell you, but I know you'd want to know. We need money for our little brother and sister. Maria has all her money tied up in her own children, Desmond is giving what little he can, and Rachelle is useless."

Shawna reached for something on her side, her hand disappearing from the holovid. When she pulled her hand back to her face, she held a handkerchief. She wiped her eyes and nose.

"Allergies?" TrysKa asked.

"No."

Great, she was crying.

"Well, I have to go now," TrysKa said, "let Mom know–"

"We miss you, and we're worried to death about you."

"IAS has taken care of me."

"Not like your family would." Shawna blew her nose into the hankie.

But Shawna was wrong. Growing up, Mom and Dad had had no clue what to do with TrysKa's adapted touch. They thought it was some sort of sickness like eczema. When TrysKa reacted to temperature changes or movement around her, they asked politely, but firmly, for her to get over it. If not for the sharp eye of her kindergarten teacher, who knows if IAS would have ever discovered TrysKa.

But she couldn't tell Shawna that.

"I take care of myself now," TrysKa said. "And if Mom needs money, I'll send some back from one of my jobs."

Shawna's head popped up like a snoop sniffing gossip.

"You have work? For IAS?"

"Not yet, but I'm looking."

"Will you have to-" Shawna looked right and left, checking for anyone on her side of the holovid. Then she leaned in close and whispered, "Will you have to shoot other people?"

"I'm a pilot."

"So, you have to shoot people out of the sky, right? I mean, you're a pilot for IAS. That's Institute of Adapted *Soldiers*, right? Soldiers shoot people. Are you really going to shoot someone you don't know?"

"If they threaten those I care about."

"You can do that?" Shawna's eyes went wide, but not with admiration.

"I do what I have to do. Do you have problems with the military protecting our country? I thought you admired their sacrifice."

"Oh, I do! I do! It's just, well, you're not really a *military* soldier, you know?"

Willow curled her hands like claws and pantomimed snapping Shawna's holographic neck. Shawna couldn't see Willow, but TrysKa could. It sent a shudder through her gut. TrysKa nudged Willow's boot with her own, and Willow put her hands back in her lap. But the gleam of the hunt didn't leave her eyes.

16

"What if you had a pilot's job *and* didn't have to shoot anyone?" Shawna asked.

Amalie and Willow both bolted upright. As one they pointed at the holoball mouthing, *End the call.*

"I can get my own job with IAS, thank you."

"But you don't have to!" Suddenly Shawna's tears were gone. "Maria found this planet-to-shuttle job with awesome pay, they'd *love* to hire an IAS graduate, you'd get to see space without shooting anyone. Wouldn't that be great?"

Shawna gasped for air after blurting out that stream of words.

A shuttle job? Space shuttles flew one route. Blast off from a planet launchpad, dock to a space station, load passengers and cargo, return to the same planet launchpad, unload, load. Repeat. Forever. That was not the space pilot job TrysKa had trained for.

"And if you take that job," Shawna added like she was sweetening the deal, "you can live at home, so you don't have to waste any credits on living expenses."

Live at home. TrysKa was not trapping herself back where she was still the six-year-old doormat that everyone counted on to sacrifice and keep the peace.

"Mom is *so* worried about you." The tears started again. "We *need* you."

"TrysKa," Amalie said.

She'd been flicking her fingers over her scroll during the conversation. Now Amalie leaned from Willow's cot to TrysKa, passing it to her. A quick glance told TrysKa everything she needed.

"I have a job," TrysKa said.

"What kind of-"

17

"One that fights slavery, needs a pilot, and pays well. I'll send you a cut of the credits if the family needs it so badly. Tell Momma I called, and I love all of you."

TrysKa cut the connection and could finally breathe. Her shoulders had been strung tight, and now they released their tension. Amalie and Willow both leapt from Willow's cot and squeezed in on both sides of TrysKa. Her adapted skin tingled at the rush of air from their movement and the pulse radiating off their bodies.

"So, you like the job?" Amalie asked.

TrysKa scrolled to the bottom of the form to the "Submit for Job" section. She touched the "Pilot" spot.

"TrysKa Carter."

Her voice signature spiked and fell like a heartbeat scrawled across the screen. She'd done it. She'd found a job just for her.

"Thank you." TrysKa hugged Amalie. "Not everyone can be a soldier like-"

TrysKa faced Willow, strong Willow, kick-ass Willow. Willow shrugged.

"Not everyone can be a pilot."

"Technically, I'm not graduating to a soldier's job either," Amalie said. "I'm going to be an IAS doctor."

"But even that took a lot of negotiating with the Council," Willow said.

"Negotiating." Amalie rolled the word around and smiled like a fox. "I like that. The next time I argue with Dad, that's what I'll call it. Negotiating."

"The truth is, not every adapted human was meant to be a soldier," Willow said.

"IAS is the only place that will train us," TrysKa said. "So, this is the only choice we have."

18

TrysKa read the job description, eating up every morsel. Pilot of a cargo ship: Asteria-class, 841 E.E. model. TrysKa tapped the ship's stats, and a schematic spun in the air: *Maverick.* What a bold name. She wasn't a flashy fighter, but oh, the cargo ship was honest. Reliable parts, well-maintained, what an under-appreciated vessel. Judging by the replacement records, this one was truly loved.

"Those were good years, the 40s, before the spaceship companies started outsourcing their parts."

"And now you're talking in a foreign language," Willow laughed. "I know English and Choctaw, not spaceship parts. But you look happy, and I'm glad."

"One day, you have to stand up to your family," Amalie said.

She picked up the holoball and put it in a cubby in the wall. The hole sucked the holoball into tubing that ran inside the walls, taking it to the supply room in the IAS basement.

"Well, I have a job to keep me busy for now." TrysKa closed the scroll and handed it back to Amalie. "Now, let's see if I can sneak into the kitchen and cook up something for just us."

"Now you're talking!" Willow jumped up and opened the door.

TrysKa and Amalie joined her in the hall. The cots flipped up against the walls, and the door slid closed behind them.

#

Tiny drones, the size of fireflies, zoomed and dived in an attempt to destroy each other. Sann stared past the holovid of the drone battle, past the off-white ceiling, at something only he could see. And couldn't stop seeing.

The mission had ended four days ago. Four days Sann had confined himself to his apartment, lying on his cot staring past the walls of his cell, trying but failing to forget. He blinked. In that instant of darkness, a head exploded, blood flew, brains scattered. Sann forced his eyes open. He couldn't close them.

Sann's scroll beeped. Another job opportunity. Another chance to "save good people" by "killing bad people." His teachers at IAS had used more nuanced language, of course, more sophisticated verbiage. But at the end of the day, at the end of his operation, that's what it boiled down to. Sann blinked again and shuddered.

He sat up, had to stay awake, and cracked open his scroll. The details of the mission slid by, senseless. Sann shook his head and tried again. Who needed to be killed in this mission? *Protecting a village from pirates... getting shields... setting them up...* Sann pressed the meat of his palm into his closed eyes and they lit up with fireworks. Then he read it again, dissecting every word, every phrase. Where was the attack? Where was the assassination?

None.

Sann read one more time, verifying before he hoped too much, that this op was indeed a mercy mission. At the bottom of the application TrysKa's voice signature was recorded next to the Pilot job. Two blanks remained, two chances for escape, so Sann tapped Sniper.

"Sann Dalise."

The flatline spiked and fell, his name, his commitment. Sann closed the application with a swipe of his fingers and checked his scroll for calls, news, anything.

Brant Mallet called 22 times.

Willow Poloma called 26 times.

If he didn't answer soon, Brant would barge over and beat the door down. Subtlety wasn't his strong suit. But what would Willow do? Sann's cheeks warmed a touch, but his stomach soured at the same time. Enjoyable feelings felt out of place right now.

"Holovid off."

The buzzing drones vanished, leaving a thin white trail in the air. Sann closed his scroll, attached it to his hip, and stood. His legs wobbled but held.

"Where's Brant Mallet?" he asked the room's computer.

"Teaching in the gym."

"When will his class be finished?"

"In thirty minutes."

OK, Sann needed to break out of his apartment, and this was as good an excuse as any. Maybe it would be good to visit the familiar halls of IAS and see friendly faces. He left his apartment high rise and dragged his feet down the sidewalk, still chained to his memories.

Sann could travel faster by riding the people mover, but that would involve packing next to other bodies. The sidewalks breathed free and open except for three exercise addicts. At the tram stop, he paid for a private ride.

The large public tram, a bus-sized opal bullet, was free, and the pedestrians squeezed inside. But with the paycheck from this past job, Sann could afford to hide away.

A sphere the size of a ping pong ball floated down from the sky. The closer it came, the bigger it grew until it stopped before him. Sann folded his legs in and locked out the world. The door closed turning off the chatter.

"IAS," Sann said.

It rose, and the city fell away.

3

The Prodigal Returns

A week later, Knox rode the shuttle from the space station down to the planet, New Terra. More than 800 years ago, Earth had kicked humans off with her extinction event. North, South, and Central America brought their space ARKs to orbit New Terra, and within a hundred years, broke ground on their first terraformed dome. The other continents picked their own systems with just the right sun and planet: Aurora, New Islam, Siku Mpya, Naya Surya, and Yichen. Altogether, that made the Six Planets.

And then, around 500 Earth Exodus, some explorers decided to check out Earth. Wouldn't you know, the planet had made a comeback. Not only had a few humans survived, though certainly not thrived, but a lot of plant and animal life had rallied as well. The Six Planets were desperate for ecological diversity, and Earth was desperate for technology. A perfect recipe for Knox's profession: trade.

He wove through the familiar crowd of the planetport to the hovertram stop. On the public tram, his clothes blended in with the mixture of humanity crammed onto the seats and aisle.

At the edge of New York, he changed rides, and it got personal. On the tram to the Institute of Adapted Soldiers, the school's beige uniforms flanked Knox, his past invading his present.

Graduated soldiers, back from their most recent operation, caught up with old colleagues. Students who lived off-campus grouped together, catching the last lift before their morning classes. Two parents huddled with their daughter between them. The little girl's blond ponytail drooped down the left side of her head. All of them eyed the faded jacket and rough exterior of the space trucker who obviously didn't belong.

The filled transport rose through the air and charged down the tube leading to the IAS dome. New York's half-sphere fell away as Knox's fist tightened around the bar. Rarely did he lose money on a job, but if Knox had to take a loss, he still followed through on his commitments. He was not a quitter.

But he'd quit IAS.

I made the choice that needed to be made.

The tram whizzed down the clear tunnel. The untamed ground below was a writhing black. Knox could almost smell the mantle mud below them, covering the planet's surface, churning the soil, growing bacteria in the sterile land, forcing life into its skin. The window to Knox's right displayed the IAS dome, a cold crystal half-sphere in the distance.

Its dome widened until it conquered the view. The curved electromagnetic field trapped the clean air inside and blocked out the noxious fumes of the unterraformed planet. Tunnels, made of the same electromagnetic field, branched out and connected to other city-domes around the world. A gigantic crystal spider web.

The grass inside IAS's dome advanced right to its swirling edge. Trees grew up the side, leaning against it, fighting to pierce through to the sun. The tram shot out the tunnel into the dome and passed over those trees. The glassy roof soared so high overhead that clouds formed within the umbrella.

The tram turned, and the IAS tower jutted up to that sky, dominating the window. The ride lowered to its landing platform at the front entrance.

"Institute of Adapted Soldiers. Thank you for riding Public Air," said an automated voice. "Remember your possessions. Please stand clear of the sliding door. And remember to leave a five-star review on the Galactic DB. Our low-cost service only continues if you rate us well."

Knox stepped down onto the epoxycrete walkway and let the throng part around him. He craned his head back and took in the twenty-five floors. Vines trailed down the building from the rooftop garden. Bees buzzed up and down the green ropes. His dorm had been on the nineteenth.

Quitter.

The skyscraper glowered down on him. The afternoon sun baked Knox's back, and his shirt stuck to his skin. He could shuck the jacket, but Knox was not walking around IAS with wet spots under his armpits.

Screw pride.

Knox had a job to do. He rolled his shoulders, cracked his neck, and marched up the wide steps to the front lobby of IAS. He stepped inside, and the stiff indoor air chilled the sweat on his skin. The student entering behind him shivered. Knox didn't. Spotlights drilled down on him, nagging him about his past. White and gray swirled around the epoxycrete tiles to imitate old Earth marble—the floor of a cold courtroom.

24

Inside the lobby, soldiers and students funneled into the gaping doors that led to the school beyond. The father and mother from the tram talked to a grandmotherly receptionist behind the counter. She stood and looked over their heads, her mouth falling open.

"Knox? It can't be!" She said. "Knox, is that you?"

Her familiar voice warmed the frigid air.

"Hey, Becky."

Becky smiled, her white curls trickling around her soft, crinkled face. After hearing her welcome, the room softened, as if it now remembered Knox and decided he wasn't a threat. He had thought Becky was old when he'd started at this school, but he'd only been six at that time. Even forty had looked old then. Forty didn't look old anymore, and Becky didn't look like she'd aged a day.

"Don't disappear." She wagged her finger at him. "Stay right there."

Becky returned to the family and handed the girl a candy from the jar on her desk. The mom was trying to put her daughter's hair back into the ponytail.

"Ow!" her daughter said.

"You need to look nice."

Knox tucked his thumbs into his pockets. The walls brandished art from floor to ceiling, all inspired from the different countries represented at IAS. Knox's gaze traveled from a woven rug to a cubism oil painting to a digital hologram. There. A traditional Scottish crest. Even in the array of masterpieces, Knox still wedged in.

The family left the front desk and perched on the edge of the couches filed along the wall.

"OK, your turn," Becky called.

Knox swiveled on his heels and strolled to the counter. Becky tapped her scroll.

"I've told KaeHan you arrived," she said. "But before he whisks you away, what have you been doing all these years?"

"Shipping."

"Space shipping, right? Between the Six Planets?"

"And Earth. KaeHan told you, I assume."

"No." Becky's eyes creased around the edges. "I remembered that was your father's trade."

Knox cleared his throat. Of course Becky would remember. All the kids at IAS were hers, even after they grew up, even after they became space truckers.

"How long has it been?"

"Since I was here?" Knox narrowed his eyes at a Navajo tapestry and calculated. "About nineteen years." *Had it been that long?*

"No, I meant since you lost Liam."

"Twelve years." Knox knew that by heart.

The door into the facility slid open, and KaeHan walked through with a young instructor. The teacher walked straight to the family on the couch.

"Hello, my name is Celeste Yawisaki," she knelt before the little girl. "And I'm going to give you a tour of the Institute. After that, we'll visit Councilor KaeHan Lee in his office."

KaeHan waved to the family.

"And he'll answer all your questions. My adaptation is better eyesight, what's yours?"

The girl perked up and smiled at her dad. "Mine's seeing too!"

"High-five," Celeste said. She walked backward and opened the door behind her, "We're walking, we're walking."

With a waving hand, she led the family into the facility. The girl's hair had begun its slow slide downward, but no one noticed. KaeHan waited until the door closed behind them before turning to Knox.

"Good to see you." He stuck out his hand.

"Likewise."

Knox shook hands with Councilor KaeHan Lee, Head of Recruiting. KaeHan stood straight in his crisp beige uniform. He wore the flexible military-grade boots unique to IAS, and the shield remotes strapped around his biceps. Silver had shot through KaeHan's black hair since Knox had last seen him.

He must be pushing fifty. No, probably passed it.

"Can't believe it's been almost two decades since I've seen you face to face."

Knox shrugged. "I've sent you regular info."

"It's not the same."

KaeHan motioned to the door which opened for him, and Knox entered. The broad, clean corridor was the main artery of the building and ran from the lobby clear to the back exit. A lift and large loo were the first doors to Knox's left with hallways at regular intervals branching off in that direction. The right wall ran smooth and straight, interrupted only by two massive double doors.

Ahead of them, halfway down the main tributary, Celeste pointed to the first door on the right, and the family stopped to listen to her introduce the heart of IAS, the gym. She finished and backed further into the school.

"This way," Celeste said.

She led them toward the exit and the last door on the right, the stomach of IAS, the cafeteria. The girl's excited questions and Celeste's answers echoed down the vacant corridor.

27

"You received my plans for the operation?" Knox asked.

KaeHan nodded and kept walking without changing his pace.

"And Jefferson approved?"

Again, nod and walk.

"Mind if I ask how you sold it?"

KaeHan's pace faltered a split-second then recovered. "Purpose of operation: Gather shields and information from companies participating in human trafficking. Deliver shields to protect towns and information to me."

Knox halted. "I only said we were gathering shields."

KaeHan tried to keep going but finally had to stop and face Knox. "It doesn't change your mission. Do your part, and if you stumble on something, send the information my way. You would've done that anyway."

KaeHan was technically right, but the slight of hand didn't sit right with Knox.

"It sold the operation," KaeHan said in further defense. "And looks good if anyone from Caravan Suppliers or the Commune of Planets needs answers."

"I don't plan to be detected," Knox said.

"No plan survives first contact," KaeHan said and tried again to walk to the gym. Again he had to turn back to Knox, who wasn't budging. "Is there a problem?"

"I don't know, is there?"

Most adaptations manifested themselves physically: larger nasal passages, more rods in their eyes, faster reflexes, clearer vision. But KaeHan had a rare adaptation of herd-instinct prediction. Given the right pieces of information and a large enough "herd," KaeHan could calculate, with a heaping dose of gut intuition, the overall direction of society. Wars, bankruptcies, and collapses were foreseeable waves of human nature to his mind. But what had he predicted about Knox's mission?

With a sigh of resignation, KaeHan returned to Knox. "I actually haven't run calculations on your op... at least not extensive ones. I did a back of the envelope prediction."

"And?"

"You'll bump into some nasty stuff as you get the shields. I would appreciate if you record what you find." KaeHan tried again to step toward the gym, and this time, Knox joined him. "If Caravan Suppliers come questioning our methods, your information will be damning enough they'll leave us alone."

"But your predictions show a quiet operation?" Knox asked. "I'm not in this to put my wife or ship in danger."

"It looks smooth," KaeHan said. "What gossip from the shipping industry?"

Did Knox notice the sudden change in subject? Yes. And he let a pause linger just long enough to let KaeHan know. Then Knox shrugged it off. KaeHan had to keep his predictions close, even with the IAS Council, so of course he wouldn't let Knox in on all its intricacies.

"The wasps in Nuevo Port Alegre were poisoned," Knox said.

KaeHan stopped, his eyes flicking back and forth as if he were in REM sleep. Knox's information had triggered a prediction. KaeHan's eyes stopped twitching, and he meandered down the hall. He past the science wing that broke off to his left. Or at least that hallway had held the science classes nineteen years ago.

"Those are key pollinators for their Agricultural Domes," KaeHan said.

"Local fruit supplies are crashing," Knox said. "They'll need a new stock of pollinators."

"Who poisoned them?"

Knox's left eye twitched. "They poisoned themselves."

KaeHan groaned. "How?"

"The new fertilizer they used. It didn't kill the wasps, so they thought it was safe. It wasn't until three insect generations later that they discovered the fertilizer genetically handicapped the embryos. All the wasp hives are dying out."

"And the soil is now soaked with this fertilizer."

"They'll need to dig up the crop, mantle mud the soil to break up the toxin, and start over. At least a two-year process."

"Tragic," KaeHan said. "Well, good to know. So, where's Ximena? I've always talked to her over holocomm, never in person."

"You know our ship is her baby. It would take an emergency to rip her away." Knox stepped up to the gym doors on the right and motioned toward it. "But you're always welcome to visit us."

"IAS keeps me too busy for social visits. I guess it's my baby."

"Then you understand."

KaeHan sighed. "All too well."

The large double doors swooshed open. The cacophony of voices rolled over Knox as an arena of jumping, tumbling, racing kids welcomed him. Beige uniforms stuck to wet, slender backs and gangly legs. Sweat fogged the air, and a rush overcame Knox to bench press weights like he was seventeen again.

To his left, the familiar jungle gym grew out of the floor like a mighty redwood. Children clambered over the bars close to the ground, but older teens continued up the structure that stretched to the ceiling. Overhead, the bars continued like branches of the tree, and the oldest swung like lemurs.

One guy got a little too cocky showing off for his lady and slipped. His drop surprised him, but soon slowed to a gentle landing thanks to the hoverbelt he wore. The teen glared at the bar that betrayed him and let out several choice phrases in German.

"Falke," KaeHan tutted. "Watch the language when the little ones are still in the gym."

"Tell that to Instructor- Oh, hi Instructor Lee."

"Hello," KaeHan said.

"Sorry."

"I don't mind after hours when the gym is all older soldiers."

"Yes, sir."

The teen sprinted to the jungle gym and up its bark he loped with long arms and legs.

Knox followed KaeHan around wiggly six-year-olds practicing tumbling and footwork. Preteens lounged on the floor, waiting for their turn with student-grade plasma guns and programmed shields. At the far end of the gym, KaeHan pointed out older teens engaged in one-on-one battles. Their instructor stood back, interrupting as little as possible, guiding only when necessary. The remote-controlled drones dive-bombed like well-trained falcons. A proud papa, KaeHan's eyes shone over his students.

"Two of your crew are in here," KaeHan said, and a door slid open.

Knox entered a quieter, mid-sized gym, designed for advanced one-on-one duels. Bleachers lined one wall, so students could observe battles and demonstrations. Large boulders, scaffolding, piles of sand, and other strange mechanical objects waited behind a gate at the far end of the arena. Had it been fifteen years since Knox had dodged those very obstacles during battle demos?

To his right, two soldiers practiced their drills. In rhythm, they stepped, crossed, rolled, struck, dodged, stepped back, crossed again. Knox unconsciously shifted his weight, his body recalling his own years of repeating those fundamentals. The young man caught Knox's attention. His hair parted above his left eye, and his olive face was heart-shaped. But he wasn't an Islander from New Terra. Maybe Naya Surya?

KaeHan clapped his hands. The concussions echoed off the epoxycrete walls.

"Sann, TrysKa."

They jogged to KaeHan, bowed their heads to the councilor, and faced Knox. KaeHan motioned to Sann.

"This is Sann Dalise, your sniper, gifted in distance and nocturnal vision with faster reflexes."

Knox shook Sann's hand and inhaled. An air of depression hung over the soldier.

"Why sign up for this op?" Knox asked, but Sann tensed up like he was being interrogated. Knox softened his voice. "I like to understand my crew's motivation."

"Oh..." Sann relaxed and chewed on his answer. "My family comes from a community of poor farmers and fishermen. Human trafficking has stolen from my country, and I want to fight it whenever I can."

Farmers and fishermen? That would be rice patty farms.

"So, the Indonesian dome? Naya Surya?"

Sann's left eyebrow flicked up between his part.

"Yes sir. Khmer actually. But most people on New Terra don't know that planet very well."

"I shipped rice from Khmer to Aurora just last week. Good to have you on board."

"Thank you, sir."

Sann stepped back, and his shoulders relaxed. Good. Level heads made for less drama. KaeHan motioned to the other soldier.

"And this is TrysKa Carver, your pilot."

She'd swept her black hair into a ponytail that blossomed with corkscrew curls. Her eyes stayed downcast as she stuck her brown hand out and shook Knox's. Her grip had the steady strength of a pilot. Black tattoos curled and traced down her arms with calligraphy-style animals, land, and sky dancing around a muscled woman. The fierce designs struck a similar chord to the art of Atienna's country, Kikuyu.

"From Siku Mpya?" Knox asked.

TrysKa covered her arms with her hands. "Oh, no sir, I'm from South US. But Siku Mpya is my heritage."

"So, you like history?"

"Love it!" TrysKa lifted her face, her eyes shining.

"Then you and Knox have something in common," KaeHan said.

TrysKa stared back at the floor, and long eyelashes covered her eyes. But a smile peeked from her lips.

"I'm curious why you picked my *Maverick*," Knox said. "It's not a flashy fighter."

TrysKa shuffled her feet. "I've trained on many flashy fighters, but they don't bring help or aid to the hurting and suffering. Charity is a cargo ship's job, and that's what I fly."

"Perfect." Two down, one to go.

33

KaeHan nodded to Sann and TrysKa who returned to their drills. Knox followed KaeHan back through the door leading to the large gymnasium. Loud music with a heavy bass beat vibrated Knox's chest.

Thump. Thump. Thump.

A young instructor and his dozen students bopped and danced to the hip-hop. It stopped, and the leader switched to foot drills. The kids struggled to keep up as he turned to the left, forward, then to the right, always pumping his feet up and down. The beats started again, and the children cheered as they danced one last time. When the song stopped, all the kids collapsed to the floor, laughing and gasping for air.

"Why didn't I have that teacher?" Knox asked KaeHan.

"That's Brant Mallet."

"Lucky kids," Knox said.

KaeHan's right eye twitched like he was in REM sleep. KaeHan was having another intuition.

"What did you just see?" Knox asked.

"Don't know yet."

KaeHan strolled across the gym as if nothing had happened, but Knox lingered and sized up Brant. He was lean and tall, taller than Sid, and a giant compared to his students. His mane of fine blond hair reached just past his shoulders and was pulled back in a low ponytail. Brant's blond eyebrows and eyelashes blended into his fair complexion. Black eyes danced with pride over his panting students while he hardly broke a sweat.

Brant pointed and called the name of one of his students.

"Jesilya!"

After a quick high-five, the girl began her flips and spins. Brant knelt and held out his arms for support on the more difficult moves.

"Begin... good... jump big... plant your feet... very good... shift your weight... and finish strong... Good! This time, shift your weight sooner and you'll earn your high-five."

She succeeded, beamed, and high-fived Brant.

"Awesome!" He snapped and pointed at the next student. "LeDavien!"

Knox caught up to KaeHan who was chatting with a panting student, pretending not to notice that Knox had fallen behind. Together, the two left the gym.

"I need just one more soldier," Knox said, keeping his voice casual, but his gaze keen.

"You'll get your last one soon."

"Gut feeling?"

"Sure."

If Brant was going to be the last member of this operation, the team would be solid. That felt good. Like checking off an on-time delivery.

"Are you going back to the spaceport now?" KaeHan asked.

"I'm not sure." Knox spun on his heels, taking in the hallway spotted with students, soldiers, and instructors. "Been a long time since I was here." Knox turned back to KaeHan. "Is it the same as before? The bullying? Have things changed?"

"Ah." KaeHan smiled at the gaggle of students sprinting past. "You want to know if your stunt helped."

"I was just a stupid lad."

"With a good cause," KaeHan said. "And it did start change. After you left, I had to finish the job, of course."

"Real change takes many hands."

"Always."

Knox stared off past the ceiling, to the rooms and floors

beyond his vision. To the life he'd lived when he was here. To the choices he'd made, and the accusations he'd thrown at the council. Wow, Knox had been a punk.

"You know," Knox said, "I think I'll wander for a bit if that's OK with you."

"Take your time," KaeHan said.

KaeHan waved and turned toward the lift to his office. It was time for him to meet with the new recruit.

Almost dinner now, the current of students and adults flowed toward the back of IAS, to its cafeteria. Knox leaned up against a wall and watched the faces go by. A short head of black curls bobbed past cutting against the stream.

Knox narrowed his eyes. The boy snuck to the lift, looked over his shoulder like a thief checking his tail, and slipped inside. Yeah, that wasn't suspicious at all.

When the lift door closed, two twelve-year-old boys turned a corner and sliced through the tide toward the lift. They reclined on both sides of its closed door, sneering with their arms crossed. They watched the number above the lift click up until it paused at sixteen. One cut his eyes at the other and pushed the button. The numbers stepped back down to one, the empty lift opened, and both entered.

Something's rotten here.

It was Knox's turn to wait for the lift to drop off the teens on the same floor. Then he pushed the button calling the lift back, entered, and hit sixteen.

4

Alex

Everyone else was at dinner in the cafeteria. Except for Alex. He was rooting around in André's dorm. André's mom had baked homemade brownies. Must be nice having the money to afford cocoa. André had then savored one in front of Alex at lunch today. He would pay.

The remaining brownies weren't in any of André's cubbies above his cot nor under his pillow. Alex stood up, his fists on his hips, his head cocked.

"Of course!"

Alex ducked his head under André's cot, and *voilà*, brownies. Alex untaped the package, peeled it open, and nibbled the corner of brown heaven. His eyes rolled into the back of his head. Wow, André's mom had put a LOT of cocoa in there. Alex wrapped up that brownie and opened the next one. He nibbled that one too. He took a corner out of each brownie, put all of them back in the packages, and taped them under André's cot. That would teach him.

Alex wiped his mouth and opened the door. And came to a halt.

A man leaned against the wall outside André's dorm room. He was short, black, and muscular with a shiny, shaved head. His clothes made him look like a space pirate. The space pirate looked familiar. The gym. He had walked with KaeHan in the gym just now.

Alex waited for the pirate to speak or move, but he did nothing. Alex shrugged. Weirdo. He walked away from André's dorm room and froze. His sensitive hearing picked up breathing around the corner. Could it be André? Probably.

Alex turned around, walked past the pirate again, got a few steps away, and froze once more. More breathing around another corner in front of him: NC, André's roommate. Alex was trapped. He rubbed the big, new bruise under his left rib. He had more than one reason for sabotaging André's brownies.

How to get out of this trap?

"Mind if I walk with you?"

Alex yelped. The pirate had snuck up behind. He motioned down the hall, past NC hiding around the corner, to freedom. Alex nodded. The pirate stuck his hands in his pockets as he strolled next to Alex.

"What's your name?"

The man had a deep voice and thick accent. Rory, a boy a year older than Alex, had an accent like that. All the girls liked it.

"Alex." His voice sounded strange to his ears. How long had it been since he'd heard it?

"Well, Alex, I'm Knox."

They strolled past NC who sneered at Alex. Alex stuck his tongue out, and Knox whacked him on the back of the head.

"Don't poke the anthill," Knox said.

What? Alex scrunched his eyebrows and cocked his head at Knox.

"Don't stir up trouble when you don't have to."

He deserves it.

Alex waited for Knox to guess what he was thinking. That was what all the other adults had done since his mom had died, answered for him. But Knox didn't do that. Well, Alex wasn't going to let Knox correct him without defending himself.

"He's a jerk."

"Maybe, but making him madder won't help you."

Alex shrugged. "Don't care." As long as he was talking to Knox, might as well sniff out some gossip. "What mission are you leading?"

"Some people I know need shields to protect them. I'm getting some for them."

"Will it be dangerous?"

"Probably not. A small op."

Knox had walked with Alex down to the next branch in the hallway. Alex's room was down this short hall. He could escape, but... but...

"How did you get adapted soldiers to help you?" Alex asked. "Soldiers are only sent on big important missions."

"Protecting a village from pirates isn't big and important?" Knox asked.

There was no anger in his voice, more of a challenge. Like Knox was testing him.

"Depends," Alex said. "How big is the village?"

Knox's eyes winced. A tiny movement, but there, just the same.

"It's not big," Knox said. "Listen, in the future, don't go out of your way to attract trouble."

Knox turned. He was leaving. He couldn't leave yet.

"Are you adapted too?" Alex asked. "You aren't carrying an IAS gun."

"Not every adapted carries the same gun."

Gotcha. "So, you are adapted."

"I didn't say," Knox stopped and narrowed his eyes. "Oh, you're good."

Alex smirked. "So, what's your adaptation?"

"You first."

Fine.

"Sensitive hearing and some nocturnal vision. I'm a sneak."

"A sneak? Curious nickname. Did you pick that or did someone else label you?"

Alex didn't answer.

"OK fine, my turn. My adaptation is sensitive smell."

Alex hadn't bet on that. He backed up and crossed his arms over his chest.

"So, you can smell emotions?"

"Smell emotions?" Knox's eyebrows raised. Did his lips almost smile? "Smell emotions. I've never heard my ability put quite that way before."

"What do you smell about me?"

Alex held his breath. Would Knox know? Would he figure it out? Knox took a knee and leaned his thick arm on it. He narrowed his eyes and flared his nostrils. Alex waited.

"Chocolate."

Alex giggled. Immediately, he touched his fingertips to the dimple on his right cheek. He hadn't smiled in so long, the dimple might have disappeared. It should have disappeared. Some things were supposed to go away after a boy lost his mommy: like giggles, homemade brownies, and adorable dimples.

"And grief," Knox said.

Grief? What did this man know about grief?

"When did your mommy die?" Alex spat out.

"I was wee, it was an accident."

Really? Alex shifted his weight from his left foot to his right.

"And your daddy?"

"I was older than you, twenty-one."

This man understood! Of all the people Alex knew, Knox understood being an orphan.

"Take me with you."

"Whoa, whoa, whoa." Knox back-peddled, his hands up. "Lad, I'm a space trucker."

"Space truckers have children."

"They don't take them into the spaceports," Knox said. "A spaceport is not a safe place for a child."

"Do you have children?"

Alex held his breath. *Please say, "no."*

"My wife and I," Knox twisted his wedding ring, "don't have any."

Sadness. That was sadness. Alex couldn't put his finger on how he knew. Maybe the way Knox looked away for an instant. Just like Knox could detect a hint of chocolate, Alex could sniff out sadness. He'd been there.

"Would you like to have me then?"

"You stay here where you're safe."

And that ended it. Except that Alex had one last card to play.

"But I'm not safe here."

Alex lifted his right sleeve, showing off the purple and green bruise on his shoulder. The bruise under his rib wasn't his only one, just his newest. Knox's jaw set on edge.

"You have to report this."

"No! It's no one else's business. I just want to get out of here!"

"If you won't report it, I will," Knox said. "I have a meeting tomorrow with KaeHan, and I'll tell him."

"But-"

"I don't tolerate bullying or hazing. Ever."

"But-"

"And you're not coming with me to a dangerous spaceport."

That was that. Knox spun on his heel and marched to the lift. Still, before he entered and disappeared forever, he hesitated. Alex waved. Knox waved back, but still left.

You're not coming with me to a dangerous spaceport.

"We'll see about that," Alex said.

If Alex couldn't convince Knox, then he'd convince KaeHan. If he couldn't convince KaeHan, Knox had mentioned a wife. Maybe she was sad too. Maybe she would take Alex.

He closed his eyes and strained his ears. No more breathing around corners. NC and André must have abandoned their stake-out and gone to dinner. Quiet as a shadow, Alex slipped down the hall to the lift at the other end. He rode it to the twentieth floor, and stood before KaeHan's office. With a breath in and out, he knocked.

"Yes?" KaeHan answered the door then looked down. "Alex?"

"I talked to Knox, and he said I could go on the mission with him."

#

Ximena didn't hear the ship's call the first time. Or the second. She was putting together another Phase Burner. This one had more of a dragonfly design. Deadly and delicate.

"Ximena," Liam's voice said.

"Oh, sorry!" Ximena jumped up from the breakroom table and ran to the cockpit. "Coming, coming, coming. Who is it?"

"Councilor KaeHan Lee from IAS."

"Why's he calling me? He must think Knox is here. Put him through."

KaeHan floated above the cockpit's controls. Next to him hopped a little boy with a head of black curls and puppy dog eyes.

"Hello Ximena," KaeHan said. "I'm afraid there's been a bit of confusion I need to clear up."

"Uh-huh," Ximena answered, but didn't look at KaeHan.

She was transfixed with the little boy. His lips were parted like he wanted to ask her a question, a deeply important question, and she yearned to blurt out *yes!* Ximena smiled at him, and he smiled back. When his lips spread, his round right cheek creased with the cutest. Dimple. Ever. Her hand, as if with a mind of its own, found the cross around her neck, and her thumb rubbed its metal, warmed by her chest.

"Ximena? Did you hear me?" KaeHan asked.

"What? No, sorry, what was that?"

"Alex says Knox told him-"

"Who's Alex?"

"I'm Alex!"

The boy waved big, like he thought she wouldn't see his image unless he exaggerated his movements. Ximena melted and waved back.

"Back to the point," KaeHan said. "Alex claims Knox asked him to come on the operation."

"He's coming with us?" Ximena caught her breath.

"Yes!" Alex yelled.

"No!" KaeHan said. "At least-"

Ximena must have looked disappointed because KaeHan paused. He looked from Alex, to Ximena, to Alex, back to Ximena.

"I assume," KaeHan said, more carefully now, "that Knox would have asked your opinion before making a decision like that."

"Of course, he would have."

So the boy isn't coming.

Ximena released the cross and picked at her thumbnail. She'd chipped it doing repairs earlier today. It was irritating.

"I suspect Alex isn't being honest about Knox," KaeHan said.

Alex stared down at the floor now, instead of meeting Ximena's gaze. She bit her thumbnail and ripped the loose part off.

"You're probably right."

A light on the controls blinked. Someone had opened the back ramp.

"Ximena?" It was Knox.

"In here," she said.

Knox's boots clicked, clicked, clicked from the cargo bay to the cockpit then halted.

"Hello KaeHan," Knox said. "Hello Alex."

"So, you two have met?" KaeHan asked.

"Aye."

"Then maybe you can help us."

Ximena couldn't stay for this.

"I'll be in our room," she said and squeezed past Knox.

She wouldn't cry before she got to the room. She wouldn't cry before she got to the room. She wouldn't cry before she

44

got to the room...

#

Knox didn't need to smell the snot and tears to know *exactly* what Ximena was going to do once their bedroom door closed. She was going to cry.

Fuck. Fuck. Fuck. Fuck. Fuck.

He had left a perfectly happy wife on this ship. Now she was on the brink of tears. The bedroom door closed.

"What the hell just happened?" Knox threw himself into the pilot's chair.

Alex startled. KaeHan didn't flinch.

"Alex informed me that you two agreed he was going on the operation with you," KaeHan said. "I think I can safely assume that was a misunderstanding."

"Misunderstanding my..." Knox cut his eyes at Alex. "I did *not* agree to let him come with me. The spaceports are too dangerous."

"Other adapted kids go to the spaceports with their mentors," Alex said. "In the one-to-one program."

Knox blinked. *One-to-one program?*

"Am I missing something?" Knox asked KaeHan.

"It was a trial program started by IAS seven years ago. A one-to-one program matches a particularly talented student, or a student with special needs, with a mentor, a trained IAS graduate."

Graduate? Well, Knox didn't qualify for that.

"Those kids go to spaceports all the time," Alex said. "Besides, the pretty lady likes me."

Knox winced. "KaeHan, can I talk to you without the interruptions?"

"Good idea." To Alex: "Wait outside my office while Knox

and I talk."

"But–"

"Go."

Alex bowed his head, his curls drooping over his dejected face. He dragged his feet out of the office as torturously slow as possible. When the door finally closed behind him, Knox slumped in his chair.

"Knox, I'm sorry," KaeHan said. "I'll tell Alex, 'no' and that will end this."

"It might for you, it won't for me."

"Why not?"

Knox closed his eyes. In his mind's eye, he could see his wife blowing her nose into tissue after tissue.

"Ximena."

"I noticed she got attached rather quickly."

"That's putting it mildly." KaeHan waited, so with a sigh, Knox continued, "KaeHan, she can't have children."

"Ah, I see."

"It's never bothered me. I love her, and children would complicate our space shipping life. A lot."

"But it bothers her."

"Off and on. She'll be fine for a year or two then one of her sisters pops out another baby and..."

Knox growled. Damn, it tore his insides out when Ximena cried, but this was one of those uncontrollable facts of life. He couldn't make her womb work. Heaven knows, they'd tried. They'd paid plenty of doctors. But a simple space trucker couldn't afford the more expensive procedures, the ones that really worked. Knox's gaze drifted back to KaeHan.

"I can't believe I'm about to ask this." Knox sucked in his breath and let it out slow. "Would the IAS Council actually allow me to mentor Alex? Even if I didn't graduate?"

KaeHan leaned back in his chair. "I could work up a temporary contract, a test period if you will."

Knox shook his head, coming to his senses.

"No, KaeHan, what am I saying? What are *we* saying? We have to do what's best for the kid. Spaceports aren't safe."

"Neither is training to be a soldier at IAS." KaeHan let that statement linger. He leaned forward and clasped his hands over his desk. "Knox, do you know what Alex has been through these past three months?"

"I figured out he lost his mother."

"He did, to terraforming cancer. And he hasn't spoken a word to a soul since then."

Knox said nothing.

"And then, just now, he knocks on my door and spills out this story about how he wants to go with you. Knox, I haven't heard the boy speak that much in a *year*."

Again, Knox didn't have an answer.

"You might be just what he needs. But I have a question."

"Go ahead," Knox said.

"What did *you* share with him?"

Knox opened his mouth then snapped it shut. "Well, now that was personal."

"You shared something personal with Alex?" KaeHan fell back in his chair and laughed. "Knox, you two were meant for each other." Pause. "Will you keep him safe?"

"I'll protect him with my life."

"Then I'll write up the paperwork tonight." KaeHan pinched the bridge of his nose with his thumb and index finger. "Monique will kill me for staying up late again." He chuckled. "But what else can I do? See you tomorrow."

"Tomorrow."

KaeHan reached his hand forward and pushed a light on his desk. He vanished, and Knox was left alone. Well, almost alone. Knox got up, crept down the hall, and stared at the door to the captain's quarters. His wife was sobbing on the other side. He was sure of it.

Dammit.

"Open."

The door swished open, and Ximena scooped up the wads of cloth handkerchiefs.

"Oh, I'm sorry, I just lost it back there, but don't worry about me."

Knox walked to her, gathered the handkerchiefs, and put them in the cleanser. The captain's quarters came with certain luxuries like a personal cleanser and toilet.

"I'm a mess." She smeared snot down her sleeve.

She was beautiful. The cleanser beeped, and Knox brought the cleaned pile back to her.

"He's coming onboard with us for a trial training period," Knox said.

Ximena stared at him, mouth hanging open.

"He?"

"Alex, the boy."

"He's coming on our ship?"

Her face had the pleading look of a child begging her daddy *please, please, please, can I keep the puppy?* Knox couldn't refuse.

"IAS has a training program, a one-to-one program. I can mentor the boy on the ship." Suddenly Ximena was in his arms, her face buried in his neck. "There, there." He rubbed her back.

Ximena lifted her face and pressed her warm lips to his. How long had it been since they'd fooled around?

"Umm... Ximena..."

"Uh-huh?"

She kissed down his jawline, and Knox craned his head back. What had he wanted to say?

This is going to be hard.

IAS could take Alex back.

Screw it. Knox lifted Ximena's shirt and rolled her onto their cot. Consequences would wait until tomorrow.

5

Brant

Back at IAS, Brant taught his last class of the afternoon, his eight-year-olds. He'd reserved a larger mat in the corner of the gym for today's lesson. Best place to corral his students and keep them from accidentally rolling into other instructor's territory.

"The first step to shield practice is to give yourself plenty of room." Brant stretched wide his arms. "Go on, spread out. When you turn your shields on, you don't want to bump into your neighbor."

Instructor Celeste, next to him, giggled. She knew the evil plot for this lesson. They'd concocted it together. Brant winked at her and faced the kids again.

"The second step to shield practice is to make sure the armbands don't come off." Brant waved his arms furiously around, but the bands stayed strapped to both triceps. "So, wiggle and see if your shield bands come off."

The kids gesticulated like a bunch of puppets whose strings had gotten tangled. Then they started laughing. All part of the plan.

"Now!" All the kids froze at Brant's call. "It's time to turn on your shield."

He twitched his left and right arm in a quick circle, and a shield whooshed to life, shining like a halo around him. All the kids' eyes went wide, and their arms started flopping. A shield popped on. All the kids yelped in surprise then returned to arm waving. Another popped on. And another. And another. Celeste, her own shield activated, covered her mouth with both hands, her laughter spilling around them.

"OK, Micah and Jesilya." Brant pointed. "Go to Celeste, and she'll help you get those shields on. Oh, wait, let me come get you."

Brant turned off his shield and pushed open a path through the shields. Every time he touched one, the static electricity gave him a zap. By the time Micah and Jesilya got out of the electromagnetic bubbles, his ponytail had fluffed like a pompom. He stepped back, smoothed his fine hair, and smiled his crinkled grin.

"Alright. Now you're going to learn how to keep your balance in these things. Try *not* to fall over. If you do fall, try to get back up."

With that, Brant turned on his shield and barreled through the center of his class. The whole group squealed as their shields went rolling, and they with them. One ball went shooting out of the herd. Brant turned his shield off and leapt through the gaps. He pushed the escaping sphere back toward his flock.

"Oh no you don't!"

His student, Desmond, died laughing as he tumbled inside his shield. Brant raced around the class, corralling the hamster balls that had become his students. Nearby instructors glared at him and sniffed at his lack of dignity.

Don't care. These kids are having a blast.

Micah and Jesilya figured out how to activate their shields and joined their friends. Celeste raced past Brant to catch another fleeing child. Before thirty minutes had passed, his students had regained their footing. They bounced off each other on purpose, knocked each other over, and recovered when they fell. By the end of the hour, they were running, rolling with the punches, and recovering their footing to charge again, all in stride.

This lesson had been a grueling month-long drill when Brant was nine. He liked his way better. Kids learned faster when they were playing.

Aubrey, the meditation instructor, strode up. Brant cupped his hands around his mouth.

"OK, everybody, the last step of shields is turning them off."

He demonstrated with a quick roll of his arms. The kids flopped their arms around for several minutes before all the bubbles popped.

"Time for meditation," Aubrey stated.

His kids groaned.

"Wait!" Brant said. "I need my high-fives from every one of you!"

That got them moving. The students lined up and gave him a high-five as they filed past. The boys tried to slap his hand really hard. The girls giggled. Brant and Celeste waved as their last class of the day skipped out of the gym. The other instructors funneled toward the teacher's lounge at the back of the gym, but Brant waved to Celeste and ducked out. No need to hear advice on how to be a more dignified and quieter teacher.

Brant rode the lift up to the third floor. In the silence, his earbuds allowed more sound in. Normally they had to filter out the raucousness of the gym for his sensitive adapted hearing, but in this lift, he could hear the buffer of air whooshing past the outside of the wall.

The special adaptations of the students at IAS were simply increased predator senses. When humanity had moved to the new Six Planets, the complex code of human genes sensed the change. So, some children were born adapted, evolved to their new environments. Their genes had tapped into ancient reflexes, senses, and strength. In Brant's case, he heard like a bat-eared fox.

The door swished open, Brant exited and turned left. He almost reached his hallway.

"Brant."

It was a whisper from behind him, down the hall in the empty cove leading to the stairs.

"I know you hear me," Ed said.

Of course, Brant heard him.

"Brant, do you want to talk privately now or publicly later? I can do public if that's what you want."

Brant wrenched his boots away from the hallway leading to his dorm, and pointed them instead toward the stairs. Thunk, thunk, thunk. He stomped down the epoxycrete floor to his waiting father. Around the corner, Ed stood, hands clasped behind his back, suit pressed, teeth clenched.

"I don't like when you ignore me."

"I don't like when you stalk me."

"I'm your father, I have a right to know what my son's up to."

"Newsflash: I'm a graduate now. A legal adult, with a job,

and a place to stay, and food to eat. I don't need you or your money anymore. So, unless you have something to add, I'm going now."

Brant turned on his heels.

"What about your mother?"

Brant didn't turn back to face Ed. "You leave her alone, or so help me..."

"Oh hell, Brant, I'm not going to hurt her. I've never-"

Brant spun, grabbed Ed by the suit, and slammed him against the wall.

"You bruised her all my childhood, you asshole!"

At first Ed tried to grab Brant's arm, but as big as he was, Brant had grown strong enough to finally challenge him. He couldn't budge his son. Ed blinked and his grip faltered. Was he surprised? Afraid? Good.

But Ed's face slipped into a sneer, and his eyes flicked to the camera standing watch in the ceiling corner.

"Temper, temper," he said. "You wouldn't want the parents to see a video of their kid's teacher punching his own father."

Brant's blood pressure shot up, ringing in his sensitive ears. A small pill, surgically inserted just within his right jawline, administered a dose of calming drugs. Some adapted children needed medical help to stay in control, and IAS had decided Brant was one of them. Brant forced himself to breathe. His fingers reluctantly wrenched open, and he stepped back.

"One of the great hypocrisies of this school." Ed straight-ened his jacket and wiped down his sleeves. "They train soldiers and killers, but the instructors of the little ones have to be gentle kittens."

"Abusing young children causes lifetime trauma," Brant said through clenched teeth. "There's a reason intensive training doesn't start until the last two years of school."

Ed swooped his bangs to the side and went on as if Brant hadn't spoken.

"As for those bruises, your mother got them at her daycare job. She's clumsy, and those two-year-olds like to sneak up behind her knees. You did that when you were little too, as I recall. She had a lot of bruises then."

"She didn't get them from me, or do you think I don't remember?"

"No proof, no case. You know how the courts hate unfounded allegations. The fines for those are quite costly, and you can't afford that right now. Not on an instructor's income."

"What about Mom?" Brant's voice was coarse sandpaper.

"She can't afford her rent." Ed fluffed his cravat. "Did she not tell you? I've been footing the bill for her place for the last four months."

The pounding blood drained from Brant's head, straight to his feet. Mom had been taking payments from Ed for four months? Of course she wouldn't tell Brant that, wouldn't want to burden him.

"How much does Mom need?"

"Apparently she's hit the end of the month with no credits in her account. She never was the best at budgeting. If she doesn't get a full months' rent in three days, it's off to the Commons."

The Commons. Government housing. Or more accurately, epoxycrete boxes stacked one atop the other with hallways between. Cameras monitored the hallways to protect the tenants, but the nastiness happened inside the cubicles. *No right to my privates* had been the rally cry to keep prying governments out of private spaces.

The downside of the privacy meant Brant's mom could be raped or hurt in the Commons with very little legal recourse. No proof meant no case. A by-product of overwhelmed, underfunded courts and overflowing jails.

Brant reached for the scroll on his hip, but Ed chuckled in a coughing way.

"You don't have enough to cover her rent. Believe me."

"You checked my account?"

"Didn't have to. I know how much instructors get paid, and I know the cost of the campus dorms for the staff. I can subtract, Brant."

"So then, pay her rent like you always have. Out of the goodness of your heart."

"I planned to, until you rubbed in my face that you're an adult now. So, if you want to take care of your mother, as all good sons should, you will need a higher paying job."

Soft footfalls approached the stairs, Brant's sensitive hearing picking up the pad, pad, pad. The person approaching was rolling the sole of their boot to muffle the sound. Unaware, Ed snapped the scroll from his hip, unrolled it, and handed the screen to Brant. Brant didn't take it, but the words, hovering an inch above its surface, cut into the air.

A security job.

"A high-ranking member of the Commune of Planets needs an escort. If our company offers him an IAS graduate, we win the bid. You'd have a nice addition to your resume."

"Did a councilor approve of this?"

Ed flicked the application to the bottom, and Head Councilor Jefferson's signature scrolled into view.

"Just sign right here," Ed said.

"He's got another job already," Sann said.

Brant could have hugged Sann. "Whatcha got?"

Sann nodded to Brant's scroll. "Pull up the *Maverick* op."

Brant opened his scroll, navigated to the IAS job applications, pulled up the *Maverick* operation, and, without reading it, flicked to the bottom. He jabbed the Fighter slot.

"Brant Mallet."

His voice signature squiggled across the form, and the deed was done.

"So now I can pay for Mom's rent." Brant turned his back on Ed. "And we're done."

"For now," Ed said.

Instead of falling in next to Brant, Sann stared down Ed with a flat, calculating look. His eyes traveled up and down Ed's body, and Brant could almost see him identify the fatal hit points.

"Well," Ed said. "Look who's become a man on his last mission." His gaze pierced Brant. "Maybe this job with Sann will be good for you after all. When you need more money, and you will, my company's always hiring."

Ed slunk down the stairwell's maw, his footsteps clicking further and further down its gullet until even Brant couldn't hear them.

"Thank you," he said to Sann.

"Welcome."

With his heart rate even again, Brant started back to his dorm, and Sann strolled by his side. A guardedness shrouded Sann's face that hadn't been there two months ago.

"I've been calling you the last few days," Brant said.

"Yeah, I know."

"I was about to come break down the door."

"Yeah, I know."

"What's up?"

Sann shrugged. This last mission had raised an invisible but very real shield between them.

"If you need to save some money," Sann said, changing the subject, "you can room with me. I have two walls programmed for cots."

"My dorm is inside IAS. If I roomed with you, I'd have to travel from your apartment."

"That's what the public trams are for. It takes ten minutes, tops."

"I got this."

Brant had taken care of himself and his mom since he was little. He didn't need any help. Sann sighed so low it was almost a growl.

"You're so stubborn."

"I just like to take care of my own. Is that so wrong?"

"Not everybody's like you. Not everybody's 'got this.'"

"Yeah, well, I've got this." Brant might be slow, but something felt off. "Do *you* need me?"

"I didn't say that."

"OK then." *Wait a second.* "But you didn't say that you didn't."

Crap! Why wouldn't Sann tell it straight?

"OK, fine!" Brant said. "I could save some money. Rooming with you would be a great idea."

He pulled out his scroll and cancelled his dorm. A transfer request popped up, and Brant narrowed down the selections to Sann's apartment. Sann smirked and made Brant sweat for a second or two before accepting.

"Thank you," Sann said.

So Sann did need the company? Why couldn't he just come out with it? The door opened to reveal Brant's former dorm, and Sann's gaze swept the battle zone.

"Well, I didn't know this before I asked you to room with me. I'm certain there's a floor under here somewhere, but there's no evidence."

"Very funny."

Brant scooped up his instructor uniforms, extra boots, sheets for his cot, bath towels, and miscellaneous stuff. A niche opened on the back wall. Brant crammed his stuff in with his elbow while the hatch slid closed over everything. Off his belongings whooshed to their new home.

"Now that's going to be all over my floor," Sann said.

"Our floor." Brant grinned big then threw out his hands. "Come on! I'll clean it up while I room with you, I promise."

Did a grin tug at the corner of Sann's lips? A touch of his old twinkle light up his eyes?

"I'm hungry," Brant said. "Let's get some food."

"You're always hungry," Sann said.

They headed back to the lift.

"Of course I'm always hungry. Food is required to stay alive."

"Yeah, but, you're *always*— never mind."

They exited the lift and bumped into TrysKa, Amalie, and Willow leaving the cafeteria.

"Anything good today?" Brant asked, eyeing Amalie.

She smirked and arched her eyebrow. "Willow and I thought so, TrysKa was disappointed."

"They didn't let you into the kitchen?" Sann asked.

"The school meal needed all the burners and hydrators today."

The way TrysKa grimaced, Brant would have thought they'd made her eat fried slugs. But then, she so loved cooking her own food, her own way.

"Saw you signed up for the Maverick op," Sann said.

TrysKa perked up. "Are you signed up too?"

"Yup."

"So, will you stay cooped up in your apartment alone until the operation?" Willow asked. "Or are visitors allowed?"

Sann stuffed his fists in his pockets and stared at the floor. "Brant's rooming with me now, but anyone can visit if they like."

"You're roomies now?" Willow asked Brant.

"Saving rent," Brant said. "And I'll be going on the Maverick op too."

All three women's faces did a doubletake.

"What about teaching?" TrysKa asked, the first to recover.

"It'll be waiting for me when I get back."

Willow sniffed the air. "I smell Ed."

Sann snickered. The snicker surprised him, but then he seemed pleased.

"Ed's reek does cling to the clothes."

"Enough, guys," Brant said.

But seeing Sann smile was worth a little ribbing, so Brant let it pass. Amalie pursed her full lips.

"My Dad could help if Ed's trying to play the finances card."

Brant bristled. "I got this."

Amalie backed off. Brant opened his mouth to apologize or smooth it over, but nothing came out. She smiled in that knowing way.

"OK, I get it. Have a good dinner."

The three ladies walked away. Brant and Sann lingered a

few seconds. After all, the view was lovely. But Brant didn't want to be seen as creepy, so he and Sann turned back to the cafeteria.

Brant grabbed two bean burgers with almond-flax buns. The cafeteria staff had prepared broccoli and cauliflower in six different ways. The first apples of the season were out but still too tart.

"Cherries!" Brant scooped a heaping spoonful onto his plate.

Cherries were only in season in the local Ag-Domes once a year, and July was it. The students in front of Brant took their lunches without paying. Their fees were covered by the school. Brant paid the discounted price for instructors, and Sann forked over the soldier's rate.

"It shouldn't cost more for soldiers," Brant said and set his tray down at a table reserved for instructors and soldiers.

"We make more, so they can get away with it," Sann said and pulled up a chair. "If IAS could charge you more, they would."

"But then they'd have to pay me more."

Brant and Sann swallowed their Vitamin D supplements then Brant bit off a hunk of his burger. Conversation stopped for food.

6

Meeting Prep

Brant reported early the next morning to a small meditation room, simple with five large pastel pillows tossed on the floor. Sann and TrysKa sat on their pillow meditating while Brant paced its perimeter... multiple times.

"Why don't you meditate while you wait?" Sann asked, keeping his eyes closed.

"I am meditating."

"You're pacing."

"This is how I meditate." Brant finished his first turn around the room.

"Perhaps we should've picked a bigger room," TrysKa said. Her voice had a lilt to it.

"If it bothers you..."

"We're fine," Sann and TrysKa said together. Sann waved his hand at Brant.

"Pace."

Brant stepped out the measurements of the room. He learned the length by heart, and closed his eyes. His arms swung in rhythm with his feet, and his breathing and heartbeat synchronized. Brant's lesson plans stopped nagging him. The sneering face of Ed retreated. Brant's tongue relaxed and fell from the roof of his mouth, and his sore jaw unclenched.

When Brant rounded his sixteenth lap, KaeHan entered. Sann and TrysKa jumped to attention, and Brant took his position by their side. Knox walked in and stopped next to KaeHan. The short, broad captain had the calloused exterior Brant expected from a man who made his living from space shipping. Knox's eyes gleamed obsidian, and his shaved head and jawline were cut from dark granite.

Then Alex burst into the room. He checked Sann's posture then clasped his hands in front of him and bowed his head in imitation. His curls trickled down covering the front of his round face.

"What's this?" Brant demanded.

"Knox is being assigned as Alex's Mentor," KaeHan said.

"Alex in the...?" That didn't make sense. "But Knox isn't adapted! He doesn't qualify as a mentor."

Knox's right sleeve clicked, and a gun shot out into his right hand. Brant's muscles moved on instinct, drawing his own gun and pointing it between Knox's eyes. Knox's stare went over the barrel and bored into Brant.

"I was going to hand you my gun," Knox said, his voice low. "Sorry... I... habit."

Brant holstered his gun. Knox wiggled his plasma pistol free from a wire contraption attached to his arm. Knox's roomy jacket sleeves didn't just give him easier movement, but hid a weapon too. He presented the butt of his gun, and Brant accepted.

Brant spun the custom weapon in his hand, admiring its craftsmanship. He'd never held a plasma gun of this make before. It was thin and flat, designed to hide in Knox's sleeve, yet the trigger and handle were wide enough to fit the captain's hand. Brant weighed it in his hand to find the heavy spots: the gas chamber, plasma inducer, and compressor. This device had once been a Langmuir XI, but someone had tweaked and customized it to fit Knox perfectly.

Wait. The insignia along the barrel. IAS?

Only adapted soldiers could carry an IAS-marked weapon. Brant flipped up the gun and checked its butt. There was the chip. That metal sliver allowed IAS graduates to take their weapons past any customs: space, or planet-side. Very few organizations had a blank check when it came to carrying weapons, and IAS counted itself as one of the privileged.

Independent space truckers, like this Knox, normally had to turn over their guns the instant they stepped out of the shipping sector of the space station. Some truckers never left the hangar simply because they refused to check their weapons before joining civilization.

But here was Knox carrying an IAS-marked pistol. That wasn't possible without the authorization of a Head Instructor, and whose name was sketched in Korean symbols?

"Councilor Lee?"

"Knox is adapted, and has been my personal informant on the space shipping business for years."

Brant suddenly felt the heat of everyone's stares. He handed the weapon back to Knox with a muttered apology. His face flushed and then, to top it off, the drugs from his pill slipped into his system. An artificial calm swept over him as shame struck back harder.

"With all due respect," Brant said to KaeHan, "even though Knox is adapted, he doesn't know what Alex has lived through."

"I know," Knox said.

"How?"

"He told me."

"He told you? *He told you?*" That was too much. "Alex hasn't spoken a word in months and he just told you? Do you two know each other? Am I missing something?"

Knox opened his mouth, but Alex cut in.

"I can tell anyone anything I want."

Brant caught his breath. He hadn't heard Alex's voice in so long. Was it his imagination or had it lowered since the last time?

"You don't even know the man."

"You're not my mom! You don't get to choose who I talk to!"

Ouch.

Brant knelt. "Alex, I didn't say I was your–"

"I hate you," Alex whispered.

He might as well have slapped Brant. Hard. The room went silent. *I hate you?* Brant had visited Alex's mom when she was sick, promised he'd watch over her son. And Brant had. He'd been patient with Alex in class, made the older kids leave him alone, and this was his reward? *I hate you.*

Brant forced his numb legs to stand and fell back in line.

"Am I missing something?" Knox asked KaeHan.

"Nothing I know about." To Alex: "Would you care to tell us what's going on?"

Alex shrugged. "Nothing. I just don't like other people acting like my parents. That's all."

"Will you listen when I act like your mentor?" Knox asked.

Alex straightened. "Of course."

65

Why? Why was Alex OK with Knox?

"Is this going to be a problem?" Knox asked both Brant and Alex.

"No, sir," Brant said.

"No, sir," Alex said.

Knox cut an I-don't-like-this look at KaeHan, who only sighed.

"Nothing in life is perfect, Knox."

"Fine, I'll figure it out," Knox said. "Can we get back to discussing the mission?"

Everyone nodded.

"Good." Knox tugged his jacket straight. "We'll be collecting the three shields along with fuel cells to power them."

Knox scanned each of their uniforms.

"This is an undercover operation, so dress in clothes befitting a spaceport. Look up images from the public feeds for your outfits, not holomovies. Those don't have a clue about real space trucker life."

Knox closed his eyes and ran through his mental list.

"Only two sets of clothes, plus what you're wearing. Hide the IAS markings on your guns." He opened his eyes. "I'll cover more details about each individual job on my ship. Understood?"

"Yes, sir," they all answered.

"Then I'll see you all tomorrow morning, 0600 New York time." Knox looked down on Alex and the hard lines around his eyes softened. "Not you, you come with me now."

"Really?"

"*Maverick* needs to be refueled, repaired, and restocked. If you're going to be my student, you'll have to learn."

"Yes!" Alex fist-pumped the air and trailed Knox and

KaeHan out.

Brant was left with TrysKa and Sann again.

"Well, that went well," Brant said.

"I know once Knox gets to know you, he'll recognize what a hard worker you are," TrysKa said.

But Brant had more going against him than she knew.

"Catch me up on this op. Quick."

"You seriously didn't read it," Sann said.

Who did Sann think he was? Brant's father?

"I've had weeks of lesson plans to prep with Celeste. Back off."

Then it hit him. This was Sann. Throughout the years, whenever Brant didn't live up to Ed's expectations, Sann was there.

Brant lowered his head.

"I've been busy."

Sann winced. "I should have known that."

An awkward silence descended and lingered. Brant shifted his weight and finally had to blurt something out.

"I have class in an hour," he said, avoiding eye contact with Sann. "Help me out here."

"It's a mercy mission," Sann said. "Three villages on Earth are being plundered for the slave trade. Pirates kidnapped their children and teens. We're collecting shields for them."

"Who are we 'collecting' from?" Brant asked.

"The application didn't say, probably because it couldn't." Sann sat down on one of the pillows, and TrysKa sat next to him. "Maybe some rich business that can afford to help, but isn't. Probably a company profiting from slave trafficking."

"But slavery's illegal on all the colonized planets," Brant said.

"Oh wow, it's illegal," Sann said. "Well, let's make murder and rape illegal too, so they won't happen anymore."

Brant towered over the seated Sann, but TrysKa's eyes went wide. She shook her head, and Brant forced himself to shrink back.

"So even though it's illegal," Brant said. "Slavery is still going on?"

"Thriving. It's thriving, and not just on old Earth, the Six Planets too."

"How? If it's illegal, we just find the fields where slaves are working and free them."

Sann snorted, and TrysKa winced. Once again Brant had said something stupid. TrysKa stepped in.

"Since it's illegal," she said, "slaves aren't being worked out in the open. Normally they're working locked inside warehouses."

"So, raid the warehouses."

"Which ones?" Sann snapped. "If this was an easy problem, we'd have solved it by now. It's not. Many warehouses are legit, the workers are fairly paid. The reason they sleep and eat there is because it saves on housing and food. From the camera's point of view, it looks the same."

Sann swallowed and closed his eyes.

"Poor governments can't afford to police every sweatshop," TrysKa said, keeping her tone soft. "Some corrupt governments are bribed by the owners. Shipping companies buy the products without asking how they were made. It's one long messy trail of cover-up."

"OK," Brant said. "I can see that. I get it now."

Brant stared at the door for a few seconds, groaned, and turned back.

"I have one more question."

"Shoot," Sann said his eyes still closed. He didn't sound as defensive.

"Why are human slaves still used," Brant asked, "when robots and automated machinery can replace them?"

"Robots are expensive, and machinery has a high initial cost. Both need maintenance from techs, engineers, and AI psychoanalysts, all expensive employees. With human slaves, owners don't have to pay income, taxes, or health care. Just enough food to keep them alive and a hard floor at night. Nothing's cheaper, even in today's economy."

"That sucks."

"Yup."

Brant raised a questioning eyebrow at TrysKa. *Do you think Sann's OK with me?*

She nodded her head an inch and cut her eyes toward the door. *Leave while you're ahead.*

So Brant did.

7

Douglas

Douglas Winward, CEO of Caravan Suppliers, leaned in to catch every word and inflection of the speaker's voice. Douglas sat behind a curved table that wrapped around the center stage. The tables behind him circled outward in the auditorium like ripples in a pond after a stone is dropped. The stage perched at the center of the bullseye, and Vittoria Corrigan gave her presentation. She spewed feel-good ideas to change the way Caravan Suppliers did business.

"That's exactly what this company needs," Douglas said, taking advantage of a pause in her speech.

She beamed and continued. He took notes on her speech and wore his best attentive face. It didn't matter if he changed anything based on this meeting. People just needed to *feel* heard. So here Douglas was, deeply interested in everything she had to say.

Sir, can we talk outside?

The words scrolled across Douglas's screen. He rose, and Vittoria fell silent.

"You've done some great work, but-"

Douglas cut his eyes at the suit nodding off next to him. "I'm afraid some of us have begun to doze off." The junior VP startled with wide eyes, and a snicker rolled over the assembly. "I want everyone alert, so I propose a bathroom and caffeine break. Reconvene in thirty minutes?"

Vittoria waited then realized he was asking her permission. "Oh, yes, thirty minutes."

It was a shame the company would lose her. Vittoria had been assigned to a project that, due to no fault of hers, was tanking. An outbreak of locusts on a terraformed crop had devastated the hemp for a new clothing line. The project needed a scapegoat, and she had an inconvenient habit of voicing her concerns about Caravan's ethical work practices. Douglas *hated* to fire her, but sometimes life happened.

Light chatter bubbled up as Douglas excused himself to the hallway.

"Sir."

Evie Nakamura, Douglas's lead analyst, beckoned with a wave. She wore no makeup, a tight bun, and tailored pants suit. The model of efficiency in bright red heels.

"On my way," he said.

Evie had a team of analysts that crunched and trended company profits and more importantly the perception of those profits. A massive money-evaluating machine. Everybody assumed, therefore, that Evie was the lead data cruncher. Everyone assumed wrong. Her underlings calculated the mundane stuff. Evie handled Douglas' off-the-books analysis.

Douglas pointed to a private conference room across the hall. They entered and stood before the one table that spanned the room. Only three chairs remained, the rest stolen for other breakrooms. Douglas locked the door, but kept his smooth salesman mask on.

The truth is: there were no "private" rooms for "private" discussions. Cameras canvased society, recording everything in this room, all over his company, covering the trams, and every hallway. He had to fool them all. They wouldn't record and document his real self for their viewing pleasure.

"What did you need?" he asked.

"We have a problem," Evie said, tapping her scroll. "I need proof Caravan Suppliers wasn't involved in something."

Douglas straightened his cravat while he waited. Evie liked leading with a dramatic pause before dropping a shocking statement. He wasn't going to rob her of that joy by interrupting.

"The attack on Taluk."

"Tal-what?"

"A country on Old Earth." Evie handed her scroll to Douglas. "Serving Hands helped three towns to develop sustainable farming and education. After they left though-"

"The towns were attacked."

"How did you know?"

The suspicion in her voice was lathered on thick, the way his grandmother used to heap butter on homemade bread.

"It's not uncommon," Douglas said. "A charity helps a community in a violent country, but when the charity leaves, the neighbors invade for the spoils. How does that involve Caravan Suppliers?"

"All three towns were producing goods for the Nichev Shipping Company"

Nichev!

That pompous, snooty company that sold everything non-GMO, organic, Fair Trade, vegan, and any other high-horse label Nicolai Nichev could grab. Douglas kept his opinions buried deep and his face neutral.

"I'm sorry for his loss, but that doesn't involve us."

Evie pursed her lips. "You know better, Douglas. The only three towns hit in Taluk happen to be the new markets for our hated competitor, Nichev Company? Coincidence? You know the Commune of Planets won't buy that. Proof, Douglas. Give me data, a trend, something."

Fine. He handed her scroll back.

"Look up the country's history," Douglas said. "See if attacks are common, especially after charities have left an area."

Evie dragged her fingers across her scroll. Her eyes darted back and forth as she raced through trends and over graphs.

"Earth's data isn't as organized as the Six Planets."

"They're not all on camera like the rest of us."

"Inconvenient," she said, still scrolling through numbers.

"Privacy generally is."

"Ah-ha, found some trends on violence in other countries, and you're right. That's proof enough. Sick, but proof." She rolled her scroll closed. "I can't believe pirates follow charities around to undo all the good."

"That's why efforts against human-trafficking aren't successful long-term." Douglas tugged the lace on his jacket sleeve. "Protection is needed around the clock. But if that's all you needed to talk about?"

"Yes," she said. "That's all I needed to discuss."

But Evie's eyes flicked to the middle button on Douglas's jacket. Douglas squeezed the stud inside his suit, and the cameras were no longer recording. A holovideo of the two of them talking business jargon was feeding around and around in a loop uploaded into the public database. Evie relaxed like puppet strings attached to her had been snipped.

"What else?" he asked.

"Serving Hands has asked for shields to protect the three towns. As you say, 'protection is needed around the clock'."

"Good for them. Why do I care?"

"The shields are being collected by Captain L.L. Knox."

She handed him her scroll again.

L. L. Knox

The absence of information on the captain screamed of classified secrets. This Knox probably shipped the exclusive, rush jobs of a wealthy business like say, the Nichev Company. The documented shipments were all Fair Trade. Oh, this definitely smelled like the undercover transporter of Douglas's competitor. Interesting.

Married to Ximena Knox for 10 years

Father, Liam Knox, killed in spaceport crossfire 13 years ago

Volunteers with Serving Hands

Followed by a long list of shipments.

"And he's hiring a crew too," Douglas slid his finger along the scroll's surface. "Collect donated shields to protect Taluk."

Douglas would bet his pension those shields weren't donations. They were going to be stolen. This Knox was a regular Robin Hood.

"So, I assume those donations will be coming from us," Douglas said.

"I can't be sure, but probably."

"Where would he likely target?"

Again, Evie paused for effect. "Our supply warehouses."

The temperature dropped a few degrees in the room.

"We don't own the supply warehouses. We just ship from them. It's not our fault how the warehouses are run."

"You and I both know the people in them are trapped, barely fed, and never paid. If Knox reveals we ship from slave owning warehouses regularly-"

Douglas closed the scroll with a snap. "It's not our job to police the galaxy. The governments we work with have made slavery illegal. It's not our responsibility to enforce their laws."

"The Commune of Planets won't see it that way, and you know it." Evie held out her hand for her scroll. "We will be held responsible for the workers' mistreatment just like the warehouse owners. Just last quarter, they buried Galactic Express under fines. We could be next if this Knox digs too deep."

Douglas put the scroll in her hand but didn't let go. Instead he pulled her scroll back to himself, bringing her close.

"What do you suggest we do?"

"Stop using those suppliers."

Douglas released the scroll with a laugh.

"Some of the warehouses are legal. They pay their workers the minimum five credits a day, or whatever it is now, but some of them don't. Do we stop shipping from all poor countries? That will cut off much needed income from legal operations. And even if we did stop using the illegal ones-"

Douglas paused for effect. Two could play at this game.

"Even if we did stop, Bottom Dollar Shipping or any other competitor would step in. Slavery would still exist."

Evie pursed her thin lips.

"You're right, of course."

"At the end of the day, customers want cheap products, and

they don't care how they're made. Until they care, slavery will persist."

"Fine," she said. "Then how do we handle this Knox?"

"Give him a shield."

Evie's mouth dropped open, and Douglas grinned. He'd won the shock contest this time.

"What?" she asked.

"Schedule a new shield generator to pass through one of our company's space sheds. Let Knox try to take it. And if something of high value happens to be shipped at the same time. Something like, say, a rush shipment of rainforest samples to New Terra?"

"Which would be accompanied by a patrol of security guards..." Evie nodded.

"The guards would shoot to kill any thieves trying to steal valuable rainforest cuttings."

Douglas put on the facade he'd use if testifying for auditors. "We didn't know their mission was for good. For all we knew, a bunch of pirates were trying to steal precious plant life needed for terraforming."

"Perfect." Evie made a note on her scroll.

"It would also be a shame if Knox, after trying to steal from us, was linked back to Nicolai Nichev."

"Mmmm." Evie made a sound like she was eating fine chocolate.

Douglas slipped the smooth salesman mask back over his face. He pressed the middle button, and the cameras resumed live recording. He shook Evie's hand, and they parted ways.

Employees filtered back into the auditorium. Douglas glided through the managers, shaking hands, and patting backs. He settled into his seat and nodded encouragingly at Vittoria. She bounced on her toes, a beaming smile on her face. She *could* inspire a crowd.

Douglas half-listened to her cheerleader speech while still grinding away at the conversation he'd had with Evie. Knox might dig up a lot of dirt, but in the end, the hole would be his grave. And Knox's connection to the Nichev Company was strong. Could he be the private space trucker Nicolai used for their new markets and high-end products? Oh, that would be a loss for his company. *Splendid.*

Douglas clasped his hands on the smooth desk before him, and devoted his full attention to Vittoria. It was important she *felt* heard.

8

The Maverick

Knox and Alex went to Alex's old room, and loaded the few belongings, including some handwritten notes from his mom, into the niche in his wall. The door closed, and Alex's stuff was whooshed away to be shipped up to the spaceport. The two then left IAS and boarded a large passenger tram. Alex snaked his way to a window seat and pressed his forehead to the glass, still chilled from nighttime. IAS grew smaller and smaller, and disappeared. Good riddance.

"Ready to meet *Maverick*?" Knox asked.

"You bet."

When the tram landed at the New York Space Shuttle, Knox held Alex's shoulder and guided him through the crowd. Alex's head whipped right, left, and around like an owl's. People were everywhere! One man wore a maroon cloth wrapped around his head and a fluffy beard on his face. A woman muscled past wearing space trucker clothes like Knox and a gun on her hip. Alex's earbud kept translating snippets of conversations in different languages. A businessman read the documents floating before his face instead of watching where he was going. And he had funny puffy pants! What planet had that style?

Knox steered Alex toward the space shuttle. When the doors cracked open, Alex bolted from Knox's grip, ducked under elbows, and plopped down at a window seat. A strong hand grabbed Alex's arm and started dragging him away.

"Hey!"

Alex bit the skin, but his small teeth couldn't pierce the leathery toughness.

"Come back with me," Knox said. "We need to talk."

"Oh."

It was Knox. Alex followed back off the shuttle. Knox led him away from the line and knelt down. Alex rubbed his arm.

"Did I hurt you?" Knox asked, brushing Alex's arm with the back of his calloused fingers.

Alex shook his head. "I'm fine."

"OK." Knox sighed.

He's nervous.

Alex didn't know what to think about that. His mom had taken care of Alex so naturally. It's what she *did*. Brant had sucked. But Knox had seemed so confident like he had a gut feel for it.

The look of nervousness passed, and a firm resolution replaced it.

"Alex, I told you the spaceport is a dangerous place."

"We're not in the spaceport."

"Ah." Knox cocked his head. "So, you intend to listen to me in the spaceport, but not anywhere else?"

"No. I mean yes. I mean. I intend to listen to you all the time?" Knox was tricky.

"Alex, either make a habit of listening or a habit of ignor-

79

ing."

"OK?"

"So, start now." Knox stood and held out his hand. "Stay close, listen, follow directions, and then I'll trust you with more important things when it matters."

Alex hadn't held anyone's hand for months. He shuffled his feet, opened his eyes wide at Knox, and frowned back at the open palm. Knox didn't budge.

Alex stuffed his hands in his pockets and glared at the crevices etched around Knox's thumb and over the meaty muscles. The seconds ticked by, and the queue shuffled into the beckoning shuttle. If Alex didn't agree, he'd have to go back to IAS.

Fine.

Alex laid his palm on the rough skin. Knox closed his fingers, secure but not too tight. If anyone wanted to hurt Alex's hand, they'd have to get through Knox's first. Together, they walked back to the shuttle and stepped inside. Knox shouldered his way through to a window seat. Alex crawled up and pressed his forehead against the clear plexicast.

"Thank you," Knox said and sat down next to him.

Alex didn't answer. He couldn't. He crossed his arms, stuffing the hand Knox had held up under his armpit. His mom wasn't the last person to hold that hand anymore. That was a little thing, right? No big deal.

Then why did it hurt so much?

Alex blinked away stupid tears. The shuttle tilted on its side, and the artificial gravity inside adjusted. For Alex, the floor of the shuttle still felt like "down", but according to the outside world, he should feel "sideways." Weird. The blasters started, the shuttle vibrated, and off they shot to the sky.

"Is this a spaceship?" Alex asked.

"Space shuttle," Knox said.

"What's the difference? A spaceship is a spaceship, right?"

"The shuttles have big blasters." Knox pointed out the window at the bulbous rockets pouring flames. "They need those to get this ship off the planet. Gravity is strong."

As the horizon fled, the shuttle entered a tube. They shot out of the safety of the dome into the toxic air of the planet. The green gases billowed outside the window. It thinned as they rose, and then fire licked the shields. The rockets, belching flame, pierced through the dangers, moving upward.

"So, what's a spaceship like?" Alex asked, curling up to Knox's side.

Knox wrapped his thick arm around Alex's shoulders.

"A spaceship only travels in the vacuum of space using tiny bursts of gas. Once it gets moving in the right direction, it never stops."

"Never?"

"Space is empty. The ship keeps going."

An inferno clawed over the shields, scraping for a weakness, but found none. Finally, the last remnants of atmosphere dropped away, and the fire demon lost its hold. A black blanket enfolded them.

Alex pressed his forehead to the window again, and cupped his hands around his eyes to block the indoor lights. The darkness of space soothed his sensitive vision. His contacts, which normally remained shaded, cleared, and his pupils dilated. The stars twinkled brightly, and Alex's sharp eyes picked out the tiniest ones. A dust cloud of diamonds.

Below him was New Terra, a huge black rock with patches of green and blue. It reminded him of the Petri dish his science instructor had showed the class. Alex peered through a microscope at the billions of bacteria on the dish, but with the normal eye, it looked like specs of fuzz. That's what the giant city-domes looked like now, splotches of green and blue bacteria on a vast black Petri dish.

The shuttle rolled away from the planet, and the spaceport cut across the window, a complex snowflake. It grew and spread. At an outer corner, space slugs stuck to the white tubes, sucking on the spaceport with their mouths.

"What are those?" Alex pointed to the slugs.

"Space barges."

"Are they spaceships?"

"Aye, big ones. Too big to land inside the station. That's why they dock on the outside of it."

"What do they have in them?"

"Anything this planet wants to buy from the other planets."

"Wow."

The edge of the station grew larger and larger until the barges slid off the side of the window. The middle tunnels expanded until all Alex could see was a small hole in the spaceport's side.

The shuttle aimed its nose toward the niche. Alex pressed his cheek to the cold plexicast, but couldn't see their goal anymore. He was about to curl up his knees and close his eyes, embracing for impact, when a strong arm wrapped around Alex's shoulders, and drew him to the safety of Knox's side.

"I've ridden this shuttle before." Knox's breath warmed Alex's hair. His deep voice echoed from his chest. "We're going to be fine, you'll see."

A thud echoed up and down the shuttle's interior. Alex curled up tighter into Knox. Out the window, the spaceport sprawled. How had it once looked so small and fragile? It was massive! The air slurped loud then clicked.

They were safe. The shuttle had entered its tube and was inside the station. Alex took a deep breath. He smiled at Knox who was smiling back, or at least Knox's eyes were smiling.

"That was easy," Alex said.

Knox almost chuckled. It welled up in his chest, but got caught in his throat. He shook his head.

"Let's get your stuff," Knox said. "Stay close."

Knox held out his hand, and Alex took it. Together they entered the spaceport. Alex rode people movers down long tunnels with lots of windows showing off space, the planet, and stars. Spaceships, repair bots, and sometimes suited people floated by the windows. Alex followed Knox through a market where the smell of food made his tummy gurgle. Was that fire-roasted fish? Crisped potato slices? Mmm, melted yeast spread. But Knox didn't stop for food.

Alex followed Knox to one of the collection counters. Crates bigger than Alex floated behind space truckers.

Holy moly, those gates are huge!

"Holy moly" had been a favorite expression of Alex's mom, and it fit here. The barriers in front of the landing dock were at least three stories high. He'd never seen electromagnetic gates that enormous before. How big was this spaceport anyway? The gateway swirled with light like oil on the surface of water. Through the shimmering curtain brimmed space fighters, cargo ships, robots, and lots and lots of truckers. Knox stopped at a checking station.

"Alex Mason," he said to the robot attendant.

A scan lit up Alex's face and hurt his eyes. He slammed them shut and snapped his face away.

"Confirmed," the robot said.

A minute passed, then two. Alex bounced on the balls of his feet, but Knox didn't budge. Instead he scanned the crowd, flaring his nostrils sometimes. What was Knox looking at? All Alex saw was boxes. In his boredom, his eyes traveled across all the different types of uniforms: pilots with their perfectly creased pants, hired hands with sweat stains under their armpits, security guards with their hats and showy guns, and space truckers dressed somewhere between the hired hands and pilots. His eyes traveled up to the ceiling then widened.

"Snakes!" Alex pointed.

That actually stopped a few people who then broke into laughter.

"New here, eh?" A woman winked at him then continued on her way chuckling.

Alex's checks warmed, and he stared at his boots. "They look like snakes."

Knox knelt down. "Vines run all through the station. They help with CO2 removal. That gas naturally builds up as we breathe, and it becomes toxic."

"Isn't there a way to get rid of it with, I don't, technology?"

"Get rid of it?" Knox said. "Yes. It can be captured and released into space, but over time, the lost gases need to be replaced with oxygen. The plants help to do that while reducing the strain on the technology."

Alex crinkled his nose. "But why use plants that look like snakes?"

"Vines are the easiest plants to grow. They only need a small pot of soil and some mist."

Through the crowd of crates, a small box bobbed forward

and stopped in front of Alex. Knox pulled the hover-brackets off the corners, hoisted the box over his right shoulder, and tossed the brackets back to the robot. He held out his left hand to Alex.

"Now we have your stuff," Knox said. "Stay close. The dangerous part's on the other side of those." Knox nodded to the barriers.

He got in line at the smallest gate. Above it, a sign glowed '0-10 crates, 250 kg limit.' Alex scanned the beefy men and women around him. Some of them could tip the scales past 250 kg without any cargo. When Knox's turn came, a beam scanned Knox, Alex, and the crate.

"Admitted," the guard said and pushed the button to lower the glimmering sheet.

Knox and Alex stepped across the threshold, but a second energy wall was still active before them.

"Why are there two gates?" Alex asked as the screen behind them reactivated.

"When truckers on the landing dock break out in a fight, it stops their gunfire from shooting into the rest of the spaceport."

The drapery before them dropped, and Knox stepped forward. Alex clung to Knox's side.

"Why aren't the crate pick-up stations on this side of the gates?" Alex asked, craning his neck over his shoulder to watch the big gate turn off.

"In some spaceports, they are on this side." Knox hooked his index finger in Alex's collar and tugged him forward. "Always watch where you're going in here."

Fighters!

Alex bolted toward the flashy ships, only to choke himself

on his collar. Knox had a firm grip. Alex stumbled back and coughed.

"Sorry, forgot." He smiled sheepishly up at Knox, who just shook his head.

The tightness on his collar eased. Alex could turn his neck now. Pharoah-class fighters held first place in line, small pyramid ships with a sphere cut into the center. The pilot sat in the sphere, and twisted all around like a carnival ride. Guns and accelerators aimed from the four points of the pyramid.

The Gyro-class fighters occupied the next spot with their circular tubes running around the spherical ship. In battle, those tubes lined with guns and accelerators would spin and twirl faster than the eye could see. Further down stood the Hornets, the Star-Shooters, Sting Rays, and even one or two Pteranodon-class!

Alex had flipped through page after page of spaceship specs at IAS, but now he was close enough to reach out and touch one. If Knox would let go of his shirt.

"What have we got here?" That voice was deeper than even Knox's.

Alex faced the biggest guy he'd ever seen. No, the second biggest, instructor Tom was actually bigger. The giant smiled at Knox, showing off bright white teeth and pink gums.

"Ximena have anything to do with this?"

Knox didn't answer. The guy threw his head back and guffawed. Alex could see the roof of his mouth. The dark guy squatted down to Alex's level, and held out his paw.

"The name's Sid."

"Alex."

Alex put his hand into Sid's palm, and it was swallowed past his wrist in the warmth of Sid's grip. His hands were softer than Alex expected.

"Good to meet you, Alex." Sid shook very gently. "Listen, if anyone ever gives you trouble, you just tell them you're Knox's boy. OK?"

Alex nodded.

"And that Sid will not be happy if you're hurt. Got it?"

Alex nodded again, his curls flopping over his face. Sid chuckled and stood. He patted Knox on the back so hard it *thumped.*

"You got yourself in a world of trouble."

"Thanks," Knox said.

Thanks? Alex crinkled his nose.

Knox started walking, and hooked his index finger in Alex's collar again. Alex shrugged his shoulder at Knox's hand, but in answer, Knox gave a little jerk. Cough. OK, he wasn't letting go.

A Gyro fighter behind them launched straight up to the ceiling. Alex let his head fall back. Five fighters, three small cargo ships, and near the end of the dock, a mid-sized transport hovered up high.

"How do they keep from running into each other?" Alex asked, his mouth hanging open.

"They follow flight patterns sent to their computer."

"So, they never crash?"

"Oh, they don't always follow the plans, and then, yeah, they run into each other."

Alex clutched Knox's side.

"Oh, we won't be hurt." Knox pointed back at the ceiling. "See how the ceiling flickers?"

"An energy barrier?"

"When the ships take off, the safety net is turned off, but

once they're on the other side, it's turned back on. If they crash, the net will catch the wreckage."

"Have ships ever crashed while the safety net was off?"

Knox cleared his throat. "Look, we're almost here."

They passed a row of small cargo ships. Small, as in, the size of a private gym back at IAS. How much stuff could fit into one of those? They resembled squatty bugs, like space ants with short legs.

Knox turned down the next row of cargo ships, and Alex's heart raced. One of these ships was *Maverick*! One of these ships was going on a secret mission to steal shields and save people and–

"That's it?" It popped out of Alex's mouth before he could catch it. "I mean, *wow!*"

Too late. Knox deflated as he rested his palm on the scratched hull.

"I'm sorry," Alex said.

Someone under the ship giggled then snorted. "It's OK."

Ximena coasted out from under *Maverick's* belly. She hadn't been the prettiest woman on the holoprojector and wasn't much better in person. But then she smiled bright, and Alex's chest warmed. There was something beautiful about her after all. Ximena leaned in to whisper.

"It's not supposed to look impressive on the outside." Her clothes smelled of machine oil. "That way no one knows all its awesome secrets."

"It has secrets?" Alex caught his breath.

Ximena backed away and studied Alex with a calculating stare. "Do you like buttons and numbers?"

"You bet!" Alex yelled so loud truckers up and down the aisle stopped to stare. Knox winced; Ximena beamed.

"Follow me," she ran up the ramp of the ship and smiled back over her shoulder. "Let me introduce you to the real *Maverick*."

"Cooooool."

And Alex raced after her. He didn't look back over his shoulder, so he didn't see the corners of Knox's mouth tug into the tiniest smile.

#

The next morning by New York time, Brant and Sann followed TrysKa past the rows of space fighters to the small cargo ships.

TrysKa, dressed in a crisp pilot's jacket and slacks, turned a corner. Sann followed, sporting a stained sleeveless shirt and faded jeans. His outfit did "hired hand" justice.

Brant came last. He'd chosen a more blast-resistant look. A non-Newtonian fluid coated his pants and jacket covering a lightweight, black hemp shirt. Some sweaty workers eyed Brant's reinforced wardrobe with envy. He hadn't thought he'd overdressed for the job, but maybe he was wrong.

They turned down a row of giant metal insects. The things looked like they could eat an elephant for breakfast. Gray ship after gray ship passed by before TrysKa finally stopped at a random one.

"How do you know this one's *Maverick*?" Brant asked.

"Isn't it obvious?"

Brant raised his eyebrows in answer.

"Upgraded blasters." TrysKa pointed at the bulges on the sides. She pointed at pods gathered under its abdomen. "40s model Tesla FTL nozzles, more reliable than the modern versions that are contracted out." TrysKa pointed to the ion accelerators. "But these are upgraded to the more efficient modern models. The older versions clogged."

Brant squinted at the ship. "OK, yeah, I got it."

He didn't have it. A petite woman walked down the ramp and stuck out her greasy hand.

"Oh, wait," she said and searched the bounty of pockets on her overalls.

She checked a pocket filled with styluses.

"Nope." The flap latched back to her overalls with a soft ping. Another pocket held bolts and screws.

"Nope." She rummaged past a pocket of bulbs and another with crystals before finding what she wanted.

"Ah!"

She pulled out a stained shop towel and wiped off her hands. After rubbing them on the cloth then wiping them briskly on her overalls, she held out her hand again.

"Ximena Knox, engineer of this ship and glad to meet you." Her r's had a slight roll.

Brant shook her hand, followed by Sann, and finally TrysKa.

"So," Ximena said to TrysKa. "You were the one giving the run down on my *Maverick*?"

"Oh, umm..." TrysKa blushed.

Before she could finish though, Alex burst from the back-door, bounded down the ramp, and stood before them with his hands on his hips, ready to crow like a rooster. He had transformed overnight into a true space urchin. Where had Knox picked up this outfit? Space Brats Anonymous? Faded jeans, a worn jacket, and scuffed boots composed an ensemble that would blend in with any spaceport. Shoot, if Brant didn't know better, he'd thought Alex was trying to look like a miniature Knox.

"I have my own room!" Alex announced.

The boy's stare challenged Brant to say something.

"Bet you love that," TrysKa said.

"Damn straight!"

"Alex!"

Alex dropped his head and looked up at Ximena through his curls.

"I'm sorry."

Ximena melted, but then her eyes hardened with *that* look.

"Knox!" she called back up into the ship.

"What?" his voice came back.

"What have I told you about cussing around Alex!!"

Knox's boots ran to the ramp. He pointed Alex onto the ship.

"Get back in there."

"Yessir."

Alex skipped onto the ship and flashed a grin at Ximena. Knox closed his eyes and worked his jaw.

"I'm a Scottish space trucker."

"Who's mentoring an adapted student."

"The IAS instructors cuss all the time around the kids!"

"Not around the little ones, thank you very much!" Brant said then swallowed. "Sir."

Knox sucked in his breath and held it, his chest puffed out. Then he exhaled.

"Fine, he didn't learn that from IAS, but he's picking up worse all over this spaceport. In multiple languages."

Ximena put her hands on her hips and cocked her head. The light glinted off the cross around her neck.

"Those truckers aren't his mentor. You are."

Knox winced. He'd lost, and he knew it. "I'll work on it, but I make no promises."

"Fair enough."

He turned with a squeak of his boots and strode back onto the ship. Over the landing dock screaming with people, robots, and ships' engines, Brant's adapted ears caught Knox mutter under his breath.

"I'm fucked."

A smile spread wide across Brant's cheeks. Sann raised an eyebrow. *What's so funny?* Brant shook his head and tried to pinch his lips back together. The last thing Brant needed right now was to laugh in Knox's face.

"So, you've studied my ship's stats?" Ximena asked TrysKa.

"Oh yeah." TrysKa's eyes lit up. "You've done some amazing work. Some of your tweaks to the foundational engine parts are pure brilliance!"

Ximena clapped her hands. "Then you'll understand the significance of this: we found a junked 20s-model Asteria-class ship and bought its distributor."

TrysKa's eyes went wide like Ximena had announced they had a lifetime supply of chocolate.

"You mean this ship," she pointed, "has a one-piece, hard titanium, cool-conductive distributor?"

Ximena nodded vigorously and smiled even bigger. TrysKa grabbed Ximena's hands.

"That means its power efficiency-"

"Forty-five percent higher."

"If you have a variable gateway-"

"I installed one."

"So you can-"

"Yes!"

"Oh. My. Goodness!"

Ximena leaned in. "You want to see the system?"

"Can I?"

"Come in!"

Ximena and TrysKa raced up the ramp hand in hand. There was a snap and whoosh from inside the cargo bay followed by more girly chatter. Brant blinked. Sann's mouth hung open too.

"What just happened?" Brant asked.

"I have no idea." Sann looked up the ramp. "Think we're allowed to go aboard?"

"I guess."

The ramp opened under what looked like the ant's butt. Inside, a cargo bay opened wide on both sides, bigger than a meditation room. Two small rows of crates lined the walls, but judging by the dust grid on the floor, it was normally packed wall to wall.

Brant spun, taking in the network of doors. "So where do our suits go?"

Alex popped out from behind one of the crates, shoved Sann and Brant apart, and ran up to a cabinet. He tapped it, and the door, the same size as Alex, flung open to reveal shelves housing black folded slick suits.

"You put them here."

Alex puffed out his chest. He owned a spacesuit, he knew where it belonged, and he was rubbing it in Brant's face. Brant searched through his duffle bag for his suit, and Alex got bored. He ran to the other end of the ship.

"He has a spacesuit," Brant said through clenched teeth and pulled his out.

"Play it cool," Sann said. "Knox won't throw the kid out the airlock."

"Alex has been through too much. He doesn't belong out here."

Sann didn't answer but instead lifted out his neatly folded suit. He smoothed out any air pockets and fit it perfectly onto one of the empty shelves. Brant crammed his suit into the one remaining slot with his elbow.

"Well," Sann said. "Everyone will know which one is yours."

Brant laughed, and Sann grinned back. Good.

But Sann's smile vanished as he knelt to his duffel again. Piece by piece, he pulled out the parts to his gunpowder rifle, untraceable by modern technology. His face lost some of its color as he assembled the parts and sighted it. Brant unbuckled his holster and gun, eyeing Sann the whole time.

What had happened on his last mission? Brant opened the cabinet labeled 'Weapons.' Two hooks had pistols, Knox's Langmuir and a handheld Beretta Pico Plasma, probably Ximena's. Five other hooks waited, empty.

Sann hung his rifle on a larger hook, but Brant couldn't leave his gun in a strange cabinet. He didn't know Knox and Ximena. Sure, KaeHan had vetted them, and they were great people on an important mission. But this was *his gun.* Brant fitted the belt back around his waist. Until Knox commanded otherwise, Brant's pistol would stay on his hip or under his pillow.

Brant led the way down the narrow hallway and Sann followed, walking single file. This must be the middle bulb of the space bug-vessel. The first door on the left was locked open with a ladder leading down to the gunnery in the belly of the ship. To his right, a plaque marked 'Captain's Quarters' hung on the door with '& Engineer' scribbled in black below that—Knox and Ximena's room. Those two were an odd pair. The second door on the right once read 'Engineer's Room', but 'Engineer' had been crossed out and 'Pilot' written above it in the same scribbly handwriting, TrysKa's room. Brant turned again to his left: a bathroom and one last door labeled 'Hired Hands.'

"Here's home."

Brant entered his room and nearly hit his chest on the top bunk. He sidestepped to the left, so Sann could get in the room. Sann was talking to Alex over his shoulder and smacked into it.

"You found what? Oof. Well, this is a tight fit."

"Where does our stuff go?" Brant craned his neck to look around the tight space.

"I think below the bottom bed."

Brant pressed flat against the wall and peered down. Sure enough, two drawers hid below the bottom mattress.

"I'll leave, you put your stuff up, and we'll swap places," Sann said. "You want the left drawer or the right?"

"Left, I guess."

Sann stepped out, and Brant slid to the right and knelt down as best he could, folding his long legs under him. What he wouldn't give for his open gym, room to run, and students hanging on his every move. He unzipped his duffle only to whack his right funny bone on the edge of the bunk.

Sonuva!

Brant shook his arm to work out the pins and needles. He tapped the front of the left drawer. It flew open and smashed against the wall. Brant jerked his hand back just in time. Wow, this ship was touchy!

He unpacked, but his wadded mound didn't fit. With a groan, Brant neatly folded and flattened his clothes. But what about the odds and ends like his laser tooth cleaner, comb, translator earbud, and deodorant?

"Oh well. Who needs deodorant on a tiny ship anyway?"

Brant threw the deodorant in Sann's drawer, stood up, made a tight one hundred and eighty degree turn, swiped the panel to open the door, and fell out of the room. Right into Sann's arms.

"Your turn."

Sann squeezed himself and his duffle into the room.

After the tight hallway, the breakroom felt almost airy and spacious. Brant's shoulders relaxed. To his right, the table followed the curve of the rounded middle section of *Maverick*. Benches lined the curved sides and chairs pulled up to its exposed straight edge. Brant folded himself onto the bench seat next to Alex.

Opposite the hallway, the cockpit door was closed. Steps were cut into the wall along both sides of the door leading up to what must be the engine room. Though judging from its small entry door, it probably felt more like an engine closet. Brant remembered the ion nacelles that lumped to both sides of the head like strange antennae. The small hatch above the cockpit probably led to that tiny compartment in *Maverick*.

Wait, Brant had the whole ship backward. The huge cargo bay wasn't the ship's butt; it was its front. The tiny engine with its accelerators was the backside. The space ant flew backward. Good thing TrysKa was the pilot and not him.

"You see the wiring?" Ximena's question echoed out of the engine hatch. Her voice traveled with metallic reverb through tubing and pipes that ran inside the walls and ceiling.

"You changed all of the connections to super conductive conduit?" TrysKa's voice rang in surround sound.

"Every. Single. One. Took me *years*."

Brant ignored the geeky chatter and finished taking in the

room. Along the left side, a counter stuck out of the wall with a warming plate welded on top. Could this be the food prep area? Cabinets decked out every available wall space, squeezing in a heating unit, freezing unit, and a hydration/dehydration box too.

"Oh!" TrysKa said as she climbed down from the engine closet. "It has a kitchen."

She flew to the shelves and opened drawers.

"Hmm. Laser knives need to be realigned. I would've put that over here."

Sann joined Brant and Alex at the table. Alex had poked around the ship earlier and found a deck of cards. He passed out cards to Sann, Brant, and himself, and they started a game of poker. The boy flashed his deep-dimpled grin over a win when Knox entered the room studying his scroll, his bald head down.

Knox halted, crossed his arms, and narrowed his eyes at TrysKa fluttering around the kitchen. Sann glanced at her over his cards and cleared his throat.

TrysKa lifted her face. Both her jaw and the laser knife in her hand fell. The laser switched off before the handle hit the metallic floor with a clang.

"Oh, I'm so sorry." TrysKa scooped up the knife. "This is your kitchen, and I've been messing it up."

"You can cook?"

"Well, yeah. From a big family, learned to cook, never cared for the food at the Institute cafeteria."

"The galley's yours."

Knox then strode to the cockpit, all business. TrysKa lost her breath at his abruptness. She called to the cockpit timidly.

"Are you sure? I mean, who normally cooks?"

"We normally fend for ourselves," Knox said. "And pray we don't get food poisoning."

TrysKa clapped her hands like she'd won a medal and turned back to gut the kitchen.

"Not so fast." Knox stuck his head out of the open cockpit door. "You're a pilot first."

"Oh right!"

TrysKa stowed the loose kitchen utensils back into drawers, locked them, and ducked into the cockpit. She took her post in the pilot's chair and lit up the Asteria-class controls, all familiar friends from her training.

Some of the controls were hard-wired switches and levers, specifically the jump lever. The rest of the system lit up before her as holograms. The control panel, previously dead and black, came to life at her touch and birthed buttons and switches, numbers and graphs, all floating above the panel. With a brush of her fingers, she changed which systems she viewed.

A thrill ran up her spine as she sat upright, leaning into the bright switches and graphs. *Home.* The middle child in a large family, TrysKa had always felt forgotten. The lone pilot in a class of soldiers and a doctor, she'd always felt outside. But here? Ximena had gushed over the ship's details with her.

Then there was the gift of the kitchen. In her family, she'd been shoved aside, not allowed to make food the way she liked. "You're too little." In IAS, students weren't given the luxury of a personal kitchenette, and their food was so bland and soggy! She'd befriended the chefs and kitchenbots to garner limited access to the cafeteria kitchen. But on this ship? She ruled her own kitchen. No questions asked, and no orders given, except for hers.

Now TrysKa warmed the pilot's chair, a chair typically occupied by Captain Knox. Would she be good enough for him? She may not know him, but she knew this ship. The systems warmed up for launch, and the engine chomped at the bit to take off. On the graphs, the line for power revved to life, the shields activated, and the ionic propulsion charged. TrysKa felt it all. Her adaptation reached beyond her body and connected with *Maverick*.

"Alright, girl," TrysKa said to the ship. "Let's get to know each other."

"Knox doesn't normally call me a girl, but you're welcome to, my lass."

The baritone voice startled TrysKa. "I'm sorry? Who's there?"

"I'm the ship's computer," he answered back. "Call me *Maverick*. It's easier that way."

Most ships used digital sounding voices, though TrysKa had trained on two fighters with breathy sopranos. That had been annoying. But this deep Scottish personality gave her pause.

"It's an honor to meet you," she said, a lift at the end of her sentence making it almost a question.

"I knew I'd like you," *Maverick* answered.

Knox grunted with approval and leaned his head back to rest. Another thrill ran up her spine straight to her cheeks. *Home*.

Knox reached for the comm button to request a flight path to leave the landing dock. The blue line lit up, winding through a miniature model of the hangar. With a steady hand TrysKa piloted the ship up and out.

When *Maverick* was a safe distance from port, TrysKa started up the controls for the jump. The FTL nozzles, little orbs gathered like egg sacks under the ship's belly, separated and distributed around *Maverick*. With the coordinates for Yichen entered, the balls aligned into their spherical configuration. If the curvature was off, even by a human hair, *Maverick* would smear across the galaxy in subatomic-sized sparkles. TrysKa double-checked the shape. Perfect.

With steady pressure, she eased the lever forward. The nozzles, powerful magnets, fired off. Hydrogen injected into their center, and the forces sliced open neutron from proton. A pinprick of light brighter than the stars and a shadow deeper than space itself pushed back and forth on each other. A delicate strand shot from one sphere to another and another and another, connecting in an intricate web. Over and over the threads wrapped until the cocoon completely enclosed the vessel and its crew.

Then reality hiccuped, and *Maverick* was across the galaxy.

"Wow, that felt weird," Alex said from the breakroom.

"That's why it's called the Jump Hiccup," Ximena said.

"Or the Star Barf," TrysKa yelled back over her shoulder.

"Or the–"

"*Alex!*" Knox yelled.

"What was Alex going to say, sweetheart?" Ximena used her sweetest, deadliest tone.

Knox grumbled deep in his throat. "After the mission."

9

Two Storage Units

For the rest of the morning and past lunch, the crew lived the normal shipping life. Picking up crates here, dropping them off there. Knox alternated between taking Brant or Sann with him when he picked up goods. Brant stepped lightly and scanned the crowd, but no one was interested in messing with guarded crates.

When would the operation begin? Brant could be teaching his kids right now instead of working as a hired hand for a space trucker. Knox tapped his scroll, and the stack of crates floated into *Maverick's* cargo bay.

"Why are we doing this again?" Brant asked.

"Waiting on a call," Knox said.

He marched through the crates that zipped a millimeter from his head. Brant flinched and jumped forward to get out of the way.

"Walk at an even speed," Ximena said from the hallway. "My program will calculate your pace and avoid you."

"But they're flying at my face!"

Brant made a fatal twist, and hugged a heavy crate straight

in his chest. All the boxes halted mid-flight like humming-birds hovering above a flower. Brant crawled out of the cargo bay, and the goods finished loading and settled into their spots.

"So what call are we waiting for?" Brant brushed the dust off his navy jacket.

"The shields we want are in a Yichen space station," Knox said, "in the Caravan Suppliers hangar right now. I'm waiting on an invitation inside."

"You have an insider?"

"Nope. I know how space warehouses are run."

Knox spun on his heel and strode to the cockpit. Brant lifted then dropped his arms.

"That wasn't helpful."

"Crates are forgotten or left behind all the time. Hundreds a day in fact." Ximena rolled up her scroll and put it on her hip. "For the important shipments, the company workers will quietly call independent truckers, like Knox, to rush deliver it for them. Some truckers make their entire living off of the left behind orders."

"Oh, so we'd get a call."

Sure beat breaking into a building that orbited in space.

"But it's even more brilliant than that," Ximena whispered so Brant had to lean in. "They don't keep records of the forgotten shipments. Knox's name is written on a piece of paper, the call is on a private line, and the payment is cash."

"So, we'll be allowed in, and no one will know we were ever there."

"That's my husband's brilliant plan."

She spun, her braid wrapping around her waist, and Ximena skipped to the breakroom. Before Brant could take a step,

Maverick lifted to head to its next destination, faltered, and landed right back down.

"What just happened?" Alex asked TrysKa.

"We got a call from the Caravan Supplier hangar," she said over her shoulder. "Hush."

Knox talked quietly with a hologram in the cockpit, his deep voice rumbling. A click at the end of the call, and Knox strode in, took a chair, turned it backward, and straddled it. Alex slid over to make room for TrysKa on the bench. Ximena leaned against the wall, her nose stuck in her scroll.

"Can you put that up?" Knox said.

Ximena kept staring at it, so Knox waited. As if on a time delay, her head popped up.

"Did you say something?" Ximena blinked a few times and stared off. "Oh, put up my-" She closed her scroll and latched it to her belt. "What did I miss?"

"Got a call from the Yichen space station," Knox said. "I knew it wouldn't take them long to leave something important behind."

Ximena sucked in a big breath and let it out with a nod. Was she nervous? TrysKa nudged the chair next to hers. Ximena turned the chair around and straddled it right next to TrysKa. TrysKa gave her a reassuring smile. Sann and Alex inched down the bench to make room for Brant. He perched on the edge of the flattened cushion.

Knox pressed on.

"I noticed a shield generator parked in Caravan Supplier's hangar three days ago. I checked their schedule, and the shield won't be transported down to the planet for 2 weeks. So, I left my contact information for when they needed a rush delivery. Which is now." To Ximena. "Would you get the projector, please?"

"Of course."

Ximena reached behind Brant. "Sorry."

"It's OK."

Ximena's hand reached into the cabinet behind Brant, rummaged around a bit, and drew out the holoprojector. She placed it in the center of the table as it swirled to life with color.

"Lights down," Knox said.

As the cabin dimmed, Alex lifted his left arm to scratch his armpit. TrysKa gasped. Brant's sensitive ears caught the noise, and he followed her gaze. Alex's sleeve had slipped down his arm revealing the purple, green, and brown. A big, ugly bruise.

One second the breakroom was quiet, everyone listening. The next, Brant leapt from his chair with a roar. Blood throbbed in Brant's vision and pounded in his ears.

"How dare you!"

He yanked Knox up by his jacket, set his feet, and–

Pushed against a mountain. Brant had intended to slam Knox against the wall but slammed into Knox instead.

"KaeHan trusted you with Alex, and you hurt him!" Brant yelled. He would break through Knox's hard exterior one way or another. "Not even twenty-four hours and you-"

"I already had those bruises from IAS."

Alex's soft whisper sliced through Brant's shouts. The blood drained from Brant's face. The pill had been pumping meds into Brant's system, and now overcompensated. The world swished back and forth.

"Kids from that school beat me up right under your nose," Alex said in the shocked silence. "So much for watching me like I'm your own."

Brant's knuckles had turned white clutching Knox's jacket. He pried his fingers open and stepped back. His palms throbbed.

I'll watch him like he's my own.

Brant had used those exact words when promising Alex's mom he'd watch over him. He'd thought the boy was asleep on the hospital couch when Brant had whispered that vow to her. But Alex must have been awake. And heard it all.

I failed her. I failed Alex.

"Follow me." Knox's voice rumbled deep. "TrysKa, remember what we discussed?"

Tears welled in her eyes as she slipped off her chair to the cockpit. Sann's hands covered his face. Ximena, though, looked like she wanted to shoot Brant on the spot. The only word to describe Alex was victorious. The boy had set a trap, and Brant had jumped right in. Stupid.

With a shaky breath, Brant trudged to the cargo bay.

The ship took off and flew. Knox hadn't told TrysKa where to go, yet she already knew. Somehow he'd known Brant would lose his temper. Was Brant really that predictable?

Knox stood, thick arms crossed, by the ship's ramp. Brant wanted to collapse against the wall, but resisted. Instead he stood, head high, arms by his side, waiting for whatever came. A voice sneered in his head.

You didn't last long.

A failure already.

Crawl on back home. You can work for me.

It sounded just like Ed. The ship jumped across the galaxy then flew for a few excruciating minutes. It must have entered a hangar somewhere, because TrysKa landed it with her signature soft touch. Knox hit the ramp controls with his fist, and it creaked open, slamming into the floor like the striking of a judge's gavel. Brant flinched despite himself.

"This is a space warehouse for Nichev Company," Knox said.

"Are the shields here?"

"No, but you will be until you get control of yourself."

The warehouse wasn't like the spaceports, a bustling city of activity with ships and people coming and going. Instead it held excess shipments. Since planet-side land was scarce, storage could wait in orbit until needed. Crates piled high everywhere. Vines hung in thick braids from the ceiling straight to the floor. They sprawled along the ground like roots and crawled over the boxes. A rotting stench topped it off.

"The robots that organized shipments got an AI virus and are out for repairs. Hence the disarray."

Disarray? That was an understatement.

"You'll organize it while we get the shields."

Brant's cheeks warmed, and he cursed his fair skin that betrayed his blush. The implant slipped Brant meds.

"We'll pick you up when we're done." Knox paused. "And you've calmed down enough to *not* attack me."

"Yessir."

It was more than he deserved, but that didn't make it any less humiliating. Brant strode into the dappled green lighting and halted on the warehouse floor. *Maverick* closed its ramp with a resounding clang. And left.

Brant leaned over and supported his hands on his knees. "This is messed up."

"You must be the loud-mouthed guard."

Brant jumped at the deep voice. He normally heard the breathing of enemies approaching, but his ears still buzzed from the temper crash. Brant circled a small hill of crates and heaved a trailing vine away from his face. A big man in linen overalls lumbered from the small office at the back of the warehouse.

"The name's Sid." He extended his dark hand.

"Brant Mallet." Brant shook it.

Sid smiled showing off his bright teeth. "What did you do? Pop off at him?"

"That about sums it up."

"Did you disrespect his lady?"

"Ximena?" Brant asked. "No, no, of course not."

"Good. Then he'll take you back. Knox just needs his respect, you understand." Sid scratched the bristles on his cheeks and groaned at the mess. "Until then, whatever you can clean up will help me out."

"With what?"

Sid pulled a thick tablet out of his front pocket. Brant hadn't seen one of those since he'd visited his grandmother as a kid. A 2D model of the warehouse lit up on the screen instead of illuminating above it.

"This," Sid said.

He poked the picture of one of the crates next to them. The box hovered in the air, and Brant backed up. Sid smeared his finger across the display, and the box flung at the spot next to them and plopped down.

"You sort," Sid pointed at the boxes, "And cut those down," he pointed at the vines. "I assumed your drones can handle that?"

"Easily." Brant was going to use his cutting-edge attack

drones to clean up overgrown vegetation. Great.

Sid handed Brant the old tablet. "I have stupid calls to answer."

On cue, the warehouse computer, with a generic woman's voice, announced over the speakers.

"Request for the manager. Request for the manager."

Sid jerked his thumb over his shoulder. "Stupid calls."

He took off toward the back of the warehouse. Brant had expected him to lumber, but no. Sid glided smooth as silk then accomplished the impossible. He squeezed his large body into the minuscule cubicle that represented his office. How?

Brant shook it off and rolled his shoulders. He had a job to do. With a three-hundred-and-sixty-degree spin, the jungle glowered back. It was overwhelming. The same overwhelming Brant had felt when confronted with mapping out lesson plans for all his different classes.

"We'll start with the easiest part," Celeste told him. "Then untangle from there."

OK. If Brant could teach a bunch of ten-year-olds to stand on their heads, he could organize this place. And he would. Better than it ever had been with robots. Brant tensed his triceps, and the two attack drones on his armbands popped out, one from his left and one from his right. Their blades sprang open before they hit the floor, and the bots helicoptered up to eye level. The breeze from their fans blew his loose hair back from his face.

"Cut down the vines that hang down more than one meter," he said.

Up they bobbed to the ceiling and down came the plants. Brant threw up his hands as the cables tumbled over him.

"Not the ones right over me!"

He chucked the leafy cords to his side, and the drones raced to the edges of the warehouse. After each shot, a trunk of vines toppled down with an echoing thunk.

"Gather them in that corner!" Brant yelled and pointed.

The drones stopped shooting and dive-bombed the ground. Up they flew with the green streamers trailing behind them. Brant wiped the tablet clean with the back of his jacket sleeve until it squeaked and shone.

Take the easiest part first.

Brant started with the pile nearest the air lock.

"I'll show Knox."

#

Alone in the cockpit, TrysKa piloted *Maverick* out of the air lock leaving Brant behind. With a quick swipe of the back of her hand, she wiped her cheeks. Knox had stayed at the breakroom table, thank goodness, giving her a chance to process what just happened.

She knew what it was, of course. Alex had set Brant up. Poor kid, TrysKa didn't blame him for being angry. That was a normal part of grieving. But Brant! He'd done so much for Alex, only to be the target of the boy's outrage.

But isn't that how it normally works?

Still, Brant needed this job. As usual, TrysKa felt stuck in the middle, understanding both points of view and helpless to heal either. Compassion sucked sometimes.

She steered the ship away from the warehouse into wide, open, empty space. After setting the ship adrift, she joined the oppressive silence in the breakroom.

"As I was saying," Knox said. "The shields and batteries are being held in this space station."

"Are we breaking in?" Sann asked.

109

"We don't have to. That's the advantage of being a trusted independent space trucker."

Knox nodded to Ximena who took the baton. "Since space barges are huge, crates can be forgotten and left behind. It happens. Normally those forgotten crates are loaded onto the next barge, but every once in a while, those forgotten crates *need* to be delivered now."

"That's where we come in," Knox said.

"The spaceport operators call up an independent trucker, pay us cash, and we rush the shipment to its destination."

"Sometimes we even beat the barge, because they unload slow."

"So," Sann said. "You got a call from the station with the shields?"

"Aye," Knox said. "I'll get the forgotten shipment while you two get the shields. Ximena guards the ship."

"Someone always stays with the ship," Ximena said. "Always."

Something in TrysKa's stomach twitched. She was hired as the pilot. Yes, she trained in combat, but not like Brant, at least, that's what her instructors had always said. But Knox's trust in her seemed so matter of fact. Maybe she could do more than she'd always been told.

"What about the cameras?" Sann asked.

"Your last mission was planet-side?" Knox said.

"Yes, sir."

"Cameras might be everywhere planeside, but they don't last long in the landing docks. Space truckers use them as target practice. Eventually the spaceports stop paying for new ones."

"So, no cameras."

"Nope."

"What do I do?" Alex asked.

"Guard the ship and my girl," Knox said.

Alex slumped in his chair and crossed his arms.

"Guarding the ship is the *most* important job," Knox said. "We don't get out of here alive without *Maverick*. You take care of it, you hear?"

"Yes, sir," Alex grumbled.

Knox narrowed his eyes, but he didn't have time for more. Ximena gave TrysKa's shoulders a squeeze, and TrysKa smiled tightly back.

"Are you OK?" Ximena asked.

TrysKa blinked. "Of course."

Lie.

"I mean, I'm glad to help however I can."

Ximena cut her eyes at the choice in wording. She'd used that look before on the engine diagnostics on her scroll, the look of troubleshooting a sticky problem. Only now it was directed at TrysKa.

"I'll go fly the ship now."

TrysKa practically ran to the pilot's chair. Yes, she'd become friends with Ximena quickly. Yes, it was breathtaking to finally be respected, even admired. But her thoughts had always been her own, to wrestle with alone.

The controls for the jump lit up. TrysKa entered the coordinates for Yichen. *Maverick* jumped, and a space station floated on the screen with the planet Yichen as its backdrop, a dead, black rock with speckles of terraformed land.

TrysKa requested entry to one of the six points, the one owned by Caravan Shipping. After receiving the flight trajectory, she entered the air lock then landed in the assigned spot.

The whole time, she held her breath, as if the hangar owners could see into her soul and detect her intentions.

"You're with Sann," Knox said.

TrysKa followed Sann down the ramp and across a bustling warehouse. The signs were written first in Mandarin then followed by the other languages, and the ferns were juecai.

Sann blended into the human mix with a bored confidence. He slouched his shoulders, cutting his eyes at people passing with a "don't mess with me" look. This was a man who didn't care what he did as long as you paid him.

Yet TrysKa knew the purpose of this mission struck a deep chord in his soul along with hers. How was he able to pull off the act? She followed him, her back too stiff and straight, her hands fidgeting for spacecraft controls that weren't there. She kept checking over her shoulder too quickly. One glance behind her lasted too long and she bumped into Sann. TrysKa stumbled back and blinked rapidly.

"I'm sorry, I'm screwing this up, Brant would be better at this."

"No, he wouldn't."

TrysKa's face popped up. "Yes, he would. Both of you are so natural at the hired hand thug."

"Thanks," Sann said, a smirk tugging at his mouth. "But you're not dressed like a thug. You're a pilot, so just be you."

TrysKa's neck relaxed. Of course, how could she be so stupid? She nodded and took the lead. After all, a pilot would know what she wanted in a space station. A hired hand is just there to follow orders and lift heavy loads.

As TrysKa sliced down the aisle between transports, hired hands parted to let her pass. No one gave her a second glance, except that one creep who checked her out. Sann gave him a glare that ended that. Mechanics worked on their ships without so much as noticing her, as if she was a natural part of the station. That strange feeling of welcome TrysKa had experienced on *Maverick* resurfaced. She brushed it aside to focus on her task, steal shields.

Her adapted skin picked up the eddies of movement around her. That was her adaptation. In addition to faster reflexes, she could feel the tiniest of air changes. Heat waves, wind currents, movements of life, breath, it all wafted against her skin. In school, she'd studied the duckbill platypus, an underwater animal with her sense. Some instructors had compared her adaptation to smell, others to highly sensitive touch. Neither were exactly right. It felt closer to swimming than anything else for TrysKa.

When she almost reached the far end of the hangar, a calm current settled around her and Sann. No one was watching or following them now. She glanced over her shoulder to verify her sensation, and indeed, they were completely unnoticed. With a silence sprint, she jumped left and hid between two transports. Sann stood by her side.

"Was it just me, or did you look like you knew what you were doing back there?" Sann whispered.

TrysKa touched her finger to her lips, but couldn't help a smile. A slight current of wind told her that a worker was coming. Both she and Sann held their breath until he passed.

"Clear," TrysKa said.

"My payment?" Knox said over her earbuds. So, he'd reached his contact and was gathering the shipment. A woman's voice came muffled over TrysKa's earbud, Knox's contact.

"How many different countries?" he said.

113

TrysKa blocked Knox's voice from her attention and peeked around the scuffed up transport's nacelles. This aisle ended at a wall with sorted piles of crates. Three aisles to her right, workers unloaded crates from an air lock, the same two aisles to her left. Caravan Supplier's barges must be latched to the outside.

"Something's not right," TrysKa said, pointing to the boxes collected before them.

There sat the shield generator and photocells, innocently waiting for a new owner, but not a few meters away stood a patrol of guards around twenty potted plants.

"I can distract the guards while you get the generator," Sann said softly in her ear.

"I guess so but..."

TrysKa shook her head. It didn't feel right. Shouldn't valuable plant life be in a more secure holding area instead of the open hangar? But maybe Sann was right, and she was being paranoid. TrysKa faced him to work on a plan when her earbud crackled. Instead of transmitting Knox's voice, it transmitted a message from *Maverick*.

"I'm sorry, Knox." Ximena's voice was high-pitched with panic.

TrysKa and Sann tensed.

"I didn't know what to do," Ximena continued. "I couldn't leave the ship, Sann and TrysKa left according to plan, but then Alex followed him, I'm sorry, I can't-"

"It's fine." Knox said to the woman on his end, but the double meaning was clearly meant for Ximena. "The crates and cash look good. I'll do my part now."

TrysKa clutched Sann's shirt and pointed. A slight breeze, the size of a child, had rippled her way, barely reaching her hips. Sann motioned for TrysKa to lead, and out she ran, ignoring the stares. Down the aisle and around the nose of a Gamma-class cargo ship, she grabbed Alex's jacket.

"Sann, TrysKa, I don't know where you are, but get back to the ship, now!" Knox said over her earbud.

"We're on our way," Sann said, as TrysKa dragged a sheepish Alex back to *Maverick*.

"Tell me you have Alex with you," Knox said.

"Yes, sir," Sann answered.

When TrysKa and Sann walked up the ramp, Alex in tow, Knox was sitting on the floor with Ximena in his arms.

"It's not your fault," Knox said in her ear. "You had to stay with the ship."

"But-"

Ximena couldn't get out more. She buried her head in her husband's chest.

"Where's Alex?" Knox asked and stood.

Ximena covered her mouth, but before anyone panicked, curls and big brown eyes peeked around TrysKa's legs.

"Get onboard," Knox said. To TrysKa. "Get us out of here, quickly."

"Yes, sir."

As she slid into the pilot's chair and pulled up the controls, TrysKa's chest felt empty and her stomach sick. She'd failed. They didn't have a generator or photocells. Why hadn't she felt Alex following them? She should have. But then TrysKa had been focusing on adult-sized air movement, not a child's.

Maverick lifted and followed its assigned trajectory to the air lock and exit. The feeling of belonging had abandoned her. TrysKa might as well be honest with herself. She was just as much of a misfit here as with her family and her school.

10

Pick Up and Drop Off

First Knox kept his word and delivered the forgotten crates to their destination. It gave him space to think. Gave him time to decide. Afterward, Knox retreated to the cockpit. He leaned around the doorframe and watched Alex chatting away with Sann in the galley.

"He's not remorseful," Knox said, keeping his voice low.

"No, he's not," TrysKa said.

"He's going to run away again, isn't he?"

TrysKa focused on launching *Maverick* instead of answering.

"After we pick up Brant..." but Knox couldn't finish.

"I understand."

The ship entered and exited the air lock, on its course out of the spaceport. Alex's voice tripped from the breakroom into the silent cockpit.

"Where does *Maverick* get its power?" he asked.

"From helium-three," Ximena said.

Oh no, Ximena was in the breakroom now too.

"He-Le-Ummm three?"

Knox could almost see the boy wriggling his nose as he

sounded out the word. Wow, this sucked. The ship put enough distance between itself and the spaceport for a safe jump.

"It's a gas made of helium missing a neutron," Ximena said. "Great for fusion."

"A gas? Is it in air?"

"Not air on the terraformed planets. There's not a lot there." Chair legs scratched across the floor. Ximena had sat down and inched next to Alex. "But the gas planets have TONS."

"How do we get gas from them?"

Knox pushed a button, and the door to the cockpit closed.

"I'm so sorry," TrysKa said.

Knox said nothing. *Maverick* jumped.

TrysKa guided the ship to the Nichev warehouse. Knox didn't move. She got permission to land, and they entered the air lock. Knox remained seated. The ship landed with a soft touch, like TrysKa was afraid to disturb him. Knox closed his eyes.

I never should have brought Alex onboard. Too late now.

Knox pushed up from his chair and nodded at TrysKa. She tapped a floating light, and the door opened. Knox stomped past the breakroom keeping his gaze fixed forward. He marched down the hall, through the cargo bay, and down the opened ramp. Right into a brightly lit warehouse floor.

Knox blinked as his eyes adjusted. The dark canopy was trimmed back. Two attack drones whizzed in from Knox's left. He flicked his gun out from his jacket sleeve and aimed. Then let his arm fall. The two drones coasted by, oblivious, with ivy trailing behind them.

Brant had used his attack drones as garden shears. Clever. Boxes from the tip of the mountain in the far left corner swarmed over the warehouse floor and dropped into their place. It was like watching a controlled avalanche. Sid glided out of his office and waved to Knox.

"You didn't have to come back so soon," Sid said and slung his arm over Knox's shoulder. "A couple more hours, and Brant would've done the whole place up nice."

Knox shrugged Sid's arm off. Normally he would have been impressed, but the job of returning Alex loomed ahead. Knox stomped down the cleared aisle and around the row of boxes.

"Time to go," he said to Brant's back.

"I'm not done."

"I have another trip to make after this."

And I want to get it over with.

"I hate leaving something half-finished." Brant dragged his finger across the tablet.

"Of the four people I got from KaeHan, fifty percent refuse to listen!"

If Brant had given a stupid or lazy reason for not obeying Knox, then he would've been fired on the spot. But no. Knox hated leaving a job half-assed too, and here was Brant using it against him.

But Brant did stop. He spun away from the towering mess.

"Who didn't listen? Did Alex do something?"

Knox pivoted. "Let's go." And marched back to *Maverick.*

"Wait!" Sid rushed to his office. "Don't forget what I owe you."

He ran back out of his office toting two massive jars of beans. Knox took one in both his hands and nodded to Brant who took the other.

"They're seasoned for Ximena, so don't eat too much or-"

"Colon cleansing by fire, got it."

Knox resumed the procession to his ship, and the next

difficult duty.

"Thanks for the help," Sid called after them.

Knox boarded the ship, but Brant hung back on the ramp.

"Come!"

The two drones shot back from the warehouse, folded up, and attached to Brant's armband. Knox put the jars away in a compartment of the galley reserved for Sid's beans.

"How spicy?" Ximena asked.

"Just for you."

She hugged Knox, but he couldn't hug back.

"What?"

Knox didn't answer. Understanding spread across Ximena's face. *Alex.* She knew what Knox had to do without a word spoken. Her eyes misted, and she shook her head, backing away from him.

Ximena could argue if she chose. Cut into Knox and drill her point home. Instead she fled to the captain's quarters. Alex stood in the middle of the breakroom.

"Why is she sad?"

Again, Knox couldn't answer. He brushed past Alex to the cockpit.

"IAS," he said to TrysKa.

"*No!*"

Alex rushed to the cockpit. Knox rose to stop him, but then relaxed. Brant had Alex in his arms. He'd been in the hallway waiting. Alex writhed and bit and gagged on tears, but Brant held him firm. Then Alex's body fell limp. The only movement came from his body shaking with sobs. Brant raised his face to Knox, and the question was written clearly across it.

Maybe he should stay?

Knox shook his head. Quite the opposite. Alex's outburst

wasn't an admission of wrongdoing, just an attempt to manip-
ulate. He wasn't sorry for what he did, just that he got caught.
Knox turned on his heel and collapsed back into the co-pilot's
chair. TrysKa tapped a light, and the cockpit door closed out
the sobs.

"I know it's hard," she said. "But you are doing the right
thing."

Was he?

Knox stared straight ahead as the ship took off, jumped, and
landed on the N.T. spaceport #2. He took one deep breath, let
it out, then rose. He adjusted his jacket, and TrysKa opened
the door.

Alex was a heap on the floor. Brant stood back, his arms
crossed and head down, in the corner of the galley.

"He didn't want me anymore," Brant said to the floor.

Knox scooped Alex up in his arms and carried him across
the landing dock. Alex curled up in a ball on Knox's lap during
the shuttle ride down. Neither spoke.

Alex, I told you to listen. I told you I would have to do this.

But what good would that do? Alex would argue that
he would listen, with wide eyes and a sincere face born of
desperation. And he would mean it. For these five seconds, at
least.

But not tomorrow. Tomorrow, he would run off and
wouldn't be so lucky.

Knox couldn't explain. He couldn't argue. Because if he did,
he would pick Alex up and take him right back to *Maverick*. No,
he couldn't speak, but he could hold him.

So, Knox wrapped his strong arms around Alex and pressed
his cheek against Alex's soft curls. The shuttle ride ended
too soon. The hoverbus raced at high speeds. IAS rose in

the window and condemned Knox. He never should've been entrusted with Alex.

Knox delivered a hiccupping quiet child to KaeHan.

"Sorry it didn't work out," KaeHan said.

"Me too," Knox said. His throat felt like sandpaper.

Alex didn't say anything. In a daze, he let KaeHan lead him into IAS. Knox couldn't turn back to the hoverbus until they were both swallowed inside the tower and lost from sight. There were no enthusiastic questions on the trip back.

Knox stood inside his ship, staring at the door to his quarters.

"Ximena in there?" he asked no one in particular.

"Yessir," Sann answered from the breakroom.

"Where's TrysKa?"

"In there too."

"Good." Knox walked down the hallway to the breakroom. "Brant?"

Sann jerked his head to the hired hands' room. Knox grunted.

"I'll sleep on the bench tonight," Knox said.

He certainly wasn't disturbing Ximena. Sann nodded and pushed up from the table. He took his glass to the sink and cleaned it.

"TrysKa made soup." Sann walked to the door to his room. "You should try it."

When Sann entered his room, Brant's snoring boomed until the door closed and cut it short. Mushroom broth simmered on the heating pad on the counter. Knox ate it out of the pot.

11

Clever

Douglas strode down the boring beige hall from one late meeting to the next. The only meeting that could in theory start on time was the first one of the day. But even that one found a way to push itself back thirty minutes. At least Douglas was compensated with yeast pastries with sprinkles for the late morning meeting. The rest? They had no guilt, no apologies, and no sprinkles.

"Sir."

Evie pushed aside the gaggle of "important people" tagging along behind Douglas, and ran to his side. Today she wore blood-red lipstick, her mouth a thin crimson ribbon. She slipped a piece of paper into his hand. Paper. Convenient for passing along information without the relentless data trail. Douglas opened the scrap and glanced down without missing stride.

Nothing was stolen. Knox smelled the trap.

Douglas swung into an open office door. Three employees snapped to attention when he entered. One unlucky chap spilled green tea over himself.

"May I borrow this room for a moment?" Douglas smiled.

"Of course!"

"Yes, sir!"

"Umm..." The last employee scooped up her scroll and whatever incriminating goof-off game the three were playing on it. "Absolutely."

And the office was empty save for Douglas and Evie. The entourage following Douglas gawked through the doorway.

"Go to the meeting without me," Douglas said. "I'll join you shortly."

They ogled until Evie closed the door.

"What happened?" Douglas asked.

He threw the scrap of paper into the trash can. It disintegrated with a flash of blue light. Then he pushed the button in his jacket, and the cameras were off. Douglas was free from all those mechanical spies.

"It's a little-known shipping procedure," Evie said. "One I wasn't aware of."

"Do tell."

She sighed. "Apparently when shipments get lost or forgotten, our people hire an independent trucker to cover their tracks. And pay him cash. Knox had permission to land and a shipment *of ours* to pick up. But the batteries and generator were untouched."

This Knox was good.

"So, what do we do now?" Evie asked. "Knox still needs those shields. The more he pokes around our company, the more likely he'll uncover the slaves in those warehouses. We can't have him reporting that to the Commune."

"Quiet, quiet, I need to think."

Douglas paced in the tiny office, a luxury he rarely indulged.

Around the desk he circled, clicking his teeth with his finger-nails, another bad habit.

"This Knox wouldn't hit the same target twice. He's clever, more than I gave him credit."

"So what-"

"Shh-shh-shh."

Click-click-click, Douglas's nails tapped his teeth. Talking out loud, hearing his thoughts. Cameras never let him do this. Ahh, the freedom.

"Knox is a Robin Hood. He doesn't want to steal necessary shields, ones that serve a purpose. No, he wants the frivolous ones, the ridiculous ones, the ones we'd be embarrassed to report as stolen."

"Like the ones protecting our suppliers' warehouses? With slaves?"

"No." Douglas snapped his fingers. "The islands!"

"The islands?" Evie leaned in.

"The deserted islands our high-ups bought for themselves on Earth. They're isolated, have alarms, fences, shields, over-board security. Way too much, and absolutely unnecessary."

Talk about a frivolous shield, ripe for the picking, and insured so the owner would get a new one. That had to be Knox's next target.

"So Knox is attacking one of those?" Evie was hooked.

"Not attacking." Douglas waggled his finger. "If Knox was the attacking type, he would've pulled out the guns at the spaceport. No. This man doesn't like to risk his life or the lives of his crew."

"That's nice of him."

"It's his weakness." Douglas licked his lips. "It's his weakness, and it gives him away. Knox will pick the least guarded, never-used island. The one that doesn't need shields because no one ever visits it."

"Grivet's island!"

"Bingo!"

"Oh, Grivet hates when his stuff is taken away. Even if he never uses it."

Some managers knew how to delegate work to their best employees while taking all the credit. At least the job got done and done well. Other managers sat on their asses and earned a fat income with benefits and stock options. Grivet was the second kind. But Douglas couldn't fire him thanks to family ties to vital investors.

"Grivet's useless," Evie said. "He's sat on that Fair Trade project for seven years with no progress, but the instant someone offers to finish it for him..."

"He destroys them!"

"But still doesn't finish the project."

Douglas and Evie were nose to nose.

"So," she said. "If Grivet were to get wind that his unused, unmaintained, unwanted island was going to be raided by pirates..."

"He would man it with more guards than the sum total of guests that have ever visited."

"Warning arranged, sir."

Knox had picked the perfect shield to steal. No one would have missed it. Too bad Douglas figured it out first.

No one dug up dirt on his company. Or more accurately, no one survived digging up dirt on his company.

Evie closed her scroll. "Anything else?"

"I'll handle everything else," Douglas said.

Evie stiffened. That was one of their codes. *You don't want to know what else I'm doing.* Her lips parted to probe further, but Douglas pressed the button inside his jacket. The cameras resumed their scrutiny of every second of his life, and Evie pursed her scarlet lips with a glare. Together they left the room.

His minions had waited for him in the hallway, directionless without his leadership. Douglas stepped out, and they all fell in line. Evie, however, made her own way against the flow. She could do real work instead of warm a seat in meetings all day. Lucky girl.

As the next meeting droned on, Douglas opened his scroll and drilled down several layers of files through multiple passwords to a vault-protected commlink.

Teacher? he typed.

It took fifteen minutes before the reply materialized under his.

You need me?

A thorn in my side needs removing.

Medical procedures aren't free.

Douglas typed a credit amount.

That will cover expenses, the Teacher typed. *Tell me about the thorn.*

Douglas touched the file on Knox and sent it.

I've set a trap for Knox, Douglas typed.

I'll clean up when your plans fail.

The insult didn't sting, but the Teacher had an ego that needed massaging. It was important the man *felt* like Douglas cared.

Remember who pays your bills, he typed.

Remember who does the work.

Good. Douglas closed the scroll. Plan A and Plan B were set

in motion. This was fun.

12

The Teacher

Ophelia sat cross-legged on a cold epoxycrete floor and watched as Juliette practiced her flip. The little girl landed with wobbly legs.

"Again," Ophelia said.

Juliette tried, but her footing still shifted. The girl was scared of falling on the hard floor. That was the problem. Ophelia and the other adapted kids, her sisters and brothers, didn't have a cushy gym with flexible plastimat floors. They couldn't afford that. They lived in an abandoned parking lot on the bottom floor of an ancient business building. The bottom two floors had been locked up and emptied years ago. Then her Teacher had found it, and their family had moved in.

"MacBeth," her Teacher said.

"Coming," Mac answered.

Ophelia whispered to Juliette, "Sit and meditate."

Ophelia peeked over her siblings' heads to her Teacher. He stood in one of the stairwells, dim light trickling around his dark silhouette. The lifts didn't go down to this floor anymore, so everyone, including Teacher with his bad knees, used the stairs.

"Yes, Teacher?" Mac said.

Human cruelty had shredded the Teacher's face, but his soul burned bright through his eyes. Love brimmed in them and spilled out onto Mac. If only Ophelia could be washed by that adoration too.

Teacher had saved her from hell. A locked room. Ruthless visitors. Bruises and screams and needles. She pushed those memories back down and locked them away. She remembered instead the day Teacher had walked through the door and rescued her. Raised her with her brothers and sisters, all children he'd saved.

A fly buzzed in the garage's corner by Ophelia, rudely interrupting her worship. It was fat on rotten food from a nearby compost pile and bumbled around noisily, smacking into the wall. The insect glowed in the soured yellow light, but Ophelia didn't move to attack. The spiders would take care of it.

"Now is the time for you to give back to this family," her Teacher said to Mac.

Ophelia's adapted ears caught the low conversation over the irritating bug.

"Anything." Mac's low voice echoed off the stairwell walls.

"A man in the space trade business has been a thorn in the side of our Supplier."

"Space trade."

He spat those words out like they were rancid meat. Space traders bought products made by slaves in one country then sold those tainted goods to countries where slavery was illegal. Scum.

"So, our Supplier has asked that we remove the thorn."

"Yes, sir," Mac said. "But not for free."

"What have I told you?"

"No human works for free," Ophelia recited under her breath in unison with Mac.

"Exactly," Teacher said. "Our Supplier is paying handsomely."

"Then we can afford food and power for another month."

Ophelia gave Juliette a squeeze around her bony shoulders. Teacher always brought too many back with him. Like going to an animal shelter and melting at all the adorable puppies, Teacher couldn't say *no*.

But then the food ran out. Or someone got sick and needed a doctor. Or they needed supplies for one of his jobs. The Supplier gave some money, but never enough. With a heartbroken limp, her Teacher would lead the weakest children away from their home.

And come back alone.

But he gave them a better life than they had before even if for just a little while. That's what Ophelia told herself at night as she listened to the rhythmic breathing of her family, snuggled in sleeping bags on the floor. He gave them his family.

But with more income from the Supplier, the Teacher could pay for more food, clothes, and energy. Ophelia wouldn't have to say goodbye!

"What thorn needs removing?" Mac asked.

"L.L. Knox," Teacher said. "He's captain of an Asteria-class cargo ship named *Maverick*."

Teacher handed Mac a scroll. His eyes scanned the information.

"He has a wife."

"She isn't a threat, and we don't take life for fun."

"Of course."

"MacBeth." The Teacher put his damaged hand on Mac's shoulder, and the two stood proud. "When you succeed," Teacher said, "you will have saved many in this family."

When would Ophelia hear those words? When would she have a chance to go on a mission and earn money for her family? Mac bowed and strode up the stairs. With a sigh, Ophelia returned to Juliette, noticing the quiet.

The webs had done their job and silenced the gross fly. Good. That's why Teacher taught Ophelia to leave the spiders alone. Such useful, misunderstood creatures.

13

Welcome to Earth

The next morning, Earth filled the viewscreen. Sann shared the cockpit door with Brant. Alex normally would have leaned his head on TrysKa's chair, but that spot was empty.

"I'd seen it in history vids," Brant said. "Holograms don't do it justice."

TrysKa nodded. Sann just tried to take it all in. Earth. A planet covered in color: vibrant blues, intense greens, and brilliant white. Too lavish. Like the life of the entire galaxy was showered on this one rock.

"That's an ocean?" Brant said. "Ocean." It rolled off his tongue. "The word isn't-" Brant spread his arms wide. "Big enough."

India and the northeast of Africa spun slowly by. Sann leaned in to get a better view of his original country, Cambodia, the one that had become Khmer on Naya Surya. It was hard to distinguish one country from the other without the convenient dividing lines. Humans cared about borders; planets didn't.

There. There was the mountain range, forests, and rivers, the borders of so long ago. Of course, since the Earth Exodus, lines had been redrawn. Entire countries had abandoned old Earth and relocated to the colony planets.

TrysKa pointed *Maverick* toward a shining spec orbiting Earth. The glowing dot grew larger and larger until a tiny web system came into focus.

"A spaceport?" Sann asked.

For some reason, he imaged Earth full of rundown cities with no technology. Then he winced at his own naivety. This planet was full of diversity, both rich and poor, both technologically advanced and undeveloped, just like everywhere else in the galaxy.

"Three space stations orbit," TrysKa said. "Earth still has an abundance of resources that the Six Planets need."

Knox tapped a light that pinged the spaceport. "*Maverick* calling Spaceport of the Holy Cities. *Maverick* calling Spaceport HC." His voice sounded thick and low, like his throat was constricted.

"Holy Cities?" Brant asked.

Knox didn't answer. Probably missing Alex. The kid would've loved to see Earth. Sann could almost see Alex bursting with questions and straining on his tiptoes to see the planet. Brant grimaced and shifted his weight. He knew why Knox wasn't speaking too.

TrysKa answered instead.

"Jerusalem and Mecca." She didn't draw any closer to the spaceport, pointing the nose toward the planet below instead. "Someone had to stay behind and rebuild the monuments of faith and human history."

Sann moved away from the cockpit and sat at the table. What monuments of Cambodia had survived? Maybe he would visit them one day.

"HC port here, state your purpose," said a flight coordinator from the spaceport.

Sann craned his neck to peer back inside. The bust of a young man wearing a white skullcap floated above the control panel. His beard was neatly combed without a touch of gray.

"Requesting permission to land planet-side," Knox said. "Working with Serving Hands on the Taluk Project. Authorization scan commencing."

The ship scanned Knox's face and brainwave pattern. The coordinator checked information on his side, staring off at a point in space between TrysKa and Knox. He nodded.

"Authorization granted. Proceed on the provided course."

"Copy that. *Maverick* out."

"I didn't think cargo ships could survive the Gs of atmospheric entry," Brant said.

"*Maverick* originally couldn't." TrysKa veered along the approach trajectory. "But Ximena's upgraded a lot of parts. The blasters have the power to launch, the shields can withstand the plasma and friction, and the artificial gravity and inertial dampeners can handle the Gs."

"Mostly," Ximena said and buckled herself into a chair. "There are still some hiccups, so you will want to strap in."

Her gaze drifted down to her hands and stayed there. Her nose was rubbed pink, and her eyes were puffy.

Brant left his spot by the cockpit door and slid in next to Sann. He pushed a button above the bench and energy restraints wrapped around their chests.

Sann couldn't breathe. He clutched the table's edge and pushed air down into his lungs. The restraints slacked as his chest expanded. But when Sann exhaled, the restraints tightened again. He closed his eyes. Breath in. Wince. Breath out.

I can do this.

Breathe in. Hold. Breathe out. Hold. Brandon howled outside the ship. No, no, that wasn't Brandon. It was wind. They were descending into the atmosphere of the planet. Breathe in. Hold. Breathe out. The guards had Brandon. They were making him kneel. The ship rocked, and Sann's stomach slammed into his lungs then fell on his bladder. Breathe in. Breathe out. Breathe in.

Brandon shouldn't have come for me. Leave him alone! He wasn't the sniper. I was! It's me! Don't-

The ship jumped. Brandon's head burst open. The break-room lights seared into Sann's vision. He slammed his lids shut against the brightness. Brant's hand pressed down on Sann's shoulder.

"You're not alone. I'm here. You're not alone."

And the nightmare fled. Sann's heartbeat, which had been pounding in his ears, softened. He opened his eyes. Blue sky lit the cockpit's viewscreen, and a horizon peeked over the edge. Higher and higher the horizon rose, and the ship steadied in TrysKa's sure hands.

Before *Maverick* touched down, though, a pale-lipped Ximena deactivated her restraints and bolted to the bathroom.

Whhhhoooaargggg!

"Oh, poor thing," TrysKa said from the pilot's chair.

She peeked around the edge of the cockpit door. Knox stood, pointed TrysKa back to the controls, and straightened his shoulders.

"This is my job."

While Ximena loudly emptied the last of her breakfast, Knox inserted filters into his nose and strode to his wife's side.

TrysKa touched down *Maverick* with the gentleness of laying an infant down for his nap. Sann released his restraints and filled his chest with oxygen. He'd made it.

A door swished open then closed, and Knox's boots clicked their approach back to the breakroom.

"Ximena's settled. Time for everyone to meet Taluk."

Sann followed Knox to the cargo bay and Brant fell in line. TrysKa came last, pausing by the captain's door and running her fingertips along it.

"When I come back, I'll make a ginger soda for you," she whispered.

Knox opened a compartment door and pulled out a tub of lotion. He tossed it into Brant's chest.

"Sunscreen?" Brant read.

"You've lived under domes all your life," Knox said. "They filtered out the UV light."

"UV light?" Sann asked.

"Harmful light from a star. If you stay out in the sun without protection, the skin will burn like hell, blister, and peel."

That was all Brant needed. He squirted a heaping dose into his hand and started slathering.

"Alright." Sann held out his hand. "My turn."

"You, TrysKa, and I will be fine," Knox said.

"What?" Brant asked, his face looking like a clown's.

"High concentration of melanin." Knox held up his hands, the light gleaming off his dark copper skin. "Protects from UV light. Oh, and one more thing: you won't need Vitamin D supplements while you're here."

"The sun makes vitamin D?" That was too much for Brant. Knox might as well have said fish climb trees on Earth.

"Sure does," TrysKa said. "Better than any source we eat.

It's the way our bodies were naturally meant to absorb it."

TrysKa sounded so certain that Sann dared not cross-examine her. No matter how strange it seemed.

"Learn something new every day." Brant finished smearing the white goo around his nose. He rubbed his ears and checked his hands. "Did I miss a spot?"

TrysKa raised up on her toes and tilted her head this way and that. "You rubbed it all in."

Knox passed out water bottles. "All of you, drink. If you pass out from heat exhaustion, I'm not carrying you back."

Sann took the bottle, drank half, and strapped it to his belt. When Knox punched the ramp controls with his fist, the humidity rolled into the cargo bay. Brant and TrysKa ripped their bottles off their belts and chugged. Sann's skin oozed sweat, and his clothes clung to every nook and cranny. Just like back home.

Almost monsoon season.

Knox led the crew down the ramp into an open field. The morning sun burned hot on Sann's back. Brant swayed to his right, swayed left, and started stumbling. Sann grabbed his shoulder before Brant keeled right over.

"What's wrong?" Sann asked.

"Not used to the sky being so far away." Brant set his feet and shaded his eyes with his hand. "It gives me vertigo."

"Oh."

Sann tilted his head up to the blue expanse, his hair tickling the back of his neck. The birds soared through the air with no shields to contain them. What would it be like to live with that weightless freedom?

"Don't do that!" Brant clutched Sann's arm. "How does it not bother you?"

"My country is under one huge dome instead of the smaller ones used on North and South US. The sky feels this far away back home."

"Why does it have an enormous dome?" Brant shook his head like he had water in his ears. "Is Khmer that big?"

Brant's trying to distract himself from the sky.

So Sann talked while Brant blinked and breathed in through his nose and out through his mouth.

"The Reparations Act required all colonizing countries to terraform countries they'd controlled," Sann said. "So France had to terraform and dome Viet, Khmer, Laos, and Indonesia. But they didn't break us into four tiny bubbles."

"They stuffed you all in one?"

"Four different cultures, faiths, and languages crammed into one enormous cage. And we were left to draw up dividing lines the old-fashioned way."

"War."

"You got it."

Sann lowered his face back to Earth, and Brant dropped his arm. *You OK?* Sann asked with a raised eyebrow. Brant nodded.

A breeze relieved the oppression as it raked through Sann's thick hair and lifted his tank top. TrysKa fluffed her shirt and rubbed her arms. The wet wind, thick humidity, and swaying crops were probably scratching against her adapted touch.

One stalk bent down and caressed Sann's chest. He cupped its head. The grains had ripened to a full blood-red for their harvest.

"What is it?" Brant asked, pointing up at the maroon seeds.

"Jowar," Knox said. "A good source of nutrients for humans and a common feed grain for livestock."

"Livestock? As in animals? As in meat?"

"Meat is Earth's main export."

"So Taluk has lots of animals?"

"You'll see soon enough." Knox tapped his nose with the filter still inserted. "You'll smell them before that."

A jowar stem arched against the wind. Brant snapped his face up, turning one ear in the direction of the stalk and then the other. He cut his eyes at Sann. Someone or something approached through the field.

Through the gaps in the shoots, a shadow filtered through, a shadow with the same brownish red as the grains themselves. Then the stems bowed and let past a middle-aged man. His taut skin stretched over lean muscles. His shoulders slumped from hard labor and grief. His clothes hung limp.

"Klundah." Knox shook the Taluk's hand.

"Knox," Klundah said.

Knox clicked his tongue for the "Kl" so it sounded like <click>unduh.

"I wanted the crew to meet your people," Knox said. "I wanted them to know why we are on this mission."

Klundah leaned his head to peer up the ramp into the cargo hold. Knox shook his head.

"I didn't get a generator or photocells this time, but I have other plans. One setback can't stop us."

Klundah sighed then nodded. "Follow me."

He led the crew to a narrow irrigation ditch between the stalks. Sann reached out and let the heads, both scratchy and soft, brush along his palm. With resilience, they sprang back straight and tall behind him.

It had been so long since he'd strolled through a field. Back home, his family grew rice patties instead of grains, but still this place brought back memories. Plants and humans and animals mingled together with no shields sanitarily separating them. He'd forgotten the smell of growth and soil.

"Oh wow!" Brant retched and held his breath.

Sann smiled so big his cheeks pushed up into his eyes. Speaking of smells...

The breeze carried the perfume of nature's fertilizer. Sann inhaled with eyelids fluttering. Strange that manure could be nostalgic. Brant, red in the face, finally released his breath and sucked in air only to hunch over in a fit of gagging. He stood up, tears streaming down his cheeks.

"It *burns*."

"Welcome to the animal pens," Sann said with a chuckle.

The fields parted, and the crew walked between two wire fences. The fences ran from post to post enclosing herds of goats and sheep. The animals grazed, unaware of their smell or their importance to the community as suppliers of wool, milk, and Earth's main export: meat. Beyond the goats' enclosure, another fence circled a larger animal.

"Mmm, steak," Brant said.

How could Brant inhale manure and want steak at the same time? Sann shook his head.

"No steak here," Knox said. "Those cattle are beasts of burden, used to pull the farming equipment."

"What about hovertractors?" Brant asked.

"They have a few, and some tractors with wheels. But these are their main equipment."

Brant winced again at the pungent odor. "Don't they eat any of the cows?"

"No."

"Why not?"

"Their faith," Sann said.

The crew left the animals behind, and the smell of chimney fires and morning oats cleansed Sann's palette. The road changed from packed dirt to broken black slabs. Sann picked his footing along the shifting chunks.

The town's buildings rose and crumbled along the roadside. A solid brick house rubbed shoulders with a ruin. The earth-quakes that caused the Earth Exodus had knocked down an ancient city. A few buildings had been rebuilt while others had rusted steel spikes protruding from toppled walls. Between two houses, a noble statue stood guard, its left arm gone and its face half-shattered. Fresh paint covered the ancient watchman, but fresher graffiti decorated its legs and damaged armpit.

Some houses had new doors, but most had off-kilter openings that no door could fit. Faces peered out at the crew and Sann. Split lips. Cracked fingers. Suspicious glares.

One of the faces–

Sann did a double take. No, of course it wasn't his little brother. His brother was safe at home in Khmer. Yet, the face had looked so similar. Something about the eyes. Sann turned away and put one foot in front of the other.

Brant whispered. "What just happened?"

The houses bowed and parted to present the town square. In a traffic circle, an ornate fountain spouted putrid water. A pump somewhere in the city was operational, pumping water through the ancient pipes. Soil, rust, fertilizer, and filth streamed through the frothy spray.

"I didn't–" Sann shook his head. He couldn't speak.

"Take your time," Brant said.

Klundah led Knox to the fountain where a Serving Hands volunteer held a purple mangosteen fruit and instructed the

141

townspeople on the operation of sanitizers. Sann took a shaky breath.

"I didn't realize how much this place would remind me of home."

"This place?" Brant's eyes swept the scene. "Your home?"

"Khmer is not a wealthy nation, Brant."

"But these people don't even have clean water. The Reparations Act required France to filter the water coming into your dome."

"It did, and they did."

Sann closed his eyes. He could see the market in Manado, the town near his family's rice patties.

"But the river coming from India isn't filtered. France was only required to filter water coming from the assigned plankton ponds."

"And the river from India isn't clean?"

"Polluted." Sann could see the river, algae-filled and murky. "It's a boundary marker between countries, poor countries that fight each other. Filters have been built by one side only to be blown up by the other."

Pavement hunks grated against each other. Sann opened his eyes. Brant was rocking his feet, scraping the black slabs against their neighbors.

"I never knew," Brant said.

"I never told you."

"How did you ever make it to IAS?"

"Serving Hands. They came to our town, taught us about the human traffickers."

Brant stopped fidgeting with the concrete under his boots. "But I thought human traffickers only kidnap from Earth. How do they steal people out of the domes?"

"They lie."

Sann strolled to the fountain, his hands clasped behind his back, the breeze in his face. The Serving Hands volunteer held high the fruit and detailed the right times for planting seeds. Brant stepped to Sann's side.

"The traffickers say we'll get a paying job," Sann said. "All we have to do is go with them, to a different country, to a different planet, and once we pay off the 'transportation fee' we can send our paychecks back home. But once we're in a different country with no passport and no ID-"

"They never come back home, do they?"

Sann shook his head. "Dad almost took one of those jobs, almost got on that transport, but Serving Hands stopped him. Taught us about the traffickers' lies. And discovered a farm boy who could see distances far too clearly."

"You?"

"Me."

Sann sat cross-legged on the ground with the Taluk farmers. The volunteer's alto rose and fell as she taught the necessary depth of soil. A girl wearing a beige sari dress translated the lesson into the town's native tongue, full of clicks and whistles.

Sann closed his eyes and drifted back fifteen years. He could hear the charity worker at his hometown teach about rice. He curled up in his momma's lap, his ear pressed to her heartbeat. Footsteps crunched up behind her, and Sann raised his eyes over her shoulder to the strange man standing there.

"So you're the one," KaeHan said.

Serving Hands called KaeHan, and he answered. For one little five-year-old boy, he came.

14

Play ball!

Sann and TrysKa had settled in to listen, but Brant stood alone and unnecessary. Until a movement caught his eye.

Through a gap in the buildings, a ball shot past followed by a teen. Brant circled back and crept past the buildings lining the town center. He pressed his left shoulder against the scalding brick and peered through the gap. An alleyway ran between two shop buildings. Several teens, around fifteen years old, raced back and forth on the epoxycrete kicking a homemade rubber band ball. Half the boys showed off their glowing tan chests while the other half covered their chests with wrapped scarves.

Brant turned his ear toward the court, so his earbud could translate their language. It stumbled.

"Bahasa from Indonesia. Correction, a form of Telugu from India, a form of Czech from Czech Republic. Correction, an unknown mix of original Earth languages."

The translator switched off. But Brant didn't need a translator to understand perfectly. Their tone said it all.

"Man, you can't win. Give up now and save yourself the

time!"

And, "You were born already beaten by me."

The words were universal no matter the language. Brant had yelled them himself at Willow and DeVaun. The hairs on the back of Brant's neck prickled. Someone was breathing behind him.

"You going to stand there and stare?" a voice asked.

"You gonna stand there and stare?" Brant asked back.

"You want to play?"

Behind Brant stood a Taluk teen, wispy frame and shoeless feet. His trim arms were crossed and his eyes narrowed.

"Am I allowed to join you?" Brant asked.

"You with Knox, right? What's your name?"

"Brant. And yours?"

"Devdan. Or at least, that's the version you can say. Follow me."

Devdan slipped through the gap and waved for Brant to follow. The brick on both sides of the alleyway baked Brant to his bones. When the teen stepped out onto the dirt court, Brant wanted to hang back but couldn't tolerate being cooked alive. He slipped out of the radiating waves and kept his face down.

The game froze as the teens huddled together and eyed him. The children along the sidelines gathered too, watching him with the eyes of prey prepared to escape its predator.

These kids just wanted to be left alone. Brant started to back away.

Devdan motioned for everyone's attention and spoke. While he didn't speak in English, the word "Knox" slipped in. The other kids studied Brant with more interest, and he paused, holding his breath. The pack of children loosened as some peeked at the "alien from another planet."

Devdan finished, and the group burst out laughing.

"What did you tell them?" Brant asked, stepping onto the court now.

"Nothing, just that you would keep your shirt on."

A teammate kicked the ball to Devdan who passed it to Brant. Brant rocked back on his heel, and the ball gripped to the sole of his boot. The ground was packed solid but with subtle shifts and the occasional crack. Brant tapped the ball between his feet to feel for its hold with the surface.

"Sure, that's all you said." Brant lobbed the ball along, sauntering up to Devdan.

"You ever lose, Brant?"

"Nope. You?"

"No."

Brant tapped the ball to the teen who appeared to be the captain of the "shirts." The captain stepped back, sized Brant up, and pointed at the tallest boy on the other team.

"Cover him," Brant said. "Got it."

At each end of the court, two stakes poked into the ground with wire strung along their tops. Goals. Buildings stood sentinel on both sides of the court. Two older boys stood guard at the edges, their stances loose, their gaze piercing, and their guns held close. Beyond it all, the stalks swayed. Would animals attack from the stalks? Maybe, but the greater danger came from pirates.

The captain kicked the ball to Brant. Instantly two shirtless boys charged. One threw his elbow at Brant's chest. Brant whipped around and lunged for the ball. The other shirtless player kicked it to his gang.

The game began.

Most of the shirts hung back to guard their goal. Only one ran with Brant to the shirtless side of the court. The opposing squad surrounded the ball. Brant spotted the two weakest boys but didn't barge them. He wasn't going to use his height and strength advantage on the smallest of the pack.

Brant charged the biggest teens. They faltered, accustomed to being untouchable. Instead of bowling them over, he squatted down on his left leg and shot his right one out, hitting the ball. It popped out of the scrum. Brant's teammate sprinted for the escaped prize, and the shirts burst after him.

So distracted were they by Brant's friend, that they lost track of Brant. He set up at an angle to the goal and whistled. It split the air and froze the players. His partner recovered and kicked the ball hard, too hard. Over everyone's head it flew.

Brant crouched and sprang. His head slammed into the ball, sending it right back to his cohort. The group of shirts had barrelled toward Brant but all skidded to a halt. Dust flew. So did curses. At least that's what it sounded like.

Brant's ally planted his foot into the ball's side. Straight into the unguarded goal. Brant back-peddled with arms out.

"What??? I think that's a score."

Brant's team cheered, and two more joined him. The shirtless team all stared at their goalie. He jogged back to his post, swearing under his breath. With his foot, he hit a rocket to the other end of the field.

No more easy scores. The shirtless team formed up and played their positions. When the fight went to the shirts side, Brant let the boys play. But when the battle crossed to the shirtless side, Brant jumped into the circle of kicking feet and flying elbows. A leg clipped him, and Brant hit the dirt. The shirtless faction made a point. Brant leapt to his feet. Yup, that was Devdan.

"Thanks a lot!"

"Anytime!"

Dust ground between his teeth. Brant spat and galloped beside his teammates. It was glorious. The sun rose, and the game played on. Brant fist-pumped the air after another of his gang scored when Knox stepped to the sidelines.

"Grumpy captain here," Brant told Devdan. "Gotta go."

Brant marched off the court, and the teens' voices taunted. He didn't need his translator bug to understand.

"Leaving so soon?"

"Scared of losing?"

"Can't handle it?"

Brant faced the players and pointed at Devdan.

"I'll be back to beat you again!"

"Oh! We'll be ready for you!"

Brant jogged over to Knox, who wore a stony expression. Brant put his hands on his hips, and caught his breath.

"What?"

"Congratulations."

Brant startled.

"If you wanted to get on my good side," Knox said. "This was the way to do it."

Brant's chest puffed out against his sticky shirt, and he followed Knox out of the village. On the edge of it, Sann loitered, waiting for his friend. But when Brant ran up, Sann winced.

"Oooooh."

"What?"

Brant's hand followed Sann's gaze and touched the top of his head. His part stung like a wasp attack. *Ouch!*

"Hopefully TrysKa has something for that," Sann said. "I didn't think about the sun burning the top of your head."

"Knox should have. His whole head is one big part."

Sann bit his lower lip, and the hairs on Brant's neck bristled for the second time that day. About fifty meters away, someone with big lungs was breathing. Brant grimaced and inch by inch, peeked over his shoulder. Knox stood with arms crossed.

"So much for getting on my good side."

Yeah, Knox had heard what Brant had blabbed. Brant hung his head, and Knox's throat cleared.

"But when you decide to burn yourself, you give it your all."

"Yes, sir," Brant said.

"We grow aloe onboard to convert the carbon dioxide, Ximena will cut you a piece."

"Thanks."

Knox walked along the irrigation canal to *Maverick,* and Brant and Sann followed. Behind them, the town settled down for their afternoon nap. The sun set ablaze the tops of the grasses like an ocean of blood. It reflected onto Sann's shirt and turned his skin a deep crimson.

When the cool air from the ship rolled over Brant, he almost collapsed on the cold cargo bay floor. TrysKa cut a tip off a squishy leaf from a spiny plant growing out of one of the cabinets.

"Here you go," she said. "Hold out your hand."

Brant did, and TrysKa squeezed plant snot into his palm. What was he supposed to do with this? Sann laughed.

"I know it looks weird," TrysKa said. "But it will cool the burn."

Brant dipped the tip of his index finger into the gunk and placed the dab on the front of his part. Instant cool breeze.

"Oooh." Brant's eyes rolled up into the back of his head.

"Told you."

He scooped up the rest with three fingers and smeared it down the burn line.

"Woooow."

He wiped his hands on his pants and started toward the hallway.

"Wait," TrysKa said, apologetically. "Would you boys be willing to shower before entering the kitchen?"

"Sann?" Brant asked.

"Yes, Brant?" Sann mirrored.

"What do you think TrysKa's hinting at?"

"Perhaps that we stink."

"Ya think?"

Brant stepped into the bathroom and pushed the *shower* button. The incinerating toilet lowered through a hole in the floor and sealed shut. Brant spun. Where was he supposed to hang his clothes? And how was he supposed to get them off? The cubby was too narrow for his long arms to pull his shirt over his head.

A horizontal blue light turned on above his head, covering the entire ceiling.

No! No! No!

Brant buried his face in the elbow of his right arm and covered his goods with his left hand. Zap! The light dropped to the floor, sterilizing Brant's body along the way. The room smelled of ozone, his skin tingled, and static lifted his hair. He stepped out of the bathroom in a daze.

How deep did that beam sterilize?

"It only cleans the outside of the body," Knox said.

The captain stood in the hallway, leaning against the wall.

Brant couldn't tell, but his stony eyes seemed softened around the edges. Like he found Brant's reaction funny.

"Are you sure?" Brant asked. He needed to *know*.

"Let me put it to you this way, back when I worked on the space barges, all the men used these showers." Knox pointed at the door. "On breaks they would have too much fun at the local pubs and brothels. Nine months later, they got the paternity bill with DNA proof. The showers only sterilize the outside of the body."

OK, Brant didn't want to hear anymore. He didn't want to think about that shower anymore. He didn't want to deal with the fact that he'd have to use that thing again and again and again on this mission. He just wanted lunch.

TrysKa must have planned ahead this morning. A pot of stew simmered on the stove, its smell saturating the entire *Maverick*. Brant inhaled half the bowl within seconds of sitting down.

"Is this lamb?" Brant was in heaven.

"I traded for some today," TrysKa said and ladled a bowl for herself.

Her step faltered on the way to her seat, and she gazed down the hallway.

"Is Ximena still in her room?" Brant asked around a hunk of steak.

"Yeah," TrysKa said.

"Is she sick?"

"No."

"Then what's wrong?"

TrysKa sat down at the table instead of answering. Brant took another bite and checked out Knox. He looked pissed, so Brant dropped the subject. None of his business.

"Do you believe in second chances?" TrysKa asked instead of eating.

15

Second Chances

"I guess so, why?" Brant asked.

TrysKa took a sip of her soup and flicked her eyes at Knox.

"Depends," Knox said.

"Wait now, are you talking about Alex?" Brant brought his fist down harder than he'd meant to. The bowls all clinked on the metal table, and the liquid inside sloshed. "He's safe at IAS."

"He needs family."

Had Sann said that? Brant twisted, so his chest squared off with Sann. He was supposed to be on Brant's side. Sann slumped over his bowl and twirled his spoon in the broth.

"I know *Maverick* isn't safe if Alex doesn't listen." TrysKa murmured it under her breath. If Brant didn't have adapted hearing, he wouldn't have caught it.

"You're right, it's not," he said.

His voice sounded like a yell after her whisper. TrysKa blinked like she was going to cry in her soup.

"What were you going to say?" Knox asked her.

"But if Alex does listen, then you and Ximena are exactly

what he needs right now."

"And how will we know if he's going to listen or not?" Brant asked, his face heating up.

"Only by giving him another chance."

"And getting him killed?"

Knox raised his hand. "Enough."

Brant bowed his head. A hunk of meat meandered around his bowl. He shoveled it in his mouth, and ground his molars on it. The salty, fatty flavor rolled over his tongue and soothed Brant's temper, almost against his will.

"There are ways that Ximena and I could keep a better eye on him." Knox finished off his stew. "We weren't prepared the first time."

Knox took his bowl to the kitchen and dropped it in the sink. A blue flash sanitized it.

"Where does this go now?" he asked TrysKa.

She lifted her eyes and pointed at one of the cabinets.

"I'm sorry for arguing," she whispered to Brant.

She didn't have to apologize. It was Brant who'd lost his cool at her. He tried to say that, but the chunk of lamb wedged in his windpipe. Brant wheezed and gagged on it until Knox whacked him on the back. The food skidded, leaving a wet trail across the table.

"Chew first, swallow second," Knox said and went to the cockpit.

TrysKa left her meal unfinished and joined Knox in the cockpit. Awkward silence filled the galley, as thick in the air as the aroma of the lamb stew.

"I'm a jerk," Brant said.

"But you're a good-hearted one," Sann said.

"Thanks?"

"Anytime."

Brant chucked the half-eaten lump across the breakroom into the sink. It incinerated. They finished their food and cleaned the dishes. As a peace offering, Brant brought TrysKa's bowl to her in the cockpit. She set it on her lap and squeezed his hand. Apology accepted.

"I'm calling KaeHan," Knox said. "We'll get his thoughts."

Fine. KaeHan would agree with Brant. IAS had been a safe haven for him growing up, and it was the same for Alex.

"I was just about to call you," said KaeHan's miniature image.

"What's wrong?" Knox and Brant asked simultaneously.

Brant leaned into the cockpit over Knox's shoulder to get a better view.

"Alex has disappeared off our camera feeds and is hiding somewhere in IAS."

"If he's off the feeds then how do you know he's still in the school?" Knox asked.

"He can't get out of the school without being recorded."

"Yes he can," Knox said. "Unless you've installed more cameras in the loading storage shed out back."

"No one knows about that area but you."

"And anyone who's worked with me. We'll be right there."

Knox tapped a pinprick star hovering above the controls, and KaeHan disappeared.

"TrysKa-"

"On it."

Maverick launched. She lunged toward the air lock, and Brant had to reset his feet.

"Sorry," she said and smoothed the acceleration.

"No need to apologize." Knox rose and adjusted his jacket.

"Brant would be halfway into the breakroom if I were flying."

Knox marched to the captain's quarters and Ximena. When he entered his room, Brant stared down the hall, the walls blurring out of focus. Where could Alex be?

He didn't have much time to wonder. TrysKa landed the ship in N.T. #2 in record time. Brant beat Knox to the spaceport's shuttle stop but had to wait for it to unload. Knox was by his side in time to ride down together. The hoverbus to IAS, however, flew through gel instead of air. It was like the IAS dome was frozen on the horizon.

"Breathe, Brant," Knox said. "We'll find him."

I'll find him.

Finally, the hoverbus touched down, and Brant raced into the foyer. KaeHan startled.

"You got here fast."

"Where did you last see him?"

"Shouldn't we wait for—ah, Knox, there you are."

Most others would have been winded trying to keep up with Brant's long stride, but no. Knox's legs might be shorter, but he could hold his own in a marathon.

"Let's go," Knox said.

They all hurried, but the lift took its sweet time rising to the ninth floor. Knox exited first and measured off fifteen steps.

"Here." Knox looked straight at the camera over the lift, then the one at the end of the hallway, and lastly the one one-third of the way down. "This is the blind spot."

"And where we last saw Alex," KaeHan said coming to stand next to Knox.

"And you know where the blind spots are how?" Brant asked, trying to imagine the lines of sight and failing completely.

156

"Needed privacy from time to time when I was a student here," Knox said.

He pointed his toes at a sixty-degree angle toward the lift and took three steps. "He could get back to the lift this way."

"He wouldn't go there," Brant said.

"And then from the third floor, he could take the other lift down to the loading docks."

"Again, how do you know this?"

"Had to get out once for fresh air."

KaeHan cleared his throat. "So, you think Alex tried to leave?"

"No." Brant didn't budge toward the lifts. "He's still here. If he couldn't get to Knox, he'd make Knox come to him."

Brant pointed toward the hallway that branched off between the lift and himself. "His room's that way. Odds are he's in there."

"His roommate would have seen him," KaeHan said.

"He's in one of the empty rooms then!"

Brant hadn't meant to yell. He sucked in his air and closed his eyes.

"He's just worried about Alex," Knox said to KaeHan and pointed his boots in a new direction. "And Alex could get down this hall while avoiding detection."

Knox walked a zigzagged pattern to the intersection and then down the hall. He ducked and slid to his right then followed the wall to the end. He looked like he was maneuvering around an unseen laser security system.

"Anyone in this room?" Knox nodded to the one at the end.

KaeHan pulled out his scroll and checked. "Nope."

Brant bolted to the door and barged in. Empty. Two cots were folded up against the walls. The floor, walls, and ceiling

157

had the high shine from a cleaning-bot. Brant spun to face Knox and threw his arms out.

Knox entered and flared his nostrils. "Oh, he's in here alright."

Knox punched the top of the cot to his right. It folded out. Nothing. He punched the top of the left one. Only air. Then he narrowed his eyes. He strolled around Brant and studied the back wall. It had a closed niche like the one that had delivered Brant's clothes to Sann's room.

"Open the cabinet," Knox told the computer.

The hatch opened, and Alex rolled out like an energy bar from a cafeteria food dispenser. He plopped on the floor and blinked his eyes. Knox took a knee in front of him.

"Hey lad."

Alex lunged at Knox and lassoed his arms around his neck. His fingernails dug into Knox's jacket. Knox closed his eyes, cupping Alex's head in his right hand and wrapping his left around the boy's back.

Brant's stomach soured. What had Knox done right and he wrong?

"Let's take you back home." Knox rose, holding Alex in his arms. Alex hooked his ankles around Knox's waist and buried his head in Knox's shoulder.

"About that," KaeHan grimaced.

"About what?" Knox dropped his voice even deeper than usual.

"The first time Alex went with you, I handled things quietly. Just me and Councilor Perez."

"But now?"

"When Alex went missing, Wright heard and started sniffing around."

"So Councilor Wright now knows I'm mentoring Alex."

"And Head Councilor Jefferson."

Knox didn't say anymore. The silence thickened and raised goosebumps on Brant's arm.

"What's wrong with the Head Councilor knowing?" Brant asked.

KaeHan cleared his throat. "Jefferson and Knox had philosophical differences."

"When I was a student here, I called him out on mismanaging IAS." Knox shifted Alex's weight in his arms, but didn't let go.

"You what???"

"And he was only ten," KaeHan said, smirking at the memory. "Imagine a ten-year-old Knox going head-to-head with Jefferson."

Brant was reminded of the holovideo of two bison circling each other before they charged head first.

"IAS had a ring of boys that were hazing students," Knox said. "It doesn't now. I did the right thing."

"But that gang wasn't Jefferson's fault," Brant said.

Both Knox and KaeHan went quiet for a little too long.

"Was it?" Brant asked. "Was it?"

"It's complicated," KaeHan said. "And then Knox left IAS at sixteen years old which put him squarely on Jefferson's bad side."

"*You quit?*" Brant turned on Knox.

The full realization of the bomb KaeHan had dropped hit him. Alex froze. Knox looked like a knife had wedged itself under his right shoulder blade, and he didn't know whether to remove or leave it. He inhaled deeply against the pain.

"I can explain."

"You don't owe me anything, *sir*," Brant said. "And Alex stays here."

Every syllable shot the word hypocrite straight and true, and from the look on Knox's face, every arrow hit home. Brant stomped down the hall and around the corner. He made it to the lift and his finger reached for the *down* button. But it couldn't push it. He slammed his fist into the door instead, over and over and over. Sann would have hated Brant's resemblance to Ed right now. But Alex gave his adoration to this phony instead of Brant.

Bootsteps echoed down the hallway toward Brant. They paused for a second before turning the corner. Brant leaned against the wall and crossed his arms, refusing to face Knox. Knox leaned against the wall next to him. Neither spoke.

The silence didn't rattle Knox. He breathed steadily, and Brant found himself matching Knox's rhythm. Had he done that on purpose? Brant's stomach had relaxed at some point, but when? Knox slowly twisted off his wedding band and rested it in his palm.

"Dad left me two things when he died," Knox said. "His ship and his wedding band."

Brant kept his arms crossed, but did shift his eyes. The golden circle caught and reflected the lights from the ceiling. Knox slipped his father's ring back on and admired his left hand.

"While I was training at the Institute, I discovered that I have a touch of predictive adaptation... sometimes. I get a gut feeling when someone I'm close to is about to die." Knox crossed his arms again and stared at the wall. "When I was sixteen, I got that gut feeling about my dad. I had a choice: finish my training or leave with him. I made my decision, right or wrong. After my dad visited the Institute one day, I stowed away on the ship with him."

That wasn't exactly quitting. Brant's neck relaxed, and his gaze shifted from Knox's ring to his face. How many knew this?

"What did your father think?"

Knox chuckled. "I have never seen him so hot, but I wouldn't budge. And I wouldn't tell him why I left. I couldn't." He paused. "After a few years, Dad and I saved enough to afford his dream, our ship. The memories he and I made on *Maverick*, they're priceless. I wouldn't replace them for anything. Even a diploma."

"Can't blame you," Brant said. His voice sounded strange to his ears, choked. "If I had a dad worth spending time with," Brant shifted his weight and stuck his hands in his pockets. "Why didn't you go back after?"

"After Dad died?" Knox said. "Because the loan wasn't paid off on *Maverick*. No way in hell I was losing Dad's ship. I worked until the debt was paid, and *Maverick* was mine. Unfortunately, by that time I'd run *Maverick* into the ground. I was desperate for a mechanic."

"Was your dad the original mechanic?"

"Ay, Dad was a mechanic and a damn fine one. I couldn't believe my luck finding another one as brilliant. Ximena's the best thing that happened to this ship, or me, since Dad died. When we married, I didn't need to go back to IAS. I had a good job, a ship I was proud of, and a wife I adored. I was happy."

"Then Serving Hands had a mission for you."

"Then Serving Hands had a mission for me. A mission Dad would've loved to support. Made me face my past." Knox turned, leaned his head back, and looked Brant in the eye.

"Now you know. The question is: can you trust me with Alex?"

Brant stared off into empty space. Knox was a cunning man who hated quitting, *hated it.* And yet, Knox had done the very thing he hated for the good of his family. If Brant's mom needed him to quit IAS to care for her, could he? Again, Brant shifted his weight. He hoped he would but wasn't one hundred percent sure.

"Yeah, I can trust you," Brant said. "You didn't quit, not really. You chose to sacrifice for someone you loved. I can respect that."

"OK." Knox's right shoulder relaxed.

"But I do need to think," Brant pushed away from the wall and started pacing the long corridor.

Stomp, stomp, stomp. It was too quiet. *Stomp, stomp, pivot.* Must be during class. *Stomp, stomp, stomp.* Celeste would have the eleven-year-olds right now.

Knox joined Alex and KaeHan, still waiting just outside the room. Alex climbed back up into Knox's arms and buried his face.

Brant paced the hallway two more times before returning to them. He studied the floor instead of facing them. The hallway tiles were worn gray in the middle from years of traffic. The scoring lessened near the walls and was the original pristine white along the edge. Brant swallowed the lump in his throat.

"What if TrysKa, Sann, and I vouch for Knox?" he asked.

Brant flicked his gaze up. Knox's face said, *thank you* crystal clear. It filled Brant up and satisfied him just like TrysKa's soup, which surprised Brant. Why did he care what Knox thought?

"That might work." KaeHan pulled out his scroll and flicked his fingers through his documents. "Jefferson has a soft spot for you, and we could play that to our advantage."

"Jefferson likes me?" Brant asked. "He doesn't even know who I am."

"Oh, he knows," KaeHan said under his breath, more to himself than anyone else.

He turned the scroll to Brant, the line for a signature blinking. Brant's stomach soured a second time, but he pushed past it.

"Instructor Brant Mallet."

The voice signature rose and fell, committing Alex back into Knox's care. KaeHan flipped the scroll back to himself, but Brant kept staring at the space his signature had occupied.

Had he done the right thing?

"If you'll get TrysKa and Sann to call me," KaeHan said to Knox.

"I will."

"Then I think I can work things in your favor."

As if a magic curse had been lifted, Alex leapt from Knox's arms with a shout. He bounded down the hallway to the lift and spun back to face them. His dimple beamed.

"Well, someone's happy," KaeHan said.

But Knox didn't puff out his chest in joy. Instead he strode to the boy, and Alex's smile wavered.

"What?" Alex asked, a tremble in his voice.

Knox knelt to eye level. "You will listen to me?"

"Yessir! I promise! I-"

Knox raised his hand, cutting Alex off.

"Don't promise me," Knox said to Alex. "Let your *yes* be *yes*, and your *no* be *no.* Will you listen to me and Ximena?"

"Yes."

"Will you run away again?"

"No."

Knox held the boy's gaze for a few seconds more then rose with a grunt.

"Let's go then."

Knox held out his strong hand, and Alex put his soft one inside. Together they walked to the lift. Brant followed. Maybe Alex would like him now, or at the very least, not hate him.

Brant, Alex, and Knox didn't notice KaeHan falter mid-stride. The lift door closed the three of them inside and KaeHan out. So, they didn't see him tilt his head to the side. They rode down, and Alex asked questions about Earth.

They didn't witness KaeHan's eyes flick back and forth under his thick lids.

16

Predictions

That night KaeHan couldn't sleep.

His back slumped over his tiny desk, in his darkened, cramped office. He should be in his bed now. His apartment was only a ten-minute walk from the main IAS building, and Monique would fuss at him in the morning. But as usual, grim predictions weighed on KaeHan, making his mind race, chasing away sleep.

All around the office, glowing predictions floated—a few were only strings but others were twisted star clusters. The numbers held the secret probabilities of success and failure of IAS missions, government movements, and cultural up-heavals. But for KaeHan, the most important probabilities they calculated were the likelihood of his soldiers' return.

KaeHan rubbed his stinging eyes before pressing the call button on his holograph ball.

"Amalie Fontenot," he said.

Colors swirled like a tiny waterspout in the heart of the small crystal ball as it made the connection.

"Yes?" Pops, Amalie's dad, coalesced in miniature above

the ball.

"Is Amalie there?"

"KaeHan, can it wait 'til morning? It's... hell, it's after midnight."

"I'm afraid it can't wait. I ran calculations concerning a new mission and need your daughter's take on it."

"It's not Brant's, is it?"

KaeHan sighed. Normally he never talked to anyone except the Council about his predictions, but Amalie had been sharing her calculations with her father since childhood. Pops had helped his little girl cope with burdens most adults couldn't bear. KaeHan didn't bother denying the truth.

"I'll get her," Pops said.

It took a few minutes before Amalie's face appeared floating above the ball. Her image lit up the cave, brightening even the dark corners. She'd neatly pulled back her hair into a ponytail and covered her nighty with an attractive robe. She must have taken a minute to get fixed up.

"Something's wrong with Brant's mission?" she asked, her eyebrows puckered.

"Before I talk about my calculations, have you run any on his mission?"

Amalie's face fell. "Yes."

"When?"

"After TrysKa signed up for it. Something about it, about the mission, I couldn't stop thinking about it, worrying about it."

"Why didn't you tell me?"

"Because I couldn't get a straight answer!"

Amalie raised her voice and set a stern face like her mother's.

"But you calculated something?" KaeHan asked.

"Yes, a dozen different somethings: complete failure; death of everyone; everyone comes home safe and sound; the IAS is attacked by a rogue group of soldiers with the adaptation; and everything else in between." She pursed her lips. "But all of them had high chaos factors. None of them had decent probabilities. I've never had this problem before."

"That's because you've never been as attached to the results before."

Amalie tried to hide any reaction, but her blush betrayed her. "Why would-"

"Amalie," KaeHan said in a fatherly tone. "Even if Brant weren't going on this mission, this is the first mission you've calculated that involved your fellow classmates."

"Should I distance myself from them?"

He could tell from the pleading in her voice, she didn't want to. Oh, she did not want to.

"No," he said. "If we disconnect ourselves from the very people we love, then the motivation for every prediction comes into question. If we don't love a specific human, how can we claim to love a generic humanity?"

"But what about Brant's mission? How can I calculate that if my emotions are all messed up?"

"Lucky for us, you're not the only one with the prediction adaptation."

"What did your calculations say?"

Now the lack of sleep pressed down. KaeHan's spine ached, his feet had fallen asleep, and the prickly pins-and-needles pain was traveling up his calves.

"The Shadow is finally going to show itself."

"The Shadow? On Brant's mission? Why?"

"Knox has hidden his IAS training for more than ten years

now. He's ordered Sann, TrysKa, and Brant to hide their identity as well. The Shadow doesn't know it's revealing itself to us."

Seven years ago Amalie had found the anomaly KaeHan had dubbed the Shadow, a small influence here and there that swayed results against their predictions. At first KaeHan had dismissed it as an error in her calculations, but she had stubbornly refused to be put off.

Thank goodness.

When KaeHan had finally placated her and considered her findings, he'd been forced to see her point. Someone out there was tweaking battle results and markets. This Shadow had the prediction adaption, but more than that, he had trained assassins for his own purposes and calculations. Some rumors even sounded like those assassins were adapted.

But where was this rogue teacher finding his students?

"We have to warn them," Amalie said, pulling KaeHan back.

"Amalie, this is the best chance we have of identifying this Shadow. What do your calculations show if he stays hidden too long?"

"He grows strong enough to attack us."

"But if we can expose him now?"

Amalie winced. KaeHan could see the truth stung, and he wished he could change the future to spare his sweet student.

"This is much sooner than any of our predictions calculated." Her voice cracked. "It would give IAS a great advantage. The mission has to go forward."

The last part she whispered.

"That's what I calculated too."

"Can we warn Knox?" Amalie asked. "Give them the best chance possible?"

"No," KaeHan said and pressed his thumbs into his temples. "Knox is fiercely protective of family. He'd cancel the operation."

"Then a different mission could expose the Shadow."

"Amalie," KaeHan looked back at her floating face. "According to my calculations, The Shadow is hunting Knox specifically. If Knox cancels this mission, then he'll be killed after it's over. He needs our soldiers, and he needs to face this threat now. While he's protected."

"Why do they want to kill Knox?"

"I don't know exactly. Something to do with money."

KaeHan's gaze traced the familiar string of probabilities motivated by starvation, need, and greed. Following the money accounted for ninety-nine percent of his predictions if not more.

"So, we let them be ambushed? Is that what you're telling me?" Amalie said.

"You don't know Knox. He's a clever strategist with contacts throughout the spaceports. With TrysKa as pilot and Brant and Sann as protection, they have a chance. A good one."

She stared down at her hands, clasped out of sight of the holograph. He hadn't convinced her.

"When do we finally tell Jefferson about the Shadow?"

"When we have enough proof to convince him."

Amalie snorted.

"He's a good man," KaeHan said. "But he isn't one to jump at..."

"Shadows?" Amalie finished.

KaeHan grimaced at her pun. "It won't be long. After Knox's operation, events will move faster than we previously predicted. We'll have a lot of recalculating."

The tendons on Amalie's neck tightened, but other than that she kept her face civil and pleasant.

"You need your rest," KaeHan said. "Never forget how important your future is to this school."

"Of course. Good night."

"Good night."

Amalie didn't agree with KaeHan on this one, but she was going to trust him. KaeHan pressed his thumb to the base of the holograph, and her image dissolved. He'd talk to her again in the morning. After he had had some sleep.

He shouldn't have let Alex go back to the *Maverick.* Too late now. Now it was all in Knox's hands. The small spiral of calculations for the fragile operation hung in the air. KaeHan traced his finger along the glowing percentages.

"Knox, I hope you've grown shrewder through the years. You'll need it."

Then KaeHan's finger rested on one knot of numbers, a high probability event. His temples throbbed.

"But even you can't stop this."

KaeHan shut off the calculations, and they spiraled down into the holoprojector on his desk. He left, and darkness enveloped the room.

17

Sann's Mission

"Noooo!" Sann sat up from his bed with a yell and hit the crown of his head against the ceiling. "Ow!"

He collapsed on his mattress with his eyelids closed. His forehead throbbed, the ache pulsing outward to his hairline and downward to his temples and behind his eyes. Warm air blew in his ear. It had a rhythm to it. In. Out. In. Out.

"Brant, what are you doing?"

"Breathing."

"I can feel that."

"Then why did you ask?"

Sann rolled his head right, and Brant smiled his crinkled grin. His arms were crossed on Sann's mattress, and his chin propped on top.

"Hi," Brant said.

"Why?" Sann asked, trying to blink the nightmare from his eyes.

"Who's Brandon?"

Oh no, Sann had been talking in his sleep.

"No one."

Then he winced. Brandon wasn't no one. He was very much a real person, who'd had a real life.

"He was someone on my last operation," Sann said. "Someone who died."

"How?"

"None of your business, and it's classified."

Sann pushed Brant's shoulder to move him out of the way, but Brant didn't budge.

"Sann," Brant said. "KaeHan instructed us to confide in a trusted friend. Even with the classified stuff. Otherwise—"

"I remember what KaeHan said!" Sann shoved harder, and Brant retreated to the corner of their cramped room.

"Well?"

"And I'm fine."

Sann dropped his feet to the floor and kicked open his clothes drawer. Sann would need room to get dressed and that would force Brant out.

"And when IAS does their psych evaluation in four months?" Brant said. "Will *they* agree that you're fine?"

Sann's knees gave out, and he crumpled onto Brant's bed. He'd forgotten about the regular psych evals. He covered his face with his hands. Sann couldn't tell a counselor about his last operation, couldn't relive it that way. Not that way.

"Or you could talk to me now, and maybe by then, things will be better."

"How?" Sann asked. "How will talking make anything better? It won't change a thing."

"Honestly, I don't know. That's just what KaeHan always says."

Brant sat down next to Sann, and tried to sit up. But his head bumped the bottom of Sann's bunk, so he hunched over and rested elbows on his knees instead.

"Personally, I always felt better after dueling my anger out," Brant said.

That's right. Brant hadn't lived a perfect life either. He'd always confided in Sann about his Ed problems.

What must an abusive father be like? Sann's family wasn't rich, but they had each other's love. Sann stared at his clasped hands. Might as well give it a shot.

"My mission was to assassinate a doctor who used human slaves for his experiments," Sann said.

"Umm, gross."

"Yeah," Sann said. "You ever heard the legends about Earth's technology before the Exodus?"

"Computer chips embedded in the back of people's heads, a net of information connecting everyone, stuff like that?"

"Yeah, he was trying to do that."

"What happened to the people he stuck a chip into?"

"Let's just say they went nuts and leave out the gory details."

Sann had seen the bodies. After the raid of the facility, the commander of the mission had called Sann to a locked warehouse.

"This is why we did what we did," the commander said.

He opened the door to row after row of bodies, carefully preserved for the demented doctor's study later. Their self-inflicted fatal wounds condemned the professor to his deserved fate, Sann's bullet.

"I don't regret killing the man. Yet he still haunts me. In my dreams, I look through the scope, and he's looking back. He says, 'You're no better than me'."

"You know that's not true," Brant said. "You saved his

future victims." Brant shifted. "Why couldn't he be arrested, though? Why hire an IAS sniper?"

Sann punched the wall in front of him then rubbed his knuckles. The pain felt good.

"He had money and influence in his government, and no cameras in his high-tech lab. No proof. Arrests weren't an option," Sann sneered, his lip pulling back from his canines. "Even the bodies disappeared after our raid. His government threatened counter-measures until all the pictures we took went public."

"Oh, now I know which doctor. Wow." Brant shuddered. "Gruesome."

For a full minute, the only sound in the room was Brant and Sann's breathing.

"But, that doesn't answer my question," Brant said. "Who's Brandon?"

"Brandon was my back-up if things went south," Sann said. "He wasn't adapted and didn't trust my methods. Everything had gone according to plan. I snuck in, set up, and shot the doctor. Then the facility's security guards started a sweep of the area."

"But you didn't have any digital tech on you, did you?"

"No tech, my suit hid my body heat. They weren't going to find me."

Sann clenched his eyes shut. Brandon was racing down the hill, shooting at the guards, screaming Sann's name. Why?

"Brandon panicked, he thought they'd found me. They got him instead. Shot him instead. And I just watched." Sann opened his eyes, but blood still swam in his sight. "The commander and his troops came as soon as they could, but too late for Brandon."

"Could you have done anything to save him?" Brant asked. "Really, could you?"

"No." The word was so final. "But that doesn't make it hurt less."

"No, I don't guess it does." Brant uncurled and stood beside the bed. "But it makes me feel better you're still with us. Call me selfish."

"Selfish."

Brant smiled again. "You get dressed, I'll get my coffee."

Brant stepped out of their room, and Sann pulled his shirt over his head. His hair flopped back around his face. Did he feel any better now that he'd talked? How would he even know? Wrestling into his jeans proved a challenge in the tight room, but Sann managed.

It makes me feel better you're still with us.

His friends wanted him around, and that was reason enough today. Sann grabbed his shoes and socks and left for the breakroom bench. That would give him more space to lace up.

Everyone else had already gathered in the breakroom. TrysKa stood in the kitchen, sipping her coffee. Ximena straddled a chair and studied her digi-scroll resting on the table. Alex snuggled against her side. Knox's stare bored into a hologram of an island revolving above the tabletop.

Brant lounged along the bench and chugged the last of his coffee. He dropped his mug in the sink, sterilized, and handed it to TrysKa.

"I should've been drinking your coffee all these years," Brant said to TrysKa. "IAS has nothing on you."

TrysKa wrinkled her nose. "They buy the cheap stuff already ground instead of whole bean. You have to fresh grind it, and—"

175

"I'll take your word for it." He winked. "Even if I knew your secret, mine would still taste like burnt dirt." To Sann, "My turn?"

Sann motioned to their room. "All yours."

Alex yawned big and stretched his arms out like a cat. Then he balled up his fists and rubbed them into his puffy eyes. Did that kid do anything that wasn't adorable? But more importantly, did he know he was doing it? Sann pulled on his socks.

"Coffee?" TrysKa asked Sann.

"More of a green tea guy, myself."

"Oh, wait!" TrysKa opened a cabinet just to her right. "I found some, let me get the water boiling."

Knox broke his trance over the hologram.

"We have green tea?" he asked Ximena.

She stared at her digi-scroll. Five... four... three... two...

"What?" she asked. Blinked a few times. "We have green tea?" Ximena swiveled in her chair to face TrysKa. "Where did you find it?"

"Buried behind some expired protein packs."

Ximena raised her right eyebrow at Knox. "Learn something new every day." And returned to the ship's diagnostics.

TrysKa put the mug in the sterilizing sink. The sink's spout filled the mug with water, stopped, and flashed its blue beam. TrysKa pulled out the steaming mug of hot water and dipped the bag of tea leaves in.

As Sann laced up his other shoe, the smell enveloped and swept him back home. His mom hummed over the stove, brewing tea, filling their tiny epoxycrete house with its fragrance. His brother and dad played elephant chess in the corner. Sann lounged on the woven grass mat and listened to the clink as his dad set the Advisor piece down on the polished wood board. TrysKa brought the tea to the table.

Thank you, Sann mouthed.

TrysKa's soft smile reflected understanding. Did she know what she'd just done for him? Probably. Sann closed his eyes and took a sip. *Home.*

Brant strode in fully dressed. "What now?"

"Now we plan," Knox said. "Lights down."

The lights dimmed. TrysKa pulled up a chair beside Ximena and Alex. The hologram of the island lit up the faces around the table with a ghostly glow. The beaches rose steeply then flattened out. The mansion sprawled on the plateau with a pool, pool house, and game court. Knox pointed to the slab of epoxycrete with basketball goals.

"This will be the best place for *Maverick* to land." He slid his finger to the left, and the image pivoted. "They have at least one back-up generator and maybe even an older one. What records I could find indicate they bought two new ones, but didn't dispose of the old one."

"It's a reliable model with decades of operation left in it," Ximena said.

What must it be like to have that kind of money to throw around? Sann would never know.

"We don't know exactly where the generators are, but they're most likely kept in this shed near the pool. I seriously doubt they waste room in their main residence with a generator."

"Only one person lives here?" Alex asked, leaning over the table and almost touching the hologram with his nose.

"One family," Knox said. "Except they never actually visit."

"*What!*" TrysKa, Brant, and Alex said in unison. Sann gulped too much green tea.

"The island's only maintained by three robots," Ximena said. "I dropped one of my cameras there right before Knox went to IAS. I wanted to verify no human visitors."

"One ship flew by yesterday," Knox said. "But other than that, no activity, no visitors, no nothing."

"So, when we land to find the generators and photocells, we won't have to worry about guards or family members," Ximena added.

"We'll also perform the raid at night," Knox said.

"Then why'd we get up so early?" Brant asked.

"Because, on this island, it's already midnight."

"Right, different planet, different time zones."

Brant sat back from the hologram and crossed his arms. Space travel still wasn't his thing. Sann was accustomed to changing planets, countries, and time zones. Since five years old, he'd traveled back and forth from IAS to Khmer. But Brant had never left the planet. He was a fish out of water, or more accurately, a teacher out of his classroom.

"So," Knox said, "I'll search the storage unit, but just in case, Brant and Sann can go through the house. TrysKa" he faced her. "I'll need you piloting the ship."

She nodded.

"And Ximena," to his wife, "I'll need you to coordinate the op. All our transmitters will feed to you, and you follow our locations on the hologram here."

"I can do that."

"What about me?" Alex asked.

"Stay on the ship and help Ximena."

Brant coughed, and Knox eyed him. Brant shrugged as if to say *it was just a cough*, but Sann knew better. So did Knox.

Brant didn't believe for one second that Alex would stay on the ship where he belonged. Knox eyed Alex. The boy refused to make eye contact, focusing instead on the hologram.

"Think of it, Alex," TrysKa said. "You'll get to boss Brant around."

That perked Alex up. Brant winced, and Sann took another sip of his tea to hide his smile.

"So," Ximena said. "Is that it? Seems pretty simple."

Knox crossed his arms and leaned back in his chair to get a different view of the hologram. His eyes darted back and forth like it was a complex chessboard, and he was facing a cunning opponent.

"I don't like it. Something's irking me, but I can't put my finger on it."

"Knox nervous?" Brant asked. "Didn't know that was possible." Awkward pause. "Did I just say that out loud?"

"Yes, yes you did," Knox said without looking up from the image. "But I owe you for vouching for me, so I'll let this one pass." He pivoted toward the cockpit. "Screw it. The mission's easy, let's go."

"No."

Ximena's voice was flat without a hint of anger. Simply a statement of fact, like math.

"You have these gut feelings for a reason, and we're not ignoring it. Let's assume something is wrong with the plan. How do we handle it?"

Knox didn't balk at her for daring to argue. Instead he grunted, pulled up a chair, and let his eyes flick over the hologram again.

"Honestly? I'd walk away and find a different target."

"Knox," Ximena said. "We've watched more than just this

island. The other one's are visited all the time. This one really is abandoned, and the only one with multiple generators and cells."

"I know." But his jaw muscle still tensed.

"Let's assume this is the best target, what would you do different?"

"Hmph."

That's all he said. The silence stretched for a minute then two then five. Finally, Knox pointed to the overgrown hill.

"Eyes on the hill." To Sann. "You're my sniper."

"Yes, sir."

"TrysKa will fly the ship low to let you out in these high grasses. Hide out there. Got everything you need to be invisible?"

"All my gear, sir. No instruments will detect me." To Ximena. "I won't have a translator, though, that could be detected."

Sann removed the earbud and set it on the table.

"Drop me here." Sann pointed at a flat grassy spot away from the pool. "And I'll back up the hill to here." Sann traced his finger away from the house to a high spot several feet away.

"I'll pick you up there," TrysKa said. "What if there's a problem? How will you signal that?"

"Shoot the bad guy?" Tea crept back up his esophagus.

"OK, yes, that, but what if you want to send a message?"

"I'll shoot something near the problem."

"I'll set the ship's controls to detect a gunshot hit," TrysKa said.

Knox nodded, but Sann's hands tightened around his mug. When he signed on for this operation, Sann hadn't planned on pressing his cheek to the cold metal of that gun or peering down its long scope. This was supposed to be a break from sniper work.

"Blinding bombs for Brant and I," Knox said.

"Blinding bombs?" Brant asked, but Ximena was already up and rooting through a cabinet above his head.

A white ball, about the size of a lemon, rolled out of the cabinet, hit Brant's head, and clanked onto the table.

"Cover your eyes!" Knox said and buried his face in the crook of his elbow.

Sann pressed his face into his arm when the inside of his eyelids lit up like a migraine kaleidoscope. Alex fell on the floor screaming.

"Oh!" Ximena tripped trying to reach him. "Sorry, sorry, sorry."

TrysKa was already by Alex's side with the med pack. She ripped open a pain relief press and stuck it under Alex's chin. His body went limp, and his yells subsided to whimpers. Knox stood and carefully extracted two more white metal balls from the cabinet. He carefully handed one to Brant.

"If you need an escape, squeeze it hard and throw," Knox said.

Brant, still blinking from the brightness, stowed it in the inside of his jacket. "If you insist."

Knox stowed the last one in his jacket pocket. "Now, where were we?" He sat down. "Guns in the sky." Knox pointed above the house. "TrysKa, instead of landing, you'll drop Brant here." He pointed at an open spot beside the house. "And me here." He pointed next to the warehouse. "You'll then hover above us to protect against aerial attack."

"And when you have the shields?" TrysKa asked.

"Meet us at the last second for pick-up on the epoxycrete.

I don't want to give away our landing spot before then." To Alex, "Will you stay on the ship?"

"Yes."

Alex was still hurting from the blinding bomb and didn't put up a fight. But would he obey in the heat of the operation? Sann finished the last of his tea, sterilized the mug, and put it up.

TrysKa and Knox headed to the cockpit as Sann returned to the bench, resting his back against its threadbare cushion. He closed his eyes. *Maverick* left N.T. #4, but Sann was on Naya Surya, in his family's stilted home, listening to his mom's humming. His dad was winning another game of elephant chess when space enfolded the ship. He and his brother were strapping the harvester to their water buffalo, Nagpuri, when the ship jumped. Sann opened his eyes and blinked at the brightness.

"Well, time for me to get suited up."

Brant stood. "And me, shielded."

Together, Sann and Brant marched to the cargo bay.

Sann opened the spacesuit cabinet and pulled out his crisply folded suit. There was no room in his bedroom or the bathroom, so while Brant strapped on his shield arm and leg bands, Sann shucked his clothes and shimmied into his slick suit.

It clung to his thighs, remembering his form. There was the stupid wiggle he had to perform to stretch it over his ass. After that, the arms were easy, but the fingers were a pain. Sann always got his middle finger stuck in the ring finger spot. After some back and forth negotiating, he coaxed his shoulders in place and zipped the skin closed over his chest.

His bushy hair was last. He leaned his head back, and his hair cascaded down his neck. Sann pulled the hood back, tussled his hair into it, and pulled it over. Only his eyes and nose remained uncovered. He took the goggles from the cabinet and pressed the flexible plastiform against his eye sockets. It sealed to the suit.

Brant inspected his plasma pistol and holstered it. With a twitch of his right triceps, his spherical shields activated. In a rolling motion, Brant rotated his shoulders, and the shields shrank to within an inch of his body. He jumped, rolled, and drew his gun. The shields shrank and expanded to follow his movements. He nodded and stood. Brant was ready.

Sann wasn't.

Brant winced at Sann's costume. "I always hated those things. Never could get comfortable in them."

Brant's voice traveled clearly through the mesh around Sann's ears, but it still sounded muffled and far away, if that made any sense.

"You prefer shields," Sann said. The suit left a waxy aftertaste on his lips.

"That's putting it mildly. Going into battle without shields? I might as well be naked."

Not a pretty image. Sann would've made a gagging face, but the suit covered his mouth.

"I don't confront my enemy in battle," Sann said. "I hide in the shadows and kill them."

Sann opened the tall, thin cabinet holding his weapon. It felt heavy in his hand. Brant leaned against the cabinet, and his gaze traced the rifle.

"Killing someone while facing them isn't more honorable than killing them while hiding. They're still dead."

"History doesn't agree with you."

"History is written by people sitting in comfortable chairs

miles and years away from battle."

Sann didn't have an argument with that one. Maybe Brant had a point. At the end of the day, soldiers weren't fighting for a cause. They were fighting to go home. Plain and simple.

Sann prepped his rifle.

"I can't believe people used those in battle," Brant said.

"Gunpowder rifles were just as deadly as plasma, until shields became strong enough to deflect bullets."

"But they only shoot one bullet at a time. Plasma can sweep the enemy." Brant swung his hands through the air, as if spraying a water hose.

"But even when off, a plasma gun gives off a digital signature." Sann sighted down the scope. He could trace the details of the millimeter-thin plexicast seal on the cargo bay door. "I have to be invisible."

"But can't they see your heat?" Alex had snuck into the room and was peering into the gun cabinet.

Brant closed and locked the cabinet. Alex stuck his tongue out, and Brant rolled his eyes. Sann smiled at their antics.

"My suit hides my heat signature," Sann said. "And it's blast-resistant."

"It can protect you from a bomb?" Alex's eyebrows rose into his curly bangs.

Sann laughed. He couldn't help it.

"No, it only protects me from a small blast or a split-second of plasma fire. An extended shot is still deadly."

"Oh."

Alex got really quiet. He stuck out his lower lip.

"Be OK, Sann," he said.

"I will."

Sann rubbed Alex's curls. Even through his suit, the curls

slipped and wrapped around his fingers. Knox walked into the cargo bay, his thick eyebrows still furrowed.

"Let's get this over with."

Knox snapped his fingers and pointed back down the hall. Alex wrinkled his nose but still obeyed, trudging to Ximena.

"Live up to the second chance I gave you," Knox said.

Alex sped up his pace, and Knox sighed. With a twist of his right arm, a shield encircled him. Sann narrowed his eyes. Knox's jacket sleeve swelled slightly where the shields hid. What else lurked in those jacket pockets and boots?

"Time to check-in," Ximena said from the cockpit.

Brant shook his head like a cat with water in its ears.

"Lower volume," he said and stuck his pinky in his right ear.

"TrysKa, you're TK," Ximena said.

"TK here," called from the cockpit.

"Brant, you're Bravo."

"Bravo here," Brant said.

"Alex, you're cute."

"NO, I'M NOT!"

Sann and Brant exchanged grins. Even Knox's shoulders shook at that.

"OK, Alpha then," Ximena said.

"Alpha here."

"Kappa here," Knox said.

"Zed back at you," Ximena said. "We're threading the needle."

"Threading the needle?" Alex asked over the earbud.

"Slipping between space stations without being detected," Ximena said. "*Maverick's* shields can deflect the detection systems of most satellites, but the spaceports are better equipped. We've got to sneak between their coverage." Knox set his feet. "Hold on."

"Why?"

Maverick jerked under Sann's feet. He crashed into Brant, and the two of them tumbled into the wall. Sann grabbed a cabinet's handle with his right hand. Brant anchored his feet into the grippy floor and pushed his back against the wall.

The artificial gravity overcompensated for the Gs on the ship. Sann's rear almost lifted from the floor. Every organ in his gut lightened inside of him, pressing up into his ribs. He grabbed the handle with his left hand too, and balled up in the fetal position. The inertial dampeners reacted, and gravity pressed heavily on him. Sann's left thigh pressed into the floor, and his blood rushed to his legs.

"Flying low," Brant said to Sann. "Ximena says the gravity should level out now."

The world inside Sann's stomach settled back into place. Brant stood and held his hand out. Sann accepted and pulled himself up. He bounced on the balls of his feet. His legs held. OK, he could do this.

Brant tapped his ear. "Sniper, get in position."

Sann nodded. He walked to the cargo bay door and crouched down. Knox waited by the door's controls.

"Lights off," Knox said, and the cargo bay went black. Even the ship's diagnostic lights dimmed. Only the power light on Brant's gun blinked.

"See you on the other side," Brant said. Sann gave him a thumbs up.

"Sniper away," Knox said.

He punched the controls, the ramp cracked open, and Sann slipped into the velvet night. He fell into a thicket of brush and ducked below the branches. *Maverick* whooshed overhead, silent as a night owl.

It flew low with its ramp opened. When the ship swooped by the side of the house, another shadow fell out. Brant. He ran to the front of the estate without any attempt at stealth. He shot the door lock, and the *pow* echoed off the hill.

Maverick rounded the mansion and a bulky form leapt and rolled to the ground in front of the shed. That would be Knox. Everything was going according to plan.

Sann slithered backward through the brambles. His suit protected him from punctures, but the thorns still scraped his skin. He snaked up the knoll behind him, his legs weaving up further and further to the peak. Sann settled at the top of the hill and perched his rifle. He wiped the humidity from the goggles, pressed the scope to them, and manually adjusted the focus.

Maverick hovered in the sky, a mother bird protecting her young. Knox stood at the storehouse's door. He held a strange scanner, something obviously pieced together by Ximena. Knox's fingers worked the buttons.

The quiet pressed down on Sann. He'd stayed awake through many midnights back home, and always been surprised by the noise. The crickets, the wind, the scream of a mouse caught by a raptor.

But no bugs chirped, no frogs croaked, no owls called on this abandoned island. What would scare such silence?

Brant walked past a window and froze, cocking his ear, listening for an out-of-place sound. At the same time, Knox lifted his face to the wind, sniffing. Sann swept his scope across the game court.

Floodlights burst on. Stars blinded him, and his heartbeat

boomed in his ears to a rapid beat. Sann blinked to clear his vision and steadied his breathing.

Three guards had rounded the house and sprinted up the hill. They plasma sprayed down the spot where Sann had landed. The heat rolled over him, hiding uphill in the bushes. They stomped around the scorched earth, searching for his bones.

I'm up here, watching you.

"Sann!" Brant's mouth screamed from inside the house.

Through the window to Brant's left, Sann saw guards burst up from the floor. Three, four, they kept coming. At least fifteen in all. They must have hidden in a basement. Waiting. Ready. Brant ducked into a closet and picked off the attackers as they funneled one at a time down the hallway. His drones swooped around the ceiling, taking out more.

OK, Brant's fine for now.

He could escape out a window when the time came.

Sann angled his scope toward the shed. The door stood ajar. Knox must be inside already.

But why wasn't *Maverick* giving air support? Sann tilted his head to get a better vantage of the sky. The clouds shifted. Shields. The soldiers had turned on the shields, blocking *Maverick* out.

A blinding light turned night into noonday. Sann buried his face in the dirt but too late. Knox must have set off a blinding bomb inside the warehouse. As Sann blinked the stars out of his vision, the sky refocused. Knox had turned off the shields.

Sann cut his gaze to the soldiers on the hill. They were still rooting around in the embers looking for his body. He inched his scope to focus on the game court stretched between the estate and outbuilding. *Maverick* would be setting down there soon.

What was that?

A bush's shadow thrashed near the slab. Sann tightened the focus, but the shadow was gone. A foot? It had been a foot, he was sure of it.

You're hiding from me.

Whoever it was had been writhing in pain from the blinding bomb. But after recovering, this loner wasn't rushing Knox and his crew. Instead he staked out his spot. He was observing, probably watched each member of the *Maverick* team land, even Sann. This was more than a well-trained guard. This person was trained in special ops. Probably wearing the same protective skin that shrouded him from *Maverick's* heat sensors.

But why did he stake out that specific spot? No!

He was waiting for *Maverick* to land. Once down, this hidden threat could shoot the engines with a fuel-powered rocket. The crew would be grounded. Trapped.

Sann had to warn TrysKa. His scope scanned the area. Close to the concealed shooter, a tree with flame red leaves raised its branches to the sky. If Sann hit a limb, the leaves would scatter as a warning. Sann pressed his rifle to his cheek.

"Maybe up here!" one of the guards on the hill shouted.

Without twitching a muscle, Sann cut his eyes down the hill. The soldiers were closing in. Any shot would give him away.

In the house, guards had run around to the other side of the hallway. They closed in on Brant from both sides. Outside the shed, Knox ducked behind the shield generator. Plasma fire zoomed over the pool at him, its reflection lighting up the water's surface with trails of fire. *Maverick* flew toward the slab and the lurking danger.

I couldn't save Brandon, but I can save all of you.

Sann closed his left eye, focused down the scope with his right, and locked in on a single knot on the tree's bark. He evened his breathing and waited for the calm between heartbeats. His finger squeezed the trigger.

Splinters exploded, and red leaves burst like fireworks. Birds, huddling in the branches, took to the freedom of the sky. What would it be like? To be that weightless?

"Hey!" A guard yelled and pointed. "Up there!"

18

Sacrifice of a Brother

A flurry of birds swarmed the ship. An alarm flashed on the console. A bullet shot.

Sann's warning!

TrysKa banked *Maverick* back to the sky. Something was wrong with the landing spot. Just then a form darker than the night slithered away from the slab into the brush. What was that?

Fire lit up the side of the hill.

"Sann!"

Alex, his head leaning against TrysKa's seat, gasped. Ximena yanked him back into the breakroom and onto her lap. He curled up in the fetal position.

TrysKa raced *Maverick* to the hill and filled the guards with plasma fire. Her heart skipped a beat as the bodies blew backward. TrysKa blinked rapidly, and the tears cleared from her eyes, streaming down her cheeks.

She had to save her team.

"Bravo stay low!" Ximena said. "TK, give Bravo cover!"

"On it."

Brant had crashed out the house's window and was barreling up the hill. TrysKa laid down a line of fire along the ground behind Brant. A wall of dust billowed between him and the mansion. The guards shot wildly through the brown cloud but didn't come near Brant.

"Kappa," Ximena called. "Get to the landing spot, we'll—"

"No!" TrysKa said. "Something's wrong with the slab. That's why Sann shot the tree."

"Change of plan, moving the pick-up spot." Ximena swiveled the holograph of the house. "No guards behind the shed. There's flat ground, we'll land there."

"Copy that, Zed," Knox said.

Brant knelt on the smoking hill next to where Sann had been. TrysKa piloted the ship to Brant and lowered the shields. She opened the ramp, and her controls beeped. Brant had entered the cargo bay. But what about Sann?

"Bravo and Sniper onboard," Ximena said. "We're coming for you, Kappa."

"Copy that, we're in position."

TrysKa swung the ship around the storage shed, positioning the ship between the house and Knox. The guards poured around the pool, so TrysKa aimed for the outbuilding and fired. The little structure erupted into singed shrapnel, and the guards fell back.

Her controls beeped again. Knox was onboard.

"Take to the sky, TK," Ximena said.

TrysKa couldn't answer with her voice, but she could with her hands. Her fingers glided over the controls with the moves they knew so well. She grabbed the lever and pushed steadily forward. The rocket blasters fired, and the ship entered the cumulus clouds above.

The mist in the screen swam in TrysKa's vision. She smeared the tears away with the back of her hand.

Save your friends first. Grieve second.

TrysKa pressed the lever forward again. Time to send *Maverick* soaring. Black space unveiled before her; flames enveloped her. TrysKa and the ship were one, freeing her family from hate and violence, delivering them to safety.

But too late for one.

#

Knox's boots pounded into the metal floor carrying him to the cargo bay.

Where they halted.

Brant was curled over his knees. In his arms, he clutched a gun, charred black suit, and smoking unrecognizable remains. His shoulders didn't move. He wasn't breathing.

Knox's stomach shifted, the sign that artificial gravity was about to crank up. Knox closed the distance between himself and Brant in one lunge. He anchored his left knee and the sole of his right boot to the grated cargo bay floor and enfolded Brant in his arms.

The gravity squeezed down. Brant's chest expanded, taking in oxygen. He was breathing. The air escaped with a rattle. Knox held tighter, pressing Brant's ear against his chest. The erratic throbbing of Brant's vein on his neck evened, matching Knox's heartbeat.

The ship steadied in TrysKa's hands. Gravity settled.

Knox reached through Brant's arms and gathered Sann's remains. Brant fell aside limp, his eyes unfocused, like a corpse. Knox pushed up to standing, but his knees threatened to buckle. The stench of burnt meat was the same as last time. He could see another body, his father's body, a hole where the heart belonged.

But no, Knox couldn't go down that road right now. Brant needed him. Knox set his legs and forced them to work. He picked up Sann's rifle and lay it safely aside then set his own pistol to incinerate. And pulled the trigger.

All that remained of Sann were ashes.

He'd failed.

Knox withdrew his weapon back up his sleeve. With set jaw, he left the cargo bay and its judgement. The breakroom was empty. Ximena had taken Alex into the cockpit with TrysKa.

Knox searched the galley cabinets. A simple effort. He needed an uncomplicated task. There. A glass jar. He wrapped numb fingers around its cold surface.

Knox's boots stuck to the floor, refusing to move. He kicked out one foot then the other, ordering them to return to the cargo bay.

Brant hadn't moved. At least his shoulders rose and fell in the pattern of breathing. Knox knelt beside the fine gray dust, and gathered it into a pile. He cupped the powder in his hands and funneled it into the jar. Seconds spilled away, then minutes, but still Knox scooped and poured. He didn't leave a speck on the floor.

Finally he screwed the lid on the jar.

Brant leapt up. His body lurched backward, slamming his back into the wall. The air surged from his throat with a gasp.

Knox bolted forward. He grabbed Brant's triceps but couldn't hold him up. Brant was too damn tall. Knox propped Brant against the wall and waited. What was he supposed to do? Brant's eyes rolled up into his sockets.

"Brant," Knox said. His voice sounded far away.

Brant moaned and his body started to quake. Knox filled his

lungs and belted out.

"Brant!"

It reverberated off the walls, ceiling, and floor probably ringing in Brant's sensitive ears. But if this didn't work, all Knox knew how to do next was slap him. Thankfully, Brant's lids popped open, and he sucked in air.

"Breathe."

Brant's chest expanded out, then in, out, and in. "I should have been there."

Knox opened his mouth to say something, but sandpaper coated his throat. His tongue suddenly felt swollen and heavy and dry. Knox bowed his head and licked his lips until he trusted his mouth to function.

"We'll figure out what happened later."

Knox released Brant's arms and stepped back, his hands raised in case the giant fell. But Brant steadied and blinked. He would make it. Somehow.

"Right now, we remember your brother," Knox said.

He picked up the rifle and jar. Through the years, Knox had lifted many a heavy load, yet this small jar weighed him down more than any. His feet marched solemnly down the hall with Brant stumbling behind. They entered the room where Sann had slept, and Knox put the jar and rifle on the bottom bunk.

But he couldn't leave it like that. So vulnerable. Anytime the ship jerked around, the jar would go flying, shatter. Knox pressed Brant's shoulder then went to the cargo bay. He returned with a magnetic restrainer. Brant had collapsed in the corner, his long legs sprawled, his arms lifeless in his lap, his eyes glassed over like a fish.

Knox bolted the jar and rifle securely to the bed. Time to give Brant his privacy.

"Sann deserves his memorial."

Brant didn't move.

"But Brant—" Knox said.

Brant blinked and looked up.

"Keep breathing."

Knox left and Brant's yell, raw and primal, vibrated through the closed door. Then a long low moan followed. Knox shuffled down the hall to the bathroom. His hands hovered over the sink, but he couldn't sanitize them. Knox rubbed his thumb over his fingertips, the fine powder cascading down into the sink.

What just happened?

19

Found the Pirate Ship

Brant peeled his sticky cheek off the floor. He pushed his aching body up, keeping his eyes downcast. He couldn't look at the bottom bunk, at the jar and rifle.

Brant left the room and wandered like a lost ghost into the breakroom. Dead silence had devoured *Maverick*. The contents of the kitchen cabinets had spewed all over the floor, leaving no room for Brant to walk. TrysKa must have gutted it. He turned, and there sat the bench Sann had warmed only a few hours ago. A lifetime ago. Sann's lifetime ago.

Brant limped back down the hall to the cargo bay where the two generators squatted along with several photocells. Brant approached a generator until his chest was within an inch of it.

"You weren't worth the price."

The casket of twisted wires and contorted pipes didn't answer. Brant turned his back on it and measured the perimeter of the cargo bay with his steps. His feet learned the length, and Brant paced with eyes closed. His heart beat in time with his steps, and air filled his lungs again.

The morning replayed. Brant was leaning his arms on Sann's bunk, smiling. Sann was trying not to smile back. Trying and failing. Brant would never see that lop-sided smirk again. Never see Sann's black eyes twinkle; never hear his voice.

No!

Brant had a mission to complete, Sann's mission. He couldn't dig this grave, not now. Brant crammed his grief down, elbowing it into a tiny locker of his mind. And slammed the door shut.

Grief would have to wait.

The ship's ramp clicked open and lowered with a creak. Brant pushed his back into the corner of the cargo bay as Knox's boots clicked up the ramp in rhythm. Alex's quick steps padded to no beat but their own. When they reached the top, Knox knelt down and faced Alex. He whispered, but Brant's keen ears picked up every word.

"You don't have to do it now."

Alex nodded.

"When you're ready though, it'll be a help to everyone."

Alex nodded again. His eyebrows scrunched together in his over-expressive look of thoughtfulness. Whatever Knox had told him, he didn't like it. But instead of yelling, he stewed on it. Maybe even considered it?

"And if *you* need anything..." Knox said to Alex.

Alex threw his arms around Knox's neck. Knox's back stiffened at first, but then his shoulders eased. He wrapped his arms around Alex and held his curly head in his calloused hand.

"I've got you," Knox said. "You're safe here. I've got you."

Alex backed up and wiped his nose on his sleeve with a big

sniff. His eyes flicked over Knox's broad shoulder, and he stiffened.

"Brant."

"I know he's there," Knox said and fished a candy out of his pocket. He placed it in Alex's palm. "Go wait in the breakroom."

Alex unwrapped the candy in record time and stored it in his cheek. No sooner had he entered the hall than Knox pushed the controls to shut the door between the hallway and the cargo bay.

"Don't need him eavesdropping," Knox said.

His boots clicked toward Brant's corner. Brant hunched back, crossing his arms. If only the ship would swallow him whole.

"I need to ask you a question," Knox said.

Brant stared at Knox's boots. They had the softened creases of years of wear but had been polished to a high shine.

"Do we continue this mission?"

"Soldiers always finish their mission."

"I don't know if you've noticed, but I don't exactly live the soldier's life."

Was there a playful undertone to Knox's voice? Brant looked up at the captain's face but couldn't read it. At least he didn't look disappointed.

"You're as strong as any soldier that's graduated from IAS," Brant said.

"I'll take that as a compliment," Knox said, though Brant wasn't sure it normally would've been one.

"You're the captain of this mission," Brant said. "You decide its fate."

"You just lost your brother, and I'm asking your permission."

Brant's arms fell, and his heart beat out of turn. Knox asking permission?

"I have to finish-" He couldn't say *Sann*. "This mission."

Knox grunted. "That's what I thought you'd say."

"Knox!" TrysKa raced up the ramp. "It's here!"

#

Ximena ran up behind TrysKa, put one hand on her knee, and clutched her stomach with the other. Knox crossed to them in two steps.

"You found it?"

He reached his wife and held her waist. She let her head fall on his shoulders while she gulped down air. What Knox wouldn't give for a quiet moment with Ximena in their room. It wasn't a time to fool around. Hell, he didn't have the heart for it right now. But lying down on their cot with her head resting on his chest sure would feel good. Maybe she'd even whisper that it wasn't his fault.

But another time.

"We found the pirate ship," Ximena said and waved for TrysKa to finish.

Brant pushed away from the wall. "*The* pirate ship? The one that abducted Taluk's children?"

TrysKa nodded. "Ximena had *Maverick* programmed to find the pirate ship's digital signature. When we docked, it alarmed. All we had to do was track it down using her scanner."

From one of her pockets, Ximena pulled out a handheld scanner, a wire-wrapped ball with seven antennae.

TrysKa continued, "We followed the trail, and it's here!"

"So, let's break the children out of the ship!" Brant stood ready to push down the door with his bare hands.

"The children have been sold a long time ago," Knox reminded him. "But the ship might have records—"

Bang, bang, bang, bang, bang, bang, bang!

TrysKa and Ximena jolted at the knocking on the closed hallway door. Knox winced.

"Alex."

Knox left Ximena and opened the door.

"So what do we do about the ship?" Alex's eyes were perfectly round.

"What do we do about—" Knox set his jaw. "You could hear that?"

Alex's eyes flicked to Brant, Knox, Brant, and Knox again. "No."

"We need to soundproof that door," Knox said to Ximena, who smiled at Alex.

But her smile was broken around the edges. Grief was still too fresh for laughter.

"More importantly," Knox said, "what do we do now?"

"We break into the ship's computer!" TrysKa said. "Get their computer's history. Save those children."

"No!" Ximena said.

"Yes!" Brant, Alex, and TrysKa answered back.

"I'm done!" Ximena said, and her eyes begged Knox to take her side.

Danger!

Knox set his feet and let his arms swing loosely by his side, preparing for battle. He sized up the forces at play: caring TrysKa, passionate Brant, and frightened Ximena.

"Ximena."

"You're going to keep going? Knox, that was a trap we walked into." Ximena pointed to the generator. "They were

201

waiting for us. Whoever it was has soldiers and money and knew what we were going to do. Knox!" Her eyes verged on tears. "Who will this mission take next?"

Knox closed the distance to his bride and held her.

"Ximena."

What to say? He had to finish this mission. Sann had just surrendered his life for it. If Knox walked away, the young man's sacrifice was for nothing. It couldn't be for nothing.

But Ximena was crying. It broke him when she cried. He caught one of her tears with his calloused knuckle. He couldn't say *no*, but he couldn't say *yes*.

Knox pressed Ximena to his chest, and cut his eyes at TrysKa. She nodded.

"Ximena," TrysKa said, her voice soft as a caress. "I need to rescue these children. For Sann."

Ximena lifted her face to her friend. "But..." She curled up. Knox wrapped his strong arms around her, protecting her from her fears.

"You're right," Brant said, interrupting Knox's plan. "It was a trap. They were too prepared."

What the hell was Brant doing?

"But now we know someone's expecting us." Brant locked eyes with Knox. "*You* know someone's expecting us, and you can out-strategy anyone."

Out-strategy anyone.

Well, Knox had never heard it like that before, but he'd take it. He stepped back and faced Ximena.

"Well?"

She pulled a stained shop rag out of one of her pants pockets and smeared it across her wet cheeks. Then she eyed Knox like she was studying the engine's diagnostics. Her gaze dissected him from his eyes to his neck, from his fists to his stance.

"Like Brant said: no one can out-strategy my husband."

Knox's chest swelled, and Ximena gave him *that* look. Why did the rest of the crew have to stand here, gawking? Knox could use a little wifely encouragement right now. But he cleared his throat instead.

"How do we break into the pirate ship's computer?" he asked.

"Oh, well." Ximena stared off at the ceiling. "It's a Kronos Class ship, I think my Sneak could copy the ship's log and transmit it to our ship."

"Won't their ship's computer be secured?" TrysKa asked.

Ximena laughed until she snorted.

"Space truckers are not tech-savvy," she said, walking to and digging through one of the cargo bay cabinets.

"That's wording it mildly," Knox said.

"Nor do they secure any of their computers. Ever."

Now that Ximena had a puzzle to solve, she was all in. She dug through two more cabinets before finding the right one. She stuck her arm into the cabinet's recess, all the way up to her armpit. After groping around, she pulled out a glob of wires stuck to putty. Her Sneak. Ximena picked out a dust bunny, dirt, and a skinny stylus.

"I wondered where that was." She dropped the instrument into one of her pockets and held out the gooey wire-thing. "My Sneak."

"Cool!" Alex bounded up to her, and Ximena handed it to him.

He turned it in his hands and pressed his fingerprints into the putty. Brant's mouth fell open, and Knox could read the doubt clearly written across his face.

Our plan depends on that thing?

Knox cleared his throat. Brant looked up, and Knox made a slashing motion across his neck. Ximena got fired up about many things, and doubting her intellect ranked number one. Knox had just calmed her down, and he didn't need Brant stepping on that landmine.

Brant closed his mouth and tried to look amazed instead of dumbfounded. Eh. At least he tried.

"Next step," Knox said, positioning between Brant and Ximena, "is sticking that thing to the ship."

"I could do it!" Alex said, shooting his hand in the air and waving it.

"No!" everyone in the cargo bay said at once. Alex's hand fell, and his face soured.

"I can do it," TrysKa said.

"Umm." Knox did not want to lose another crew member.

He turned to Brant. TrysKa winced like she'd been slapped. Brant's gaze wavered back and forth from Knox to TrysKa.

"I could do it," Brant said gingerly. "But I would need to dress like a hired hand. I assume a spaceport security guard would get too much attention?"

The image of Brant strutting around in a hired hand outfit was too much. Knox grunted.

"You'd look like a security guard in costume."

"Blending in was never my strong suit," Brant said. "Give me a gun and a straight shot instead of sneaking around." Brant's eyes flicked to TrysKa again. "TK has adaptive touch, she's a better fit."

Adaptive touch?

"Why wasn't that on your application?" Knox asked TrysKa.

"Oh," TrysKa clasped her hands in front of her. "I wasn't

trying to deceive. KaeHan removed it from my skill set. Normally graduates with adapted touch are recruited for nighttime ops or dark cave attacks."

"Got it," Knox said, raising his hand. "You love being a pilot."

"I can still do this job," TrysKa said in a pleading voice.

She held her hand out to Alex. He pouted but surrendered the Sneak.

Knox's stomach turned. He wanted to do this job himself, but too many truckers and hired hands knew him. And Brant had as much chance of blending into a spaceport as a mustang in a pack of wolves. Blast it all! TrysKa was the best choice. She carried herself with the calm assurance of a pilot, and no one would pause when she approached a ship. They'd assume it was hers.

"She is trained in hand-to-hand combat and weapons just like every other IAS grad," Brant said, giving Knox the nudge he needed.

"Fine," Knox said. "TrysKa it is, but this plan needs more. There've been too many traps lately."

"What else does it need?" Brant asked.

A smirk tugged at the corner of Knox's mouth. "A distraction."

"Really? A distraction? Is that all I'm good for?"

"And a laugh," Alex said.

Knox chuckled then swallowed it. "Alex! What did I tell you?"

Alex crossed his arms and glared at the floor.

"A distraction?" Ximena asked, the light clicking on. "You don't mean? Certainly not a?"

"No better distraction in a spaceport," Knox said.

Ximena groaned. "So much for keeping everyone safe."

"I'll back up Brant if he needs it."

"Wait! What's the distraction?" Brant asked.

Ximena pursed her lips but didn't argue further.

"A bar fight," Knox said. "The bars inside the landing docks are notorious."

"They're a professional sport out here, really," Ximena said.

"A bar fight?" Alex asked, jumping up and down.

"No!" everyone yelled at him again. Again he pouted.

A bar fight. Brant's blast-resistant uniform would actually serve Knox's purposes perfectly. With one added touch.

"Help TrysKa load the food into the galley," Knox said. "I have to get something from the market."

"Food?" Brant walked to the ramp and leaned around the opening. "Oh wow!"

A pile of small crates stacked as tall as Alex patiently waited to be put up. Ximena tapped a light on her scroll, and the crates floated into the cargo bay.

"Put away," Knox said. "Don't eat."

"Yes, sir."

But when Brant snagged a crate from mid-air, his eyes had that hungry gleam. Knox needed to move quickly.

20

Distractions

Brant opened another crate for TrysKa. The energy bars had been unloaded a few crates back, and Brant had pocketed a few. If only he could sneak off to his room.

Sann's room. Brant's chest tightened. Not there. The bathroom, maybe?

A hand smacked the back of his head.

"Hey!" Brant leapt to a defensive stance. "Oh."

It was Knox. Of course. He held out a canvas bag, and Brant opened it. A bright orange jacket was folded inside, and a thin gray strip coiled up underneath. Brant pinched the end between his thumb and index finger and uncurled it from the bag. Bold words in red ran down the paper, but Brant couldn't read Spanish.

"Which port are we in, again?" Brant asked.

"New Terra Port 4."

That was the hub for Mexico and the Carribean countries. Back in Brant's memory somewhere, he recalled that the Carribeans had been islands on old Earth. Now they were terraformed domes just like everyone else. Maybe they had bigger plankton ponds.

"What does it say?" Brant asked.

"Dishonorably Discharged."

"Why?" Brant held the tattoo ribbon as far away from his body as his arm could stretch.

"It was that or 'Drop Out,' and you didn't strike me as a quitter."

"Thanks, I guess." Brant pressed it against Knox's chest. "I'm still not putting this thing on."

"Did I forget to mention? I can't afford a security guard, especially one from Seguridad del Espacio Exterior. I need an affordable distraction, and a discharged guard will fit the bill perfectly."

"Yeah." But Brant hadn't bet on this. "But wait... you can afford IAS grads."

"I have a wealthy client that I don't want other truckers to know about. He's the one funding this mission. If other truckers see I've hired a security guard from that company—"

"They'll get suspicious."

"Precisely."

Crap! "I need a minute."

"Don't take too long. That pirate won't stay here forever."

Knox picked up the crate and brought it to the breakroom for TrysKa to unload. Brant ducked into his bedroom. There on the bed lay the jar and rifle. Brant looked at the tape in his hand instead. *Dishonorably Discharged.* He could crumple it up, incinerate it, and dump its contents down the sink to recycle.

Or he could finish Sann's mission.

With a growl, Brant jerked up his left sleeve and placed the cloth at the top of his triceps. He smoothed his hand down over the strip, and the condemning tattoo heated into his skin.

He ripped the empty ribbon off his arm and crushed it in his fist. Then he stormed out of the room.

Right into TrysKa.

She dropped a box of dehydrated fruit, but Brant caught it. He held it out for her, but instead of taking the small crate, TrysKa hugged Brant, food and all. She didn't say anything, but she didn't need to. Brant nodded, and TrysKa carried the food to the kitchen, head down.

Knox stepped into the hallway. "Let's go."

Brant followed Knox off *Maverick* and into N.T. Port #4. They passed several transports that looked less like space ants and more like giant boxes glued together. Outside of one, a captain cussed, spraying spit on his hired hands while they loaded crates. The vessels changed again to more of a deflated balloon shape. A businesswoman, donning a suit and gun, struck a deal with a merchant for goods. A robot whipped past Brant on a cushion of air carrying tools that looked familiar. Maybe Brant had seen them in one of Ximena's cabinets? It took a tight corner, and the crash of metal parts and thud of a body followed. A wave of shouting, screeching, and cussing trailed the wreck like an aftershock.

One of the mechanics pulled out from under his ship. "Ola Knox!" He waved. "¿Cómo estás?"

How are you doing? the translator bug said in Brant's left ear.

"Fuckin' awful! And you?" Knox said back.

For the entire stroll down the aisle, Knox swore again and again, lathering fuck over it all with a generous hand. Oh, he relished the momentary freedom. As they reached the bars, Knox sighed like a man who's licked his plate clean and pushed back from the table. He cut his eyes at Brant.

"You don't have to tell Ximena about that."

"I don't see Alex anywhere," Brant said.

"Good."

'Luis and Carlos' read the sign over the entryway of the bar sitting between a payment kiosk and a bed and breakfast that probably served more than breakfast. Jalapeño, habanero, and chili peppers danced along the faux-adobe bar front, and a dark-skinned Goliath statue stood cross-armed beside the open archway. No sooner had Knox crossed the threshold than the sculpture shot his hand in front of Brant's chest. Brant grabbed his gun and took a defensive stance. The not-statue narrowed his eyes.

"¿Está él contigo, Knox?" *He with you, Knox?*

Knox cut his eyes sidelong at Brant like he was toying with answering *Unfortunately.* But out of his mouth came the words:

"He's with me, Carlos."

Carlos rotated his wrist so his palm faced up. "Gun."

Brant grabbed his weapon, his finger on the trigger. Let the bouncer try to take it away. But Carlos simply stood with a bored look on his face. If Brant didn't give up his gun, then they wouldn't get in. He was doing his job and could wait with his hand out forever.

"Would you trust me instead?" Knox asked.

Knox opened his palm. Callouses toughened the underside of each joint, and years of hard work etched deep lines in the skin.

Do I trust Knox?

Brant pulled his pistol from the holster. It was heavier than usual. He moved it toward Knox's hand, but the gun bucked back. It strained as though an invisible cable tethered it to Brant. He forced the gun into Knox's open palm, but couldn't let go.

This is my gun!

Brant had cleaned it, tweaked it, and trained with it. If it wasn't on his person, it was locked up, and only he knew the combination. It responded to his touch and his touch only. He couldn't give up his weapon. He wouldn't give up his weapon.

But I promised to finish Sann's mission.

Brant sucked in his breath. Sann's mission. He would do anything, sacrifice everything, to honor Sann's life. Brant tore his eyes off his gun. He faced his captain; he faced Knox. If anyone would guard Brant's weapon with his life, it was Knox. No one—no guard, no enemy, no friend even—would wrestle Brant's gun from this man.

Brant waged war against his every instinct and peeled open his fingers. He reeled back his hand, against the hooks connecting him to his weapon. They sank into him, yanked at his muscles, ripped into his bones. *That's my gun!*

Brant dropped his arm in surrender. Knox wrapped his strong fingers around the offered weapon then secured it to his belt.

"You, I trust," Carlos said.

With a grunt, he crossed his arms and seemed to transform back into stone. Brant fought the urge to poke him. Or punch him.

Knox entered and then Brant, who expected his eyes to dilate open and adjust to the darkness. Instead, hanging lights brightened the inside of the bar, and the yeastahol scent mingled with the climbing bougainvillea. The thorns and magenta petals spread out of clay pots on both sides of the door, vined up the wall, and interwove above Brant's head.

Customers laughed over their drinks around small tables. A

long, high counter, polished to a mirror shine, ran the length
of the right wall. Customers, most of whom wore the orange
Seguridad jacket, filled every available barstool. Luis, both
bartender and owner, strolled the opposite side of the counter
refilling drinks. He had smoky gray eyes and moved with the
smoothness of a ballroom dancer.

To Brant's left, two women in uniform had cozied up over
their drinks. They stopped chatting and glared at him. In the
center, four guys' laughter cut short. Their jackets lay tossed
over the back of their chairs. One of them had loosened the
laces on his boots after a long shift. He re-tied them with deft
fingers. All four of them pushed their drinks to the center of
their table and scraped their chairs back. Brant's right hand
drifted to his empty holster. He felt naked.

"I'll cover you if you need it," Knox said and strolled to the
bar.

The four guards marched to Brant and tried to circle like
buzzards. He backed up and walked with them, not allowing
them to get behind him. The rest of the customers, except for
the uniformed women, herded to the bar.

The guard to Brant's right had a lip that curled on the left,
a permanent smirk. His companion glared through pig eyes
from a soft face, a stark contrast to the third fellow, as thin
as a bronzed stick bug. The last one, sleek with slicked-back
hair, spoke.

"You don't belong here."

Brant didn't answer. Just side-stepped, crossed, sidestepped again.

"You're required to display that." He swiped at Brant's arm
and the tattoo.

Brant popped the hand with the back of his left wrist, but

Slick-hair flexed his biceps to keep his arm in place, inside Brant's personal space. Brant rotated his arm quick, hitting the guy's elbow. That in turn swung the guard's fist back into his own nose. The other three laughed.

"Plenty of other bars for wash-outs," Slick-hair said.

Brant tensed his shoulders at that, but then immediately loosened them. "I'm with Knox."

"Knox is safe here. You can wait outside."

"He told me to come with him," Brant said. "I'm coming with him."

"Luis!" Slick-hair shouted at the bar owner. "Shouldn't Carlos take out the trash?"

"This bar welcomes everyone," Luis said. "You know that."

"Everyone who's qualified. Junk like this will tarnish your rep."

"How many other bars have said that to you?"

Luis scanned the customers who'd gathered by the bar. Many of them had been leaning forward, anticipating the coming fight. His statement doused their fervor with ice water. They all shifted and glanced away. Some grumbled.

"That's why I don't tolerate it said here," Luis said. "Everyone's welcome."

He brought a drink to another customer who tossed a black paychip onto a growing mound of discs on the shiny counter. Knox fished a paychip out of his pocket and flicked it onto a stack of about five. Ah, the customers were taking bets. The large stack was bets on the guards and the small pile? That would be bets on Brant.

Stick-bug bowed out.

"Luis is right."

Slick-hair halted, his mouth opened as he watched his ally

retreat. Brant took advantage of the momentary distraction and shifted his weight to the balls of his feet, testing the ground: slick epoxycrete, polished to feel like wood. Brant rolled his shoulders and tightened his abs, ready for the coming storm. The shock on Slick-hair's face melted into a sneer. Molted red splotches grew on his face. His whole body clenched.

"Drop-outs don't belong here!"

He swung a punch, but it was in slow motion. Brant ducked easily and planted his fist into the guard's kidneys. His punch left a momentary impression in the guy's back. Slick-hair crumpled. One down.

Brant rolled away as Pig-Eyes kicked the air he'd just occupied. Pig-eyes and Curled-lip lunged for Brant but hit each other instead. Curled-lip shoved over Pig-eyes who slipped sideways on the glossy floor. Brant twisted his torso and tunneled his force through the meaty side of his fist in Curled-Lip's temple.

His head jerked left, and his neck cracked. The noise was sickening. Pig-eyes grabbed his friend.

"Are you OK?"

But Curled-lip didn't answer.

"He'll live," Brant said. He could've hit harder and paralyzed the guy. But he hadn't.

Still the prone guard's eyes rolled up into his head, and Pig-eyes screamed something in Spanish. Brant grabbed the chair behind him instead of listening to his earbud's translation. As the last guard charged, Brant stepped back and whirled the chair forward. He'd expected the legs to shatter against the guy's solid body, but it held firm, thunking against Pig-eye's arm and hip. His body dented left, and his feet flew off the floor. He skidded into a table, knocking the yeastahol down his shirt and pants. Nuts sprinkled his wet hair.

A gun clicked, and Brant froze.

"Isabella, check our man."

Brant moved only his eyes to locate the threat. One of the women from the other table stood a safe distance away with her gun pointed at Brant's chest. He might be able to move fast enough. Or he might not.

Knox cleared his throat with Brant's gun aimed and ready. The charge in the room skyrocketed.

"I don't want to shoot anyone," Knox said, his voice that of a parent to a toddler. "But I don't want my crew shot either."

Isabella circled Brant, giving him a wide berth, and bumped into Carlos. He must have snuck in during the fight. She walked around the clay giant, dropped to a knee next to Curled-lip, and slapped his face. He rolled his head and threw up. She jumped back but not before chunks smeared her pants.

"Shit, he's concussed."

"Well, he deserved that for picking the fight. Especially here." The first woman's grip on the gun relaxed. "But is he paralyzed?"

"Nah."

To prove her point, Isabella pinched the soft skin on Curled-lip's side. He twitched and giggled, high-pitched.

"Stop it!" His voice was breathy.

The woman made to holster her gun, but Carlos held out his hand.

"Your weapon."

"Carlos, you saw what that guy did." She held her hand out, like she was presenting Brant to a jury. "I had to protect my team."

Carlos didn't argue, but held his hand there, waiting. A pained look crossed her face, and Brant could relate. In slow motion, she unholstered her pistol and handed it over.

"It's safe with me." Carlos turned and left. His feet didn't make a sound, like an elephant tiptoeing.

Knox holstered Brant's gun. He took his sweet time dividing the winnings with the other five that had bet on Brant. This distraction was for TrysKa's benefit after all, so Knox nursed it. Counting up a handsome sum of money had its own hypnotic effect on the bystanders. Knox pinched a paychip between his index and middle finger and flicked it down the bar. It slid into Luis's waiting hand.

"Sorry for the mess," Knox said.

"You got a bargain with that guy." Luis pocketed the chip. "Now, if you'll excuse me, I have to call these kids' superiors. They have a lot of cleaning up to do."

"We can handle this without the call, thank you," the woman said. She shucked her jacket and picked up a table. To Brant, "Next time."

Brant backed out of the bar, keeping his eyes on her until he was safely out. Knox drew Brant's pistol, spun it, and presented the butt to Brant. Brant snatched and holstered it in one fluid movement. And sighed as his shoulders released their knot of tension.

His gun was safely back where it belonged.

"Why did you trust me?" Knox asked.

"Had to finish this mission."

Knox nodded, and the two began the trek back through the hangar to *Maverick*. Brant let his hand rest on his gun as he strolled, the cool handle a comfort. Fine, he'd say it.

"And I knew the only way anyone would take my gun from

you," Brant added, "was by prying it from your cold, dead fingers."

"Damn right." Knox's black eyes gleamed at that.

Ximena's voice crackled over the earbud. "Alex? Alex, where are you?"

Brant and Knox broke into a run, shouldering bodies out of the way.

#

Back when Brant entered the bar and started circling with the four guards, the news broke out.

"Bar fight!"

Like a school of fish, everyone on the landing dock funneled toward *Luis and Carlos*, and TrysKa slipped into the stream.

All the people flowed in the same direction, rippling the air. The currents rolled against TrysKa's left arm and the left side of her face, lifting the hair along her skin. She cut across the aisle and entered an eddy. After catching her breath, she ducked between two ships, making her way toward the next aisle. Again she cut across the flow, weaving through the people.

A wave brushed against her. Someone else traveled cross current with her, shadowing her. She turned downstream past two ships, then darted between them. When she reached the next aisle, TrysKa cut upstream, hugging the ships and avoiding the crowd. Between ships, she hid and waited. No upstream ripples followed. Whoever it was had lost interest and returned to following the herd.

Again, TrysKa cut across the path. This time two ripples turned to hunt her. *Ugh!* She picked up the pace to the next row, but the ripples closed in.

"*Hey!*" someone yelled behind her.

A splash cascaded through the air. Her pursuers had pushed someone over. More waves foamed and crashed. The horde was fighting back. In the chaos, TrysKa slipped between transports and entered the next current. One of the ripples still tracked her. TrysKa grabbed her pistol but hesitated.

I don't want to shoot! Why are you pushing me?

The ripple lunged forward. TrysKa drew her gun, but he grabbed her arm.

"Hey, beautiful," a gurgling voice whispered in her ear.

His breath reeked of earthy smoke. TrysKa set her feet to kick him in the groin, but he stiffened and crumpled to the ground. Stunned. A lithe woman with a gun stood over him, scowling. Three truckers halted and grabbed their guns.

"The bar fight's more interesting," the woman said.

The truckers shrugged and went on their way. The woman holstered her gun and held out her hand to TrysKa.

"Meihui."

TrysKa shook her hand. "TrysKa. Why did you?"

"You with Knox?"

"Yeah."

"Worked for him before. He always pays well." Meihui didn't let go of TrysKa's hand, instead she pulled her closer. "Never hesitate."

She let go, kicked the body in the side then slipped into the throng. Shouts rose from the bar, and the onlookers cheered. The fight had started. TrysKa ran across the last aisle, raced upstream, and found the ship.

"Unmute." Her earbud beeped. "Ximena, I'm here."

"Hold the Phase Burner up to its shields."

TrysKa pulled the Phase Burner, a gangly spider, out of her pack and held it in her open palm. It twittered then bobbed in the air. With the spastic flight pattern of a bumblebee, it plopped on the ship's shields. The spider's abdomen flickered rainbow colors as it chirped and measured the shield's wavelength cycle. It whirred for a few seconds more, and the shimmer around the ship vanished. The Phase Burner fell to the ground with a clink. TrysKa pocketed it.

"OK, shields down."

"Attach the Sneak to a communication spike," Ximena said.

TrysKa pulled the Sneak out, but her pocket came with it, attached to the putty. She peeled her pocket from the goo and stuck the Sneak to a thin rod sticking out of the ship like chop sticks. It didn't do anything.

"Is it working?"

"Oh yeah," Ximena said. "I'm receiving files. Can't read them, but I'm getting them. Alex, you have to come see this."

Pause.

"Alex?"

"Ximena, did he...?" TrysKa scanned the aisle for Alex's curls.

A few truckers turned, eyed her curves, then noticed her pilot's badge. They shrugged and melted back into the river of bodies. They weren't stupid enough to mess with a pilot, unlike some.

"Alex? Alex, where are you?" Ximena's voice rose, and a door swished open. She must be searching the ship.

"Ximena!" TrysKa yelled.

"What?" Ximena said back, out of breath.

"I'll find Alex, is the transmission done?"

"Not yet."

The cheers had died, and workers were dispersing back to their jobs. The fight had ended.

"What do we do about the Sneak?"

"It'll self-incinerate on its own, find Alex!"

"10-4."

TrysKa retraced her steps. The mass was spreading out instead of funneling in like before. The currents weren't as strong. TrysKa moved smoothly, feeling the ripples of each person, searching for an out-of-place eddy. She skirted close to the hulls as she passed, testing for the breath of a little body hiding under a ship's belly.

Her earbud buzzed. "TK, do you have him?" It was Knox.

"No."

"Dammit."

TrysKa found *Maverick* as Knox and Brant raced up. Ximena came out of the ship with a sheepish grin on her face, and Alex popped his head out from behind her.

"Are you going to send me back?" Alex asked Knox in his most pathetic tone.

"No," Knox said to Alex. To Ximena, "He was hiding?"

"Not exactly," Ximena said, pulling out her scroll and fiddling with some graphs.

"So where was he?"

"Digging around in the kitchen."

"He what!" TrysKa said.

Her shoulder blades pulled back. That was her kitchen. No one dug around in her kitchen. They asked permission. They thanked her for her cooking. They didn't "dig around."

Everyone jumped back from her. Alex froze for half a heartbeat, then bolted to the cabinet that was his bedroom. TrysKa's shoulders hunched. She hadn't meant to scare the boy.

But he'd been in *her* kitchen.

Knox patted her on the back. "He deserved the scolding."

"I scared him."

"Oh, he'll get over it."

Ximena pulled out a shop rag and covered her eyes. She was crying. TrysKa wrapped her arm around Ximena and walked her to the breakroom. Knox and Brant hung back on the hangar floor.

"I was just so scared," she said, her voice muffled by the handkerchief.

"I know."

"I've lost so many children. Before I even got to meet them."

"I know." TrysKa squeezed Ximena.

"Why can't I save Alex? Why do I freeze up?"

"It's my job to keep him safe on the dock. It's your job to make the ship safe in space. It won't do me any good to save him if we blow up."

Ximena wiped her cheeks, and blew her nose. She rested her head on TrysKa's shoulders.

"Thank you."

"Anytime. I'll make some lunch."

TrysKa pulled out a pot and set it on the electric pad. She cut dehydrated vegetables on the countertop while the tray heated the pot. Her thoughts churned.

You won't stay on Maverick after this mission is over. After you're gone, who will watch Alex?

She didn't know, but Alex needed a family. And Ximena and Knox needed him. Would it be better for Alex to return to a school that bullied him? No! TrysKa drizzled oil into the pot.

At IAS, Alex wouldn't be killed or kidnapped.

TrysKa dropped the vegetables in, and they sizzled and popped. She stirred them with a flat-tipped spoon.

221

Alex had listened today. He was doing better.

For now. But Ximena needs to pull her nose out of that scroll if she's going to be a mother to Alex.

Now wasn't the right time. That was it. Bad timing. Ximena did need more focus, but if TrysKa said that now, it would only make her defensive. Timing and grace were just as important as telling the truth.

She'd tell Ximena soon. She would. At the right time.

Sure you will. Coward.

21

Pandora's Box

The light-headed aftereffect of the drugs kicked in. Brant blinked and shook his head as he stepped up the ramp. Knox's sharp eyes caught the movement.

"The pill?"

Brant back-peddled from Knox's dissecting gaze.

"Nothing to be ashamed of," Knox said. "You do what you have to."

Easy for him to say.

"Do you have the pill?" Brant asked, an edge to his voice.

"No," Knox said. "But my muscles aren't adapted. The hormone fluctuations are more common with the adaptations of speed and strength."

"Not everyone with phys-ads needs them."

Knox stood higher on the ramp, so he could look Brant in the eye.

"Brant, you have a body struggling with an evolutionary jump of our species. It's not always going to be pretty. I trained with students who needed help controlling their hormones, and they didn't get it."

"How did that go?"

"I don't want to..." Knox stared off, seeing the ghosts of his past. "They did the best they could." He shook it off. "But you are in a healthy place. When you're in the heat of battle you keep control. Isn't that important to you?"

"Yeah."

"Then don't be ashamed of the tools that help you reach your goals."

Knox pivoted and entered the ship, but Brant remained rooted outside. Ed had always openly shamed Brant about his "weak" need for meds. Even DeVaun sneered when the subject was brought up.

Don't be ashamed of the tools that help you reach your goals.

Brant had never thought of it that way. Ever. He lowered his head, and walked to the breakroom. The ship welcomed Brant with the hearty aroma of soup. *Mmmm.* His stomach gurgled. Knox flared his nostrils and inhaled deeply.

"You're not kidding," Ximena said from the bench.

Knox sat next to her, wrapping his arm around her shoulders. Brant leaned against the doorframe when he heard the sound of fabric rubbing against skin underneath the table. With a slight tilt of his head, he saw small boots peeking out from under its edge. That Alex. What would he think of next?

"So," Brant asked, pretending not to notice the sneak. "Do we have the pirate ship's history?"

"Oh," Ximena pulled out her scroll. She'd forgotten about the transmissions. "Yes, we do. It's just..." She wrinkled her nose. "It's encrypted."

"No." Knox leaned over, glaring at the code.

"I thought space truckers didn't know encryption and codes and stuff like that."

Brant stood over Ximena's other shoulder. The symbols, letters, and squiggles clumped together into a mountain of nonsense. How did anyone read this?

TrysKa dropped a bone into the boiling pot and joined the group. "So now what?"

"Well, we do know one programmer." Ximena raised her eyebrow at Knox.

\#

Knox pulled his arm away from Ximena. No, not TG, not on this mission. Knox's plan had already derailed and crashed this morning, he was not adding more complications.

"I don't like letting her out of her box."

"You keep someone locked up in a box?" Alex asked, bobbing up from under the table.

No one startled at his sudden appearance, though Ximena snorted. Alex at least had the decency to look sheepish and mouth *I'm sorry* to TrysKa. She winked back.

"I keep her comm ball locked up," Knox said.

"Why?"

"If she can hack that pirate's ship, she can hack *Maverick.*"

"Not with Ximena's code protecting it," TrysKa said and returned to the galley.

"Even with my code protecting it," Ximena said and closed her scroll. "She's that good, which is why I made the lead room."

"We have a room built of lead?" Alex asked again, about to jump up and search the ship.

"No," Knox said, his tone sliding toward exasperation. "We have a cube with a shield that holds her comm ball."

"Now multiply those questions times fifteen and you get a picture of what I deal with every class multiple times a day."

Brant lounged on the bench with a smug grin.

"I'll get her box."

Knox escaped to his quarters. He found the Pandora's box, but instead of returning, Knox passed the cube back and forth from his left to his right hand. How many times had he been tempted to "lose" this out the airlock?

As many times as TG had saved his ass. Knox stomped back to the breakroom and set the box in the center of the table.

"I can put up a shield that blocks her from the rest of the ship," Ximena said. With a tap on her scroll, an energy bubble encircled the table. "Then TG can talk to us, but can't access our computer."

"But how can she talk to the ball through the shields?" Alex asked, leaning on the table with his elbows, straining for a closer look.

"Quantum mechanics," Ximena said, still studying her scroll.

Alex stared at her like she'd turned green and grown fuzz.

"You know how the spaceports gather energy?" Ximena asked, frowning over the diagnostics while she talked.

"The sun panels?"

"Right, but do you know how they move that energy down to the planet?"

"They pack it up and bring it in the shuttles?"

Ximena laughed until she snorted. "No. They have an electron-in-a-box on the spaceport, and they use the sun's energy to spin it."

"They spin electrons?"

"Right. And, the electron has a partner, a pair from the same atom, that's down on the planet. When the spaceport spins one electron, the partner electron down on the planet spins too."

"So both spin."

"Exactly. And the spinning electron on the planet gives off energy."

"Oh, OK," Alex said, as if that was the easiest thing to understand.

Ximena dragged her finger across a bar on her screen, something changed color, and she nodded. She closed the scroll. Brant's mouth had fallen open so wide, Knox could have stuck two energy bars in there whole.

"Why didn't you teach our quantum physics class?" Brant asked. "That made so much more sense than how Instructor Lehmann explained it."

"Oh," Ximena smiled. "Thank you. But how else would you explain that concept?"

"I honestly don't remember how he did it."

"It wasn't bad," TrysKa said as she dropped dehydrated onions into the soup. Brant's fair complexion flushed, so she cleared her throat. "But Ximena's explanation was easier."

"Science wasn't my strong suit," Brant mumbled.

"But you always knew how to help me when I struggled with landing a jump," Tryska said.

He shrugged.

"And you're good at biology."

"The human body is interesting," Brant said as if it was no big deal, but he did perk up.

Shields materialized around the table on Ximena's command, and Knox reached toward the hacker-in-a-box. He cracked open the lid. The glowing orb inside its dark recess swirled opalescent colors along the lid and inside. Alex about crawled on top of the table to get a peek.

"So this has a spinning electron in it?"

"Actually a spinning neutron," Ximena said. "Communications work better with neutrally charged atoms. Energy likes negatively charged ones."

"Again! So much clearer than Lehmann!" Brant slapped the table.

"When the neutron spins clockwise, that's a zero," Ximena said. "When it spins counter-clockwise, that's a one."

"What can you do with a bunch of zeros and ones?" Alex asked.

"I can take down governments," the ball answered.

Everyone but Knox jolted. Alex fell off the edge of the table onto the bench butt first. His hands, feet, and curls wiggled in the air. TrysKa dropped her spoon, and it clanged on the metal floor. She cleansed it in the sink before returning to stirring the pot.

"Crew," Knox said. "I'd like to introduce you to TG."

"Sorry about your loss," she said.

Knox pushed back from the table and pressed his neck into the shields behind him. The hair on his arms crawled from the static electricity. How the hell did she always know his business?

"But I assume you aren't calling me for condolences," TG said. "What do you need?"

Knox cut his eyes at Ximena, who opened the code. "Some children were kidnapped from Taluk. We found the ship that did it, but their computer history is encrypted."

"Ooooh." TG sounded like Ximena was sharing a naughty secret. "Let me see."

Ximena swiped her scroll, and the code disappeared. It didn't take long.

"This is not a nice person," TG said.

"So you can decipher it?" Knox asked.

"Already done. As a side note, Ximena, when you have your scroll inside the shield barrier, I can theoretically access all the information on it."

Ximena winced then closed it with a snap.

"Even if it's closed."

"You stay out of my head," *Maverick* said with Liam's thick voice.

Time to end this call.

"If you'll send that back to us," Knox said, reaching forward, "we can all go about our lives."

"You have time to rescue these children?" TG asked.

Knox's hand halted mid-air. No, he didn't have time. He had to gather shields, and if traps were being set for his crew, he had to gather them quickly.

"What other option do I have?"

"I could find them," TG said. "Atienna is the one to call if they're found, correct?"

Again, how did she know this? "Yes, but I can't afford your fee."

"On the house."

"No. Nothing is on the house with you, and I won't owe you."

TG sighed so loudly it came over the speaker. "Don't get me wrong. You shouldn't trust me, but sometimes it's inconvenient."

"I'm not sorry."

"What if I owe you? What if this is debt repayment?" It was her turn to sound on edge.

Knox drummed his fingers on the table. "Why do you owe

me?"

TG didn't answer immediately. The silence stretched on, and Alex picked at a blaster gouge running along the tabletop.

"Is it still on?" Brant asked, reaching out to poke the sphere.

"I'm still here," TG said.

Brant jerked his hand back like her voice had electrocuted it.

"I don't suppose you could take my word for it?" she said.

"I require at least a hint," Knox said.

"Fine. I've been following your operation."

"How? My client's systems are secure."

"Mostly. But Nichev Company and Serving Hands have a lot of talkative employees who use the Public Database."

"Of course they do." He'd have to talk to Nicolai and Atienna about that.

"And I might or might not have access to Caravan Supplier's database."

"Very handy."

"It is. And yesterday I saw a note that one of Caravan's executives was sending extra guards to a certain island."

The tension thickened like TrysKa's boiling stew. Knox's stomach tightened to rock hard. He could smell the fury pheromones radiating off Brant.

"I didn't know that was your next target," TG said. "Or I would have warned you. I'm so sorry."

Knox couldn't answer.

"It's not your fault," TrysKa said to TG. "Knox is hard to figure out."

"Caravan Suppliers predicted me," Knox grumbled.

"That's not your fault either," TrysKa said.

"Well, now that we've all decided it's not our fault, I still feel like I owe you. Do I have your permission to rescue these children while you get the shields?"

"Thank you."

And he meant it. Knox didn't agree with TG's methods, but her passion was in the right place.

"So it's decided," TG said. "Though..." Again she went silent. Blast it all, Knox wanted to end this call.

"One of the slave buyers might interest you," she said.

"Why?"

"Well, you're looking for shields, right? Several of the children were sold to a sweatshop that has an unused back-up shield generator. Two birds, one stone."

"Send us the information," Knox said, his hand raising again to end the call. "I'll look at it."

"Don't get yourself killed," TG said.

That was the closest she'd ever come to admitting Knox and Ximena were anything more than occasional clients.

"I'll do everything in my power to protect my crew. You stay alive yourself."

"Until next time."

Knox slammed the lid closed and could finally breathe. Several seconds passed before Ximena fished the scroll out from under the table and opened it with shaking hands. She tapped it, and the shield evaporated.

"It's been a hard day." Knox pressed his palms on the table and pushed up. "Let's eat dinner and turn in."

He took the box back to its hiding spot in his quarters. After TrysKa's soothing soup, he gave Ximena a quick kiss good night, and slipped away to the cockpit. One by one, everyone else retired to their rooms. Except for Brant.

22

Rematch

Brant stood outside of his room face-to-face with his reflection on the door. He pressed his forehead against the cold metal. It wasn't his room. It was his and *Sann's* room, *Sann's* bed on the top bunk, *Sann's* gun on the bottom bunk. Brant couldn't sleep in there.

He trudged to the cockpit, but Knox didn't respond to his presence. The captain was glaring out the viewfinder, eyebrows furrowed. Back and forth his eyes darted as if playing an intense game of chess against an unseen opponent. Probably replaying the raid from that morning. Just that morning. Brant winced.

"Hey," Brant whispered, not wanting to startle Knox. He didn't.

"Hi."

"I can't sleep in my—" *Sann's room.* "The room. Can I crash on the table bench? Or cargo bay floor? I don't care where really. Just not..."

"Do what you got to do."

Brant dropped a chair at the end of the long bench and

stretched out. His boots hung off the other side of the chair. He shoved it back with his feet and tried again. Good enough. He pulled off his shirt and wadded it up for a pillow. Then tossed and turned for hours until oblivion finally descended.

Brant wandered unknown planets searching for Sann but never finding him. He woke with a jerk, clutched the table, and whipped his head around wide-eyed his heart pounding in his ears. After blinking a few times, Ximena came into focus.

"Hi," he said.

"Hi," she said.

The previous day's event crashed back over him like a thundering wave. Brant yearned to go back in time to the moment before he remembered. To the moment when, in his mind, Sann was still with him. Brant sat up groggily, and noticed his bare chest.

"Oh sorry."

He grabbed his shirt and cracked it like a whip. After stretching it over his chest, he propped his left elbow on the table, and rested his chin in his hand. The coffee churned as Brant cut in and out of consciousness.

"Oh, poor Brant," TrysKa said.

When had she snuck in? TrysKa pulled up a chair, the legs barely making a sound. Her coffee mug clinked softly on the tabletop. Then came the soft padded steps of Alex. Through his blond eyelashes, Brant made out the boy's blurry form. He rubbed his hands together like a cartoon villain the instant he spied Brant. On tiptoes, Alex stalked his prey then wet his finger.

"Alex!" TrysKa hissed.

He crouched, and his finger took aim for Brant's ear. Brant launched his hand and grabbed the thin wrist.

"Hey! Leggo!"

Alex writhed to free himself, but Brant remained still as stone. In slow motion, he lifted his eyelids and swiveled his head toward his captive.

"So where should I put that finger?"

"Don't you dare!"

Alex pushed his feet against the bench to no avail.

"Brant," Ximena said.

"Fine."

Brant released Alex, sending him tumbling across the floor. The boy sprang up with clenched fists raised when something down the hall caught his attention. Alex lifted his chin as Knox entered.

"My bad," Brant said.

Brant lumbered to the coffee machine and poured himself a cup. Knox stared down at his student, and Alex's jaw dropped open.

"But he pushed me!"

Technically I let go. Brant grabbed an energy bar and plopped into a chair.

"You mess with Brant," Knox said. "You deal with the consequences."

Knox poured a cup of coffee and disappeared into the cockpit. Alex petrified. Slowly he turned big, frightened brown eyes on Brant. Crap, he was cute.

"We're even." Brant took a bite of energy bar and said with a mouthful, "And I'm too tired to care."

When coffee kicked in, TrysKa joined Knox in the cockpit and launched *Maverick*.

"Be advised," the flight controller said over the comm, "accident outside of air lock #17. Follow the altered flight pattern around the wreckage."

Brant and Alex stood in the doorway of the cockpit.

"Accident?" Alex asked.

Brant craned his neck to study the controls, but the diagrams and lights were a foreign language to him. Knox touched a pinprick light floating on his side, and a string of numbers hovered above the control panel. One strand lit up brighter than all the others. Knox grunted.

"What?" TrysKa asked. "Are the passengers OK? Did you know them?"

"That's the pirate ship's ID," Knox said.

"The pirate?" Alex looked at Brant then back at Knox. "You don't think TG?"

"Wouldn't surprise me."

"What did she do?" Brant asked.

"The vessel opened all its doors and evacuated its contents into the vacuum of space."

Including the pilot. Yuck.

"She likes us, right?" Brant asked.

The spaceport's airlock opened, and *Maverick* entered the cold void. There was no place for Brant to hide or protect himself. Where was his spacesuit again?

"We're fine," Knox said. "She destroys anyone who profits from the slave trade and helps anyone who fights it. That's her moral code."

Alex and TrysKa breathed a sigh of relief.

"And if she didn't like us, we'd already be dead."

Alex clutched TrysKa's chair as *Maverick* jumped. Luckily, Earth dazzled and distracted him before he could really panic. Brant ducked his head under the doorframe to get a better view.

"Wow." Alex let go of the chair back and tiptoed forward between TrysKa and Knox.

That's right, he hadn't been with the crew the first time they'd visited Earth. Brant tried not to think about who was missing this time.

And failed.

"Humans left Earth because of the earthquakes, right?" Alex asked. "Does it still have earthquakes?"

"It wasn't the earthquakes that pushed us off," TrysKa whispered.

"Then what?" Alex asked. "Weren't they bad enough?"

"Volcanic ash." TrysKa veered *Maverick* into orbit. "With earthquakes come volcanic eruption. That's why they put all their resources into the Exodus."

"What did the volcanoes do?"

Alex leaned over the controls, straining to see the details of the planet below. Brant's hand reflexively reached out to grab Alex, but stopped short, balling into a fist instead. Knox spanned his hand across Alex's chest and nudged him back.

"Volcanoes can kill a whole planet," TrysKa said.

"With lava?" Alex asked.

"No, by blocking the sun with its ash."

"Filling the sky with a bunch of dust can kill a whole planet?"

"Three years without sunlight is an extinction event."

Silence.

"But then why is there so much life now?" Alex asked. "I mean, look at all the green! And blue! I thought everybody was extinct."

"The ash only covered the sky for a year and a half," she said. TrysKa didn't say how much life that still wiped out. "And not everyone evacuated."

"So it was an *almost* extinction?"

"Close enough," TrysKa said. "But life is making a come-back."

"Cool."

Just as abruptly as the questions started, they stopped. Alex elbowed Brant out of his way and plopped down at the table. Out came a deck of cards, and Alex practiced shuffling them, tongue stuck out in intense concentration.

"A high price was paid for the shield generators in our cargo hold," Knox said, his voice deep. "But now they can save hundreds of lives."

He contacted the spaceport, and obtained permission for another planet-side landing. *Maverick* touched down next to Taluk thirty minutes later. While Ximena cleared her stomach, Knox wrestled down a thrashing Alex and baptized him in sunscreen. Brant smeared lotion on his face and arms then took extra care to rub down the part on his head. The crew stepped down the ramp into humidity.

Alex fell into TrysKa, and she pushed him away.

"It's too hot to snuggle, Alex."

But Alex stumbled again, squinting and covering his eyes with his fists. Brant held Alex's shoulder steady until the boy's contacts adjusted. Alex blinked, noticed Brant's hand, and shoved it off. Then snapped his head up at the approaching footsteps.

The stalks before the crew parted like a curtain. Klundah, along with leaders from the town, wove through the field to *Maverick*.

"We have your shield," Knox said.

Klundah translated to his group, and the message was passed back with a buzz of excitement.

"Would you bring the shield generator, please?" Knox asked TrysKa.

"Yes, sir."

TrysKa jogged back onto the ship, and Brant joined her. He heaved up the edge of the heavy machine, so TrysKa could slide Ximena's hover-brackets under each corner. When they were all in place, the generator lifted, floating on a cushion of air. As TrysKa guided it down the ramp, the sunset caressed its tubes and wires with a rosy glow. Klundah and his people stepped back in a hush.

"You have not been forgotten," Knox said with a catch in his voice.

TrysKa and the generator led the procession into the village. Brant followed behind her with the photocells. The previously suspicious villagers joined the parade with whispers of "shield" rippling through the throng. Knox and Klundah cleared a path through the bodies to the village center, so the cube of pipes and wires could share center stage with the water well.

As TrysKa lowered the generator to its place of honor, a finger tapped Brant's shoulder. He turned to see Devdan, flashing his bright white smile.

"Rematch?"

"Oh, sorry, I'm needed to help."

Brant faced the generator, now settled on the ground. Ximena wove her way through the pressing congregation with Alex's curls bobbing behind her. Knox lifted his head searching over the tops of the townspeople for his six-foot-five crew member and noticed Devdan tugging on Brant's arm. And it happened.

Knox smiled.

He didn't smile large, like Devdan, nor did he have Alex's dimple, not that Brant expected that. It was just a subtle spreading of thin lips with softening around his hard eyes. He motioned with his head for Brant to go with Devdan.

"What?" Brant called over the noise.

Was Knox serious? He tilted his head again, and Devdan spotted it this time.

"Looks like the grumpy captain is letting you go."

Brant winced. At least Knox hadn't heard that. He squeezed through the shoulders and arms around him and followed Devdan through the tight alleyway, packed with townspeople, to the court. Brant stepped out ready to play another round with young teens, except the guys awaiting him were not those.

Brant surveyed the twenty-somethings, confident, and ready to teach this off-worlder the true nature of their game. He cut his eyes at Devdan. Did that boy ever stop smiling? Brant shrugged and jogged onto the court. Devdan called him back.

"No, you were on Shirts last time."

"What?"

"You were on the Shirts team last time. Skins this time."

Devdan's bronze flesh glowed while Brant's pale skin only boasted freckles. Surely Ximena needed help with the generator? But no one called him over his earbud, so Brant removed his jacket and black shirt. High-pitched voices squealed. Girls only a little older than his students back at IAS had gathered on the sideline. Crap!

"Don't worry. They're here to see them." Devdan pointed to the strapping Taluk guys strutting over the pavement.

"Wow, I feel all better now."

Brant slung his jacket and wadded shirt straight at Devdan's chest. When he joined the game, the Shirts snapped to their position, sizing up their opponent. Even the Skins backed up, leaving Brant the exposed member of their pack. The most muscled of the Shirts approached and set his feet, crouching in front of Brant.

"Last time, you moved like adapted."

"That so?" Brant tugged at his pants and crouched, moving his weight on the balls of his feet. A paper-thin layer of dust shifted as his soles found a grip on the hard-packed ground.

"Ready to lose, adapted?" The player bared his teeth in a grin that was more a snarl.

"Nope."

The game began. His opponent rammed his right shoulder forward, but Brant sidestepped left, kicking the ball to his right. The player whirled back with his right arm, leading with his elbow straight at Brant's nose. Brant curled away, lifting his right shoulder. The blow planted into the meat of his tensed right triceps.

Brant backpedaled with a twist to see his teammates in formation running down the field. His rival spotted them and bolted to protect his goal. Brant matched speed, neck and neck. Their feet tangled, Brant fell backward, and his tailbone nailed the packed dirt. The pain ricocheted down every vertebra.

The ball soared his way. Pushing against the sharp throbbing, Brant launched upward and hit the ball with his hard head.

An arm swung into his periphery. Brant lowered his arm and lifted his knee to protect his stomach. Contact. Again, Brant hit the ground, hard as epoxycrete. Cheers rose from the sidelines. Skins had scored.

"You keep wasting time with me," Brant winked at his foe, "and my team will keep scoring."

Brant rolled away from the punch. In one graceful movement, he flowed to his feet and blew a kiss. Another cheer.

Brant looked toward his own goal. The Shirt's had scored. Brant's rival raced to protect his territory from the next onslaught.

"Keep flirting with me," the competitor said. "And we'll keep winning."

Brant joined his team. The captain pointed him to a vacancy, and he moved with the gang in formation. Now accepted.

The sky turned from blush to violet when Brant slammed to the ground yet again. The ball was still easy to make out, but the players' quick movements were blurred in the descending darkness.

Suddenly, all the players screeched to a halt. Instead of getting up, Brant rolled on his back as a fountain of blue light bubbled up from the middle of the village. The column of light lifted up, up, up toward the silver orb in the sky then spread outwards, enclosing the village and surrounding fields in its protective umbrella. The players all covered their faces with their arms as their eyes adjusted.

When the shield touched down beyond the dark stalks, its brightness dimmed. If Brant squinted, he could still make out its shifting energy against the constant stars. A cheer rose from the center of town and rippled outward, spilling onto the court. The big opponent approached Brant and held out his hand. Brant accepted it and was hoisted to standing.

"Thank you," he said.

"You're welcome."

This was for you, Sann.

Children burst onto the court, delivering cups of fresh water. They presented their gifts to the players who accepted with honor. Beaming like she offered the finest wine, a little girl held up a cup to Brant. He knelt and accepted the precious gift.

"Thank you so much."

He drank the water and tasted its earthy fullness. How he'd taken this simple thing for granted his whole life. The girl blushed as she accepted back the empty vessel.

"Well, you're a mess."

Brant spun to face TrysKa's iron-pressed navy slacks.

"TrysKa!" He stood and crossed his arms in front of his chest. "Where's my shirt?"

Brant scanned the sidelines for the familiar huge smile. Devdan heaved the jacket and wadded shirt in an arc through the air right into his hands. Brant peeled his ponytail off his back and checked his scraped-up chest, caked with sweat and grit. He pulled his shirt on, but slung his jacket over his shoulder to keep it clean.

"Hey Brant!" Devdan pointed back toward the alleyway. "Your grumpy captain is here!"

TrysKa bit back a giggle. She jogged toward the alleyway, and Brant trudged behind, his head down. After TrysKa passed, Knox blocked Brant's way.

"Grumpy captain?" Knox said.

"Loud-mouthed soldier?"

"You are loud-mouthed."

And you're grumpy.

Knox saw that thought clearly written across Brant's face. "Hmmm," was all he had to say to that.

Brant followed Knox to the village center where Ximena and Alex had collapsed against the generator's pipes. Grease, cobwebs, and dust bunnies caked Alex from curls to boots. He reeked of machine oil.

"What happened to you?" Brant said.

"Like you have room to talk!"

"The generator and relay stations were created by different companies." Ximena stood with knees cracking. "It took some tweaking to make them play nicely together."

She pressed the heel of her hands into the small of her back and stretched her spine with a groan.

"I was the only one small enough to fit underneath the generator to get at the switches and wires," Alex said.

"What about that?" Brant pointed. A control panel was stuck to the machine's side for easy access.

"Yeah, we had to get to the guts of it." Ximena pulled her braid free from the back of her shirt.

"All while you were playing ball! I shower first!" Alex stomped off to *Maverick*.

TrysKa and Ximena boarded the ship after Alex, but Brant kept his stench outdoors until it was his turn at the shower. Knox hung back too.

"Well done," Knox said.

"Seriously? All I did was goof off."

"How do I explain this?" Knox crossed his arms. "Sometimes accepting help can be a hard pill to swallow."

"I get that."

"The Taluk hated us when we first arrived. Civilized off-worlders condescending to save them from who? Other 'civilized off-worlders.' They tolerated Serving Hands, but Ximena and I were unwelcome."

"What changed?"

"One of my crew played ball with them, got dirty with them,

trash-talked with them. You gave them someone they could relate to."

"Bet you didn't know you were getting that when you let me join the op."

"You sure of that?" Knox cut his eyes at Brant. "I saw you with your students. You might have signed up for this mission, but I signed off on it."

Brant opened his mouth to say something, but nothing came out. Had he pleased Knox by just being himself? That had never been enough for Ed.

"I'm clean now."

There stood Alex atop the ramp, head cocked and hands on his hips. "And you stink."

"Wow." Brant handed his jacket to Knox. "You are clean."

Brant tugged at his pants and crouched. Alex scurried back into the cargo bay and peeked out the opening.

"You wouldn't dare!"

"Alex," Knox said. "What have I told you about messing with Brant?"

You mess with Brant; you deal with the consequences.

Alex's eyes flew wide open. The scene froze for a breath.

Alex and Brant bolted. Brant's muscles screamed, aching from too many hits to the dirt. Alex reached the end of the hallway and Brant lunged, grabbing the edge of Alex's boots. Alex kicked Brant's hand off with his other boot and scrambled forward on all fours. Brant pushed up and leapt after him. He squatted in preparation to tackle.

But rocked back on his heels instead.

Alex had ducked into the safe haven of the kitchen. He snarled at Brant from behind the knees of TrysKa, TrysKa welding a very large laser knife.

"Brant," TrysKa smiled tightly.

"Yes, ma'am?"

"Remove your stink from my kitchen."

"Yes, ma'am."

Brant sauntered backward to the hallway, keeping his eyes on Alex the whole time then pivoted and retreated to the shower. A massage of hot water would have been so soothing on his sore back, but a sterilizing beam was all he got.

Brant stepped out to the savory fragrance of beans and bread. He almost elbowed everyone aside for the food, but stopped himself by sheer willpower. Brant took his spot, last place in line, and dumped all the remains onto his plate.

Lunch was quiet.

"Good work today." Knox sterilized his dishes and put them up. "But we still have a lot left to do. We'll rest and regroup in a few hours."

Everyone else went to their rooms, and Brant stretched out on the bench. His muscles groaned. It had been a good game.

23

Holoconference

Call him old-fashioned, but Douglas hated holoconferences. Everyone insisted they were just as good as "in person" meetings. Everyone was wrong.

Around the horseshoe table sat three flesh-and-blood people. The rest were translucent transmissions. Most of them were high quality images, but a few flickered. It gave him a migraine, and made the whole conversation feel haunted.

To add insult to injury, the hologram attendees kept leaning back and talking to people Douglas couldn't see, or laughing at a joke told by someone on their side. And he couldn't do a blasted thing about it.

Three robots served the flesh-and-blood attendees a gourmet coffee.

"Would you like one too?" a robot asked the highest-ranking transmission.

"I'm not there." The irritation in the voice was music to Douglas.

"Of course, I'm so sorry."

When the robot turned to leave, its arm cut through the

hologram. The man jumped. Douglas took a sip of his latte to hide his smile. At least if he had to tolerate holoconferences, he could have some fun with them. The rest of the transmitted people stared longingly at the foam-topped black nectar. *Wait until the hors d'oeuvres came out.*

The conference droned on. Douglas pressed his opinions with charm and edge, but the effect was diminished. The threat of power lost something when he wasn't physically present.

Evie entered the meeting and skirted the projections. She wore a silver pantsuit, black pumps, and blood-red dangle earrings. Douglas didn't acknowledge her, but the flesh-and-blood attendees all turned. She handed Douglas a slip of paper.

They're IAS.

Two hours and thirty-seven minutes later, the last executive left and the last hologram powered down. Evie sat at a chair away from the table, virtual documents encircling her. Douglas touched the button inside his jacket pocket, and Evie collapsed her paperwork.

"IAS?" Douglas said. "How do you know?"

"At least one of them was," Evie said. "He had unaided night-vision. Another one moved with adapted speed and reflexes. The guns were unmarked, and they weren't in uniform, but..."

"One of them *was?* So at least one is finally killed?"

"One was killed, the rest escaped."

Evie fidgeted with her scroll. Evie never fidgeted.

"You know someone at IAS," Douglas said.

"Why would you..." She rolled her eyes at her attempt to hide from him. "Yes. But not personally."

"Who?"

She paused. This was technically none of his business.

"My friend's child was just accepted there. She's... excited."

"And scared."

"For obvious reasons."

Evie latched her scroll on her belt so she wouldn't be tempted to fidget with it further. She clasped her hands on her lap and cocked her head at Douglas.

"So, how do we stop Knox now?" she asked.

"We don't."

Evie blinked.

"It's personal for you now," Douglas said. "And this endeavor is no longer profitable. Let him have the stupid shields. We'll find a different way to survive any audits."

"You're going to let him win?"

She pronounced each word carefully, making it clear she didn't buy a bit of it. Douglas laughed.

"I'm a man of profit. Pursuing Knox will cost more than it gains. I'll let him have this hand. If he tries to steal something else from us, then I'll do a different profit/loss analysis. But this time, we both win."

"Really?"

"He gets his shields, and I write it off of my taxes." Douglas stood and pushed the button inside his jacket.

"Always good to work with you, Evie."

She stood and nodded. "Same here."

She walked to the door. It swished open, but she stood in its opening, not stepping forward.

"You know I didn't buy that little act."

With that, she left. Douglas stared at the closed door. She'd seen through his lies, insightful girl. That's why he kept dirt on Evie, to keep her loyal. Still, how many years since anyone had seen past his misdirection? Seen his soul? Not since his sister had died.

Douglas pulled out his scroll. Where would Knox target next? It could be anywhere. Knox would want shields that were unnecessary and unguarded. He'd target a different location from the previous ones. That left the supply warehouses that weren't owned by Caravan Suppliers.

Or the company's back-up databases. Those had frivolous shields. Along with the planet-side storehouses, but a lot of people milled around those. Maybe on the less populated planets?

Douglas could warn them all, but the inefficiency grated on his nerves. He could use Evie's insight right now. Her newfound affection for IAS was inconvenient. Douglas sent an order to his security company.

I've heard rumors of an attack on our back-up databases. Keep space fighters on stand-by. Attack any unauthorized vessels approaching.

Now his company was protected, but his suppliers? Douglas closed his scroll with a snap. They would have to fend for themselves.

He checked the time. Blast it all, he was late. Douglas fluffed his cravat and strolled to his next meeting. They could wait for him.

24

A New Trap

Mac stood at attention, but his head hung low. The faded stairwell lights traced his penitent silhouette. He'd failed.

Ophelia ladled quinoa from a bucket into Juliette's outstretched bowl. The girl took her bowl to her lap and ate quietly. Ophelia approached the next child lined up against the cold wall. Not until she stood before him did he extend his bowl. Grabbing brought discipline. They'd all learned that lesson well.

"It wasn't just Knox," MacBeth whispered to Teacher.

Ophelia tilted her head while she scooped and poured. Her adapted ears picked up their hushed words.

"He had a team of trained soldiers."

"I wasn't told about that," the Teacher said.

"I accept punishment for my failure, but I thought—" MacBeth took in a shaky breath. "I thought you would want to know for future plans."

"You thought correctly."

Ophelia reached the last child and ventured a glance over her shoulder. Teacher squeezed Mac's shoulders, but her older brother didn't relax.

"I think, since we were both deceived, we can forgo correction in this case."

MacBeth's head snapped up, but his eyes immediately cast back down, in reverence.

"Thank you."

From the quiver in his voice, he meant it. Ophelia turned her back on them. Hopefully Teacher hadn't noticed her eavesdropping. Her empty stomach soured at that thought. She strode down the line of brothers and sisters to her spot, trying to appear innocent and confident. She sat cross-legged and foraged with her spoon for morsels from the bottom of the bucket.

When the last child finished, the group stood and in a single file line, deposited their licked clean bowls into her bucket. She rose to fill it with soapy hot water, but was stopped by Teacher's call.

"Ophelia!"

She leapt up.

"Lorenzo, Katerina, Antonio, Hero, Malcolm, Beatrice, Cleon, and Benedick!"

Ophelia clasped her hands behind her, and marched in line to him. Had she been caught? The scars on her back started to itch again. Could she help that her adapted ears overheard conversations?

"I was deceived by the Supplier," the Teacher said.

The others gasped at the audacity. Ophelia sighed that she wasn't in trouble.

"Knox has hired a team to protect him. As such we need a team to defeat him." He spread his arms wide and beamed down on them. "You are my team."

Everyone stood taller under his admiration.

"What about the Supplier's payment?" Ophelia wished she could reel the words back in the instant they slipped out.

She stared at the floor, her hands clammy. The Teacher strolled and stopped before her, his boots entering the top of her vision. He slipped a scarred finger under her chin and tenderly lifted.

"Wise question."

Ophelia's muscles released their tension so quickly, her knees nearly buckled. He wasn't angry with her.

"We don't work for free, do we?" he asked.

Ophelia shook her head.

"If the Supplier needs a team, then he will have to pay for a team."

Then we can buy more food!

Her brothers and sisters would be fed for weeks with the income earned from this job. Ophelia smiled bigger than she could ever remember smiling. Teacher cupped her face.

"Sweet daughter."

He returned to Mac. "Where will you hunt this Knox next?"

"He visits one spaceport regularly. We'll find hiding places there and wait."

"Go. Finish your job." Teacher's voice softened. "And come home safely, you and all those I've trusted to your care." He rested his hand on Ophelia's silky black hair.

"Yes, sir," Mac said and ascended the stairs.

Ophelia and her brothers and sisters fell in line.

25

Databank Shield

An alarm woke TrysKa from her nap with a jolt. She ran out of her room and found Ximena in the cargo bay, putting hover-brackets on the corners of the remaining generator.

"Let me help you," TrysKa lifted up one of its corners.

"Clear," Knox said from the cockpit.

The alarm silenced, but it's echo still rang in TrysKa's head.

"Atienna's here for the second generator," Knox said as he ran into the cargo bay.

Brant lumbered in next, still weaving a little as he woke up. Alex rolled out of his cabinet-bed and rubbed his puffy eyes with his fists.

"Who?" Alex yawned.

The ramp lowered, and its opening framed a woman standing tall in the Taluk's field of jowar stalks. She swept onto the ship.

"Ah, Little Knox, Daima nzuri ya kuona wewe," Atienna said in Swahili. *Ah, Little Knox, always good to see you.*

TrysKa, Brant, and Alex all startled. Knox cleared his throat.

"Just Knox," he said.

"Of course, of course. So business-like," she pointed to several people gathered behind her. "Here is the generator and photocells. Load it onto the truck."

Five workers, all wearing the Serving Hands blue shirt with logo, boarded the ship and grabbed the generator and photocells. Everything felt rushed and unplanned. Even Knox looked a little rattled at strangers just helping themselves to his ship, but he kept his calm.

"Crew," Knox motioned. "This is long-time family friend and Senior Coordinator for Serving Hands, Ruth Atienna Kamathi."

She knit her brow. "So fussy. Just call me Atienna. Sorry we're in such a hurry."

"We were going to bring the generator later today and install it," Knox said. "Did something happen?"

"A ship flew overhead of Openyenge just now. I need those shields operational."

"Do you need my help?" Ximena asked. "To get the equipment to talk to each other?"

"I have a technician," Atienna said as she walked down the ramp in long strides. "Called in a favor from another friend. What I need from you is that last shield generator. We can't wait any longer."

"Understood." Knox hit the controls to close the ramp and signaled for everyone to gather at the table. TrysKa got her hot cup of coffee and sat next to Ximena.

"As much as we do need to hurry," Knox said. "We never had a debriefing."

He placed the holoball in the center of the table, and the fateful island haunted the air. The room fell so silent that TrysKa could hear the light whirr of *Maverick*'s air vent. Her eyes went straight to the hill where Sann had...

"I've gone back over the video footage," Knox said, "and found this."

Knox pushed play. A ship flew over the house, and the feed flickered. Ximena's hand flew to her mouth.

"Oh no! Oh no no no no!"

She buried her face in her hands.

"Did I miss something?" Brant asked.

TrysKa wrapped her arm around Ximena's shoulder. "Did you see the image flicker?"

"Yeah."

"That means someone accessed the camera and changed its feed."

Knox turned off the holoball. "The camera recorded a fake feed while all those guards dropped in and hid. That's why we didn't know they were there."

"But how did they figure out someone had dropped a camera at all?" Brant asked.

"They were looking for it," Knox said. "Must have guessed I would attack that island."

"How?"

"I'm not the only one good at strategy."

Ice shivered down TrysKa's spine. Then guilt hit and hit hard. "They laid a trap for us at the warehouse too, where we tried to steal the first shield, oh, I should have told you."

Could it have saved Sann's life? If she'd only told Knox sooner, would everyone still be alive? TrysKa was going to throw up.

"TrysKa, what did you see?" Knox's tone was unusually soft.

"In the hangar, next to the shield generator, there was a

cluster of tree samples in pots, and more than seven guards around it. I thought it was odd-"

"It was," Knox said. "Shipments like live trees would be held in a safe containment area, not out on the open hangar floor."

"That's what I thought too, but then Alex escaped, and I got distracted, and I didn't think to mention it."

"It's not your fault," Ximena said and squeezed TrysKa's hand. "And it wouldn't have changed what happened on that island."

"But-"

"Knox planned the best he could. He suspected a trap, he always suspects a trap," Ximena said. "But even so, he couldn't have planned for the sheer force of guards that were planted there."

"All of this confirms that Caravan Suppliers knows I'm stealing generators," Knox said.

"That's not good," Brant said. He stared back at the projection. "Where did you plan to get the next one?"

"The same way I stole the first. Wait for a call from a Caravan storage station, and steal it without anyone noticing."

"That won't work anymore," Ximena said.

"No, it won't, but that's why I made contingency plans."

"What are content, congen, congency," Alex twisted his mouth and nose. "Con. Ten. Gen. See plans."

With all the built-up tension, Alex's antics made TrysKa giggle despite herself. It felt undignified and completely out of place, yet everyone around the table seemed to breathe easier. Even Knox's mouth twitched with a thin grin.

"Back-up plans," Knox answered Alex's question.

"A database station to be exact," Ximena said. "The tower

is built on an uninhabitable moon. It's not in any of the Six Planets' systems."

"What's it for?" asked Alex.

"A place to back-up all of Caravan Supplier's shipment information," Ximena said. "And communications, video recordings, everything."

Why does it need shields then? TrysKa took a breath to ask, but Brant jumped in first.

"Why does it have shields?" he asked. "If the moon's uninhabited, it's not like thieves are breaking down the doors."

"Standard design practice," Ximena sneered. "Caravan Suppliers doesn't want to pay a firm to design every individual hub, so they get a one-size-fits-all over-design that will work for every location."

"And pay for unnecessary shields?"

"Cheaper than paying a design team each time."

That's wasteful. TrysKa opened her mouth to say so, but Knox spoke first.

"The shield covers the communications tower and some of the land around it," he said. "There's plenty of space to land *Maverick* next to the structure."

"How do we get inside the shields?" Brant asked.

"My Phase Burner," Ximena said. "We used one while you were fighting in the bar."

Finally, TrysKa had her chance.

"It looked like a spider."

That was her contribution? It's a spider?

"OK, sounds good. What's the gravity on that planet?" Brant asked. "Will we be crushed?"

"It's 0.95 Gs," Ximena said. "We'll be safe to land."

"But it'll take me a while to load up a generator," Brant said. "Along with the photocells."

"Can I say something *please*?" TrysKa blurted out.

She sounded like a preschooler begging for her turn. Conversation stopped. Everyone stared. TrysKa pulled her feet under her chair and hunched her shoulders.

"Sorry. I interrupted."

"That's the only way to get a word in edgewise these days." Knox cut his eyes at Brant and Alex. To TrysKa, "What you got?"

She had nothing. Really, it wasn't an earth-shattering idea. *Speak up! Why do you still think you're ideas aren't good enough?*

A lifetime of being invisible couldn't be rewritten in just a few days. Still, TrysKa took a deep breath and set her feet back to the floor.

"Most transports have a cargo cable for loading the heavy stuff." She paused, expecting someone to cut her off. No one did. "We could use that to load the generator. I assume *Maverick* has one?"

Ximena smiled so big her cheeks looked like they would pop. "Oh, *Maverick* has a cable all right. I even tweaked it."

"Shot right through a box of mantle mud once," Knox said. "Sh-stuff everywhere."

"Hey! That was a test run. I fixed it. Eventually." She turned back to TrysKa. "My cable can hit freight twenty meters away, surround it with shields, and yank it back onto the ship."

"So, Brant could use that without having to step onto the moon's surface," TrysKa said. "He'd still have to wear a spacesuit, but it should load the cargo quickly."

"Brilliant," Knox said.

TrysKa's face flushed hot. *Brilliant.* Her family had never said that, nor anyone at IAS for that matter.

"Brant." Knox pointed at him. "You'll man the cable. Alex, you'll use our gravitational bolt gun to shoot bolts at the photocells."

Alex grinned a demonic smile. *Maybe trusting Alex with a bolt shooter wasn't the best idea?* Before TrysKa opened her mouth to say as much, Knox pressed on.

"Ximena, you man the guns just in case we have company. Stations, everyone."

The tennis match of a conversation had left TrysKa almost breathless, but she needed to say one last thing.

"Ximena?"

Her friend spun back to face TrysKa. "Yes?"

"I bought a ginger pill for your motion sickness." She pointed to the medicine cabinet. "Let me-"

"I'm fine, and we're in a hurry."

Ximena turned her back to TrysKa and started her climb down the ladder to the gunnery.

"But," TrysKa whispered to herself, "I got it just for you."

Knox put his hand on TrysKa's shoulder. "She's one of those people who has to decide to do something on her own. She'll get there."

TrysKa resigned herself to her pilot's chair. Her fingers put in the request for flight coordinates as Knox settled into the co-pilot's chair.

"I'm one of those people too." Knox powered up the front guns. "You ready for this?"

"I trained for this."

"But have you ever shot a ship down before?"

"No, and I won't have to today."

That got Knox's attention. He stared at TrysKa and chewed on her answer. She launched *Maverick* and flew the assigned flight pattern through the landing dock. The ship entered the confined air lock. The pumps sucked the atmosphere out of the air lock, creating a vacuum that strained the hull.

"Do you need my help?" Knox asked.

What? No argument?

Maybe her family had over-ruled her desires more than she realized. Or perhaps IAS had tried to guilt her into specializing in covert land ops instead of piloting. Whatever the reason, this trust from Knox still felt foreign and undeserved.

But it shouldn't.

"I've got this," TrysKa said, staring out the viewscreen at the stars beyond the energy barrier.

"Alright then."

He had faith in her. The barrier to outer space dropped, and *Maverick* exited the air lock. It entered wide open space, nothing holding it back.

"Unmute," Knox said. "Engineer, you ready?"

"Oh shoot!" Footsteps ran to the breakroom. "Engineer ready," Ximena said over the earbud.

Knox cut his eyes at TrysKa and growled, but she held his gaze.

"Ximena does a lot right," she said. "All you have to complain about is that she forgets her earbud from time to time."

Knox grunted. "Alpha, ready?" he asked.

"Alpha ready!" Alex shouted over the earbud.

"Bravo, ready?"

"Bravo ready."

TrysKa followed the flight path away from the spaceport

with Knox's trust in her back pocket. The ship jumped. The universe collapsed to a pinprick and exploded back.

Knox sucked in his breath. TrysKa had dropped the ship so close to the moon, it filled the screen. Her eyes could trace individual craters along its surface. But the proximity wasn't accidental. She needed gravity's help.

Her controls beeped, and three dots appeared on the 3D grid. Fighters. TrysKa banked hard starboard. A flurry of shots grazed the ship's shields. TrysKa hit the speed. Brant grunted over her earbud. Alex yelped.

"Hold on back there!" Knox said.

Shots vibrated the floor. Ximena was returning fire.

TrysKa's hands reached into the holographic controls before her. Her adapted touch melded with the ship around her. She felt the wakes of the fighters on *Maverick's* tail, the gravitational grasp of the moon below, the rending and tearing of the vacuum above her. Tiny particles sliced along the shields, itching her skin, as *Maverick* barreled forward.

The fighters lined up aft of the ship and readied the kill shots that would take down its defenses. Knox's fists balled, but he didn't grab the guns. Even now, he trusted her. When everyone else in her life would have yanked control back, Knox trusted her. TrysKa increased the shield strength to the port side, and banked hard left.

"Brilliant." Knox had figured it out.

TrysKa cut straight across the moon's atmosphere instead of following the curvature of its surface. Her ship didn't enter the atmosphere by much, maybe only a meter, but it was enough. The moon's gravity reached out its claws, hooking *Maverick* and the fighters. TrysKa transferred power back to the forward shields and allowed gravity to reel her in. She pointed *Maverick* toward the surface and began her descent.

"Brace for atmospheric entry," she said.

"At these speeds?" Brant yelled back.

"The ship can handle it, and so can I!"

But the fighters weren't designed like *Maverick*. They were designed for space travel only, vacuum only. They'd made the most common mistake, a mistake that had "killed" many of the other IAS pilots in the simulations. *Never forget gravity*, her instructors hounded them afterwards. It's the invisible killer.

A fireball consumed the first fighter, and it fell. The other two fought to pull up, but their blasters didn't have enough power. Across the horizon they streaked, shredding and igniting. Falling stars.

"If they'd left us alone, they'd be fine," TrysKa said.

Her hands were steady, but her voice quivered.

"You done good," Knox said.

The surface rushed to meet the ship, and TrysKa steadied *Maverick's* descent. Ship and pilot were one, and the crew was safe under their wing.

#

In the cargo bay, Brant held Alex close. They both looked like shiny shadows in their black slick suits with goggles. As soon as the ship settled on solid ground, Alex pushed away from Brant. His feet were bolted to the floor, so he fell back on his bottom. Ximena had shackled Brant and Alex's ankles to the floor so they wouldn't get sucked out.

Alex stood and heaved Ximena's pipe gun up into his arms. A compressor stuck to one end of the fat white pipe with a bunch of wires crawling up and down it. If Alex pegged Brant in the back of the head with a magnetic bolt, he'd probably be knocked out.

Brant punched the controls to lower the ramp. The ship's alarm wailed as green fog rolled into the cargo bay. Yuck! Good thing the door to the rest of the ship was latched shut.

"Here comes the Phase Burner," Ximena said.

The robotic ladybug curled up in the corner took flight and fluttered out. It didn't hover smoothly, but hopped on the air. It bobbed out of the cargo bay, into the green fog, and landed on the shield like a gangly dragonfly on a leaf. An antenna with a blinking red light stuck out of the tiny insect. *Blink, blink, blink, bonk.* The Phase Burner fell to the ground as the shimmer of the shields disappeared. It incinerated in a puff of smoke, and blew off in the foul wind.

Now what?

In answer, a panel above Brant opened. He startled and tried to set his feet, but the bolts held fast. He grabbed the edge of the doorframe on his way down and managed to break his fall.

Out of the opening a mechanical arm lowered a cannon in front of Brant. He grabbed the handles on both sides and the whole assembly sprang to his touch. With ease, Brant swiveled the large barrel right, left, up, down. *Ooooh.* He got the same thrill in his gut that the speed of a classic hovercar gave. Or Amalie's blush.

Brant aimed the big gun at the first photocell. He pulled and held the trigger down. The cannon vibrated then recoiled as the cable shot. Wow, it had a kick!

A shield popped around the photocell. Brant searched the cannon and found a red button for his right thumb. Would this reel the cable back in? Probably should have gotten instructions before take-off. He pressed it.

The cell zipped back at the cargo bay door. With adapted

reflexes, Brant pulled his blaster, flipped it to pressure wave, and shot the photocell before it hit Alex, who had squatted over his pinned feet. Alex launched a mag bolt at the flying box and down it dropped to the floor with a whack! Hopefully these things were built sturdy. The machine sucked the metal cord back in.

Zip!

Brant captured the next photocell. It careened straight at his nose. Brant pressure shot it, and Alex fired a mag bolt in sync. Shoot cannon, haul cell, fire blaster, launch mag bolt, repeat. A terrifying game of flinging boxes.

"This is awesome!!!!" Alex said.

Brant's smile stretched ear to ear. He'd pulled in all the photocells, leaving just one last, big cube of wires and tubes. He aimed for the shield generator.

"Time's up!" Knox yelled in Brant's earbud. "Back-ups have arrived, and they can enter the atmosphere."

"Give me a few more seconds, and I can get the generator!"

"Close the ramp, Bravo! We're taking off."

And the ship lurched to the sky. Brant punched the ramp controls.

"Ramp closing."

"Tell us when it's sealed. We can't leave the atmosphere until it is."

Maverick flew through the upper atmosphere. The green fog thinned out. The door's gap shrunk.

Only inches.

Good enough.

"Take to space, TK!"

Brant grabbed Alex as the ship hurtled upwards. Fire scratched along the shields and glared through the slit of the still open ramp. The glow narrowed to a wedge then a paper-thin crack then click. The ramp closed.

Alex clutched the pipe gun to his chest. Plasma shots thundered from the floor as Ximena returned fire. The ship rolled, and the floor and ceiling traded places. Brant and Alex both squatted to keep stable. Artificial gravity blipped only to catch up at the worst time. His body felt crushed from every side, and Brant thanked God he had an iron stomach.

Then he hiccupped. *Maverick* had jumped.

Alex clutched Brant for a few more seconds. The vents hissed, cleaning out the poison and filling the cargo bay with breathable air. Brant released Alex, and they both stood. Black swam on the edges of Brant's vision, but before he passed out, the meds entered his system. Alex's knees were shaking.

"You OK, buddy?" Brant asked as he peeled off the headgear of his spacesuit.

"Yeah," Alex said.

"Hey, ya did good."

"Thanks."

Alex stretched his mask above his head, and the suction released with a *slurp*. His curls plopped out over his forehead. Brant unlocked the bolts from his ankles and then Alex's. They chucked them across the cargo bay.

The cargo bay doors opened in time for Brant to see Ximena run from the gunnery ladder to the bathroom. She sounded like she was emptying meals from the whole of last week. Even TrysKa turned green like she was going to sympathy puke, and she was a pilot. Oh, that smell. Nothing could describe that smell. Brant and Alex both covered their noses. Knox groaned low.

"OK, everybody else gets to hide in their bedrooms until I

knock."

TrysKa gave one backward, apologetic glance at Knox. He waved her on.

"I got this."

Alex high-tailed it into Brant's room followed closely by Brant. The boy slung his body up on the top bunk. Every nine-year-old knows the top bunk is the coolest. In the thrill of the moment, he hadn't noticed Sann's rifle on the bottom mattress. Brant leaned against the closed door and kept his attention on the beaming boy.

"That was awesome!" Alex punched the ceiling. "The photocells were flying." He held out his arms. "And then I'd shoot them." He aimed the imaginary gun and squeezed the trigger over and over. "Bang! Bang! Bang!"

Brant's cheeks stretched in a crinkled grin. Something in his chest ached to smile that big.

"Good shooting," Brant agreed.

Alex slid his hands behind his head, but then his bushy eyebrows scrunched in that grown-up way that looked so out-of-place on his soft face.

"Sorry I was such a jerk to you."

Brant caught his breath. He didn't want to look too eager to be friends. Alex might change his mind and return to being a brat.

"Don't worry about it. We're good."

But Alex's eyes misted over. "Are we good?"

Brant said nothing.

"She was fighting," Alex said. He rubbed his nose on his sleeve.

"Your mom?"

"Until you visited her, she was fighting the cancer, fighting

266

to live, fighting for me. After you told her you would take care of me..."

Alex's mom had died only a few days after Brant had visited. It had never occurred to him that the reason she let go was because she knew Alex would be OK. All this time, Alex had blamed Brant for his mom's death. No wonder the kid was upset.

Brant crossed his arms on the bunk and rested his chin on his biceps.

"I'm so sorry, Alex."

"Don't be," Alex hiccuped. "She doesn't hurt anymore."

Alex blinked rapidly and hiccuped again. Brant turned his head away. Alex needed privacy, but that was hard to do in a tiny bedroom. The boy sniffed a few more times and rubbed snot on the pillow. As Brant watched Alex snuggle up on Sann's bunk, and idea popped into his head.

"Hey kid, you want a bigger room?"

Alex looked like Brant had offered him a bowl full of candy. "Really? I mean, are you OK with that?"

Brant paused for a second and stared at his reflection in the metal wall behind Alex's bunk. Was he OK with it? Brant did not sleep well on the uncomfortable table bench, and a roommate might not be bad for Alex.

The problem was Sann's remains and gun. Who was going to carry them to Alex's room? Brant couldn't ask Alex to do it for him. The wait dragged on, and Alex fidgeted.

"Yeah, I'm OK with it," Brant said. "Let's move," deep breath, "a few things."

Brant backed up agains the wall and stared at the precious contents on the bottom bunk. There lay Sann's remains gathered in a jar, with his gun resting beside. Brant inhaled as he knelt down. Seconds ticked by, and Alex shuffled on the bed. Brant set his jaw and lifted Sann's remains like he was cradling a newborn.

"Where's your bed?" His voice choked.

Alex hopped down from the top bunk and led the way to the cargo bay and a long, low storage compartment.

"It has a latch." Alex squatted. "So I can open it from the inside."

He popped the door open. Brant knelt next to Alex's "room." A sleeping bag had been stuffed into the storage cabinet, and clothes crumpled at one end. As Alex watched Brant tenderly place Sann's remains into his modest room, his face flushed red.

"Never mind, you can't leave Sann's stuff here, I'm sorry." It came out in a rush.

"No," Brant whispered firmly. "You don't need to be sleeping in a storage compartment when there's a room available."

With the reluctance of shutting a coffin, Brant closed the compartment door. He rose, and a knot stuck in his throat. Brant opened his mouth to speak then closed it. Instead, he put his hand on Alex's curls and bent his head towards the hall.

Ximena and Knox emerged from his captain's quarters. She limped down the hall towards the galley, but Knox did a half-turn back to face Brant and Alex in the cargo bay.

"Coast is clear," Knox said.

Or at least the contents of Ximena's stomach. Alex started peeling off his spacesuit. Brant tiptoed into the break room, and watched as Knox sat down and wrapping his arm around a pale-lipped Ximena. She moaned, and her stomach gurgled.

TrysKa slipped around Brant into the kitchen.

"Oh, you poor thing," she whispered.

"TrysKa," Knox asked. "You wouldn't happen to have a magic brew that settles stomachs, would you?"

"Magic brew coming right up."

"You're an angel."

TrysKa began concocting as Brant turned back to the cargo bay. Alex was stripped down to his undies, sitting on a photocell, his suit wadded below his feet. He laughed while Brant, muttering under his breath, wriggled out of his suit. With one last mighty stretch, the suit popped off his feet and slapped his arm.

"Get dressed!" Knox called from the break room. "We still have a generator to get."

Brant ran to his bedroom and stuffed his legs into pants while trying not to bang up his knees. He grabbed a shirt and wrestled into it as he stumbled down the hall. No sooner had he pulled it over his chest than a dressed Alex zipped past him.

"Your shirt's on backward," Brant said.

Alex stopped and pulled out his collar to check. Brant brushed by and sat down at the bench.

"Made you look."

Alex stuck his tongue out and joined everyone around the table. Knox darkened the lights, and turned on a hologram of a compound. Miniature metal storehouses lined-up in a grid on top of the table.

"Easy," Brant said. "We fly *Maverick* in, and plop a Phase Burner on the warehouse shields." Brant poked his finger at the buildings. "Stun a bunch of guards, and steal the backup generator."

"I was planning a more subtle approach," Knox said.

Brant clasped his hands on the table, and did his best impersonation of a student hanging on his teacher's every word. Did the corner of Knox's mouth twitch in a smile?

"OK, Captain Knox," Brant said. "What you got in mind?"

Knox definitely smiled.

26

The Warehouse

Using a fake ship ID and calling in a favor from a contact, Knox landed *Maverick* on the planet Aurora. Conveniently, the warehouse had a landing pad out back.

"So, ships sneaking in here is normal, I take it?" Brant asked from behind a pile of crates.

"Aye," Knox answered.

He punched the button, and the ramp lowered. Knox strode down it to meet the warehouse lackey. Brant waited at the top with the fake supplies. From his height, he could just see over the roof of the nearest warehouse, a metal box with a huge sliding door. Behind it, row after row of the gray buildings lined up like prison cells. Brant squinted and looked away from the sun glinting off their surfaces.

"We didn't have any shipments scheduled for today," the flunky said, flipping through his paper records.

Who uses paper anymore?

Knox shrugged his broad shoulders. "I just deliver what I'm told."

That was Brant's cue. He guided the crates down the ramp,

careful not to jostle them.

"So where do I put them?" Brant asked Knox.

"Where? We didn't order them yet!" The wind blew a few of his pages away and he went lumbering after them.

"Perfect timing," Knox said and motioned with his head. "Go in. Quick."

Brant pushed the pile of boxes, almost as tall as himself, inside the dark of the warehouse. The temperature shot up to stifling. No breeze wound its way through the corridors in this metal oven.

"Which way?" Brant asked the empty hallway.

"Turn right," Alex said in his earbud.

Brant pivoted the pile around then evenly accelerated. No sudden movements.

"Why are you ordering me around instead of Ximena?"

"It's fun," Alex said. "And she lost her earbud again. At least she's not puking. *What?*" Alex yelled, but thankfully the earbud adjusted the volume down. He must have been talking to Ximena on the ship. "Oh, OK, I'll tell her. Ximena says: Thank you, TrysKa, for making me take the motion sickness meds."

Brant rolled his eyes while he walked. Behind the closed door to his left, his adapted hearing picked up muffled sounds like a hundred fans.

"I hear something," he said. "What is that?"

"It's a big open area," Ximena said, joining the conversation. "The workers must be in there."

Workers? No, slaves. Brant grit his teeth and pushed the crates past the door. Down the hallway, a man in company overalls stepped out around a corner.

"¿Quién eres tú?" he asked. *Who are you?*

"Delivery guy," Brant said. "Where does this junk go?"

The employee rolled his eyes and grumbled. "This is my break." But he pointed. "Down the hall, second left."

Brant followed the directions, past another door that sounded like it housed more workers, and finally arrived at a large storage room piled high with opened boxes. Brant's feet cleared a path through the energy bar wrappers and yeastahol drink cartons littering the floor. The enclosed area reeked of rotten fish.

Another uniformed guy popped out around a mound of crates. "What are you doing here?"

His pants were crisply ironed with a colorful emblem over the pocket.

"Delivery," Brant said, and lowered a box to the ground. "One of these goes to the other storage room."

Brant leaned over to look at the barcodes on the sides of the crates. They didn't mean anything to him, but he could pretend.

"Not this one." He took a crate the size of a shoebox off the largest bottom crate. "Maybe this one."

"There is no other storage room," the supply guy said.

"Yeah, there is." Brant spun the bottom crate, the one TrysKa was hiding inside, until he could see the barcode. "This one. It goes into the room with all the energy stuff."

"Energy stuff?"

"Batteries, tools, extra techno gadgets. I don't know what it's called."

"The maintenance closet," the supply guy said like he'd just guessed the answer to a crossword puzzle. "Our replacement compressor for the air coolers finally arrived. I got it, you can go."

273

The supply guy took the crate from Brant and shooed him out of the door. All part of the plan.

Brant sauntered back the way he had come while the supply guy went in the opposite direction with the chosen box. He turned the corner and lounged against the outer wall. Ouch! It scalded his back. Brant leaned against an inner wall instead. Still hot, but not enough to burn him. He was now alone in the corridor.

"How's it going out there?" he asked.

"Knox is still haggling," Ximena said.

"And TrysKa?"

"I'm watching her," Alex answered. "It looks like she stopped moving."

Since he couldn't pace, Brant counted to pass the time. At twenty-three seconds, TrysKa came over his earbud.

"All clear, you can come now."

Brant retraced his steps to the supply room and past it. "Where's the maintenance closet?"

"The tracer on the crate is straight ahead then one right," Ximena said. "All the way at the end."

Brant turned the corner to see the supply guy stunned and propped against the wall at the far end. Wires, rusted boxes of tools, and broken bulbs lay scattered around the closet door.

Brant ran up and stepped over a pile only to be handed an armful of junk.

"Take this," TrysKa said.

If the warehouse was hot for Brant, TK had it worse stuffed in that crate. Her hair, pulled back in a ponytail, had frizzed then plastered to her sweaty forehead and neck. She looked like a baseball that busted its seams.

Inside the closet, the back-up shield generator hugged the

back wall.

"Did he see you?" Brant asked as he set aside the robo-vacuum she'd passed to him.

"Nope." TrysKa lifted an exposed corner of the generator and placed a hover-bracket.

"Good." For the benefit of those listening by his earbud, Brant said, "We found the generator."

"Perfect," Ximena said. "Because Knox can't stall him much longer."

"And Brant," Alex said. "You don't have to talk louder when you're talking to us."

Brant whispered. "Shut up. Did you hear that?"

"Loud and clear, Loud-mouth."

Brat. But at least Alex had stayed on *Maverick* instead of sneaking out in a crate. TrysKa got the second hover-bracket on and wiped her curls out of her face.

"I'm going to climb on top of this thing," she said. "Can you pull it out a little so I can reach behind it?"

"Sure thing."

TrysKa hoisted one leg then the other onto the generator, and Brant grabbed the handle bars on the side. As he inched the thing back, Brant studied the wires and coils of the machine to avoid looking at TrysKa's hind side. Her sweat had plastered down her clothes as well as her hair, and she did have lovely curves. But those curves weren't any of Brant's business.

TrysKa's arms stretched behind the generator, then her head disappeared followed by her torso.

"Umm, Brant?"

"Yeah?"

Brant winced. He knew what was coming and could tell from TrysKa's tone that it was going to be as awkward for her as him.

"I need you to lift this left back corner somehow."

"OK."

How on New Terra was he going to do this? Brant closed his eyes. Probably not the best idea, but he couldn't help it. His left hand groped down the side of the generator until it found the back corner. His right hand felt past her ankles to the front right corner. He squatted and pressed his boots into the floor.

Big breath. Lift!

TrysKa attached a bracket. "Got it."

Brant's sweaty palms lost traction. The corner hit the floor. *Smack!*

"Brant!"

"Sorry. Did I hurt you?"

"I'm fine."

TrysKa's feet shimmied to the other side. Brant assumed the rest of her followed, but he couldn't exactly tell. He was busy clearing the other wall to make room for himself.

"OK, I'm ready," TrysKa said. Her voice sounded pinched, like hanging upside-down had swollen her throat.

"Here we go," he said.

Again Brant floundered around TrysKa's legs for the hand-holds, and his fair face flushed even hotter than it already was. He'd blame the blush on exertion and heat. That was it.

Set feet. Big breath. Lift!

"Done," she said.

Brant released slower this time. He backed out of the closet to let TrysKa wriggle out in privacy. His head was down, so he wasn't prepared when the generator, TrysKa and all, shot out of the closet straight at him.

"Whoa." He hugged the machine and stared straight into TrysKa's golden eyes.

"Since it was already hovering, I thought this would be easier," she said.

"Yup."

She cleared her throat. "That was awkward."

"Yup."

"Thanks for not, you know, being a jerk."

"Yup."

What else could he say? TrysKa hopped down and shoved some junk back into the closet.

"I got it," Brant said.

After all, he'd had lots of practice cramming his stuff into cabinets in his dorm all those years. Time to put that skill to good use. That, and he still couldn't make eye contact with TK. Brant shoved everything back inside while TrysKa guided the floating generator out of the way. He closed the door with a flourish.

"Tah-da!"

TrysKa silent-clapped for him. She'd taken the bottom off the crate she'd hidden in, turned it upside-down, and lowered it over the generator. It looked like just another shipment.

"Where are you?" Knox's voice came over the earbud. "Dicking off in the breakroom?"

Brant jumped forward like he'd been stabbed with a cattle prod. He sped the disguised generator down the hallway and TrysKa kept pace.

"I delivered the crates, waiting for orders," Brant said.

"I shouldn't have to tell you to come back after delivering crates," Knox said. He performed angry boss authentically, but then, he'd had a lifetime of training for the part.

"I'm not the brains," Brant said. "You are."

"Obviously. But bring all the crates back with you. This—" Knox paused. Brant could see Knox's face making clear exactly which word he wanted to use. "Professional businessman won't pay us."

"Sure, boss."

TrysKa ducked into the big storage room and grabbed their original crates. She chunked them onto the big one. Brant opened one for her to hide inside, but she didn't budge.

"Umm, TK?"

She looked over her shoulder, longingly, at one of the doors that trapped the workers.

"We don't have time," Brant said.

"Time for what?" Ximena said over the earbud.

"Mute," TrysKa said so no one could eavesdrop. "Brant, I have to free some of them while we're here. I can't just walk away and do nothing."

"Mute," Brant said, turning off his earbud too. "But we are doing something. We're getting this shield and..." Brant sighed. "There are going to be guards in there. We would have to stun them."

"I know." TrysKa pursed her lips. "But there are also people captured in there. They're being worked to death and just want to go home to their families."

Brant held up his hand. "Just wanted to make sure we were on the same page. Unmute."

"TrysKa? Brant? Are you there?" Ximena asked. "What's going on?"

"Unmute," TrysKa said. "Be prepared for some extra passengers."

"Knox was right," Alex said, probably to Ximena.

If Brant was honest, it was killing him too. He couldn't walk past those doors without giving freedom to a few.

"Quick," Brant said.

"Give Knox an excuse for stalling," Ximena said.

"Where are you?" Knox said over the earbud in a tone that nearly sent Brant racing to follow orders.

"Sorry, sir. Some of the crates were unpacked, sir. Going as fast as I can, sir."

Brant sold the performance in case the manager was listening in. Knox let fly a string of obscenities that would get him in trouble with Ximena later.

Brant sent the crates sailing to the end of hallway. TrysKa took one side of the last worker's door, her gun drawn, and Brant the other.

She nodded. He nodded. She tapped the controls. Nothing. Locked.

"Now what?" Brant asked.

TrysKa pulled one of Ximena's Sneaks out of her pocket and squished it to the panel. *How did she know to have that thing with her? Oh. This wasn't spur of the moment. TrysKa had planned to free some all along.*

The Sneak beeped, and she scooped it back into her pants pocket, a little lump on her hip. The only reason Brant hadn't seen it before was because he'd kept closing his eyes.

"Ready?" she said.

"Ready."

TrysKa tapped the controls, and the door opened. Brant stunned the two guards in his line of sight while TrysKa stunned another in her trajectory. Brant entered low as heat from plasma shots rolled over his head. A pause in the fire.

Brant stood, took down three in quick succession. TrysKa

ran in behind him and felled the last one in the far corner. They switched and stood back to back.

"Clear," she said.

"Clear."

"Uh oh."

The hallways had been so narrow, and the supply room and maintenance closet so tight, that Brant had forgotten how massive the warehouse was. The production floor spread before him like the main gym back at IAS, packed wall-to-wall with people. All skin tones, all ages, children, men, pregnant women, elderly. Easily two hundred if not more.

No way all those people were fitting onto *Maverick*. And, because life can always get more complicated, the alarms started wailing.

"That's our cue!" Brant yelled over the noise.

TrysKa raced out the door and led the way. Brant barreled the generator and crates down the hallway. He turned the last corner and jumped over the prone body of another worker. TrysKa must have stunned him. Sunlight burst into his vision as Brant shot out of the warehouse toward the ship.

Knox yelled something in TrysKa's ear. She nodded and bounded into the ship to the cockpit. Knox pointed Brant up the ramp.

Brant didn't need any more urging. He steamrolled those crates up into the cargo bay and slammed them, generator and all, against the wall. Behind him the crowd billowed in and around him. He didn't have room to breathe. Where was Knox?

Brant box-jumped onto the shipments and scanned the heads. There. Knox waited next to the ramp, pressed against the wall.

"We're full!" Knox yelled over the screaming alarm and shouting workers.

Brant's stomach balled tight, but Knox was right. There was no more room. Brant rammed his way through the packed bodies to the edge of the ramp. Knox pulled his gun, set to pressure wave, and nodded. Brant switched his to pressure too.

Together they shot a wave at the people, knocking them back. A strangled cry rose from the crowd and rolled over them, wrenching Brant's heart. He winced and stepped back. He couldn't do this.

More people ran back up the ramp, but they had nowhere to go. A hand gripped Brant's shoulder. He faced Knox and saw both the pain in Knox's eyes and the resolute set of his jaw. Brant wasn't alone.

Again Knox nodded. Brant clenched his teeth and set his feet. Standing shoulder-to-shoulder, the two knocked back the workers. Screams for mercy filled the air, but still Brant and Knox pushed back. When the ramp was free, Knox motioned Brant back to the ship. Brant ran to the door and hit the controls to raise the ramp.

As the people slowly disappeared behind the rising ramp, someone thrust a little boy into the air. Perhaps his black curls reminded Brant too much of Alex, or maybe he just had to save one more. Whatever the reason, Brant charged up the rising ramp into the crowd.

"Brant!" Knox yelled after him.

Brant grabbed the boy to his chest. He muscled through the crowd as the boy clutched Brant's neck for dear life. Brant leapt. His hand closed on the ramp's ledge. With a heave, he flipped his feet over and rode down it like a steep slide. His boots hit the metal floor, and the ramp slammed shut. The thick hull silenced the screams.

Brant craned his chin over the head of the boy and found Knox. Tears traced down the ragged trucker's cheeks and only then did Brant feel the wetness of his own face.

Maverick heaved free from the platform. Heavy-hearted, it departed the atmosphere for the cold of outer space, leaving too many, saving too few. Not a refugee spoke or dared breathe.

Brant closed his eyes and felt the rapid heartbeat of the little boy pressed to his chest. The ship jumped. It entered the spaceport of Siku Mpya, and the murmurs rose. The refugees whispered in many different languages, a buzz that filled the air.

When *Maverick* set down, Brant slid his hand along the metal wall and touched the ramp controls. Brant back-peddled, but the passengers fell out flat onto the lowering ramp. The bodies spewed out the opening, threatening to crush each other. Knox rushed out and lifted the people to their feet and out of the way. In under a minute, they sprawled out on the hangar leaving *Maverick* purged and much lightened.

Atienna stood ready with her company of Serving Hands workers. Knox hadn't just anticipated TrysKa's decision, he'd told Atienna to be ready, just in case.

The workers directed the refugees in an organized line and led the group to the waiting shuttle. Knox and his crew fell in line behind them with Brant taking up the rear guard. The first half of escapees were safely loaded on the shuttle down to Kikuyu, and Atienna stayed behind with the last group. Knox went to her side.

"You have a calling for this," he said.

"My workers make me look good."

Knox cut his eyes at Atienna, and she smiled. "And I've learned from wise mentors and my own mistakes."

Knox shook his head. "You are the most modest, hard-working woman I know."

TrysKa worked her way through the people to join them. "We have to go back. We have to save more."

"TrysKa," Atienna's smile was sad, but firm. "The Serving Hands facility is full. To take on more refuges would mean starvation for those already here."

"Then somewhere else!"

Atienna held TrysKa's shoulders with her strong hands, and pressed her forehead to TrysKa's. TrysKa closed her eyes.

"If I lose you today, then you can't save others tomorrow."

"I know."

"You must care for yourself first."

TrysKa opened her eyes, and Atienna stared deep into them.

"The Commune of Planets received an anonymous report about a recent attack on that warehouse," Atienna said. "Auditors are scheduled to investigate in a few hours, and they'll free more than you ever could."

TrysKa clapped her hands. "Thank you!" She ran off to help the other Serving Hands workers.

That call had TG's fingerprints all over it.

"If any Taluk children are recovered," Knox said, "send me a message. I'll take them home."

"Of course." Atienna placed her hand on Knox's leathery cheek. "How happy your father would be."

Knox pulled back and shoved his hands in his pants pockets. When he found his voice, he answered.

"It feels good to support Dad's cause with his ship."

"Oh," Atienna sounded surprised. "It does. Of course, it does. But that's not what I meant."

"Then what?"

"Liam always wished he could have given you a family," Atienna said. "Now you've found one."

Knox pivoted. TrysKa and Ximena wrapped blankets around the shoulders of the rescued victims. Alex found the cutest SH worker and made himself very "helpful." Brant hoisted the five-year-old he'd rescued onto his shoulders and lumbered like a giant. The boy squealed and laughed and spurred Brant on with his heels.

Knox felt his face relax into a smile. How much had he laughed and smiled over the last several days? More than he had in years. More than he had since Dad had gone.

"Perhaps I have."

And I would give anything to keep them safe.

27

Finishing the Job

Knox motioned for Brant and crew to load up. Brant lowered the boy from his shoulders back to the ground.

"Awww!" the boy whined.

Brant smiled his crinkled grin. "You're going home now, you don't need me."

Still, wouldn't it be nice to take the boy home himself? See the smile on the family's face when their lost little one was returned? He dragged his feet to the ship, turned to wave one more time, and closed the ramp behind him, and walked into a very quiet breakroom.

Spare wires and metal bits sprawled over the table's surface. Ximena, in bug-eyed goggles, took a wire, leaned over a half-assembled Phase Burner, and soldered a stick leg to its abdomen. Alex focused on trying to shuffle cards. TrysKa sniffed as she flipped a yeast-spread sandwich. Its toasted side glowed a perfect golden.

No one made eye contact.

"Did I miss something?" Brant asked. "We got the last shield? We freed some slaves? That's all good, right?"

Still no one spoke. Brant's feet itched to pace and relieve the tension. The cockpit door opened, and Knox strode out. He scanned the room and assessed the oppressive mood.

"I have rules," Knox said. "One of which is to follow orders."

"Oh!" Brant said. "That's why everyone's so quiet, you're mad about the workers storming the ship. But why? Didn't you want to free them too?"

"And endanger my crew in the process? I've lost enough on this op already."

Brant didn't have an answer to that one.

"Was it your idea?" Knox asked.

"Umm." Brant's gaze flicked to TrysKa. "Yeah, of course."

Only then did Brant register the smell of scorched bread. TrysKa startled like she'd woken from a trance and scooped the burnt sandwich off the heating pad with a flick of her spatula.

"That's not true," TrysKa said. "It was my idea."

"Normally I discipline my crew for not following orders." Knox grabbed the burnt sandwich. "But I have another rule in conflict."

"Sid's rule?" Ximena asked and balanced her new Ripper, a large hornet, on the table.

"Aye."

TrysKa layered another sandwich: bread, yeast-slice, bread, and slathered on the coconut butter she'd bought at market. It sizzled when it hit the hot ceramic plate.

"Sid?" Brant asked, inhaling the smell of toast. "You mean the manager of the warehouse I cleaned?"

"Back in the day, he was just a hired hand," Knox said. "I paid him for my long shipping runs."

"But he cooked for us too," Ximena said.

She scooped the left-over bits of her project into a pile and using her arm, swept it off the table. The stack of bolts, screws, washers, magnets, computer chips, and odd metal extras slid over the edge of the table into the open mouth of the knapsack on the floor. She tied off the linen bag, heaved it past Brant toward the cargo bay, and wiped her hands off on her pants.

"Knox never let hired hands back-talk or disobey orders," she said. "Except for Sid."

"Why?" Alex asked.

"Another one of my rules," Knox said. "I never cross the cook."

"Or the mechanic who cares for your engines?" Ximena stood and stretched.

"Da-" Knox swallowed hard. "That's right."

Knox took a bite of the half-charred bread and returned to his cave. The cockpit door closed. A smile finally broke on TrysKa's face as she flipped the next sandwich onto a plate. If it was anyone else, the unfairness would grate on Brant, but who could be mad at TrysKa? Certainly not him and certainly not while she fed him.

Alex jumped up and held out his hands with a dimple in his cheek. Food was his reward.

"To be honest," Ximena said as she accepted her sandwich, "we all wanted to free a few slaves, even Knox."

TrysKa finished Brant's sandwich and served herself last. Everyone ate and cleaned their dishes before Knox re-emerged.

"Let's install the last shield for Ngalo-ngalo."

TrysKa piloted *Maverick* to the H.C. Spaceport then pushed the shield generator to the planet shuttle. The crew followed behind with the photocells.

Riding to the planet and then the hoverbus to Ngalo-ngalo moved with a familiar rhythm for Brant. The sky blushed then started its descent to purple. A breeze blew through the field of trees and kissed Brant's skin, prickling the hairs on his arms. The air carried the sweetness of ripening mangoes on its breath. The trees' leaves rustled and clapped as the show marched past them on the broken road.

The townsfolk billowed out of homes and shops onto the streets to greet them. With generator in front, TrysKa parted the waters and led the parade into town.

The procession ended at the civic center where the mayor waited, chest puffed out beyond his normal bulk. Knox shook hands, and the two discussed plans. The townsfolk murmured as they shuffled to get a peek of the machine and the off-worlders who brought it. Knox nodded agreement to something and turned to his crew.

"They want the shield," Knox pointed up, "on top of the roof of the civic center."

"How are we going to get the generator up there?" Brant asked.

TrysKa craned her neck. "This might be more Ximena's thing."

Ximena ran up. "What's my thing?"

"Getting this," Brant pointed at the generator, "up there."

"Oh, that's easy, just boost the power on the hoverdisks," she said.

Knox cut his wife a look that said we've-done-that-before-and-it-did-not-turn-out-well.

"Oh, yeah," Ximena said. "If we do that, we might want to tie several ropes to it, and ask people down here to hold on

288

tight."

Knox grunted. While he talked to the mayor about collecting ropes, Brant couldn't resist.

"What happens if we don't tie it off?"

"It might fly up," Ximena said. "Then flip funny. And fall."

"And you know this how?"

"No reason."

The crew tied off eight ropes to the generator and handed them to strong volunteers. Brant and Knox climbed the stairs to the roof. The mayor took a few extra minutes to join them then a few more to catch his breath. When Ximena adjusted the hoverdisks, a gasp rippled across the packed streets.

The generator began to rise. When it was high enough, Brant grabbed the ropes. He tossed two to Knox and two more to the mayor.

"I got it!"

The people below released the ropes. The generator kicked upward, trying to yank all three of them over the edge. The rough cord bit into Brant's palms, but he set his feet on the ledge and leaned his weight against it. Brant, Knox, and the mayor hauled the generator over the rooftop as it fought them like an angry bull. Luckily, Ximena popped up from the ladder right then.

"I'll lower its power."

"Slowly," Knox said through clenched teeth.

"I know, I know."

She ran her fingers along some controls on her scroll, and the generator's pull lessened bit by bit. Brant guided the thing to the center as Knox and the mayor pulled the rope down, hand over hand. When it set down softly on its platform, applause burst out. TrysKa and Alex joined everyone on the rooftop.

Ximena smiled down at Alex. "Time to make the shields and photocells all play nicely with each other."

Alex groaned. "Can't Brant do it? Last time he played ball."

"Yeah, right!" Brant said. "Like I could fit under that thing."

Alex's shoulders slumped as he implored Ximena with his sad, large eyes. A sly smile crept across TrysKa's face, and she leaned in to Ximena's ear.

"Could you find four cinderblocks for me?"

"Why yes, I think I could."

Brant's grin faded. "Why do you need four cinderblocks?"

As one, Ximena, TrysKa, and Alex shared evil grins then turned to Brant.

"No."

Brant looked to Knox for help, and the captain's shoulders began to shake. A smile spread across Knox's face.

And then

Knox

laughed.

It started with his broad shoulders shaking. Then his chest rumbled low. Lastly, Knox opened his mouth and let out a deep chuckle that vibrated Brant's chest. Knox slapped his thighs.

"You don't know when to shut up." He raised his head then stepped back.

Everyone was staring at him.

"What?"

"You have such a pleasant laugh," TrysKa melted.

"Yeah, well," Knox shifted his weight and looked generally uncomfortable. "Can we install the shields now?"

Next thing Brant knew, TrysKa had found the cinderblocks, Ximena had used the hoverdisks to lift the generator onto them, and he, six-foot-five Brant Mallet, was stuffed under it.

And Alex was rolling on the epoxycrete in hysterical laughter.

Brant's head and shoulders fit under the generator, but his stomach and legs hung out like a giraffe sprawled on the ground. His long arms did not fit under the generator's belly, so anytime Brant adjusted bulbs or switches, part of his arm hit one of the cinderblocks. By the end of an hour, Brant's elbows and patience were scraped raw, and Alex had laughed The. Entire. Time.

Ximena's voice came over the earbud. "Toggle 4C for me, BB."

"Speak English, engineer!" Brant said.

"OK, OK, four over, three down. Flip that switch."

"Done. Does it work now?"

"Are there shields yet?" Ximena asked.

"No."

"Then it didn't work."

The earbud fell silent then buzzed back to life.

"OK, let's try this. Move the hot connection over to the C-shell insert. Maybe then they'll talk to each other."

Brant stared blankly at the intestines of the generator.

"Right," Ximena said. "Move the black crystal bulb, about the size of a grain of rice, to the red connection with a 'C' over it. Don't drop it."

Brant swiveled his head to find the black bulb and pulled it. A spark arched and zapped Brant's fingers. He instinctively snapped his head up and slammed his forehead into the generator's metal tubes. Dust snowed down through the machine's guts, coating Brant's teeth with grit. Alex clutched his stomach and gasped for air.

"Oh, you'll need to remove the cold first," Ximena said. "That's the white bulb."

"You don't say!"

"Oops. Sorry."

Brant removed the white bulb and put everything the way he thought Ximena wanted. Still no shields. The sun set and the moon rose to its zenith before the shields and photocells communicated.

"Finally!" Brant growled.

He pushed himself out from under the generator, his shirt plastered to his body, grime smeared across his face, and his elbows bloodied.

"I hope you wet yourself," Brant said to Alex.

Alex stuck out his tongue.

A shout rose from the ground. Families lifted their faces as the shield shot upward. It rose up, up, up, yearning for the stars, then spread its wings over the town. Everyone cheered, hugged, and cried.

Maybe scraped elbows weren't that bad after all.

Ximena's voice came over the earbuds. "Hey, Big Brother?"

"Yeah?"

"Good job."

Those two words thrilled Brant from the inside out. *Good job. Good job. Good job.* Over and over, he repeated those words in his mind. It was an addiction, a hearty beer with no hangover. Knox climbed the ladder to the rooftop and gave Brant a nod of approval. That put him over the top. Brant blushed warmly and didn't try to hide it. *Good job.*

Knox motioned for everyone to follow him back down. High-fives were shared. Brant held his hand way up and let Alex try to jump and hit it. He got a palm to the face instead. Should've seen that one coming.

Knox sent them back to the spaceport while he stayed to wrap things up with the mayor. Back on the ship, TrysKa found the medical ointment and treated Brant's elbows. Alex pouted at the attention lavished on Brant and sat, arms crossed, in the corner of the cargo bay.

After fixing up Brant, TrysKa prepped dinner with Alex's "help." Knox joined them shortly and everyone ate and laughed at the day. *Maverick* spent the night on the spaceport. Even Knox welcomed rest after the crazy several days they'd lived through. Following a slow morning, the crew packed up, and *Maverick* flew to the Kikuyu spaceport.

#

Over the next two months *Maverick* delivered refugees to their hometowns. Knox aligned the crew's daily routine with the day/night schedule on the Kikuyu spaceport. He created a spreadsheet coordinating travel to refugees' home countries, daytime hours with the spaceports, and true daylight with the destination.

TrysKa exchanged recipes with the Serving Hands cafeteria crew and bought ingredients from the nearby farmer's market. She did the local cuisine justice. It took Brant a week to master peeling the injera and wrapping up the doro wat without splatting it on his lap.

Alex wasn't as open-minded and pushed his food around his plate. The IAS lessons started, and when Alex pouted, Knox dragged him to clean the sewage tank of *Maverick*. Alex decided history and math weren't that bad after all. Ximena made science fun, and TrysKa did the best she could with history. Alex just didn't care about dead people.

Sometimes taking the refugees home was easy. The person went straight to their former home, and there waited their family. Tearful embraces mingled with laughter. They thanked the crew over and over and pressed them to stay for dinner.

Other times the family had moved. The crew asked neighbors and followed clues. Sometimes they found the family. Sometimes they didn't. Those were heartbreaking rides back to the Serving Hands facility. Atienna lifted them up and walked beside them to the job training section. Serving Hands couldn't give back their old family but could give them a new life.

One of the trips to NT #4, TrysKa led the way, taking a six-year-old girl home. The little girl held onto TrysKa with one hand and sucked on her other thumb. When TrysKa asked if she wanted to go home, the girl nodded but didn't take out the thumb. She'd lived through a lot.

As they wove through the space station hangar, heading to the shuttle stop, Knox bolted forward and shoved TrysKa and the girl up against the side of a ship.

"Knox?" TrysKa asked, holding the now terrified girl.

Knox held his finger to his lips. Brant and Alex joined them beside the ship.

"What is it?" Brant asked.

But Knox looked at Alex. "If you peek around the corner, how far can you see?"

"Not as far as Sann, but..."

"Can you see to the roof of the pastry shop?" Knox pointed in the direction of the shop.

"Sure."

Alex popped his head out around the ship, narrowed his eyes, and Knox yanked him back.

"Hey!" Alex tugged free from Knox's grip.

"I didn't want you to be targeted," Knox said. "What did you see?"

"A woman, she was on top of the roof. She saw me and ducked behind the ledge."

"A woman? Or a teenager?"

"I don't know," Alex said. "Older than me. Maybe a teenager?"

Knox squatted down and tried to peer under the belly of the cargo ship they were using as a shield.

"OK, I can see a way for us to get back to *Maverick*. TrysKa, tell me if you detect someone following us."

TrysKa nodded and carried the girl, still sucking her thumb. Altogether the crew meandered through the ships, always keeping something between the shop roof and themselves.

"What's the problem with the teen on the roof?" Brant whispered in Knox's ear.

"She reeked of that smell," Knox said. "The one a human gives off when they're about to commit their first murder."

Brant's hand rested on the holster of his gun and stayed there. Finally, everyone reached *Maverick* when an explosion burst from one of the shops along the wall.

"*Luis and Carlos!*" Ximena yelled and started down the ramp.

Knox grabbed her arm and motioned everyone into the ship. "The explosion is for us, to lure us in."

"Us?" Ximena asked as she and Knox ran into the cargo bay. "Why us?"

"Apparently our little warehouse raid upset someone important," Knox closed the ramp. "TrysKa—"

But she was already in the cockpit, requesting take off. Knox pulled out his scroll and called Luis.

"Are you OK?" Knox asked.

Luis laughed. "The local bomb was attached to the outside of the back wall. The shield barrier inside the building activated and kept us safe."

"But the cost of the damages..." Knox said. Being a businessman himself, he understood how this could sink Luis' livelihood.

"That's what insurance is for," Luis waved his hand. "But I am curious who the target was. I don't think any of my customers have a death price on them. None that I've heard of."

"It might have been me," Knox said.

"Who's stupid enough to target you?"

"I might have upset Caravan Suppliers."

Luis's smirk dissolved to the look of a man attending a funeral. "Knox..."

"I thought I covered my tracks, but they're good, better than I gave them credit."

"You stay alive, and take care of Ximena."

"Absolutely."

Maverick was already out of the air lock and entering orbit. Knox closed the scroll and looked down at the little girl, sitting cross-legged on the cargo bay floor sucking her thumb.

"We'll still get you home. Just have to go a different way."

TrysKa landed in Brazil's space station, and rode a shuttle down to its dome. It took three hours to travel across the planet's surface to Mexico, and then another three hours back. But the look of overwhelmed relief on her mama and papa's face was worth every second. As the crew turned to leave, the little girl took her thumb out of her mouth and waved.

"Gracias!"

After that, everyone was on high alert. Knox snuck a blinding bomb into the inside pockets of his jacket, and carried it with him, just in case. Thankfully, they only had a few refugees left to return home.

The last trip was the hardest one, involving a nine-year-old boy. Alex latched onto the kid his age, and they chatted happily aboard *Maverick*. As the ship landed on the spaceport, though, the youngster grew restless. Knox leaned over to Brant and TrysKa.

"Something's not right."

They followed the directions to his home, but the child dragged his feet slower and slower. When Knox and crew reached the house, the little one clung to TrysKa's legs. Knox knocked on the door. A man answered the door and locked eyes on the boy. His face flushed a splotched blood red. He reeked of fury.

"Forget we were here," Knox said.

Knox spun on his heel, picked up the lad, and left. As the crew made their way back to *Maverick*, TrysKa took the boy into her arms. Knox fell back next to Brant.

"What just...?" Brant pointed his thumb over his shoulder.

"This boy wasn't kidnapped into slavery. He was sent away."

Brant's eyes fired up, and he u-turned, murder written across his face. Knox grabbed Brant's arm and dragged him back to *Maverick*.

TrysKa called ahead to the center. When the ship returned to the Kikuyu spaceport, a worker with kind eyes waited for them. He knelt on one knee and held open his arms. The boy was wrapped in a hug.

"We've got you. You'll be safe with us."

The pair entered the shuttle together, and a message popped up on Knox's scroll from Atienna.

"I'm bringing one last group to you."

Atienna was delivering them personally? Knox dared not hope for much. Brant paced before the shuttle, and Knox's feet itched to do the same. But he resisted and planted his boots firmly to the floor. Eight children exited the shuttle with Atienna.

Eight of the children stolen from Taluk.

"Were they in the warehouse?" Knox asked as TrysKa led them into the ship.

"No," Atienna said. "The police from Texas, SUSA delivered them to us."

"Texas?"

"They received an anonymous call. When the officers checked it out, thirty children were huddled in a room together, all of whom had been reported missing. Someone had drone-delivered take-out for them to eat."

Atienna's face hardened. "Next door, the handlers were all dead. Poisoned."

TG's fingerprints were all over that, but Knox kept his face passive.

"When the police read the children's DNA," she said. "They saw these eight were in our database. Called us."

"Glad the children are safely returned," Knox said.

Brant didn't play it so cool. "Poisoned?" To Knox, "You don't think?"

"You know who did this?" Atienna asked.

So much for not tipping her off. Brant swallowed and stared at his feet.

"We weren't involved," Knox said.

Atienna held up her hand. "I don't want to know any more."

Knox and his crew took the eight children home to Taluk. Now, only thirteen remained locked away in that mega-warehouse, Klundah's niece being one of them. If only, if only, if only. Knox had known TG wouldn't be able to rescue them all, but for some stupid reason, he'd felt like life owed him. After all he'd lost, at the very least, let him save these children.

But miracles were reserved for others, and life didn't owe him anything.

28

We Failed

"How dare you?" Mac's nose was lowered to within inches of Ophelia's.

They'd camped out in an alleyway. The lights of the space-port had dimmed for its scheduled night time, a time aligned with Nuevo Mexico, the main planet-side port for NT #4. The shops were locked and barred to Ophelia and her hungry sisters and brothers.

"Knox was adapted."

"He's a stupid space trucker," Mac hissed. "IAS doesn't waste their time with stupid space truckers. They only train rich people's kids."

But Knox was adapted. He'd smelled Ophelia, she was sure of it. She'd been crouched low on the rooftop of a pastry shop, trying to ignore the smell of the rising yeast bread. He'd turned the corner into view, flared his nose, and stared straight at her. How could he pick out her smell over the caramelized sugar and fried donuts?

Then Knox had vanished. Ophelia couldn't explain it. She'd been staring straight at him when he sidestepped behind a taller person and never reappeared. She scrambled down from the building into the alley, but by the time she entered the crowd, Knox might as well have been a vision, a ghost. Gone. She sliced through the bodies, straining to catch his voice in the buzz, but nothing. Just gibberish. No Knox.

He had to be adapted.

Which meant IAS had trained a lowly space trucker. But Teacher had taught her that they only taught the privileged. That if she begged at its doors, the instructors would turn their noses up and send her away.

Mac struck her hard across the face. She crumpled to the ground, tears stinging her eyes.

"Were you listening to me?" He towered over her.

Ophelia nodded and got back on her feet. It was a lie. She hadn't heard a word he said.

"Because of your failure, I had to set off that bomb," Mac said.

Ophelia nodded again instead of rolling her eyes. He "had to" set off that bomb? No. He'd panicked and hoped blowing something up would fix it. Then he'd been shocked the masses stampeded, and the port security rushed in. Of course, a bomb would get that response on a vessel floating through the vacuum of space.

Idiot.

All this Ophelia kept locked tight in the vault of her thoughts. Tears streamed down her gaunt cheeks, and her hands writhed together.

"When we return to Teacher, I know how he'll handle you," Mac sneered.

"We're giving up?" Ophelia's head snapped up.

"Do we have a choice? He's not returning to that spaceport."

301

"Then we ambush him somewhere else."

"And where exactly do you propose we do that?"

Ophelia opened then shut her mouth. If there was anything she knew how to recognize, it was someone who had no intention of listening to her. She cut her eyes at Benedick. He smirked. She wasn't the only one who didn't like Mac.

"You said you killed one of the soldiers in your previous ambush?" Ben said.

The vein throbbing on Mac's forehead pulsed lower and lower until it lay flat against his skin.

"Do you have an idea that could save this ruined excuse for a mission?" Mac asked.

"Did the crew gather the fallen soldier's remains?"

"What does that have to do with anything?"

"One reason to gather his remains is to return him to family." Ben stepped forward, further drawing Mac's gaze away from Ophelia.

"How will we find his family? We don't even know who he is."

"I'll track his face on the public database," Ben said. "When it pops up with a family photo, we'll check the location tag. Tah-da. That's where his ashes will be taken."

Ben wisely didn't mention Ophelia's name. She was the one who knew how to search the public database for images. As long as she had a pic of the soldier's face, which Mac did indeed have, she could use facial recognition to track him down. But any solution involving her would be auto-rejected.

Mac sucked air through his teeth and pretended to weigh his options. Like he had any. With a grave expression, he nodded.

"Very good. Very good. Take the team's digi-scroll and get me that location." To Ophelia, "No food for you tonight."

After Mac lay snoring on his mat, Ophelia and Ben leaned over the scroll, his bangs brushing her left temple. Half an energy bar slipped into her fingers. With a smile, she crunched it as they ran their algorithm. A few seconds later, a name popped up.

Sann Dalise.

29

Sann's Memorial

Round and round the cargo bay Brant stomped, nostrils flaring, breathing hard. He stopped once, bounced on the balls of his feet, and started again. Knox hung back in the hallway, leaning against the wall. Brant glanced at his captain as he passed. Knox met his gaze, and he calmed his pace.

I'm not alone.

Brant had completed Sann's mission, but he didn't feel successful. Not now. How could he? How could he tell his friend's mom her son wasn't coming home and feel successful?

All too soon, *Maverick* launched from Earth's spaceport, jumped, and began its journey to Naya Surya. Alex bounded into the room, all energy and excitement.

"Alex," Knox whispered.

Alex scrunched his eyebrows then followed Knox's gaze. "Oh."

Brant knelt down in front of Alex's old sleeping compartment. It felt like he was wading through drying epoxycrete. Behind this door lay another reminder Sann wasn't coming back. Another way Sann died all over again.

Brant pushed the button, and there lay Sann's remains, resting on Alex's sleeping bag. How had they not been disturbed? Of course, Knox and Ximena had secured them with a magnetic bolt. A small gesture, but so meaningful.

With the gentleness of cradling a newborn, Brant lifted the jar and gun. He shouldn't be the one carrying Sann's remains. Brant turned and extended his arms to Knox, offering to let him do the honors. Knox shook his head.

"It has to be you, Brant. He was your brother."

But I couldn't save him.

The floor vibrated as *Maverick* entered the atmosphere of the planet.

"Everyone strap in," TrysKa called from the cockpit.

Brant and Alex wedged themselves into the recess of the ramp door. Knox leaned his back against the wall and propped his foot up. Brant couldn't find his voice, so asked with his eyes instead. Knox guessed at the question.

"I can't land on this spaceport. It's unsafe and—" Knox's voice caught.

So, this was where his father died. Knox saw the understanding on Brant's face and nodded. Brant was right.

"Councilor KaeHan called ahead," Knox said, "and cleared us for a one-time landing near the Dalise family field."

Brant clutched the jar and gun close. Alex squeezed his arms around Brant's middle as the gravity jumped and plunged. When *Maverick* landed, TrysKa, her eyes puffy from rubbing, joined them in the cargo bay. Ximena came behind with her scroll.

"You feel OK?" Knox asked Ximena, nodding toward the bathroom.

"The last few landings, I've taken that pill TrysKa bought." She smiled at TrysKa with eyes that apologized for not listening the first time. "I don't get sick now. Thank you."

TrysKa couldn't answer back, so she squeezed Ximena's hand instead. Knox opened the ramp and stood back. He motioned for Brant to lead, but Brant shook his head.

"Would you prefer I go first?" Knox asked.

Brant nodded.

Knox stepped in front. Alex, TrysKa, and Brant fell in behind. Ximena waved for them to go without her.

"You need to stay here?" Knox asked.

In answer, she hugged her scroll to her chest and kept her eyes down.

"We'll call you when we're coming back," he told her, and led the funeral procession off *Maverick.*

The crew stepped off the small ship into a downpour. Brant turned on his shields, and the water streamed around its curves. Rice patty fields spread on both sides of Brant, as far as he could see. Beyond the fields to his right, mountains rose, the veil of rain turning them a ghostly gray. Brant's boots slid on the muddy clay road, so he stared at the ground and concentrated on putting one foot in front of the other.

The Dalise's small plot backed up to the mountain foothills with their modest house wedged into the far corner. Slowly it came into focus, the triangle of its teak-style roof coming to a sharp tip. The deep shadows underneath it took shape as stilts. Knox stepped under the eave and turned off his shield. Everyone else huddled under the roof's protection, and lowered their barriers. Brant stood pinned between a wall of solid water on one side and the Dalise's home on the other. Knox ascended the steps to the front door.

"They know we're coming?" Knox asked TrysKa.

"Yes, sir," she said, tears trailing down her cheeks. "Kae-Han visited them right after, right after..." She took in a shaky breath. "When I called the Institute telling them our plans, he notified the family."

Knox put a steady hand on TrysKa's shoulder. "TK?"

"Yes, sir?"

"Breathe."

She took a few quaking breaths in and out. Brant clenched his teeth. His own tears pressed on the back of his eyelids, begging for release.

Knox knocked, and Sann's mom answered the door. Her once strong back bent under her grief, and her head was shaved in mourning. Her red eyes had cried until dry. She pressed her palms together as though in prayer and bowed her head.

Knox and TrysKa brought their hands together and bowed. Knox stepped aside, so she could see Sann's remains and gun. She shuffled to Brant, but couldn't bring herself to accept her son. Not yet.

Brant understood. She'd heard the words, *Your son gave his life*, but now she had to face his remains. Sann dying all over again.

She lifted her face to Brant instead. With his hands full, Brant couldn't bring his hands together, so he simply bowed.

"You're Brant?"

He nodded.

"I'm Leakena. Sann told us so much about you."

Brant swallowed the lump in his throat but couldn't speak. He had no right to join in this family's grieving, much less receive their comfort. The tears' pressure spread under his cheeks.

No, I don't deserve relief. I don't deserve forgiveness. I don't deserve compassion.

Leakena accepted Sann's possessions. When she lifted them from Brant's hands, a weight lifted from his shoulders, and the tension in his neck released. The dam nearly broke, but he sucked the flow in. Held it back. Brant let the struggle hurt. The family needed their healing, so he would take the pain.

"Please come in," she said.

Knox and Brant followed her inside, and TrysKa, tears streaking down her cheeks, nudged Alex. He scowled down at his feet. Maybe they should have left Alex on *Maverick*. The boy had been through so much loss already. TrysKa nudged Alex again, and he plopped down on the floor just inside the house.

Knox and TrysKa took off their shoes and set them next to the family's sandals. Brant fumbled with his laces. The knot was caked with mud. Finally, his boots leaned on Knox's, and he stood.

Most of the house was an open living area. The kitchen ran along the left wall, and amok warmed on an electric heater that doubled as a stove. The house brimmed with the smells of fresh rain, fish stew, and eucalyptus. Sann's father sat on a mat next to a low table with an elephant chess set and digiscroll. He greeted Brant and crew with pressed palms and a bow, and they bowed back.

"Make yourselves at home." He motioned the crew to woven rugs along the wall.

Knox and TrysKa sat cross-legged, but Brant's knees threatened to give out. Sann's father, in sarong pants and bare feet, was the exact image of his son. He wore a scarf with the same

308

checkerboard pattern and color of Sann's. Sann's younger brother, around fifteen, was a mixture of his parents, but Brant couldn't make eye contact with Sann's dad. It was like staring into the eyes of loss.

Leakena placed the jar in a small shrine next to the chess set. The eucalyptus smell wafted from the incense burning there, and an opal comm ball glowed in the middle. Sann's image flickered above the orb.

"He made a responsive recording for us before your operation," Leakena said. "We can actually talk to him, and he can talk back. I can still hear his voice and laugh."

Brant turned away and forced one foot in front of the other, walking with weights strapped to his ankles. He passed a door on his right, a sleeping room with mosquito nets. When he reached the rug, his legs crumpled.

Alex squirmed, and his round face pinched in pain. TrysKa leaned over, whispered something in Knox's ear, and he nodded. She took Alex and their shoes, and left. After the door closed behind them, Sann's father limped across the room. He favored his right knee as he knelt in front of Brant.

"I'm Mittapheap. You must be Brant."

The dam broke. Brant's tears burst through.

"I should have saved him, it's all my fault, all mine. I'm so sorry." But Brant could say no more. Mittapheap shook his head.

"Sann made his choice, and it was a powerful one. Don't diminish it."

But Brant couldn't accept that. He deserved blame, accusations, and exclusion, not this grieving father's comfort. Brant wept. His hands clutched his knees, digging his fingernails into his shins.

Mittapheap reached into his pants' pocket and pulled out... a handkerchief.

Brant blinked his eyes at the white cloth, his vision swimming. He wrenched his right hand free from his knee and accepted the gift. When its softness touched his face, Brant's shoulders relaxed. He breathed in the handkerchief's clean smell: linen, sunshine, and breeze. Brant brought the cloth down to his lap, rubbing it between his fingertips. The material, worn thin, slipped over his thumb. With a swallow, Brant forced his voice to work.

"I had so many years with him." The words scraped his throat. "So many memories that you didn't get."

"Share one with us," Mittapheap said.

Brant brought the cloth to his eyes, held it there, and brought it back down to his lap.

"Instructor KaeHan showed us a new kick." Brant's eyes wandered to the dried grass rug and traced its woven pattern. "We must have been twelve or thirteen."

"A twelve-year-old Brant," Knox said. "I can only imagine."

"Yeah, I was cocky." Brant smiled through the pain. "I just knew the move was easy. I would show everyone. When KaeHan asked for a volunteer, my hand popped up. I think he knew what was coming."

"His eyes twinkle when he sets someone up," Knox agreed.

"When did you get that look?" Brant asked.

"He gave it to other students."

"Sure he did."

Knox waved his hand for Brant to continue the story.

"Long story short," Brant said. "I made a fool of myself, landed flat on my back. KaeHan called on Sann next, and he was surprised. Why would KaeHan call on him when talented Brant couldn't do the move? Still he centered himself and gave it his best."

"And he succeeded?" Knox asked.

"He nailed it. First time. Instructor KaeHan used it as an example to the class of how hard work and focus trumps talent every time."

Brant smiled at the memory—so humiliating at the time, but now so precious. Brant's chest ached a little less, like the ropes cutting into his ribs had been cut. Brant lifted his eyes from the handkerchief to Mittapheap's face and saw healing there too. Through the mystery of shared grief, Brant had comforted Sann's family. He didn't understand how, but he didn't have to.

Alex burst into the house. "Something's wrong with *Maverick*."

30

Battle for Maverick

Ximena!

Brant jumped into his shoes first, but Knox was only a split-second behind. He laced up his right boot lightning fast just like he'd trained so many times as a child at IAS, but Brant was faster, already out the door as Knox tied up his left.

Knox hoisted Alex onto his back, activated his shields, and burst into the gray downpour, parting the waters, planting his prints into the clay.

"Ximena, talk to me," Knox said.

"She's probably lost her earbud again," TrysKa answered instead of Ximena.

Or she's unconscious. Or worse.

"Where are you?" Knox asked.

Brant drew further and further ahead, his shields a tiny air bubble cutting a wake into the river falling from the sky.

"I'm hiding in the brush by the ship," TrysKa said. "They haven't spotted me."

"The ship?"

"The attackers got one shot at the port side rocket, which

handled the blast. After that the shields activated. They're trying to overpower it now."

"How many?"

"Ten, but Knox, they're barely teenagers, and they're adapted." Pause. "Brant's here, what do I do?"

Knox could just make out the ghostly forms attacking his ship. Brant barged straight for the tallest of them. The whole group began evasive maneuvers and started shooting. Several plasma trails whizzed past his right and left side, missing because they expected Brant to dodge and weave. Not until it was too late did the leader of the pack realize Brant's strategy.

That hesitation cost them. Brant rammed the guy straight on, using his shield as his weapon. His opponent went spiraling into his own squad, and they scattered like struck billiard balls. Brant, however, set his feet and started firing.

"Good job," Knox said.

He couldn't have asked for a better distraction, but that surprise tactic would only work once. Knox tucked Alex into a flowing ditch between rows of rice patties. Out of his jacket pocket, Knox pulled his blinding bomb.

"Stay hidden. Only throw this if I give the code word."

Alex pouted. He wanted in on the action, but then he nodded. "What code word?"

"Darn it."

The leader had recovered his footing and shot Brant before he could roll away. His shield deflected the shot but weakened too. Brant returned fire. TrysKa poked her head out of the fields ahead and rapid-fired at one of the kid's shield until it fell. Then stunned the girl.

In the middle of all this, Alex giggled.

"That's something you would never say normally."

"Stay hidden until then."

"I give you my word." Alex sank into the irrigation water between the plants.

Knox ran low, keeping his back down. The attackers didn't fire his way. They must not have seen him, but Brant's shields were losing power.

"Ximena! I need you."

"I'm here, I'm here, I'm here! I'm sorry, I-"

"No time, they have shields. I need those shields down."

"Releasing the hive," she said.

Knox ran off the road to his left. The sludge slurped around his shield and bubbled up over his boots. He hunched down until he could just peek over the planted row.

TrysKa was right. They were just teens. Knox aimed at one of the boys and pulled the trigger ten times without pause. The boy leapt into a dazzling flip, but Knox followed him through the air. The boy's shield failed as he landed. Knox flipped the switch to stun, pulled the trigger, and flipped back to plasma.

He couldn't kill kids even if they were trying to kill him.

The fighter's body flew back into the mud with a splat. The others returned fire on Knox, but their shots missed high, leaving a trail of scalding, sizzling steam. Brant cut right, and his main attacker slipped. A few precious seconds were gained for Brant's shields to recoup.

That's when *Maverick*'s ramp cracked open. Even in the drum of rain and hiss of plasma fire, the creak echoed. The group all whirled around and wasted firepower on the ship's sturdy energy barrier. TrysKa overpowered the shield of another boy and stunned him. Knox stunned a girl.

A buzzing deafened. Out of the ship, billowed the Phase Burners like hell bees belching from a metal demon's maw.

Lopsided mosquitoes, massive hornets, and nightmare ladybugs fogged the air like smog. The youths screamed and dispersed. *Maverick*'s shield lowered to release the insect-bots, and no one shot its hull.

The scourge swarmed the gang, leaching their shields from above and below, front and behind.

The youngsters spun and slipped, trying to knock the pests off. Two fired at a Burner. But when their shields lowered to allow the shot out, other insects invaded the unprotected kid. The bots latched onto the armband, and with a crackle, fried the shield's power source. Knox stunned one, TrysKa the other.

Six down, four to go.

Brant's opponent, the only twenty-something of the group, barreled straight through a cluster of Phase Rippers, crushing a few and flinging the rest through the monsoon. He landed two more shots on Brant's shields before dodging Knox's fire. One of the mechanical mosquitos tried to alight on his shield, but the leader jerked away.

Knox concentrated on the last two boys while TrysKa leapt out of the brush to fight the last girl. Not a girl, an older teen. Burners deactivated one boy's shield, and Knox stunned him. TrysKa cut hard right, and her assailant fired at empty air. Knox stunned the last boy.

TrysKa positioned herself, so her foe was trapped between Knox and herself. Knox rapid-fired from behind, and the shield dropped. The teen froze. She didn't fire. She didn't defend herself. She didn't move. Knox heard TrysKa over his earbud.

"Come with us," she said.

The young woman didn't refuse. Instead, her arms fell

limply by her side.

"I'm TrysKa. What's your name?"

Knox didn't hear the answer. What he did hear was a roar that could only come from the chest of one person: Brant. Knox stunned the woman. He couldn't risk her shooting TrysKa.

"Which one of you is Knox?" The last attacker pointed his gun at a prone Brant and searched the brush.

Through clenched teeth, Brant wailed. He writhed in the mud with his feet gone, burnt stubs for calves. Time to end this.

"I'm Knox."

Knox rose from the field and cast his weapon aside.

"Drop your weapon too," the assassin said to TrysKa. "Or this one dies."

"No one else dies, darn it," Knox said.

It was awkward, wrapping his mouth around the code word. Even TrysKa, her chest heaving from an intense battle, did a double take. Then her eyes went wide at something in the air. Knox didn't have to turn to know what it was.

Behind him somewhere, Alex had let fly a small white ball. Knox buried his face in the crook of his arm as the leader took aim. He shot the blinding bomb dead on. Bad idea.

Migraine-bright light. Even with his face pressed against his skin, kaleidoscope colors swirled on the inside of Knox's eyelids. Two screams split the deluge. Knox charged forward and stunned the last foe. He fell silent.

"TrysKa! I need the medpack."

"Already on it."

And she was. TrysKa came racing back down the ramp, the box in hand. She knelt next to a yelling Brant, and in under a second, opened the box, ripped out the numbing patch, and slapped it on Brant's neck. His back relaxed, and his wails ebbed to moans.

"I've got him," Knox said. "You get Alex on the ship. And we need to get the Dalise family out of here."

TrysKa closed the lid with a snap, turned, and gasped. Alex stood behind them, caked in gravy-colored mud like a mini swamp monster. TrysKa took his grime-covered hand in hers and led him safely onto the ship.

"You saved Brant," she said to him.

"Will he be OK?"

"We're going to take care of him."

Alex chattered as TrysKa led him to the bathroom, their voices fading. Knox squatted to pick up Brant then hesitated. The lead assassin still lay unconscious in the mud, water flowing down his stubbled chin.

Knox couldn't kill children. He wouldn't kill children. But this young man wasn't a child.

Once *Maverick* escaped, this assassin would hunt them again. The next time, he might miss Knox and kill Ximena or Alex. No one hunted Knox's family. No one.

With a shaking hand, Knox flipped his gun to plasma, aimed, and squeezed the trigger. There was a crackle, and the sickening smell of burnt meat filled Knox's nostrils.

Knox twitched his wrist, and the pistol hid back in his jacket sleeve. He squatted, slipped his arms under Brant's back and thighs, and heaved his burden up. Knox trudged through the muck, around the stunned bodies, and up the ramp. In the middle of the cargo bay, he settled Brant's limp body on the cool floor.

"He's asleep?" Ximena asked.

"Aye, we need to get to a hospital fast."

Even unconscious, Brant twitched.

"How long to repair the ship?" Knox asked.

Ximena rolled her eyes. "They might have been trained to attack people, but those kids had no clue how to disable a transport. They shot the thickest part of the hull around the blasters." Ximena opened her scroll and wrinkled her nose. "Left a dent, but the metal integrity is fine."

Maverick rose so gently, Knox almost didn't feel the acceleration. TrysKa was good. But soon the blasters would engage and send Brant careening into a wall. Knox lifted his hand to get Ximena's attention. It shook. He stuffed it under his armpit.

"Oh," she said. "I see."

Ximena collapsed her scroll, knelt, and coaxed his hand out of hiding.

"You did what you had to do." She kissed Knox's fingers. "Whoever it was, they won't hurt us anymore."

Knox crossed his arms. "Brant needs to be secured."

Ximena pressed her soft lips against his bald head then hurried to a cabinet on the far wall. She shoved wires and tools aside, and a few Rippers fell out, only to scurry back in. Ximena reeled out a long cord with magnetic bolts attached.

"This should do it."

Together they crisscrossed the rope over Brant's body and locked the bolts to the metal floor.

"Hang in there," Knox said as the ship settled before the Dalise's home. "I'll take care of you."

31

Faith Shaken

In the far corner of the transport's cargo bay, Ophelia and her siblings huddled around Teacher. He wrapped as many as he could fit into his arms. His fingertips brushed Ophelia's arm, and he smiled brokenly at her, tears still in his eyes. Ben sat on Teacher's other side, lounging against the wall. They were all hidden behind crates and crates of food and cleansers.

The space barge shuttered as it detached from the spaceport around Naya Surya and headed back to Ophelia's home. The fort of boxes shifted and creaked.

Ophelia closed her eyes, and she was back on the planet again. When Ophelia and Ben had recovered from being stunned, he'd activated their alarm beacon. Teacher had found them and incinerated Mac's body.

"Ashes to ashes, dust to dust," Teacher said as the rain turned the remains to mud and washed them away. Then he wept, and Ophelia joined him with all her brothers and sisters in wailing for their loss. She hadn't liked Mac, but she hadn't wanted him dead either.

"One of our own has been brutally murdered," Teacher said.

Ophelia nodded and bit her lip to stop crying.

Teacher holstered his gun. "MacBeth will be avenged, just as I would avenge any of you."

Then came the long trek to a hoverbus, the shuttle ride, and bribing the transport cook to take them home. Teacher squeezed the children around him closer.

"We return home."

"Will the Supplier still pay?" Ophelia asked.

Teacher snorted. "Why would he? We did not succeed."

"But he didn't tell us Knox was adapted."

Ben stiffened and clenched his fist. Mac had been very clear that he didn't believe Knox was adapted, but Ophelia had seen the blond man and black woman fight. There could be no doubt. They were too fast. They were IAS trained.

"Adapted?"

Teacher's whisper was a cold knife slipped under the ribs. Ophelia sucked in and curled away from the hatred. The kids shivered as a group. Immediately Teacher's features melted back to kindness.

"I'm so sorry you had to face that." His voice choked. "So sorry." Then his jaw set. "But our Supplier hid Knox's training, so we will get our money. That I promise you." Teacher turned to Ophelia and caressed her cheek. "Well done with your keen observations. Thank you for telling me. Now we can provide for our family."

Ophelia shifted her weight and looked away from the intense stare. He loved her so much, she couldn't face it.

"So, IAS has seen us now." Teacher leaned his head back and stared at the ceiling. "That will force me to move before I had planned."

Ophelia closed her eyes, and TrysKa's face came into focus.

She'd betrayed Teacher and told TrysKa her name. Not Ophelia, that was the name given by her Teacher, but her *real* name. The name given by her mother so long ago. She'd forgotten her mom until she'd seen the compassion in TrysKa's eyes. When TrysKa spoke, so soft, the memories unrolled.

Her mother's jasmine perfume from the flowers in her hair. Her mother's voice reading a night-time story. Her mother's dance moves, sashaying around their tiny home while her baby sister laughed.

Ophelia opened her eyes to the softly backlit silhouette of Teacher. He'd saved her from the slavers that had kidnapped her so many years ago. Ophelia slammed her eyes shut. How could she? Teacher loved her, and she'd betrayed him. She'd betrayed him to that woman because of kind eyes. Stupid.

The barge jumped then its engines hummed as it maneuvered to dock with the spaceport. In the low vibrations of fans and mechanical gears, Ophelia heard her mother's lullaby call from a childhood lost so very long ago.

32

Auditors Suck

Retirement parties were the ultimate in wasted funds.

Hey, let's celebrate quitting!

Yeah, we're losing a veteran resource.

Oh, and everyone would be envious of the retiree too. And if the indulgence wasn't enough, bring on the politics. On second thought, Douglas rather liked that part. All the potential replacements flattering him, hinting at bribes, inviting him to hunting parties, or out for a drink.

He already knew who was going to replace the old girl, but he could have some fun for a few days. Conduct some interviews with a panel of leaders. Make it look official.

Douglas shuddered at a chill breeze. Someone needed to turn the heater up. He strolled away from the large windows and their wintry scene when his eye caught movement.

Like a salmon swimming upstream, Evie cut straight through the attendants. She wore no red today, only a grayscale outfit with angular shoes. Her eyes sliced his soul as her heels clipped against the floor.

She stepped to within a foot of Douglas, just inside his

personal space. That awkward pause, notorious in large socials, gripped the room. Evie held out her hand, and Douglas accepted the scrap of paper.

"You should have stopped when I did," she said.

With that, she turned her back to him and marched out. Conversation started back up, fitful at first then flowing. Douglas shook hands with the retiree.

"If you'll excuse me, human needs beckon."

He ducked into the nearest bathroom. In the privacy of a stall, he extracted the shred from his pocket.

Auditors are coming.

She'd written it in red.

Douglas flushed the toilet. After washing and lotioning his hands, he let the paper float down into the trash can. It incinerated in a flash. The company would survive the audits easily, but he, Douglas, might not. He would need to line up important, high-ranking sacrificial lambs for this screw-up. Perhaps Grivet. If not him, there was certainly a plethora of them eating themselves fat just outside the bathroom door.

Douglas fluffed his cravat and rejoined the retirement party. Time to gather the perfect scapegoat.

33

Hospital

TrysKa piloted *Maverick* to N.T. #6, the space hospital. After Brant was checked in, TrysKa rode the shuttle down, nabbed Amalie, and the two went to Brant's apartment complex.

"What happened?" Amalie asked as they rode the people mover from the tram stop to his building.

"Brant's feet were shot," TrysKa said. "He's in the hospital getting robotic replacements now."

Amalie kept her face neutral, and the two traveled in silence. The people chatted around them, but they were alone in their own bubble. Finally, Amalie stepped off the conveyor, and TrysKa followed.

"How soon did you get him to the hospital?" Amalie asked.

"Under thirty minutes."

"Then he shouldn't have a lot of ghost pains."

They entered the building, and the door closed out the noise of hovercrafts, audio ad boards, and pedestrians talking to their devices. The lunch crowd had returned to work, leaving the main foyer cold and empty. TrysKa and Amalie's footfalls echoed down the polished floor and off the walls as they went to the lift.

"Are you going to be OK?" TrysKa asked.

"Me? Sure." Amalie's sigh escaped with a slight shudder. "But Brant will have a long rehab, and he's not a patient man."

The lift opened and his hallway shot out in a line of identical, evenly spaced doors.

"Which one's his?" TrysKa asked.

Amalie pointed. "But how will we unlock his door?"

TrysKa slipped Ximena's Sneak from her pocket. She stuck it to the scanner, and the door swished open.

"I don't want to know where you got that thing," Amalie said. "In fact, I didn't see you use it."

Amalie pulled a pair of socks from the mountain of clothes on the floor and sniffed them.

"Clean-ish."

TrysKa dug out Brant's boots, and Amalie stuffed the socks in. They left the room only to nearly bounce off the gut of Head Councilor Jefferson, white-haired and proud.

"Head Councilor?" TrysKa said.

"Heard you were finally back," Jefferson said, his hands clasped behind his back. "That took longer than I scheduled."

"We OK'd it with KaeHan," TrysKa said.

Jefferson blocked the way to the lift. Not an easy man to ignore, and certainly not an easy man to skirt around in a narrow hallway. TrysKa inched to the right.

"I heard." Jefferson stepped in her way. "But now that you're back, having performed exemplary I might add, I've assigned you to a new op, piloting the latest in space fighters. Better suited to your level of talent."

With that, Jefferson pivoted and strode to the lifts.

Stop him! He can't choose your future!

And TrysKa snapped.

All her childhood, her father had said, *Everyone deserves to be treated with respect.* But when her sister stole her clothes, or her brother denied hitting her, what did he say?

Just this once, TrysKa, let it go.

But it was never just once. At IAS, the instructors had told her, *Everyone should train for their dream job.* But when she wanted to be a pilot, what did they say?

You have the adapted touch. We need you in special ops.

And they pressured her to fall in line. But then she'd met Knox. Finally, someone listened to her, truly listened, and trusted her with authority. Now that TrysKa knew what that felt like, no one was ignoring her ever again. No one.

"No," she said.

The air almost swallowed the tiny word. Her voice screamed in her head, but out loud, TrysKa barely whispered. Still, Jefferson halted and spun.

"I'm sorry?"

He looked at Amalie, in case she'd been the bold one to defy him. Amalie opened her mouth like a fish but nothing came out. She cut her eyes at TrysKa. TrysKa lifted her chin and pulled back her shoulders.

"I said, 'no.' I'm not going on that operation." She imagined Knox and Ximena, Brant, Alex, and Sann, standing behind her, cheering her on. "I'm staying with *Maverick.*"

Jefferson stared for a few seconds then dared to laugh.

"TrysKa, sweetheart-"

"I'm not your sweetheart."

That jolted him. "My apologies."

Jefferson tugged down the hem on his jacket and studied her like he'd encountered an unexpected predator.

326

"Would you really leave IAS and all we've sacrificed for you," he paused, "to work on *Maverick*?"

So, he was using guilt and selfishness against her. Well, her family and IAS had used that against her all her life, and now she was ready for it.

"I'm not quitting IAS, not unless you kick me out," she said. "Knox gives valuable insider information to KaeHan for his predictions."

"Shhh." Jefferson pushed the button on his jacket to turn off the cameras in the hallway.

"On this op, Caravan Suppliers attacked Knox," she said. "He'll need my protection if IAS still wants him as an informant."

Jefferson pursed his lips. "Well-played. Well-played, indeed. But will Knox pay IAS our cut?"

"Absolutely."

TrysKa wouldn't take full pay, of course. Knox couldn't afford that, but they could send IAS its piece of her pie.

"Classified informant of the shipping industry," he said. "I can put that on the books."

Jefferson's white eyebrows barely furrowed. "But that's the reason you think I'd agree to. I need to know. What's TrysKa Carter's real reason for staying with *Maverick*?"

"They're making a difference fighting human trafficking. It's a cause I believe in."

"I see."

Jefferson tapped the tip of his obsidian shoe on the epoxy-crete floor.

"Caravan Suppliers attacked Knox?" he said. "Obviously, I need to read up on this op of yours. More happened than I was aware of."

He pressed the button on his jacket, turned his back, and his shoes clomped down the hall to the lift. Only after Jefferson disappeared did Amalie squeal and cover her mouth.

"I cannot believe you just stood up to him!"

"I—" TrysKa's face warmed. "Yeah. I did, didn't I?"

"That was amazing!"

You are amazing!

She'd done it. She'd finally done it. Amalie hugged TrysKa, and the two walked elbow-in-elbow to the lift. Brant would need his boots.

#

Brant blinked. The world was white. Was he dead? No, wait. There was beige too.

Brant blinked two more times and squinted. His world divided into beige on the left and white on the right.

He turned his head to the left. The beige came down to within a foot of his face. The edge of a pillow crept into his periphery. Oh, the beige was the wall, and his head lay on the pillow. Wherever he was also smelled like bleach. Brant turned his face back up at the white ceiling.

Where am I?

"Brant!"

A person smothered him, holding him tight. Brant tried to lift his arms in defense, but lead ran through his veins. He couldn't lift his weighted limbs. The smell of apple blossom soap, craft glue, and sterilized cloth diapers billowed off the person's bleached hair.

"Mom?"

Susan kissed Brant on the forehead. Her warm lips brought feeling back to his face and neck. It seeped down his body, waking him from a stupor. She hugged him again and this time, Brant could move his arms. He wrapped them around her tiny waist. She didn't eat enough.

Susan pulled back, and Brant's arms flopped back on the bed. At first two blurry Mom faces swam back and forth, meeting in the middle, only to swing past each other.

Brant blinked rapidly and shook his head. His hair flung around his face. Where was his ponytail band? Brant imagined his hand brushing his hair out of the way, but in reality, his arm lifted only a foot before dropping. Susan smoothed his hair back, caressing his cheek with her soft hands.

"Take it easy, my love," she said. "You've been under for six hours."

"Where am I?"

"The space hospital."

"What happened?"

Images flashed in answer. No longer did Brant see his mom's smile. Instead rain poured. Teens flipped and shot. A plasma gun fired. His feet!

Sensation rushed down his body and hit strangeness at his calves. Something was below his calves, but it was wrong. All wrong. Brant thrashed to get the things off. He scraped his legs together. They wouldn't come off!

Strong hands gripped Brant's arms and pressed his back against the wall.

"Be still."

That wasn't Mom.

"Breathe."

That was Knox. Brant sucked in air, but his legs kept writhing against each other, pushing against the foreign objects clinging to the end of them.

"You have robotic feet," Knox said.

329

Brant's legs fell limp. He stared at Knox's lips, trying to string together the syllables. Trying to make sense of the gibberish.

"Robotic. Robotic. Oh."

His gaze drifted down to the end of his body, but his mom had lifted the bed sheet. She gently lowered it onto his new appendages, and the fabric grazed the manufactured skin. Nerve endings fired off. The coarseness of the material scraped. Brant jerked his feet. No, not *his* feet. The imposter replacements. The fabric ripped across them.

"Stop!" Knox said.

Again, Brant froze.

"Breathe."

Brant let out air. Sucked it in. Let it out.

"The doctors said that nerve endings are over-sensitive at first. Your brain will adapt. It will relearn how to interpret the signals sent to it."

"How long?" Brant said through clenched teeth.

Knox exchanged a look with Susan, a look that meant he knew more than he was about to say.

"The over-sensitivity should wear off in about an hour."

"When can I walk?"

Knox's gaze drifted down. Susan tapped his shoulder. Knox thumped Brant on the right triceps and pulled away to the chair against the wall, relinquishing center stage back to Susan.

"My love." She pulled a hairband from her pocket and wrapped it around her wrist. "There's a rehab procedure for this."

She combed Brant's hair back with her fingers. He leaned his head forward as she gathered it at the nape of his neck.

"Because TrysKa got you here so quickly, you didn't have much nerve damage." She slipped the hair through, twisted the band, and pulled the ponytail out again. "Your new feet took perfectly. You'll be back running, kicking, and teaching in a month."

She twisted once more and his fine mane glided over the rubber band as she pulled it free. It swung down his back.

"See, all better."

"Are TrysKa and Alex OK?" Brant asked.

"We're all fine," Knox said. "But we need to talk about your teaching job," To Susan. "The reason Brant signed on for my op is because he was told by Ed that you needed money for hospital bills."

"That bastard!" Susan spat.

She stomped her athletic shoe on the hard floor. Then put her hands on her hips and worked her mouth, like she was arguing with someone. Then she paced. Back and forth Susan stomped next to Brant's bed. Knox curled backward in his chair, as if he was trying to shrink smaller.

"Perhaps I should leave," Knox said.

For all his toughness and fight, a pissed off woman was his Achilles heel. Susan pointed for him to stay in his seat. He gripped the armrests like he was going to rip them right off. Finally, she halted.

"Did he tell you why I was hurt?" she asked Brant.

"Kids at your daycare."

They both knew Ed had lied. Her expression confirmed it. The heat rose from Brant's chest while Susan worked her mouth some more.

"You don't have to pay for me," she said.

"I don't want us to depend on Ed. I want him out of our

lives."

Susan stared. "You're not dependent on Ed."

Brant wadded the sheets between his fists. "As long as he has you on a financial hook, I am."

"I can take care of myself!"

"But sometimes life won't let you! What then?"

"I need a man who loves me!"

Susan slapped her hand over her mouth. She hadn't meant for that to come out. Maybe she hadn't even realized she felt it.

"You have a man who loves you."

Susan's tension melted. Tears brimmed her eyes and traced down her cheeks, one following another. She opened her mouth to say something, choked, then shook her head. She crept toward Brant, one timid step in front of another then took his right hand in both of hers. His long fingers spilled out of her grasp.

"You're right." Susan rubbed her wet cheek with her shoulder. "All this time I've only seen what I was missing, and I've missed what I had."

Her gaze lifted to meet Brant's. "But I can't afford a decent place on my pay alone."

"Ask for help."

"I've got this!"

Knox snorted then froze. Brant and Susan both glared at him.

"Sorry," he said. "I was just struck that I've heard those words before. Said exactly like that."

Susan cut her eyes at her son.

"Yeah," Brant said. "I might have picked that up from you."

"Perhaps now would be a good time for me to step out,"

Knox said.

He pushed up from the chair and all but ran out of the room.

"Bonding isn't his thing," Brant said.

Susan mouth twitched in her unique way as she studied the door that Knox had exited. "And yet he waited by your bedside this whole time."

"Really?"

"Never left your side except when you were in surgery." She turned from the door back to Brant. "You're determined to pay for me, aren't you?"

"Yeah."

"But I don't want you to go on ops for me. You love teaching children."

"I got that honest too."

Susan blushed hard, and the tears started again.

"Oh dear."

She grabbed the folded handkerchief on the nightstand next to the bed and wiped her nose. Both her hands clasped it like her life depended on holding onto this linen rag.

"OK, it's time for me to swallow my pride." She leaned in and kissed Brant on the cheek. "You're worth it. Your dreams are worth it."

"OK?"

"I have a coworker who just divorced. We could room together and both save a lot of money." Susan said. "I'll ask her for help."

I don't have a roommate anymore.

The thought sprung from nowhere and slapped Brant hard. He blinked back tears. Thankfully his mom misunderstood them. She got another handkerchief from the pile and wiped his cheeks. Brant closed his eyes and leaned into her touch.

"After I move I won't share my address publicly," she said. "I'll block Ed. We'll finally be free, both of us."

Susan placed the cloth in Brant's hand, gave it a squeeze, and dropped her wet kerchief into the sterilizer. It flashed, and the cloth was clean.

"Now, I think you and Knox have some catching up to do. I'll be right outside if you need me."

She stopped in the open doorway, blew Brant a kiss, and stepped out. Knox didn't enter immediately though.

Brant cocked his head. His ears caught the faint whispers of his mom and Knox's voices drifting through the closed door. If they'd used normal volume, he could have differentiated the words, but they didn't. What were they discussing out there?

Brant couldn't wait another minute. He threw his feet over the edge of the bed. No sooner did he catch sight of them, than his head jerked back. His stomach, still sick from sedatives, soured. Those weren't his feet! A stranger's feet hung off the end of his legs.

Susan and Knox's whispers continued. Her voice had that fervent tone she got when she desperately needed a favor. He had to get out there. Staring at the door and not at the fake toes, Brant hopped off the bed.

Dry ice! Steel wool!

Pins shot into the sole of his robotic replacements. The floor froze his false skin. Brant instinctively leapt and crashed onto the nightstand. He fell sideways, and the floor rushed at his left ribs. He hit hard. Air rushed out of his throat.

Knox was by his side. He squatted and hoisted him onto the bed. Brant felt a breeze on his privates.

"Oh, I'm naked." *Could this be any more embarrassing?*

Brant wasn't technically naked. He wore one of those skimpy hospital robes that didn't cover anything important. Under all those covers, he hadn't noticed it earlier.

"I wasn't staring," Knox said and pulled the sheets over Brant.

"What were you and Mom talking about?"

Knox cleared his throat and straightened his jacket. "She seems to be of the opinion that you need a male mentor type in your life."

"A father?" Brant said.

"I wouldn't put it that strongly."

"She did."

"You know her well."

"I've got this."

Brant winced, and Knox's eyes twinkled, the lights from the ceiling dancing around in those almost black irises. If Brant weren't almost naked, unable to walk, and embarrassed, he'd enjoy Knox's expression. As it was, he could only stare at his hands.

"I told you I was devastated when I lost my father," Knox said. "What I didn't tell is that I nearly ended my own life, right then and there."

"What?"

"I'd brought Dad's body to the cargo bay."

Knox took a shaky breath. In Brant's mind, he saw Knox scooping up Sann's ashes. Knox spoke, bringing Brant back.

"I was going to take his ship," Knox said. "With his body and his son onboard, and run it into the nearest star. Go out in a blaze of glory."

"What stopped you?"

"Nicolai and his father, Petrov. I didn't want them there,

but they wouldn't take 'no' for an answer."

Knox uncrossed his arms and held the headboard behind Brant. He leaned in and lowered his voice.

"Brant, everyone hits a time when life knocks them flat. Even people like you and me. I'd give the world to have my father back, but I can't. What I can do-" He cleared his throat. "What I can do is be that father for you."

Brant closed his eyes. He couldn't look into those intense black eyes one more second. It overwhelmed him. But he couldn't say, *no.* Not anymore. Life was short; Brant understood that now. Who knew if another man as strong and wise and compassionate as Knox would come around again? Brant couldn't leave that to chance.

He nodded.

"Then let's do this right," Knox said. His deep voice rumbled, and his breath warmed Brant's ear. "You are my son and I. Am. Proud. Of. You."

Knox word's cut the belt crushing Brant's chest. He filled his lungs without tightness or pain for the first time in his life. Knox's scent of sweat and pine hung thick.

"You are growing into a great man," Knox said. "And I am honored to serve alongside you. You have proven faithful in both the big things and the mundane. You defended the helpless and sacrificed yourself for others. It's a privilege to be a part of your life."

The words sank deep. *It's a privilege to be a part of your life.* Brant felt lightheaded. A weight he'd carried all his life was lifted. His jaw didn't hurt. Brant leaned his head against the smooth plastoform of the headboard.

Before Brant stood his new Dad, stood solid and strong. Knox twisted his wedding band, a legacy handed down from his own admired father. Brant had nothing to say, but that was OK.

"Now, for the more practical part." Knox strode to the far corner of the room and picked up a folded pile from the chair.

"My clothes," Brant said and held out his arms.

Knox gave him the stack of pants, shirt, socks, and underwear. Brant put them on his lap and grimaced.

"Perhaps your mother would be better suited for this task," Knox said.

"I don't want help."

"For the next few days, you don't have much choice."

Knox was right, of course, but Brant didn't have to like it. Knox left, and Susan dressed him. He felt like a toddler. His feet spasmed and disobeyed his mind. He couldn't lift his butt for her to slip on his underwear. His body was helpless and stupid.

The whole time Susan pretended not to notice when Brant punched the wall, or kicked the sheets, or yelled so loud his ears rang.

Finally, he was dressed and in his right mind. Brant pulled his mom close and held her.

"I love you."

"I know," she said. "I love you too."

And for the first time, Brant felt like his mom was finally safe.

34

Return to IAS

It. Took. Six. Hours.

Getting released from the hospital was almost as hard as escaping from jail, but finally Brant was free. Knox stood in the door, keeping it open, as Brant guided his hoverchair through the front sliding glass doors. His robotic feet wore his old boots, thanks to TrysKa and Amalie. Alex kept romping around the chair and crinkling his nose at the mechanical appendages. He reached out to poke them, and Brant kicked his hand. Alex yelped and ran back to Knox's side.

Outside the hospital, Ximena hugged Brant and waved good-bye as she headed toward the loading dock. The rest rode the shuttle with Brant down to the planet. After landing, Amalie gave him a long, slow hug. Brant closed his eyes and breathed in the lavender perfume on her hair, felt its softness against his cheek. Did he have to let go?

"I have class," Amalie said.

She waved, and boarded a hoverbus with his mom. And left.

TrysKa, Knox, and Alex stayed with Brant for the tram ride. An hour later, IAS peeked over the windowsill. Brant caught his breath, and Knox leaned back, giving him a better view of his home. IAS had always protected Brant, and now he could give back. He could teach others what had been taught to him.

Knox wheeled Brant to the gymnasium doors.

"What the hell happened to you?"

DeVaun walked up. Deep cuts etched his steel-toed boots, his right pants leg was ripped exposing his dark shin bearing a scar, and his shirt was covered with stains.

"Uhhh. Yeah," Brant looked down at his new 'feet.' "Had a run-in with adapted soldiers."

"One of our own attacked you?"

"No, no, this wasn't one of our own."

DeVaun crossed his arms and stepped back.

"You've got a story to tell."

"So do you," Brant pointed to DeVaun's leg.

"We'll have to swap." He noticed Knox. "DeVaun Matthews."

He stuck out his hand. Brant pointed at Knox then DeVaun.

"Knox, this is DeVaun, my classmate and a powerful soldier. DeVaun, this is Knox, my new dad."

"Your new dad?" DeVaun shook Knox's hand. "You can pick those?"

"I didn't like the old one," Brant said.

"You know what, neither did I," DeVaun smiled.

"But we've blocked this door long enough," Knox said. "Let's get you on your feet to meet your students."

"So, you're back to teaching now?" DeVaun asked as Knox hoisted Brant up.

"Yeah."

"Good. Where you belong."

Brant struggled to balance on Knox's arm. He felt like a

giraffe supporting himself on a rhino.

"Whoa, wait." DeVaun held up his hands. "Don't get me wrong, Knox, you might be a good guy and all. But-"

"I'm too short? Is that what you're getting at?" Knox said.

"That's exactly what I'm getting at."

DeVaun slid his muscled arm under Brant's and lifted. As Knox let go, Brant tested his new center of gravity. Perfect.

"Now you're ready to meet your students," DeVaun said.

Knox opened the door, and the smell of sweat and shouts of students beckoned. Brant's nine-year-old class practiced across the room. Instructor Celeste led them in jumping jacks. If Brant could break free from his clumsy feet, he'd sprint to them and throw wide his arms.

I'm back!

DeVaun tugged his head to the left, and Brant nodded. There was more than one way to make an entrance. DeVaun slipped along the back wall behind the classes. A few older students spotted them, but Brant put his finger to his lips. *Shh.*

Celeste was gritting her teeth over two misbehaving kids. They refused to stop wiggling and giggling. DeVaun helped Brant stand on his own, and backed off. Good thing his boots laced up tight to his calves and kept his ankles locked in place. Brant called up his sternest, deepest voice.

"Listen to your teacher." The kids snapped their heads around then leapt up as one.

"Instructor Mallet!"

The entire class piled atop him. Down Brant went under the tangle of outstretched arms.

"Give me air!"

Brant laughed as he peeled kids off of him. No sooner had he escaped from the nine-year-olds, then the rest of his students gathered from around the arena. Over forty kids pushed and shoved to reach Brant and high-five, wrestle, or question him about his mission.

"Whoa! Everyone, sit down!" Brant yelled.

And they did, except for the twelve-year-olds who were too cool to follow directions.

They had missed him. They really missed him. Brant hopped to his knees, so he could balance and see above his students. A head of silky black hair bobbed right and left, vying for a view of Brant.

Jesalya.

She was the only other student from Khmer. Brant motioned for the group to part and let her through. She backed away. Too many eyes staring at her.

"It's OK, you're not in trouble," Brant said.

He motioned for her to come. Jesalya tiptoed forward and flicked her eyes back and forth, a fawn moving into an exposed meadow. She stood before Brant and stared at the floor.

It was time to say his friend's name out loud.

"I'm so sorry about Sann."

Jesalya fluttered her eyelids, blinking away tears. She'd known him. Sann must have introduced himself to her.

"He gave his life for me," Brant said. "So I'm giving my life for you. Whatever training you need, whatever questions you have in any of your classes, you call me. Anytime. OK?"

Jesalya nodded. She stepped back into the crowd, and the other students stood by her side. Instructor Celeste waited behind the sweaty herd, her shoulders drooping.

"Miss me?" Brant asked her.

"You have no idea." She looked like she'd run a full marathon several days in a row. "How long will you stay this time?" she asked.

Forty pairs of wide eyes locked on Brant. He drank in the moment.

"I'm here to stay."

A cheer rose. Celeste threw the instructor's gun over their heads, and Brant snatched it mid-air.

"You can start tomorrow," she called over the noise.

"Tomorrow? Whoa, wait!"

But the kids applauded even louder. It was time to let them know. Brant tried to stand up, but his right ankle buckled. He crumpled to the floor, and the yells died on the students' lips.

"It's OK, it's OK," Brant said and pushed up to his knees. "I accidentally lost my feet on this last mission. Can't figure out where I put them." Some of the kids snickered. "So, it'll be a while before I can demonstrate any moves for you."

DeVaun brought the hoverchair, and Brant hoisted himself in.

"Are they AI feet?" asked one of his students.

"They're mechanical feet, yes, but they don't have a mind of their own. At least I don't think they do."

Brant arched his eyebrow like his feet might walk off without his permission. More kids laughed. The only thing that would make this moment better was to share it with his new family. Brant craned his neck around to find Knox. Where had he gone?

Knox and TrysKa chatted with KaeHan while Alex stood with arms crossed and lower lip stuck out.

"I've got to say, 'good bye' to someone." Brant tilted the joystick and the hoverchair spun. Over his shoulder, he assured his students, "Be right back."

Brant cranked the joystick forward all the way, and the chair flew forward. Nice. He'd expected it to move at a sloth's pace.

The kids clapped behind him. Brant spun it back to face them and flew backward to Knox. They loved that. With his crinkled grin, he whipped it back around.

"You're going to race that thing around the school, aren't you?" KaeHan said.

"I might."

"Good, a lot of soldiers struggle when they're strapped to a hoverchair. Seeing you flying around a corner in the thing might lift their spirits." KaeHan looked sidelong at Alex. "But now it's time for your tests."

Alex made a gagging sound.

"If you want to stay with us," Knox said, "you have to prove to IAS that we're teaching you right."

"You show them all," TrysKa said.

Alex rolled his eyes at her. He wasn't falling for that, but then he shrugged.

"Fine."

Knox chuckled, and KaeHan startled.

"Did you just laugh?"

"Your fault. You set me up with this crew." Knox swept his hand to TrysKa, Alex, and Brant.

"And I'm glad I did, Lennox."

Knox petrified on the spot. TrysKa's mouth opened to an O, but it took Brant a minute to put together what KaeHan had just said. *Lennox.* As in, Knox's first name? Oh. Oh man. Brant and Alex exchanged big grins.

"Your name," Brant said to Knox.

"Shut up."

"Is Lennox."

"Brant!"

"Knox."

KaeHan bit his lips, trying not to laugh.

"I fail to see what's so funny about it," Knox said.

But Alex knew exactly what was so funny about it. "It *rhymes!*"

That did it. Alex fell to the floor, laughing and clutching his stomach. Brant threw his head back and his guffaw echoed around the gym. Nearby kids joined the laughter even though they didn't know the joke. KaeHan put his hands on his hips, and his shoulders shook. TrysKa covered her mouth.

"Not you too!" Knox said to her.

"I'm sorry. It's not funny–*hic*. Oh no! *hic*." TrysKa covered her face with both her hands. "Whenever I try to *hic* stop laughing *hic*, I get the *hic*."

Her shoulders shook, spasmed with a hiccup, and shook some more.

"Go take your test," Knox said to Alex.

"I'll stay with *hic* him," TrysKa said as Knox stormed off.

It wasn't until the gym door closed behind him that Knox allowed himself a smirk. Why his mom had named him after his grandfather, Lennox, he'd never know, and he certainly didn't care for it. There was a reason he went by Knox and only Knox.

But he guessed Brant, Alex, and TrysKa could be in on his little secret.

#

An hour and thirty minutes later, Knox walked up to his ship. He patted its hull.

"Been a strange two months."

A ping from under the ship's belly interrupted him. Sure enough, two petite feet stuck out. He nudged one with his boot, and Ximena shot out from under the ship.

"Repairs can wait until later."

"Really?" Knox said. *Odd.*

Ximena popped up and wiped her hands on her pants.

"Atienna called."

Knox sucked in his breath and motioned up the ramp. They walked hand-in-hand into the cargo bay. Knox hit the ramp controls, and it creaked closed.

"What did she say?"

"The Commune of Planets raided that warehouse and recovered everyone captured there, including thirteen Taluk children, including Klundah's niece."

Kiara. They'd found her. From the beginning, Knox had known they couldn't rescue all of the kidnapped children. It was impossible, so why hope? But here he was, getting a call from Atienna to return the last thirteen. Including Klundah's niece. They'd done it. Life had a miracle or two to spare for Knox after all.

More than only one or two. Knox counted: Alex, Brant, TrysKa, and of course, Ximena. Knox had never had it this good. It wouldn't last forever, but he intended to enjoy every second.

"Let's call TrysKa," Knox said. "The children need a ride home."

"Actually," Ximena's voice had a sing-song lilt to it. "They won't be ready for us for about two hours."

"Two hours?"

"And I heard Alex is busy with testing? And TrysKa is with him?"

Knox did that math really quick. He scooped Ximena up in his arms, and she threw her head back and cackled. He lowered his voice and thickened his accent just the way she liked it.

"Did I tell you how sexy you look working on our ship?"

"Did it turn you on when your sexy wife saved you with her Phase Rippers?" she asked, playfulness in her eyes.

Knox strode across the cargo bay to their quarters. Entered. And took his sweet time.

35

A Brother's Goodbye

Brant lay in his bed and stared past the ceiling. Sann's stuff was gone, and DeVaun's clothes, shoes, and athletic card collection lay sprawled across the ground. Brant needed a roommate, and DeVaun had volunteered.

The previous two months washed over Brant, drawing him back.

Sann was gone. No more duels. No more joking and messing with each other. No more sitting comfortably next to each other in silence. No more. Brant slipped deeper.

Childhood: two boys wrestled in the Institute gym.

Teenage years: Sann needled Brant.

"Do you like TrysKa?" Sann asked.

"No."

"Willow?"

"Of course not."

"Amalie?"

Pause. "No."

Sann flashed his teeth in a victorious smile. Of course, he'd set Brant up. Why hadn't he seen it coming?

In that raw moment, the holograph in the ceiling powered on of its own accord. Brant got that strange feeling someone was staring at him. The hairs on the back of his neck prickled.

Then the silence spoke.

"You going to roll over and face me?"

Brant closed his eyes and covered his face with his arms.

"Hey, you," the voice said again.

Brant shook his head.

"Fine then, I'll come to you." The voice traveled closer to Brant. "Seriously, I take all this effort to make this responsive recording for you, and you can't even look up. I have to walk all the way over here and get in your face." Brant could hear the smirk in the voice.

Around the edges of his biceps entered black bangs, flickering as they swished. Brant knew those bangs.

"You going to look at me? Or will I have to poke my head through your arms. I'm made of light, I can do that, you know."

"I can't."

"Sure you can. You just use these things called muscles and lift, there you go. See, I knew you could do it."

And Brant was eye-to-eye with his best friend.

Sann smiled broadly. A shimmering light silhouetted his flickering image. Instead of a soldier's uniform, he wore a white shirt and sarong like his family, complete with the scarf.

"Thanks for finishing my mission," Sann said.

"I limped across the finish line," Brant mumbled.

Sann's head snapped back like he'd tasted sour lemons. He sat back on his former bed, now DeVaun's.

"That sounds like something Ed would say."

Ouch. Now that Sann mentioned it, that sounded exactly

like Ed, tone and all. Would Brant ever really be free of the man?

"You're right, you're right," Brant said. "I have a new dad. It's time I started acting like it."

Sann's wide smile returned. "Really? Who?"

"Knox."

"I like Knox."

"Me too." Brant's lips started to smile, but it hurt too much. "I'm so sorry."

"It was my choice, Brant. Mine."

Sann's face started to swim in front of Brant, but not because of the hologram. He blinked the tears away.

"I'll always miss you."

"You better!"

What?

Sann laughed. "But you can miss me and live at the same time. Carry my memories with you and make new ones too. Grief and laughter can go hand in hand."

Sann's smile faded, his eyes softened.

"I didn't save your life just to let guilt steal it away."

Brant swallowed. "I can honor you that way."

His chest still ached too much to take in everything Sann said, but Brant tucked it away for later, memorizing every inflection of his best friend's voice, the glimmer in his eyes, the cowlick part above his left eye.

"Wait a second. How did you know to make a message for me? Did you know something was going to happen?"

"After my last op, I recorded myself for a few days to program this AI responsive hologram. For my friends and family," Sann said, his smile completely gone. "I didn't know when my time would come, but I knew I wanted to be prepared."

His head snapped to the closed door. "Someone's coming."

Knock, knock, knock

"Who is it?" Brant asked, sitting up.

"It's Amalie Fontenot," the computer answered.

"Amalie?"

Brant turned to Sann, but only an empty bed stared back. Sann had vanished.

Brant's gut jerked like his ankles had buckled out from under him. He turned this way and that, verifying he was in fact alone.

Carry my memories with you, and make new ones too.

The soft sound of Sann's voice floated through the room. With a breath in and out, Brant straightened his shoulders and pushed the button on the collapsed hoverchair. It unfolded in the center of the room, and Brant maneuvered his bottom from the bed into the chair. Not very graceful, but he got the job done. Brant smoothed his hair.

"Open."

Amalie smiled and curled her shoulders like she wasn't sure if she was doing the right thing.

"I thought you might not want to eat alone tonight. Maybe you needed a friend for dinner?"

"You bet!" Too eager. "I mean, thanks."

Brant winced as he moved the hoverchair forward. Why did he have to be trapped in this thing? He wanted to jog backward in front of Amalie. That always made her smile.

"Is that the latest model?" She bent close enough that Brant could smell the lavender on her hair. "We only have the older hoverchairs in med class. How does it handle?"

"Let me show you."

And the door closed.

The holoprojector whirred to life once more. A chuckle echoed around the walls. For the last time, a voice spoke.

"Watch out Amalie, here comes Brant!"

And the projector powered down.

# # # # #

Want to read about the fight that Knox had with Jefferson? Want to learn about the past tension between Knox and IAS? Then sign-up for my newsletter and get the prequel, Maverick Origins, for free.

Yes! Send me Maverick Origins, please!

Acknowledgement

When I worked as a chemical engineer, every project needed a full team of people to get the job done efficiently and safely. Different types of engineers and operators and programmers. A novel is no different.

I wrote the raw material and refined it as best I could, but this book would not be the finished, polished work it is today without the help of my editors. Thank you to Odyssey Writer's Workshop for my editorial assessment. Thank you, Amanda Rutter, for gently but clearly pointing out my opportunities for improvement (aka plot holes and broken character arcs) and sparking ideas for a better story. Thank you, Beth Dorward, for your thorough final polish. And of course, thanks to Dan Van Oss and his team for an outstanding cover. Wow. (And thank you to Reedsy for connecting me with these fine folks.)

Next is my team of encouragers. Without y'all I might have given up in a heap of self-doubt. Thank you, Dad, my first and biggest fan. Thank you to my beta-readers: Dad, Holly, Missy, Anna, Sharon, Robert, Margaret, Annalisa (please thank your parents), Lynne, Ande, and... I'm sure I'm forgetting someone. Well, thank you!

Thank you to my family who lives with and loves me despite

my writer mood swings. And thank you to my library. Because libraries are secret portals to other worlds tended by magical librarians, and they deserve our awe. And because I borrowed a lot of how-to-write and scifi/fantasy books from your shelves.

About the Author

Marjorie is an Engineer turned SciFi Author who loves Firefly, Star Wars, Star Trek, and Asimov. House Ravenclaw (with a little bit of Slytherin)

On her website, www.EngineerStoryteller.com, she reviews her favorite SciFi/Fantasy books and posts pics of them on #bookstagram. Occasionally she posts recipes on her blog too. Why not?

Marjorie can sometimes be spotted in the wild... literally, since she loves hiking in National Parks across the US.

***

Want to read about the fight that Knox had with Jefferson? Want to learn about the past tension between Knox and IAS?

Then sign-up for my newsletter and get the prequel, Maverick Origins, for free.

When you sign-up for my newsletter, you'll also get 2 emails a month with reviews of my favorite SciFi/Fantasy books, updates on sales and new releases, and recipes. (Because I like to eat while I read.)

Yes! Send me Maverick Origins, please!

Also, other readers are thinking about buying this book, but they won't. Why not? Because there aren't enough reviews. People don't buy a product, especially a book, if it doesn't have loads of good reviews. So who can help me sell my books?

You can. Please leave an honest review of my book on your favorite distributor or Goodreads. When you do, you're making a huge difference in the life of this author. Thank you so much.

You can connect with me on:
🌐 https://www.engineerstoryteller.com
🔲 https://www.facebook.com/MarjorieKingAuthor
✎ https://www.instagram.com/marjoriekingwrites

Subscribe to my newsletter:
✉ https://www.subscribepage.com/GambitLP